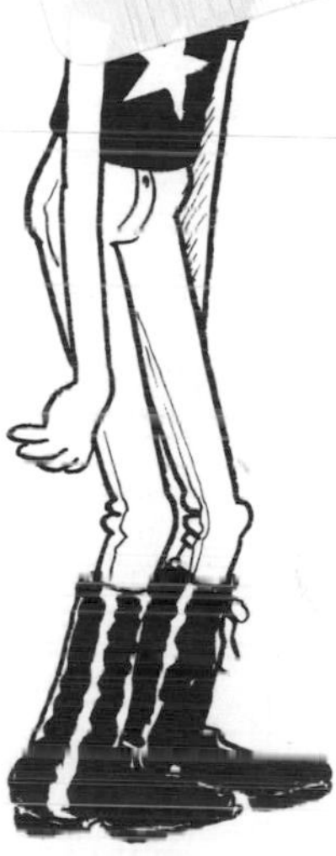

I AM NOT OKAY WITH THIS

Many thanks to Melissa and everyone who originally supported this story through Patreon. — CF

OTHER BOOKS BY CHARLES FORSMAN:

The End of the Fucking World
Celebrated Summer
Hobo Mom (with Max de Radiguès)

Fantagraphics Books Inc.
7563 Lake City Way NE
Seattle, Washington, 98115

EDITOR AND ASSOCIATE PUBLISHER: Eric Reynolds
BOOK DESIGN: Charles Forsman
PRODUCTION: Paul Baresh
PUBLISHER: Gary Groth

Library of Congress Control Number: 2019953937
ISBN 978-1-68396-331-8

www.fantagraphics.com
www.charlesforsman.com

FIRST PRINTING: January 2020
Printed in the United States

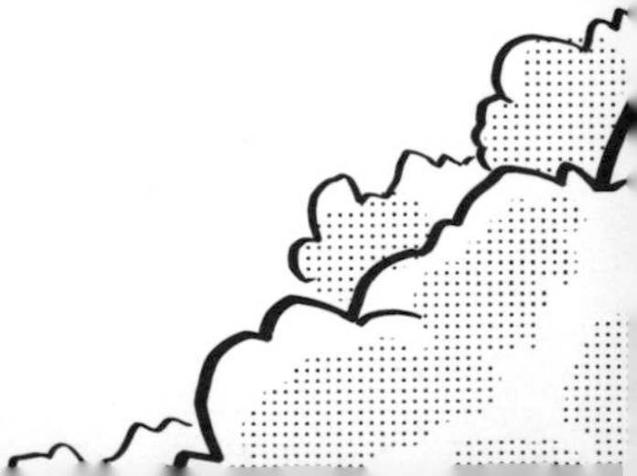

I AM NOT OKAY WITH THIS

Charles
Forsman

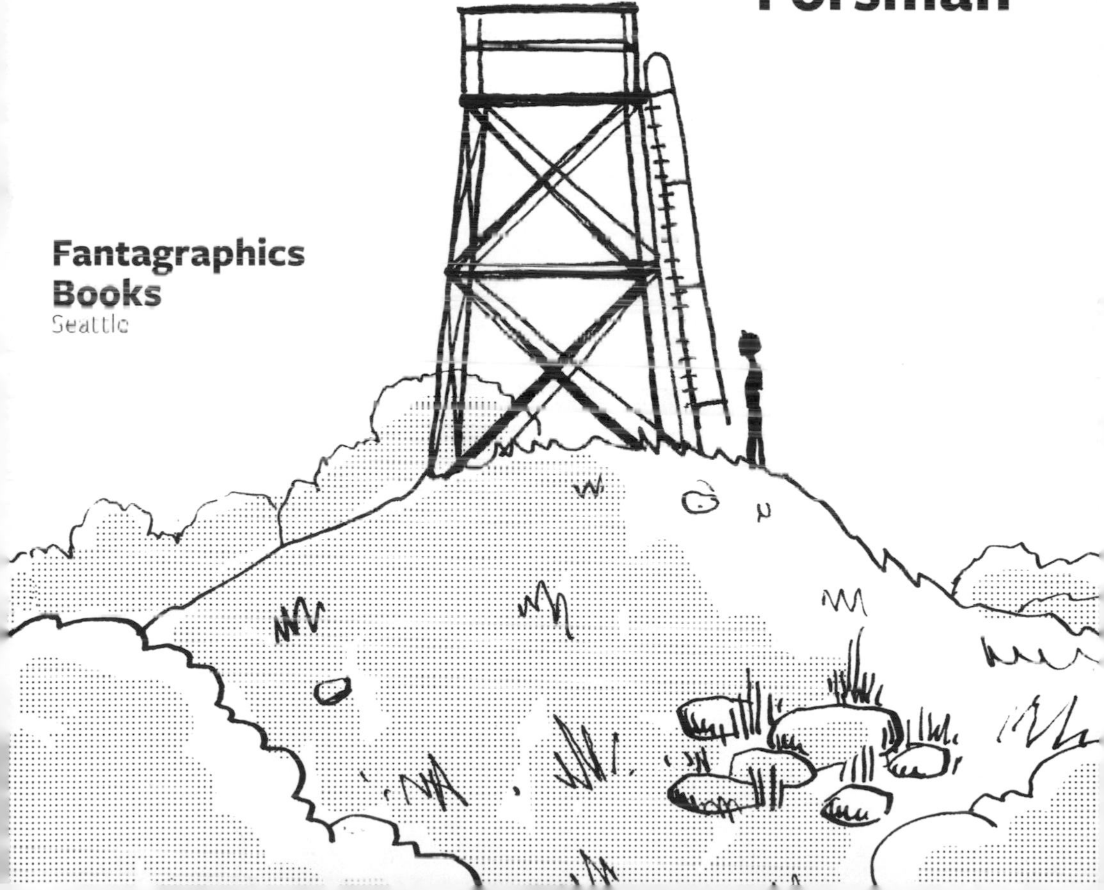

Fantagraphics
Books
Seattle

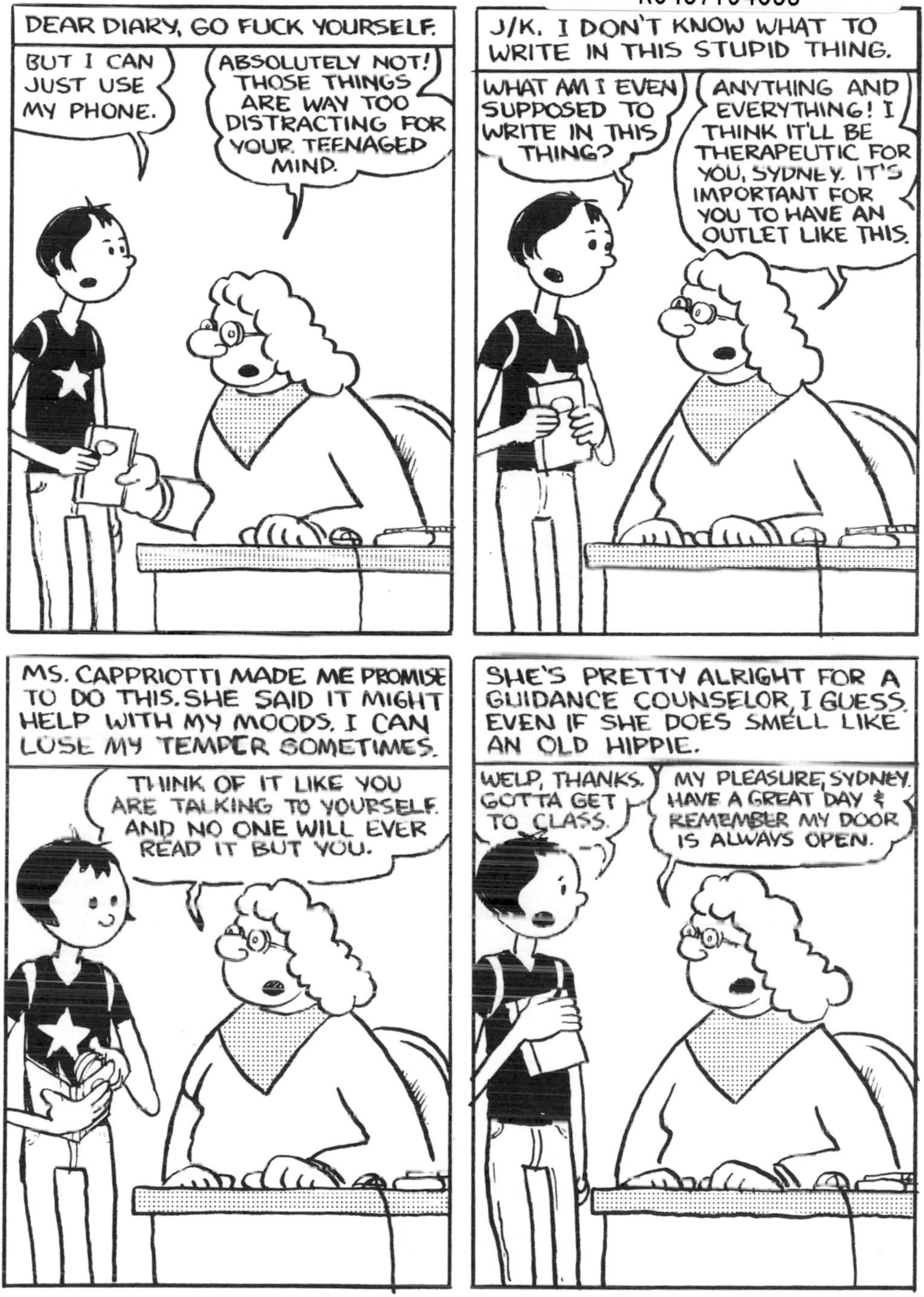
DEAR DIARY, GO FUCK YOURSELF.
BUT I CAN JUST USE MY PHONE.
ABSOLUTELY NOT! THOSE THINGS ARE WAY TOO DISTRACTING FOR YOUR TEENAGED MIND.
J/K. I DON'T KNOW WHAT TO WRITE IN THIS STUPID THING.
WHAT AM I EVEN SUPPOSED TO WRITE IN THIS THING?
ANYTHING AND EVERYTHING! I THINK IT'LL BE THERAPEUTIC FOR YOU, SYDNEY. IT'S IMPORTANT FOR YOU TO HAVE AN OUTLET LIKE THIS.
MS. CAPPRIOTTI MADE ME PROMISE TO DO THIS. SHE SAID IT MIGHT HELP WITH MY MOODS. I CAN LOSE MY TEMPER SOMETIMES.
THINK OF IT LIKE YOU ARE TALKING TO YOURSELF. AND NO ONE WILL EVER READ IT BUT YOU.
SHE'S PRETTY ALRIGHT FOR A GUIDANCE COUNSELOR, I GUESS. EVEN IF SHE DOES SMELL LIKE AN OLD HIPPIE.
WELP, THANKS. GOTTA GET TO CLASS.
MY PLEASURE, SYDNEY. HAVE A GREAT DAY & REMEMBER MY DOOR IS ALWAYS OPEN.

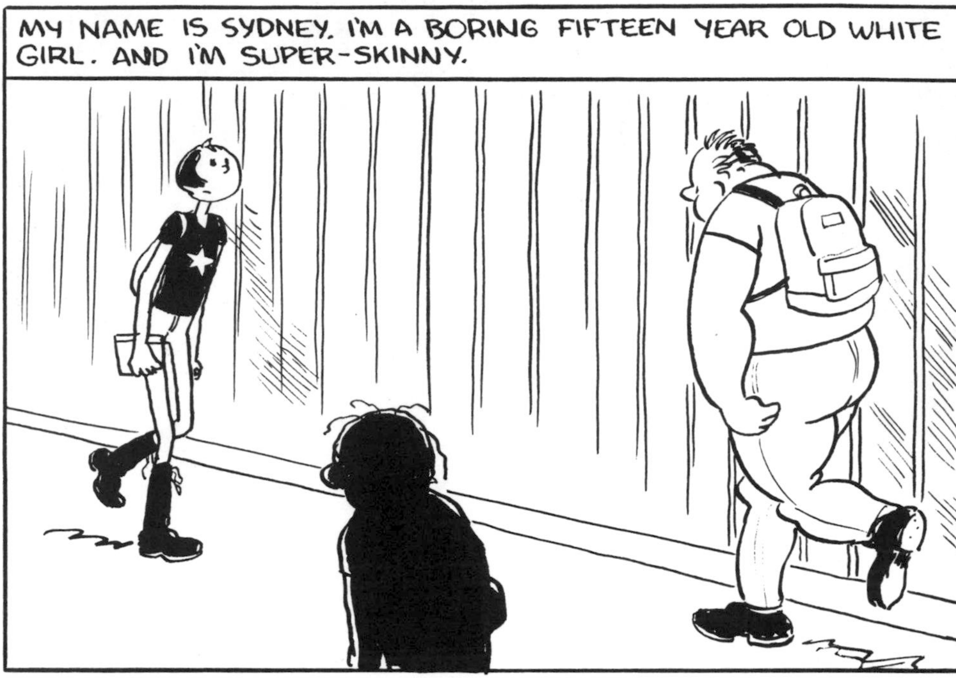
MY NAME IS SYDNEY. I'M A BORING FIFTEEN YEAR OLD WHITE GIRL. AND I'M SUPER-SKINNY.

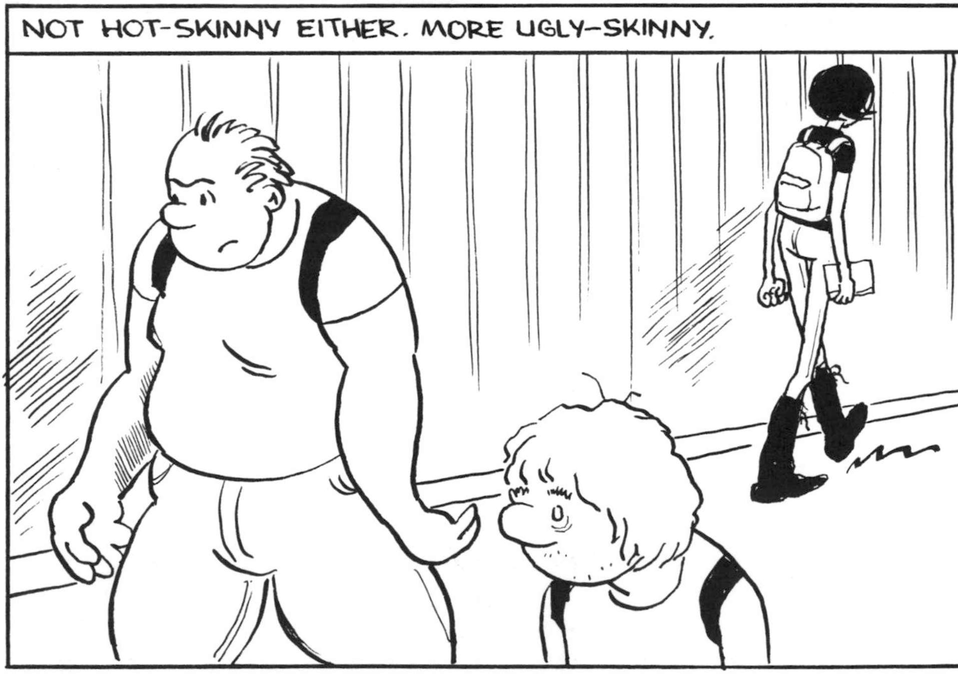
NOT HOT-SKINNY EITHER. MORE UGLY-SKINNY.

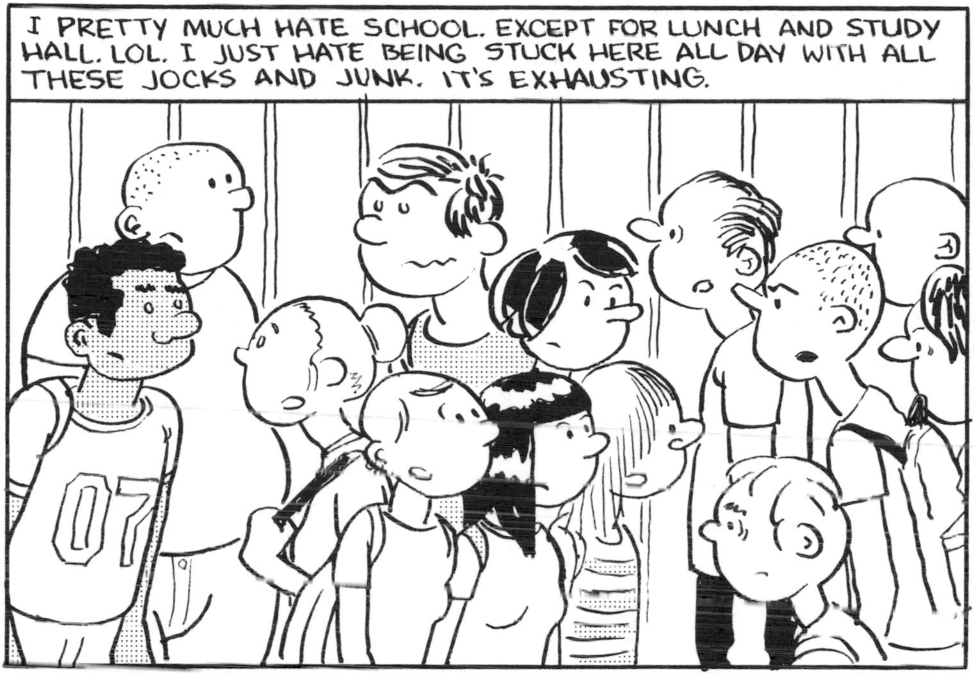
I PRETTY MUCH HATE SCHOOL. EXCEPT FOR LUNCH AND STUDY HALL. LOL. I JUST HATE BEING STUCK HERE ALL DAY WITH ALL THESE JOCKS AND JUNK. IT'S EXHAUSTING.
07

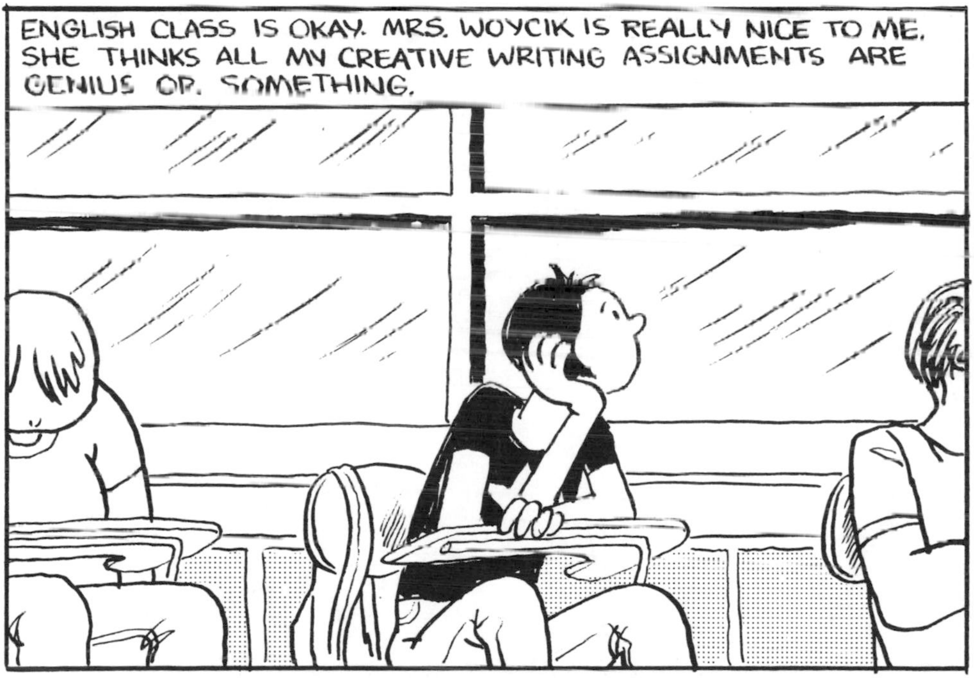
ENGLISH CLASS IS OKAY. MRS. WOYCIK IS REALLY NICE TO ME. SHE THINKS ALL MY CREATIVE WRITING ASSIGNMENTS ARE GENIUS OR SOMETHING.

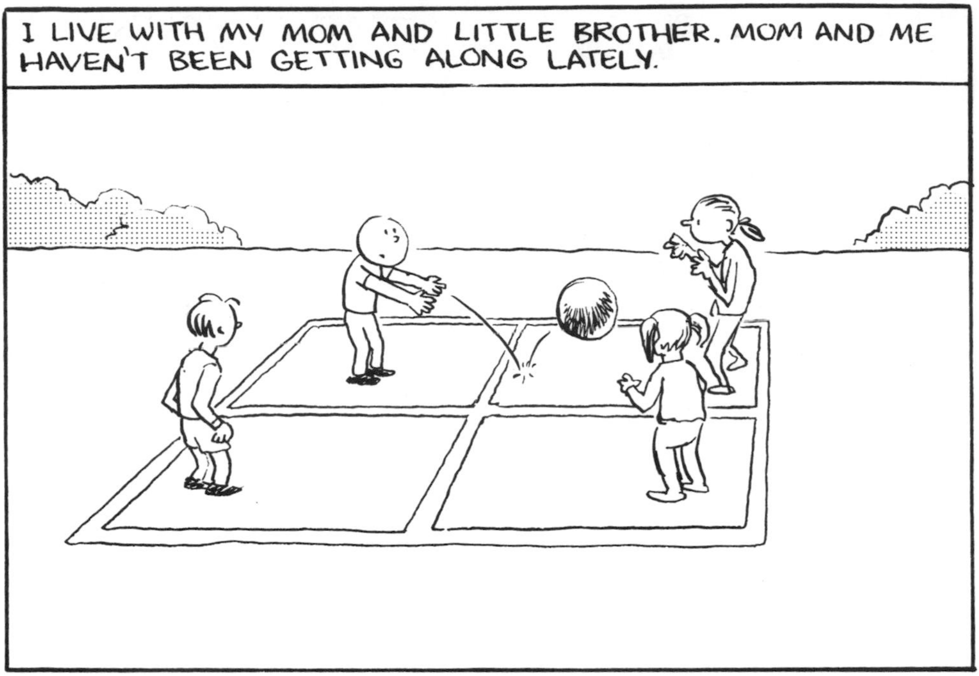
I LIVE WITH MY MOM AND LITTLE BROTHER. MOM AND ME HAVEN'T BEEN GETTING ALONG LATELY.

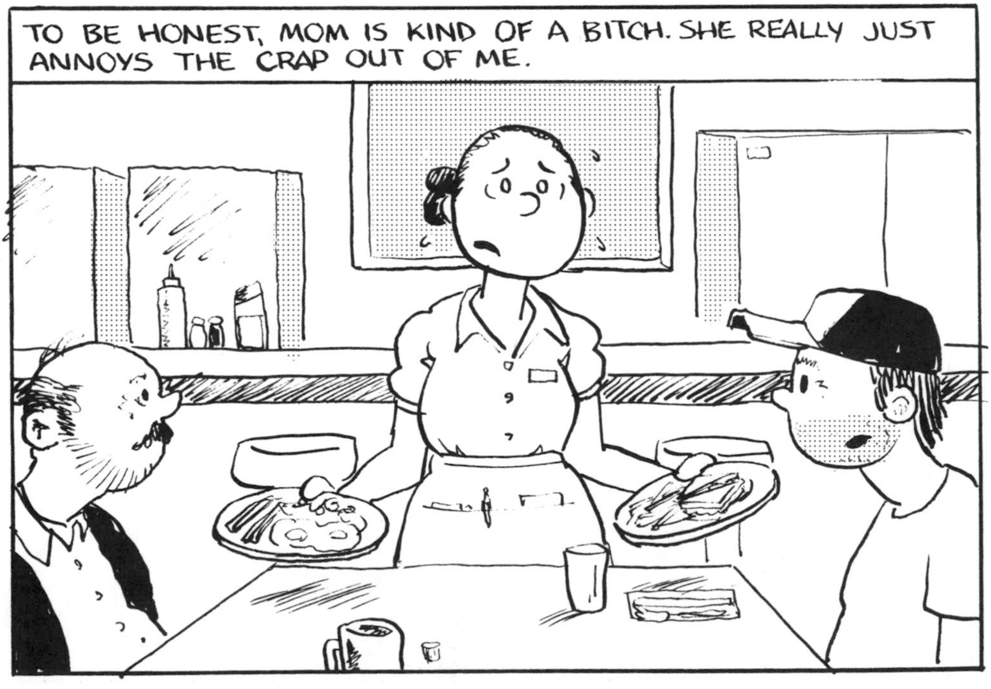
TO BE HONEST, MOM IS KIND OF A BITCH. SHE REALLY JUST ANNOYS THE CRAP OUT OF ME.

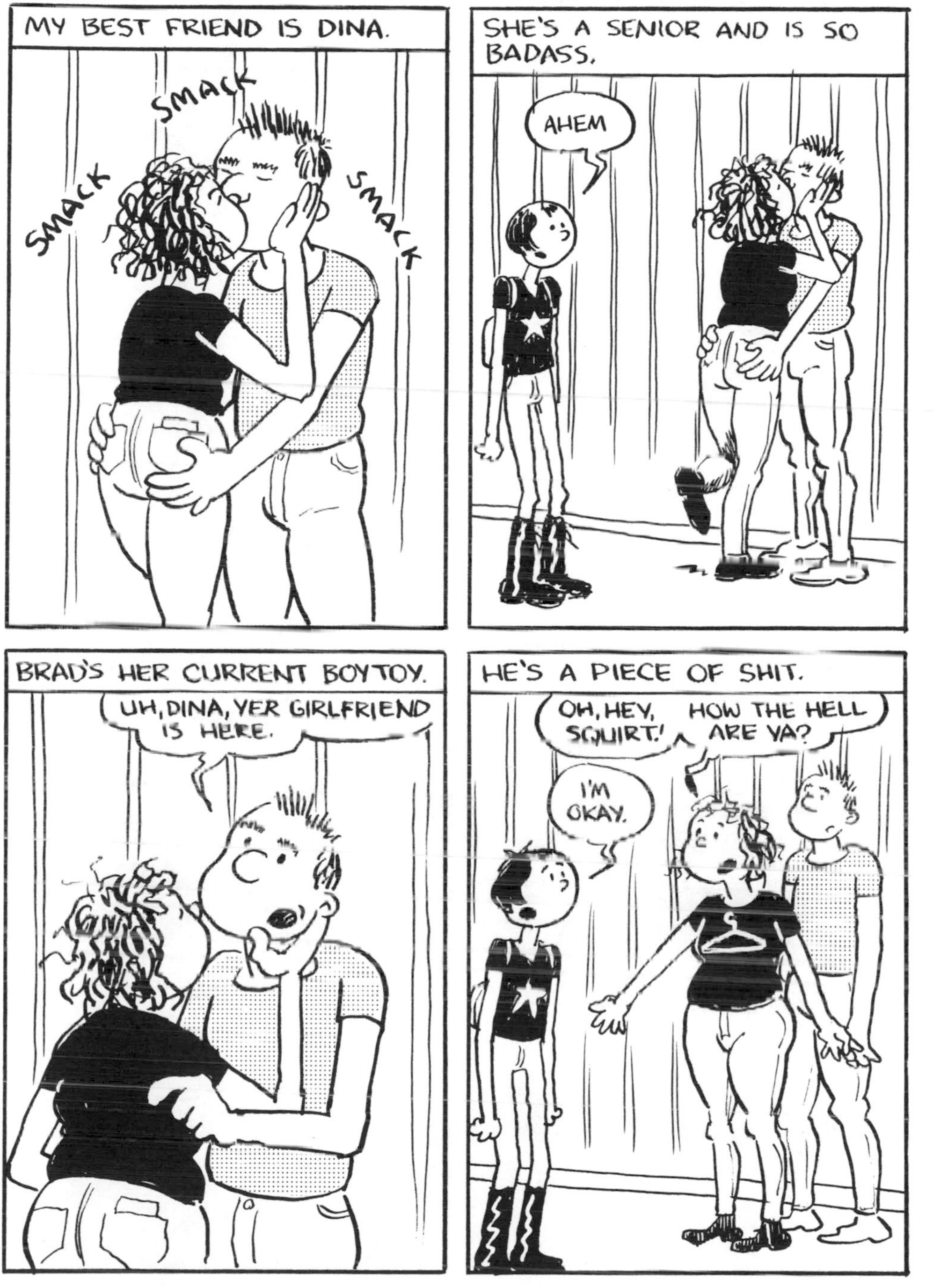
MY BEST FRIEND IS DINA.
SMACK
SMACK
SMACK
SHE'S A SENIOR AND IS SO BADASS.
AHEM
BRAD'S HER CURRENT BOYTOY.
UH, DINA, YER GIRLFRIEND IS HERE.
HE'S A PIECE OF SHIT.
OH, HEY, SQUIRT!
HOW THE HELL ARE YA?
I'M OKAY.

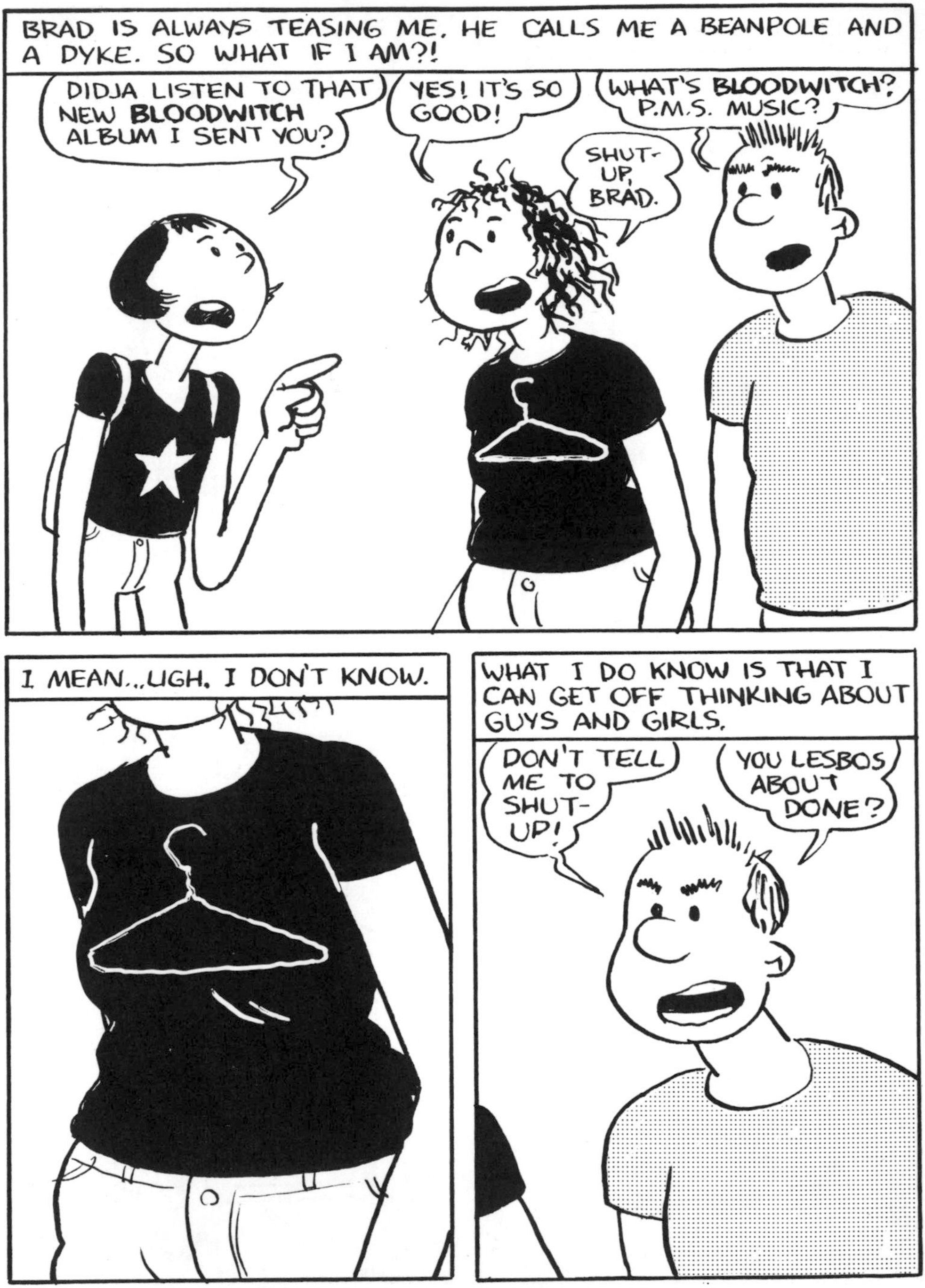
BRAD IS ALWAYS TEASING ME. HE CALLS ME A BEANPOLE AND A DYKE. SO WHAT IF I AM?!
DIDJA LISTEN TO THAT NEW BLOODWITCH ALBUM I SENT YOU?
YES! IT'S SO GOOD!
WHAT'S BLOODWITCH? P.M.S. MUSIC?
SHUT-UP, BRAD.
I MEAN...UGH. I DON'T KNOW.
WHAT I DO KNOW IS THAT I CAN GET OFF THINKING ABOUT GUYS AND GIRLS.
DON'T TELL ME TO SHUT-UP!
YOU LESBOS ABOUT DONE?

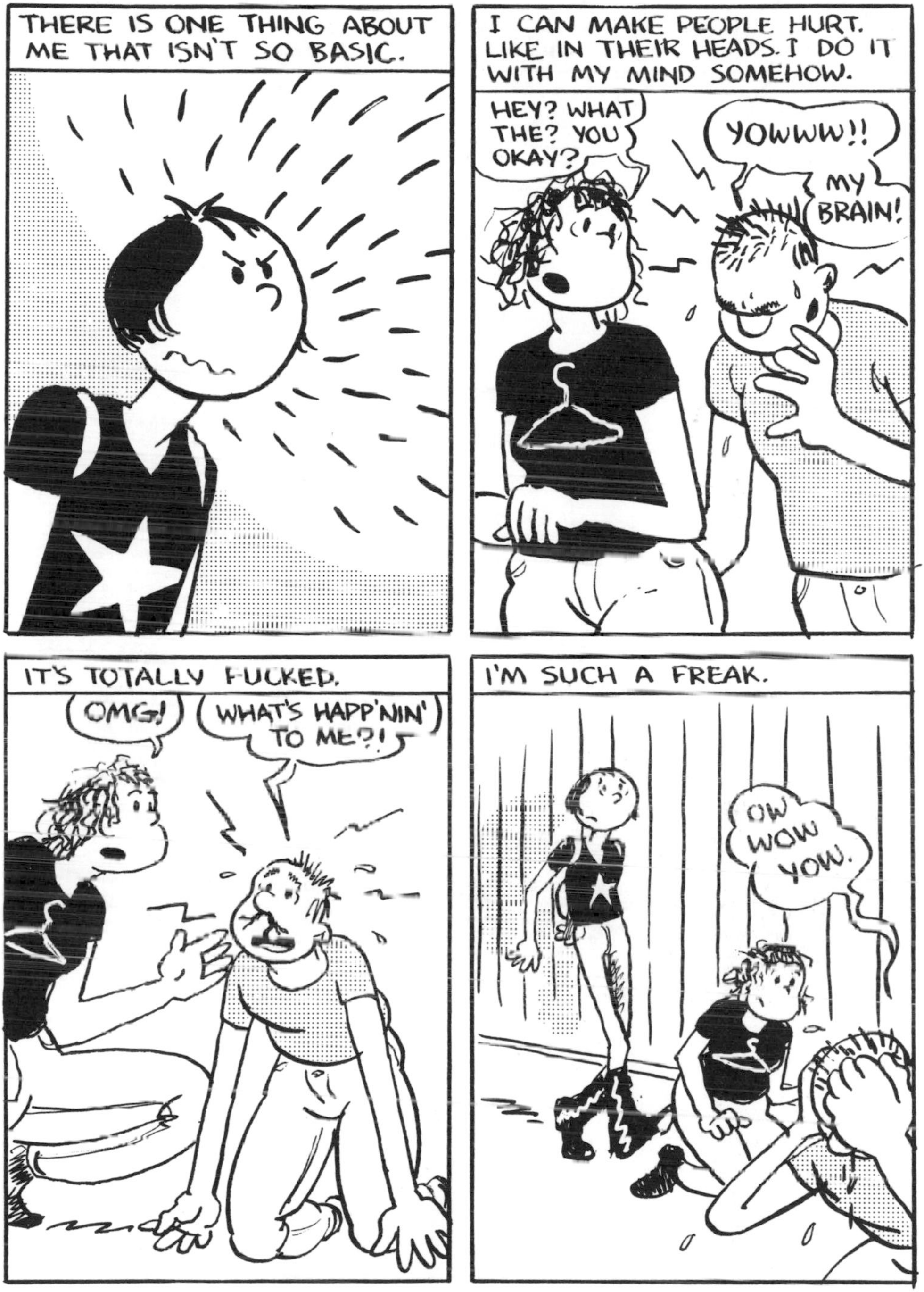
THERE IS ONE THING ABOUT ME THAT ISN'T SO BASIC.
I CAN MAKE PEOPLE HURT. LIKE IN THEIR HEADS. I DO IT WITH MY MIND SOMEHOW.
HEY? WHAT THE? YOU OKAY?
YOWWW!!
MY BRAIN!
IT'S TOTALLY FUCKED.
OMG!
WHAT'S HAPP'NIN' TO ME?!
I'M SUCH A FREAK.
OW WOW YOW.

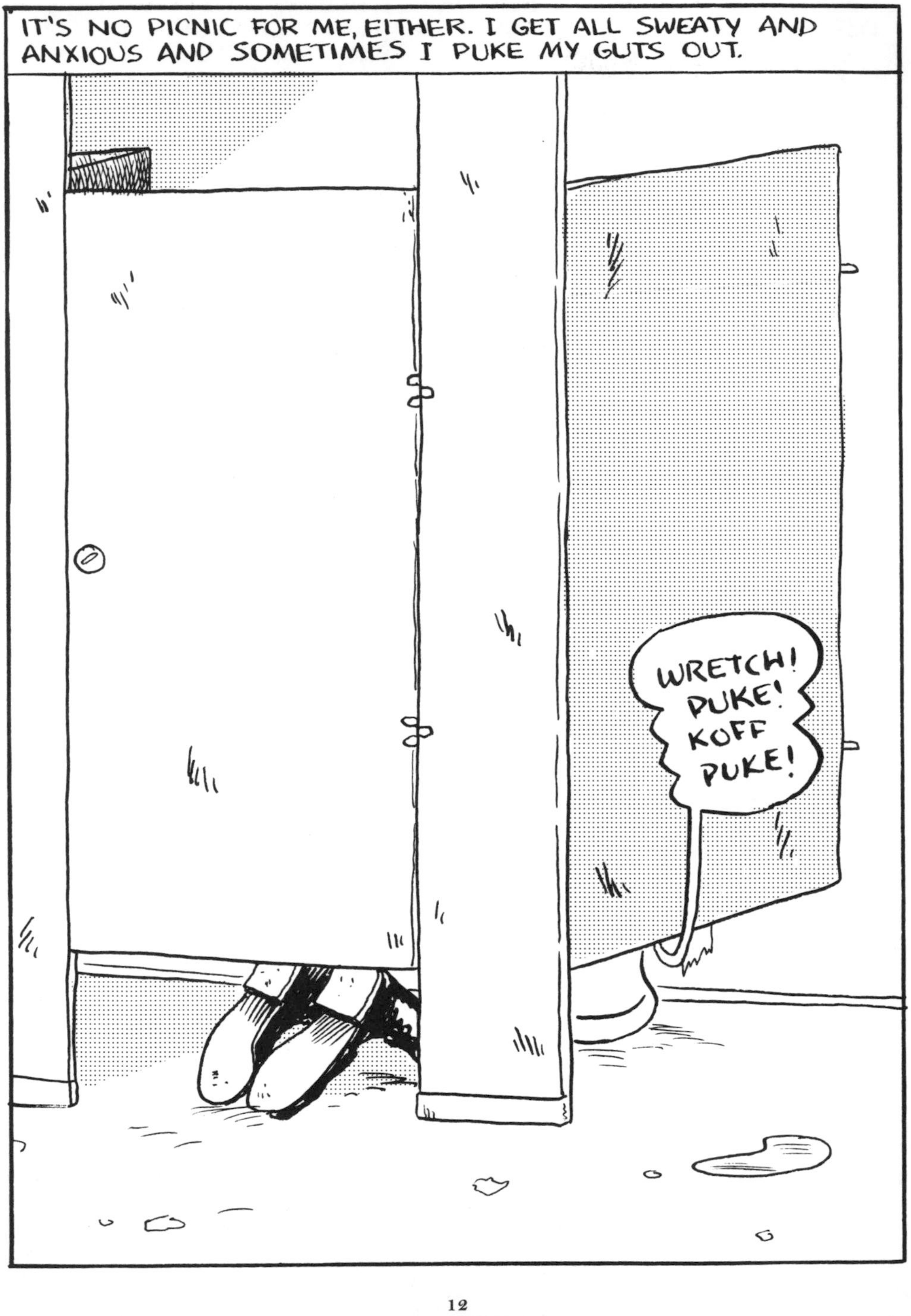
IT'S NO PICNIC FOR ME, EITHER. I GET ALL SWEATY AND ANXIOUS AND SOMETIMES I PUKE MY GUTS OUT.
WRETCH! PUKE! KOFF PUKE!

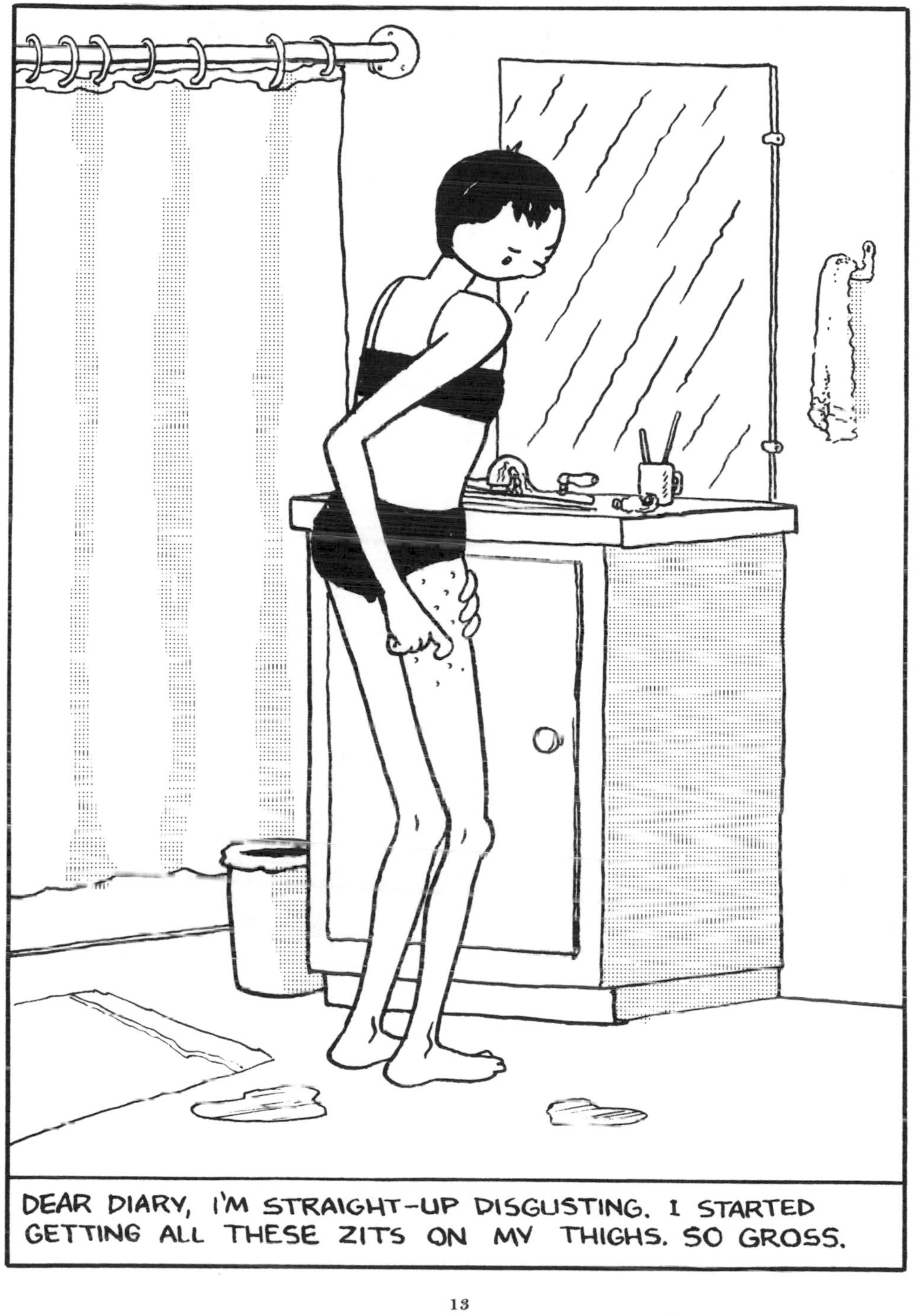
DEAR DIARY, I'M STRAIGHT-UP DISGUSTING. I STARTED GETTING ALL THESE ZITS ON MY THIGHS. SO GROSS.

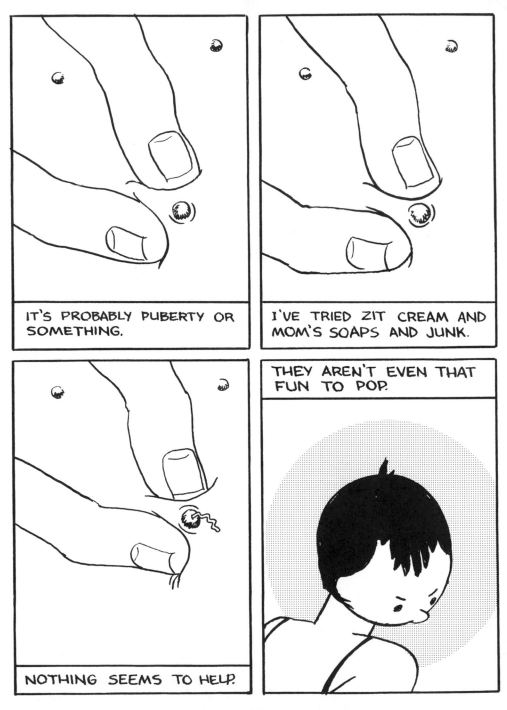

IT'S PROBABLY PUBERTY OR SOMETHING.

I'VE TRIED ZIT CREAM AND MOM'S SOAPS AND JUNK.

NOTHING SEEMS TO HELP.

THEY AREN'T EVEN THAT FUN TO POP.

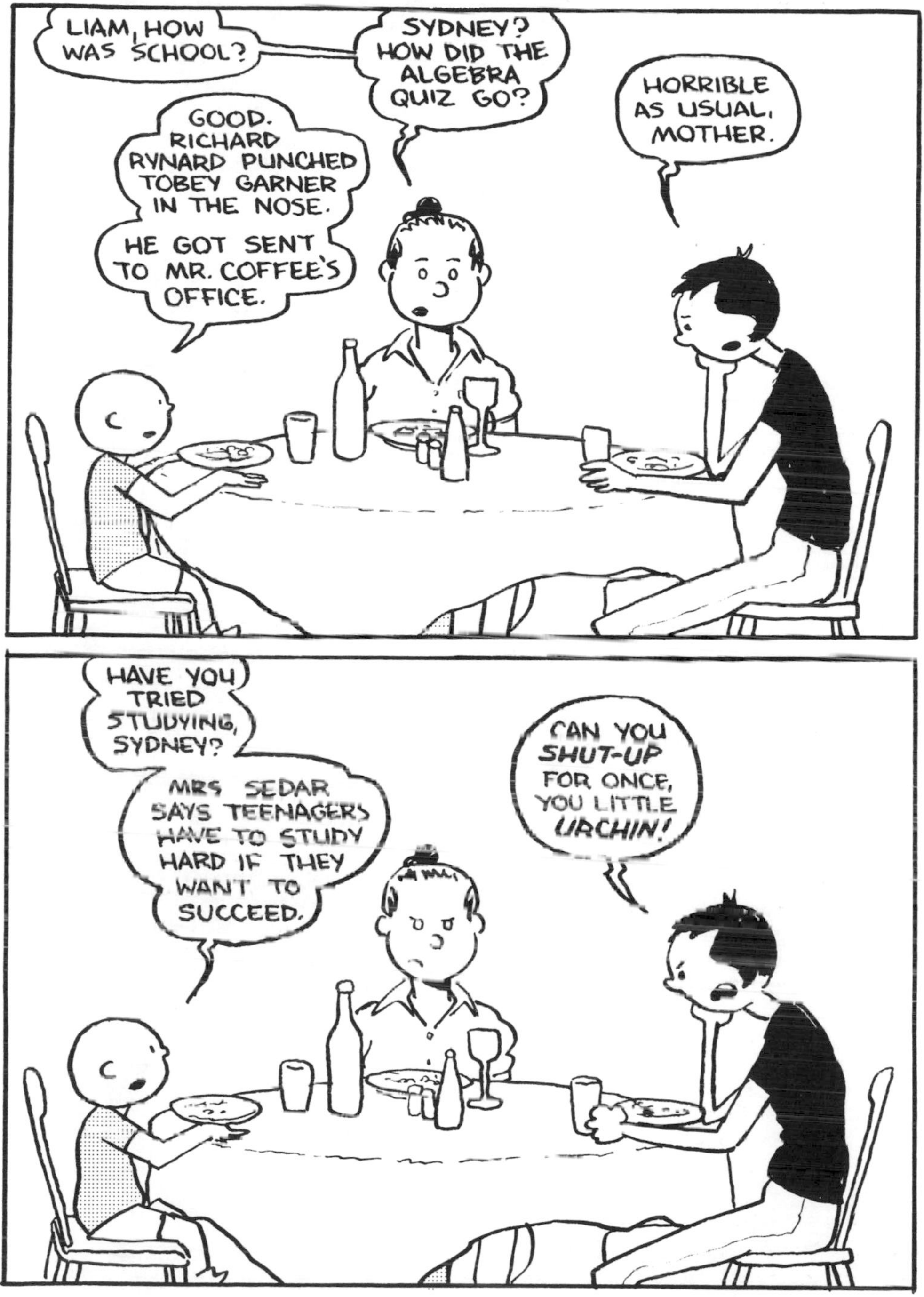
LIAM, HOW WAS SCHOOL?
SYDNEY? HOW DID THE ALGEBRA QUIZ GO?
HORRIBLE AS USUAL, MOTHER.
GOOD. RICHARD RYNARD PUNCHED TOBEY GARNER IN THE NOSE.
HE GOT SENT TO MR. COFFEE'S OFFICE.
HAVE YOU TRIED STUDYING, SYDNEY?
MRS SEDAR SAYS TEENAGERS HAVE TO STUDY HARD IF THEY WANT TO SUCCEED.
CAN YOU *SHUT-UP* FOR ONCE, YOU LITTLE *URCHIN!*

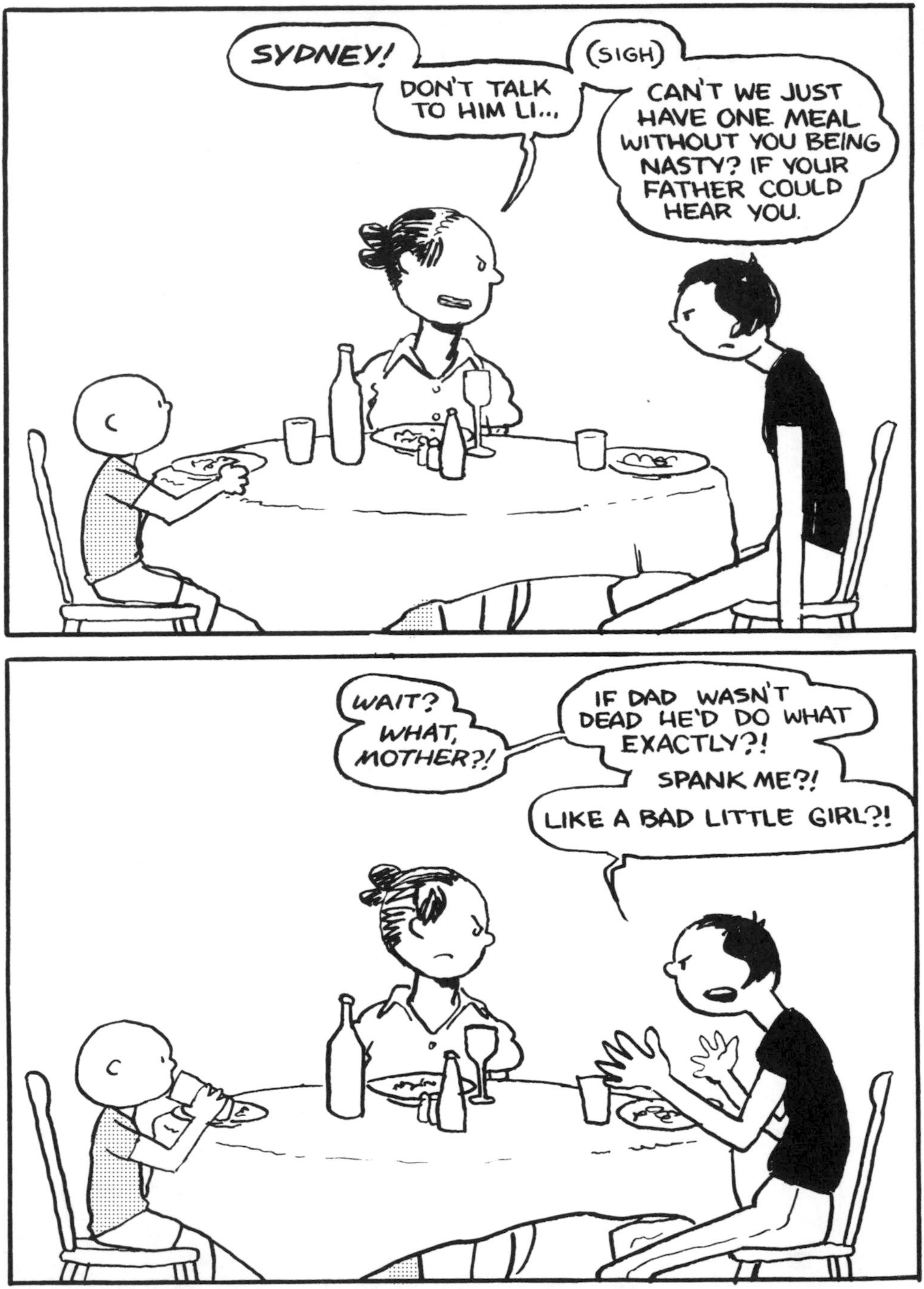
SYDNEY!
DON'T TALK TO HIM LI...
(SIGH)
CAN'T WE JUST HAVE ONE MEAL WITHOUT YOU BEING NASTY? IF YOUR FATHER COULD HEAR YOU.
WAIT? WHAT, MOTHER?!
IF DAD WASN'T DEAD HE'D DO WHAT EXACTLY?!
SPANK ME?!
LIKE A BAD LITTLE GIRL?!

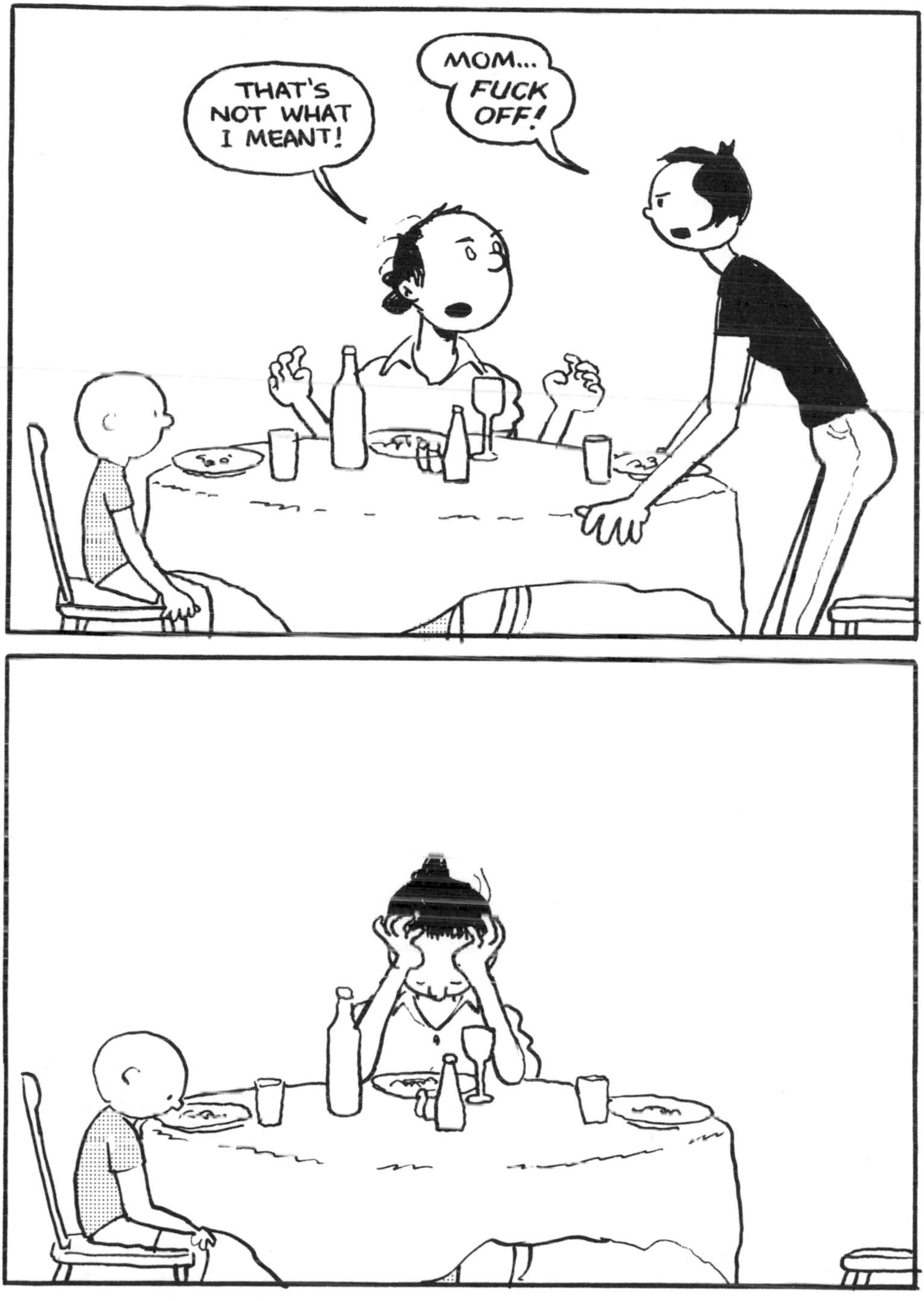
THAT'S NOT WHAT I MEANT!
MOM... FUCK OFF!

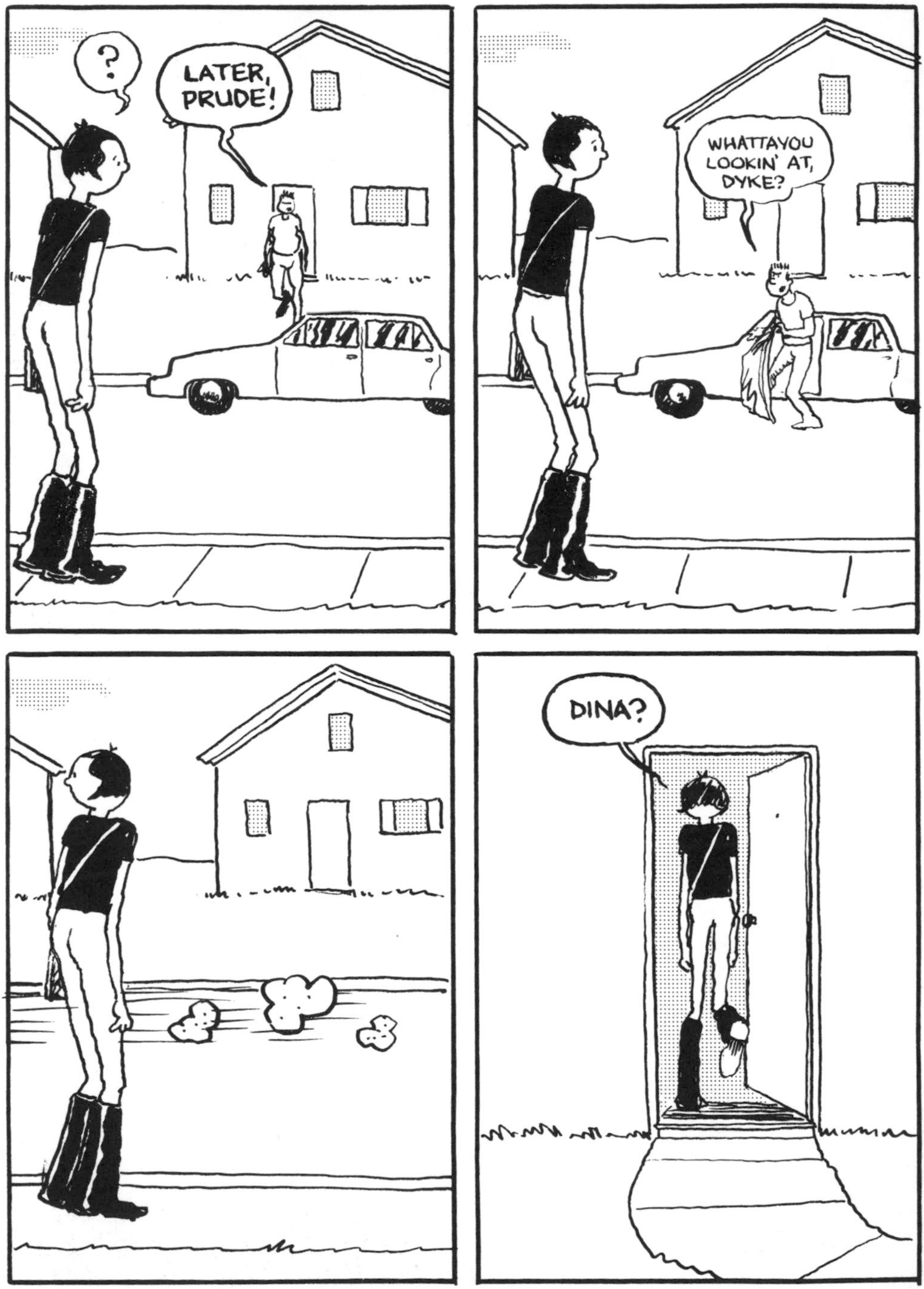
?
LATER, PRUDE!
WHATTAYOU LOOKIN' AT, DYKE?
DINA?

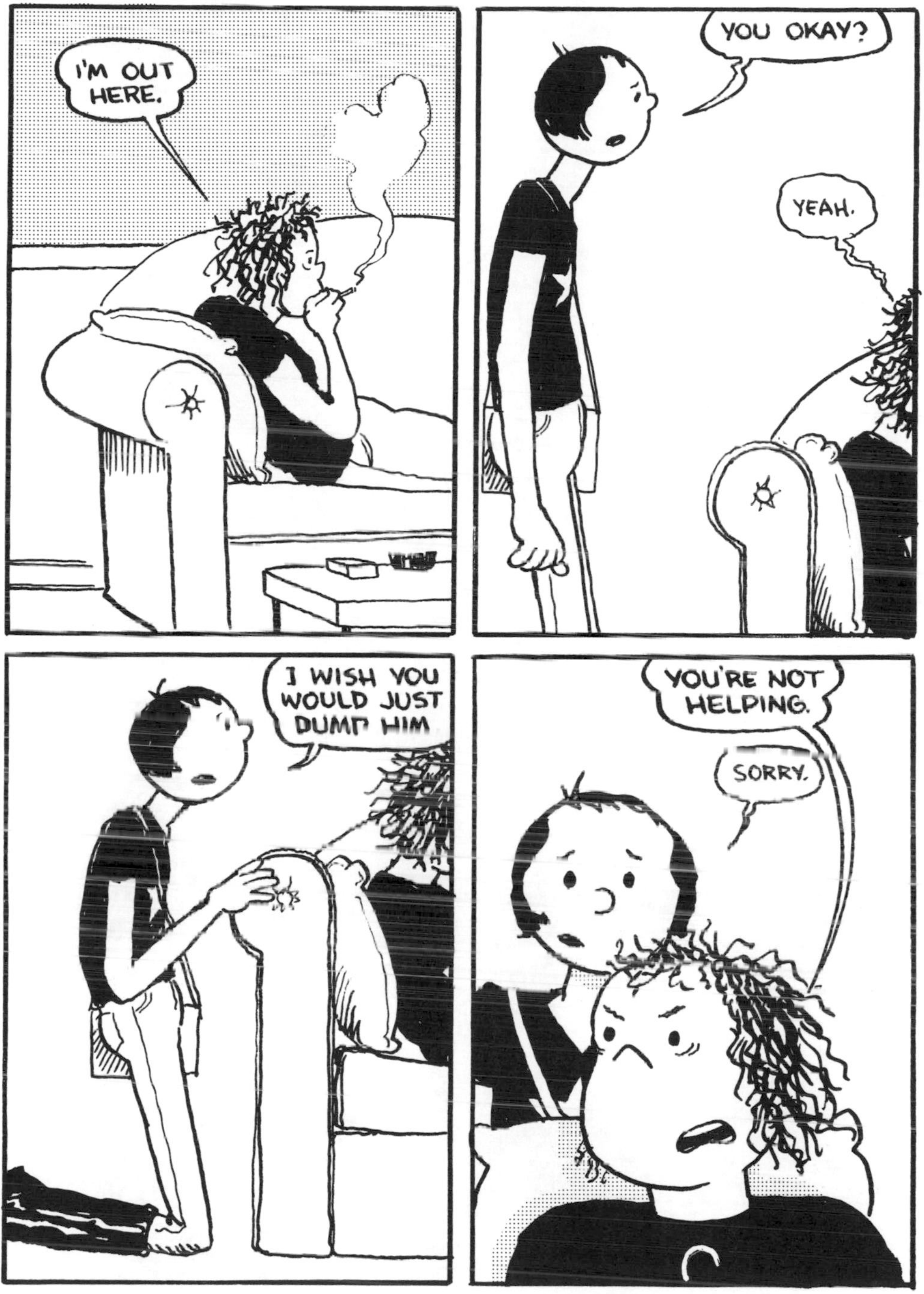
I'M OUT HERE.
YOU OKAY?
YEAH.
I WISH YOU WOULD JUST DUMP HIM.
YOU'RE NOT HELPING.
SORRY.

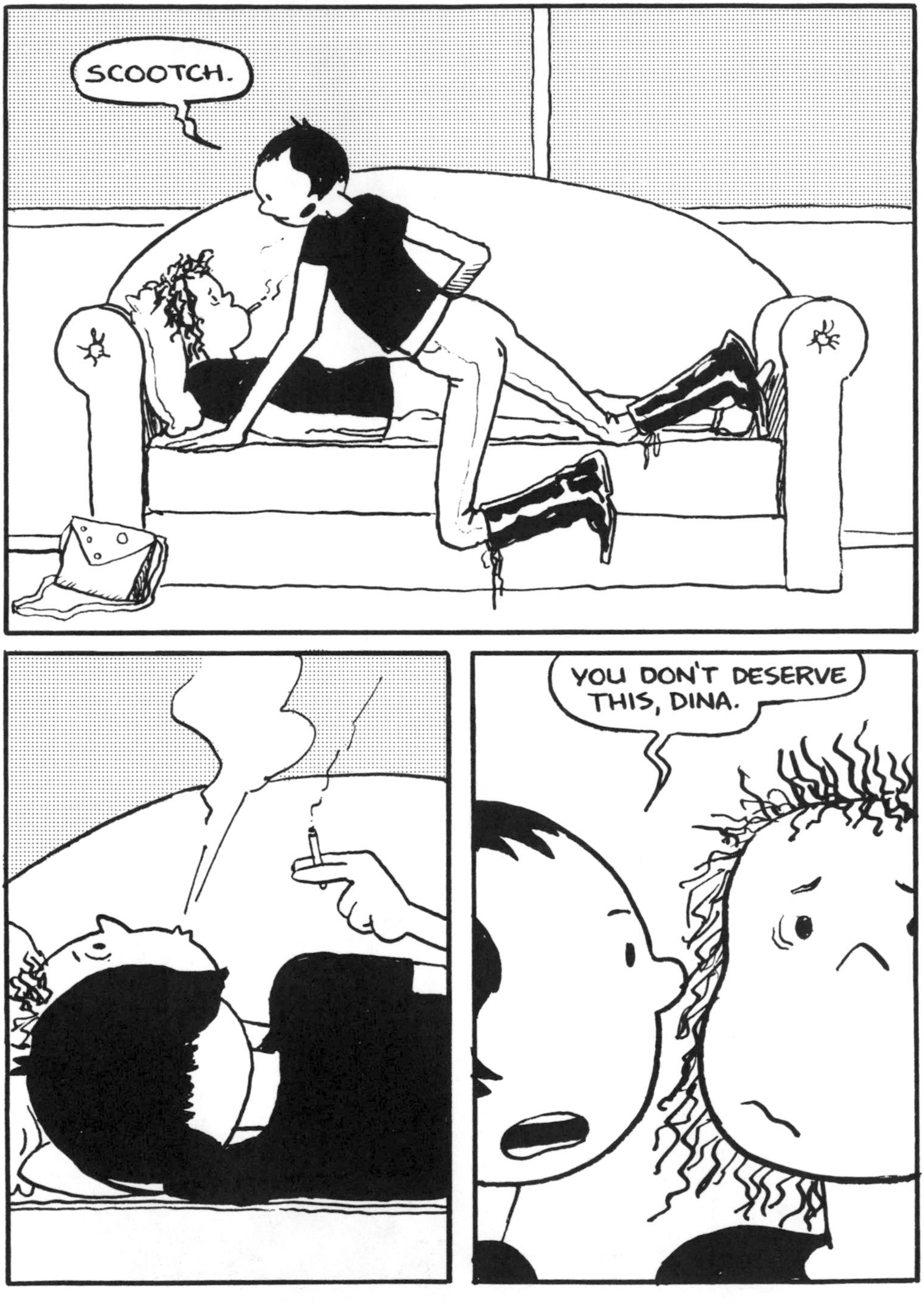
SCOOTCH.
YOU DON'T DESERVE THIS, DINA.

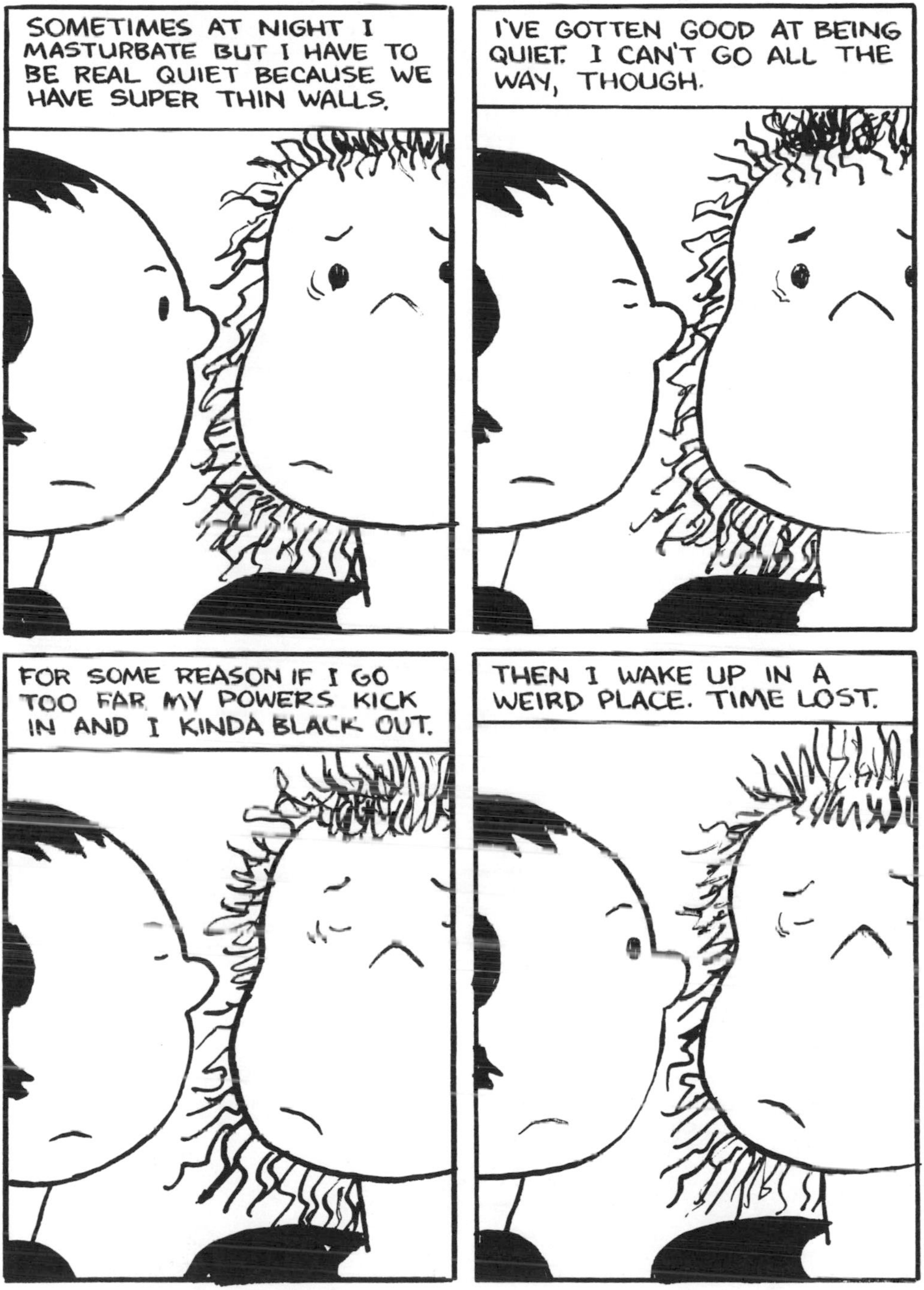
SOMETIMES AT NIGHT I MASTURBATE BUT I HAVE TO BE REAL QUIET BECAUSE WE HAVE SUPER THIN WALLS.
I'VE GOTTEN GOOD AT BEING QUIET. I CAN'T GO ALL THE WAY, THOUGH.
FOR SOME REASON IF I GO TOO FAR MY POWERS KICK IN AND I KINDA BLACK OUT.
THEN I WAKE UP IN A WEIRD PLACE. TIME LOST.

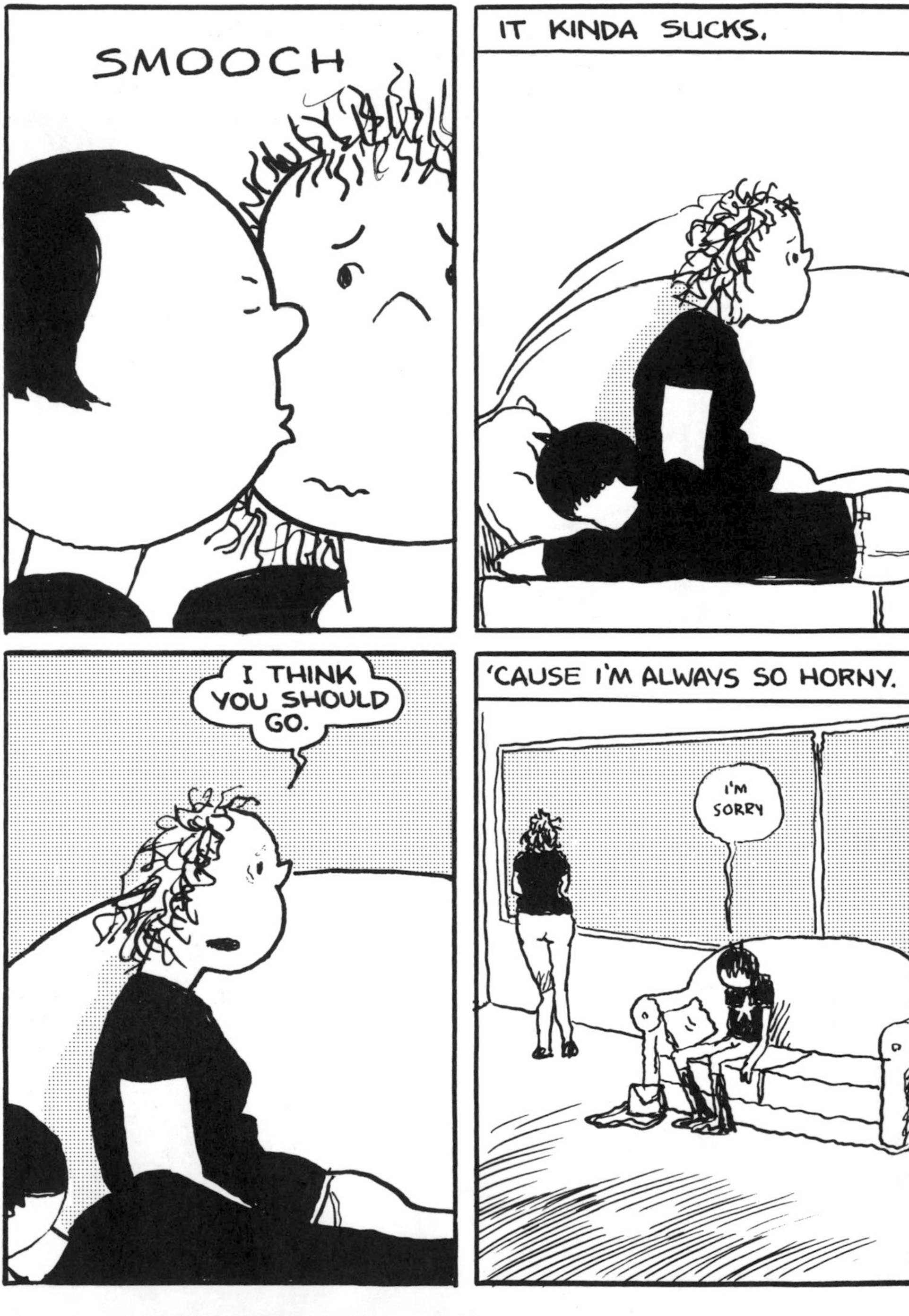
SMOOCH
IT KINDA SUCKS.
I THINK YOU SHOULD GO.
'CAUSE I'M ALWAYS SO HORNY.
I'M SORRY

I GUESS I SHOULD TELL YOU ABOUT MY DAD. HE'S GONE. DEAD. I KEEP HIS DOG TAGS AROUND MY NECK. IT IRRITATES MY SKIN. THE METAL SMELLS LIKE HIM.

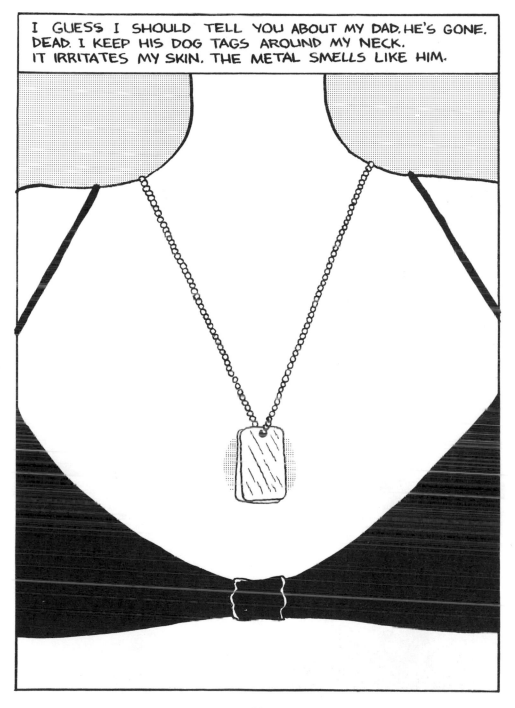

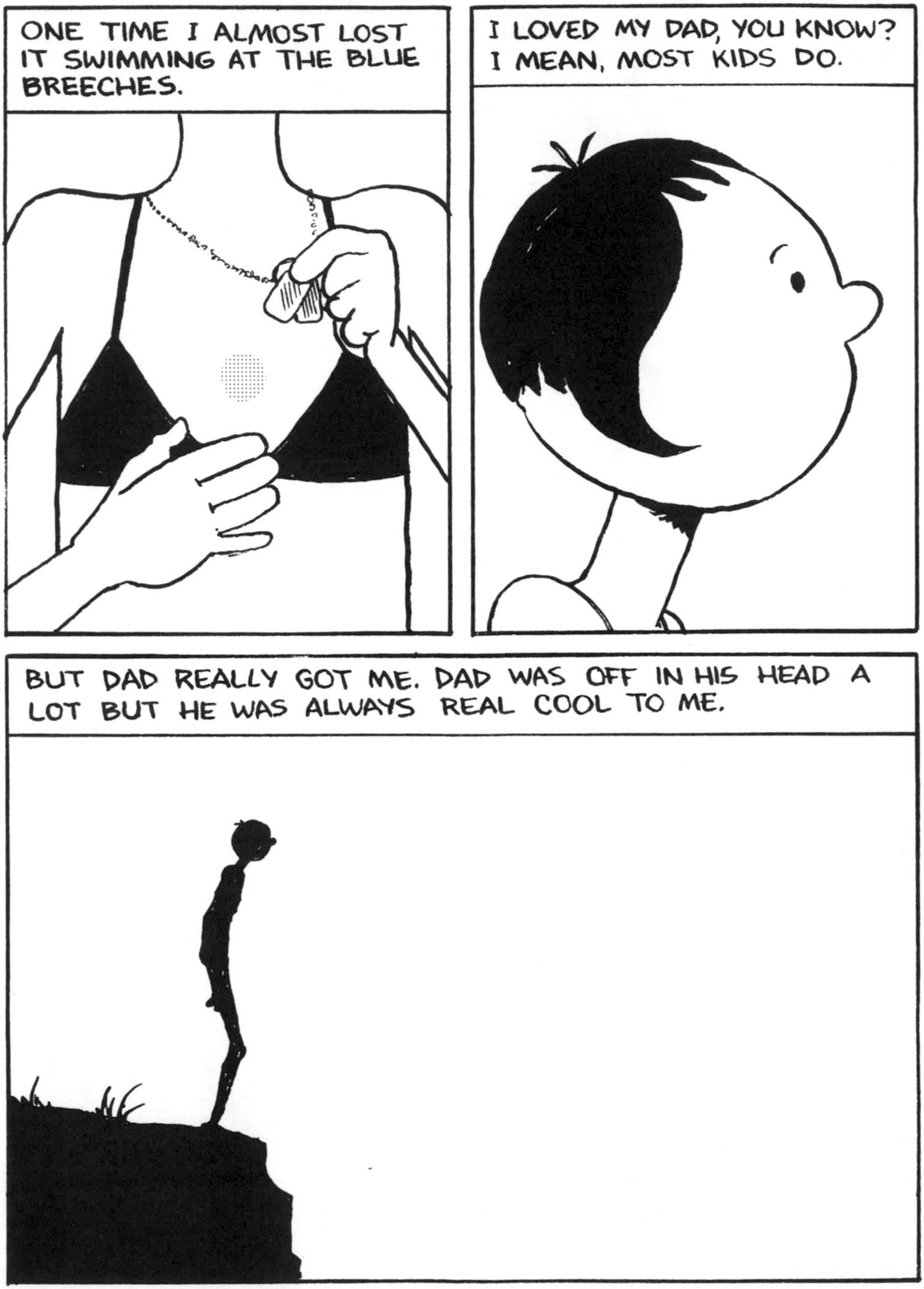
ONE TIME I ALMOST LOST IT SWIMMING AT THE BLUE BREECHES.
I LOVED MY DAD, YOU KNOW? I MEAN, MOST KIDS DO.
BUT DAD REALLY GOT ME. DAD WAS OFF IN HIS HEAD A LOT BUT HE WAS ALWAYS REAL COOL TO ME.

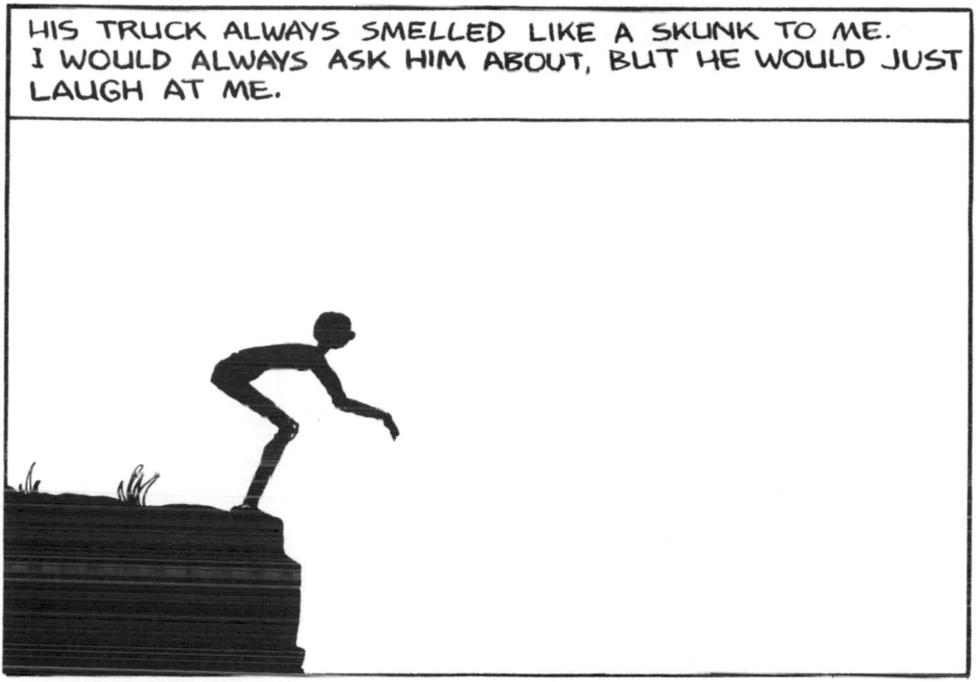
HIS TRUCK ALWAYS SMELLED LIKE A SKUNK TO ME.
I WOULD ALWAYS ASK HIM ABOUT, BUT HE WOULD JUST LAUGH AT ME.

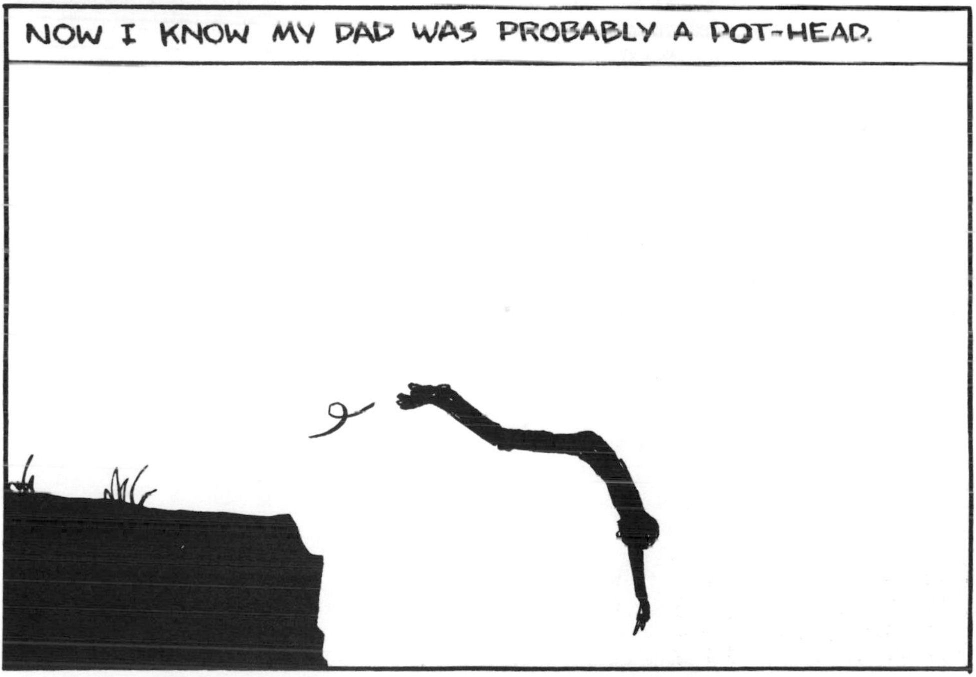
NOW I KNOW MY DAD WAS PROBABLY A POT-HEAD.

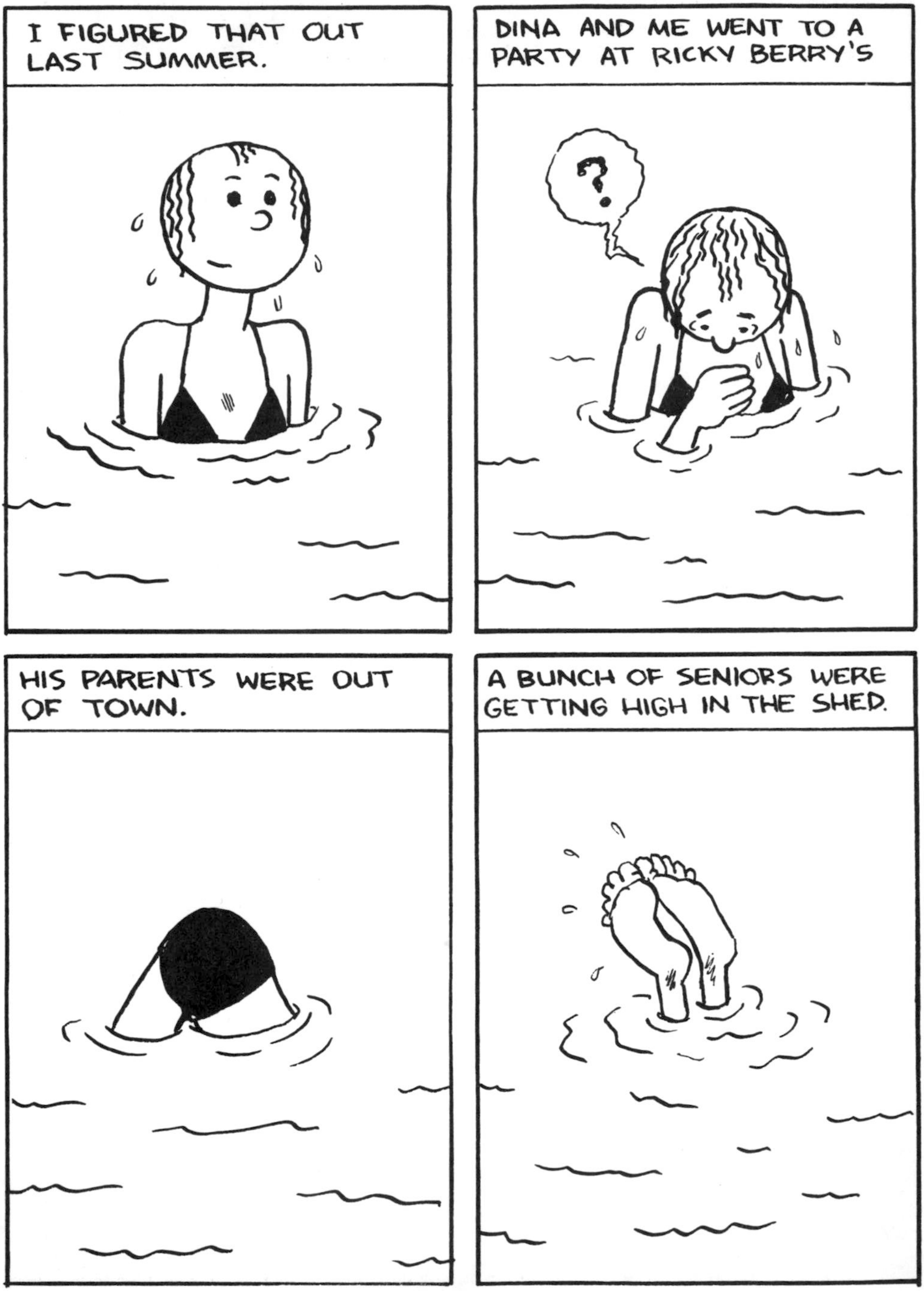
I FIGURED THAT OUT LAST SUMMER.
DINA AND ME WENT TO A PARTY AT RICKY BERRY'S
?
HIS PARENTS WERE OUT OF TOWN.
A BUNCH OF SENIORS WERE GETTING HIGH IN THE SHED.

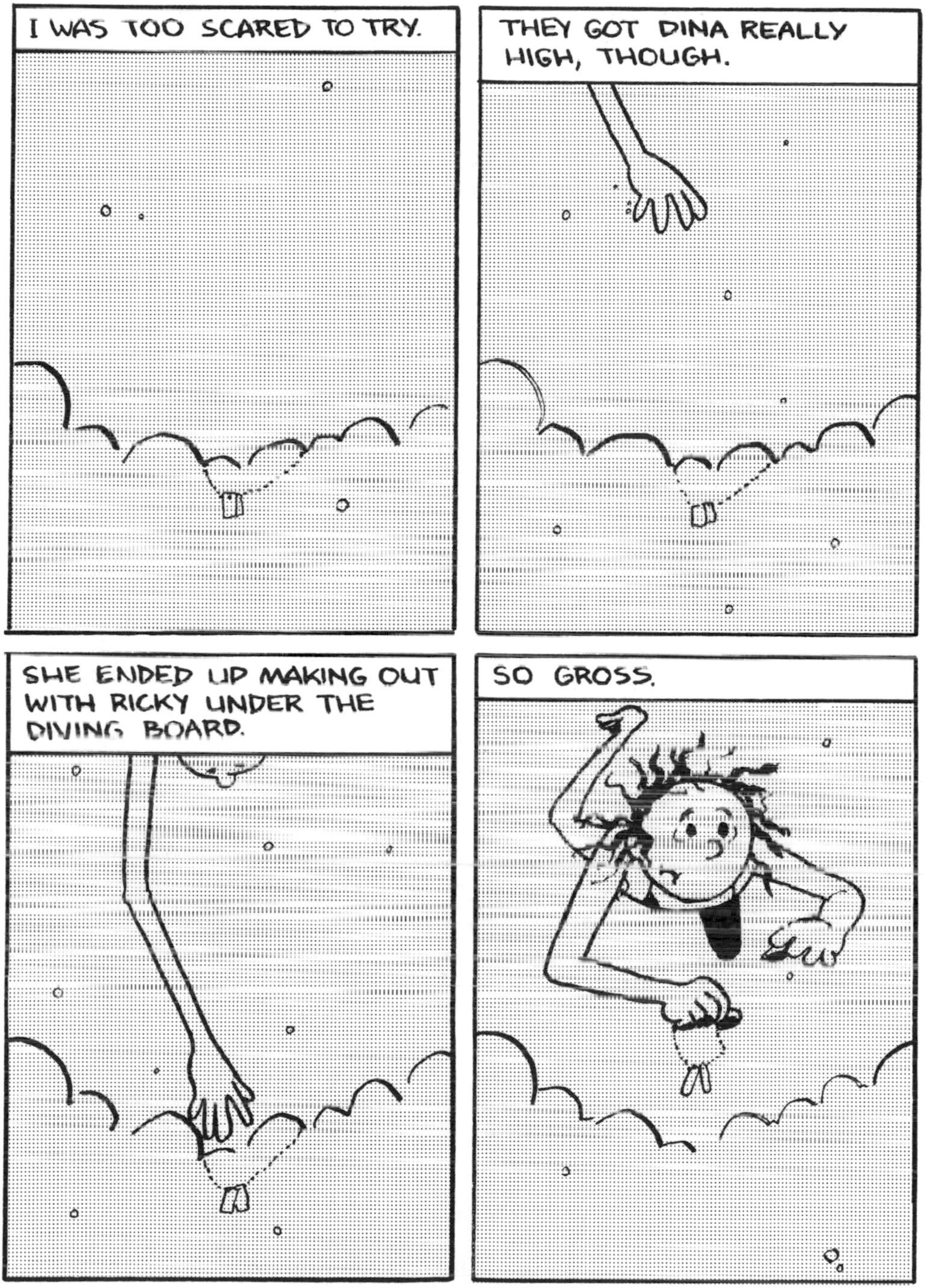
I WAS TOO SCARED TO TRY.
THEY GOT DINA REALLY HIGH, THOUGH.
SHE ENDED UP MAKING OUT WITH RICKY UNDER THE DIVING BOARD.
SO GROSS.

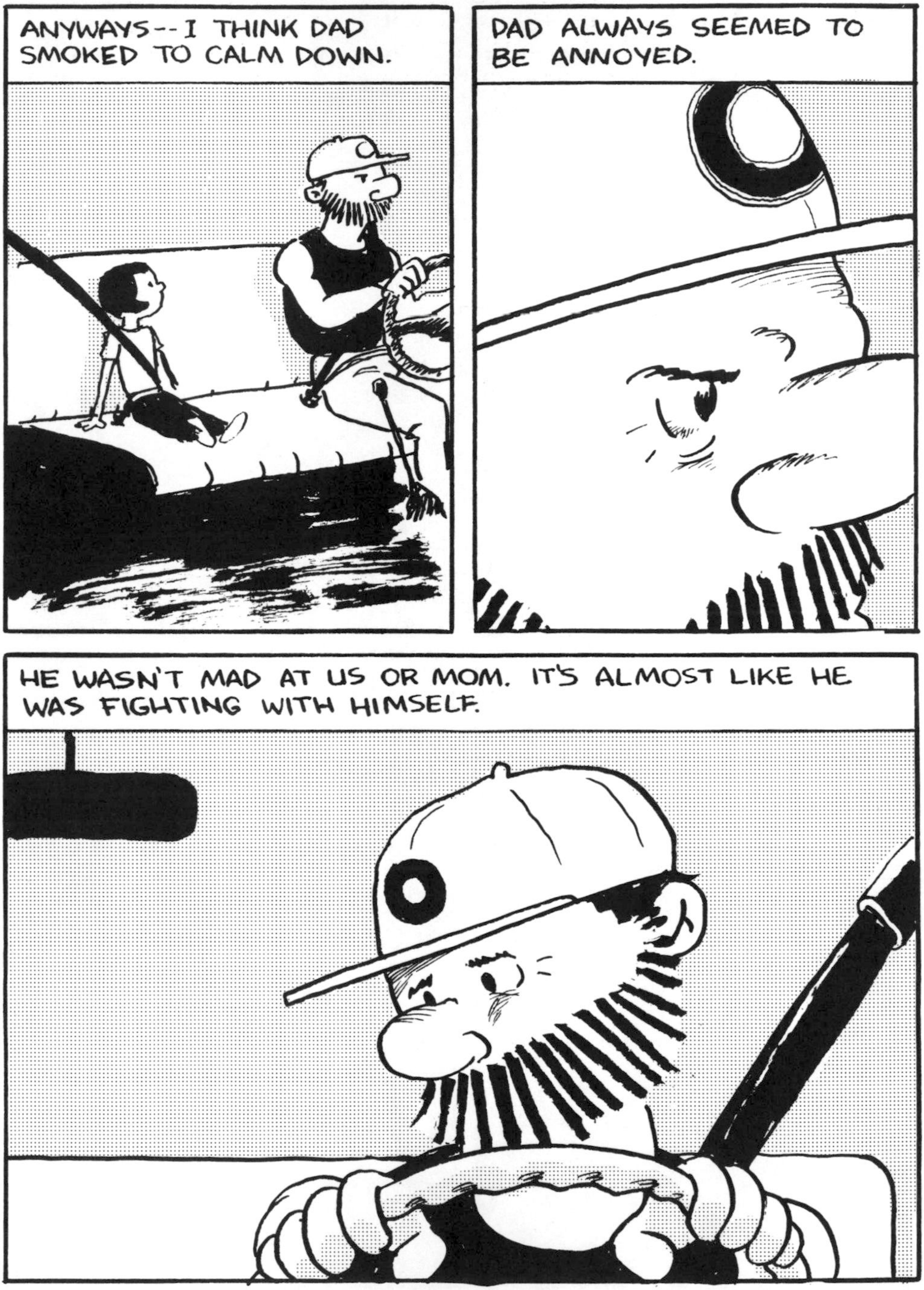
ANYWAYS--I THINK DAD SMOKED TO CALM DOWN.
DAD ALWAYS SEEMED TO BE ANNOYED.
HE WASN'T MAD AT US OR MOM. IT'S ALMOST LIKE HE WAS FIGHTING WITH HIMSELF.

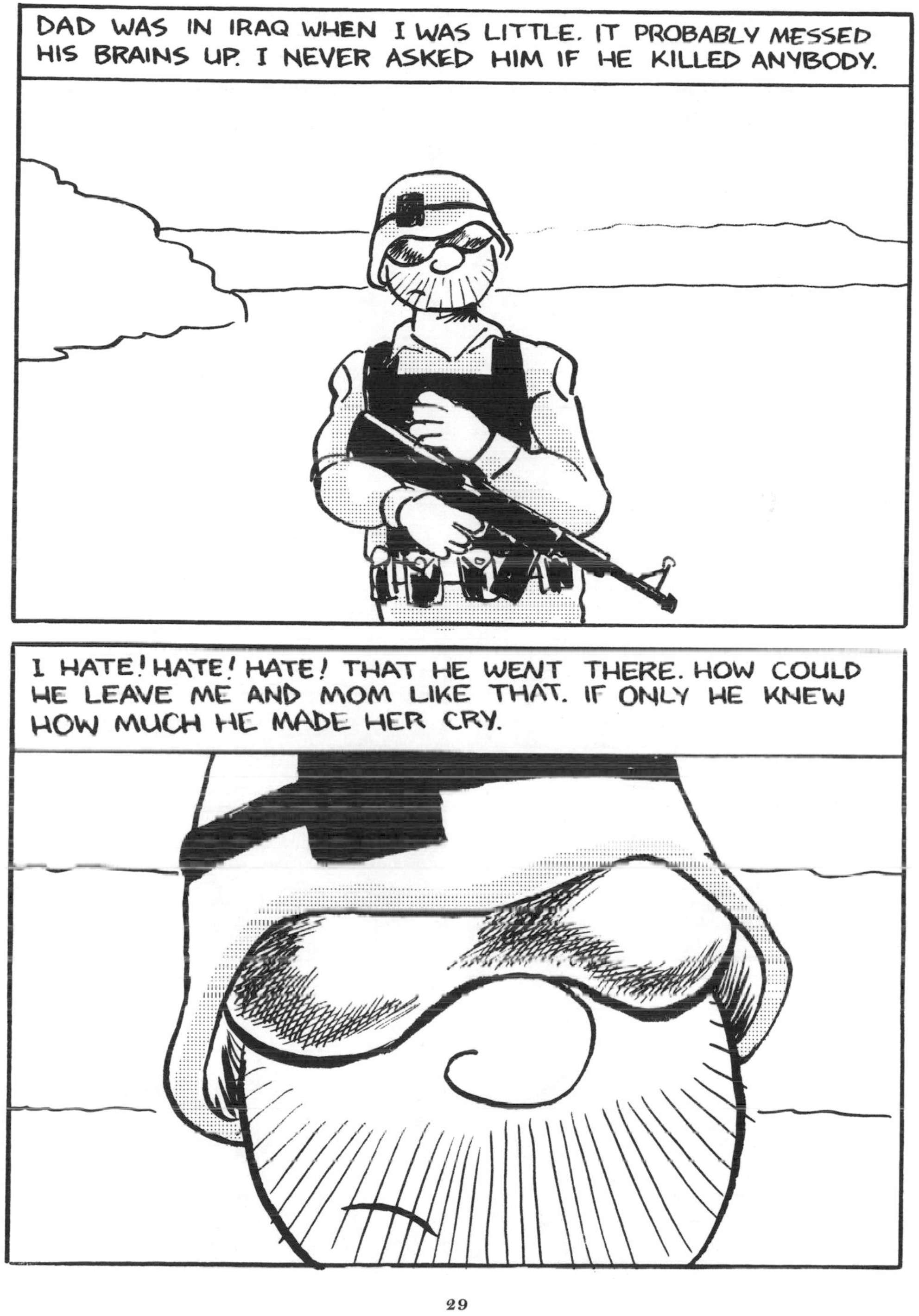
DAD WAS IN IRAQ WHEN I WAS LITTLE. IT PROBABLY MESSED HIS BRAINS UP. I NEVER ASKED HIM IF HE KILLED ANYBODY.
I HATE! HATE! HATE! THAT HE WENT THERE. HOW COULD HE LEAVE ME AND MOM LIKE THAT. IF ONLY HE KNEW HOW MUCH HE MADE HER CRY.

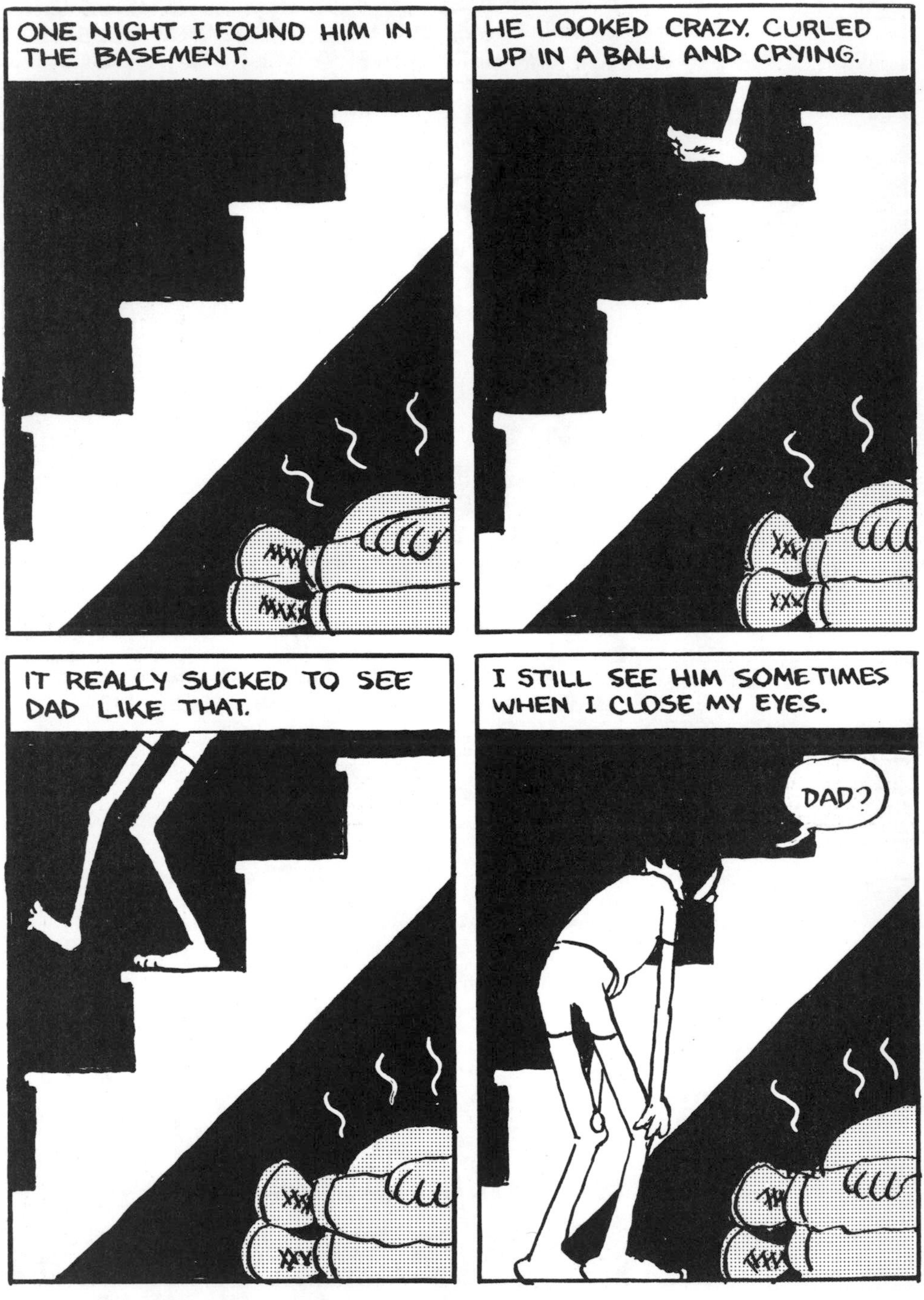
ONE NIGHT I FOUND HIM IN THE BASEMENT.
HE LOOKED CRAZY. CURLED UP IN A BALL AND CRYING.
IT REALLY SUCKED TO SEE DAD LIKE THAT.
I STILL SEE HIM SOMETIMES WHEN I CLOSE MY EYES.
DAD?

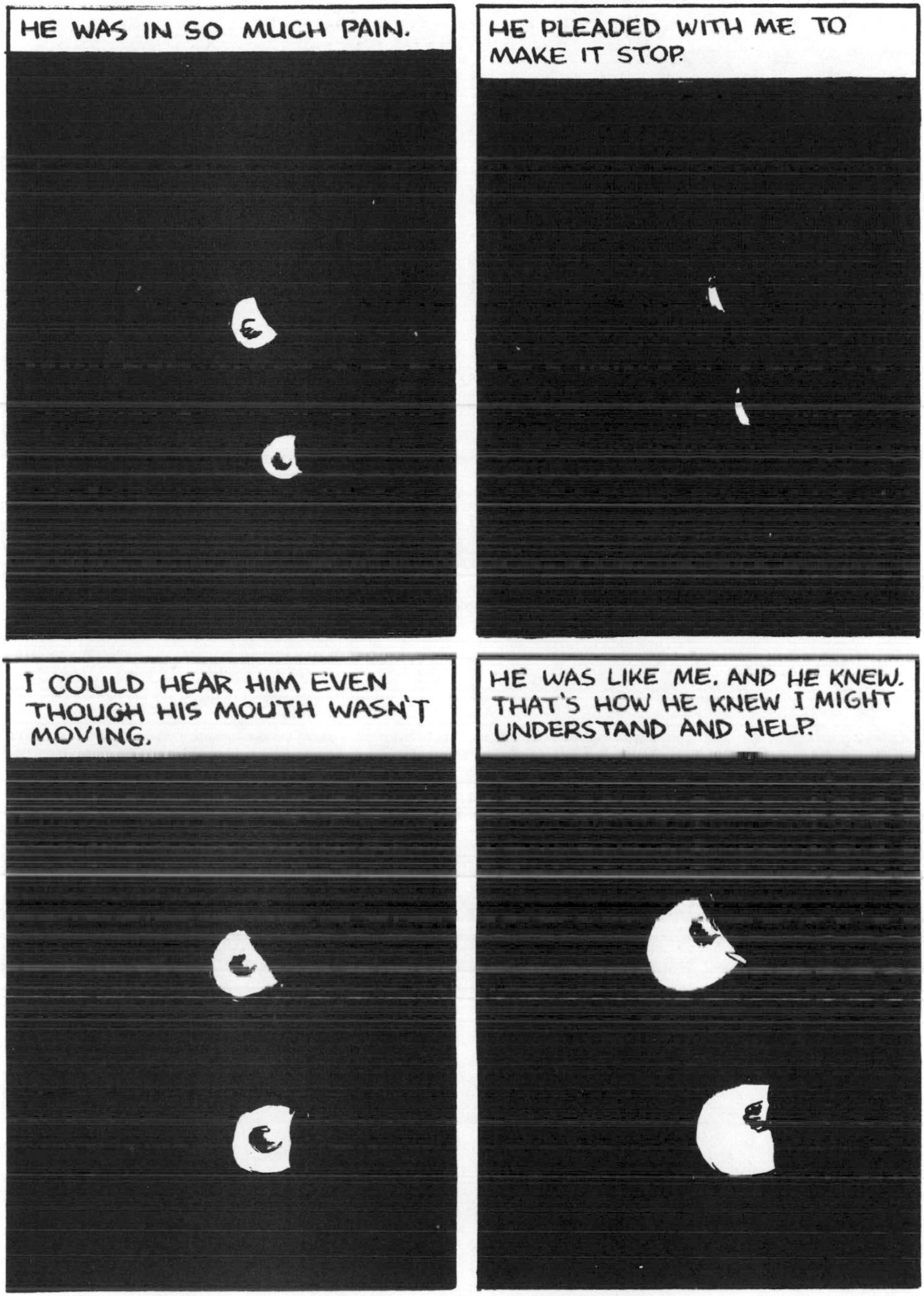
HE WAS IN SO MUCH PAIN.
HE PLEADED WITH ME TO MAKE IT STOP.
I COULD HEAR HIM EVEN THOUGH HIS MOUTH WASN'T MOVING.
HE WAS LIKE ME. AND HE KNEW. THAT'S HOW HE KNEW I MIGHT UNDERSTAND AND HELP.

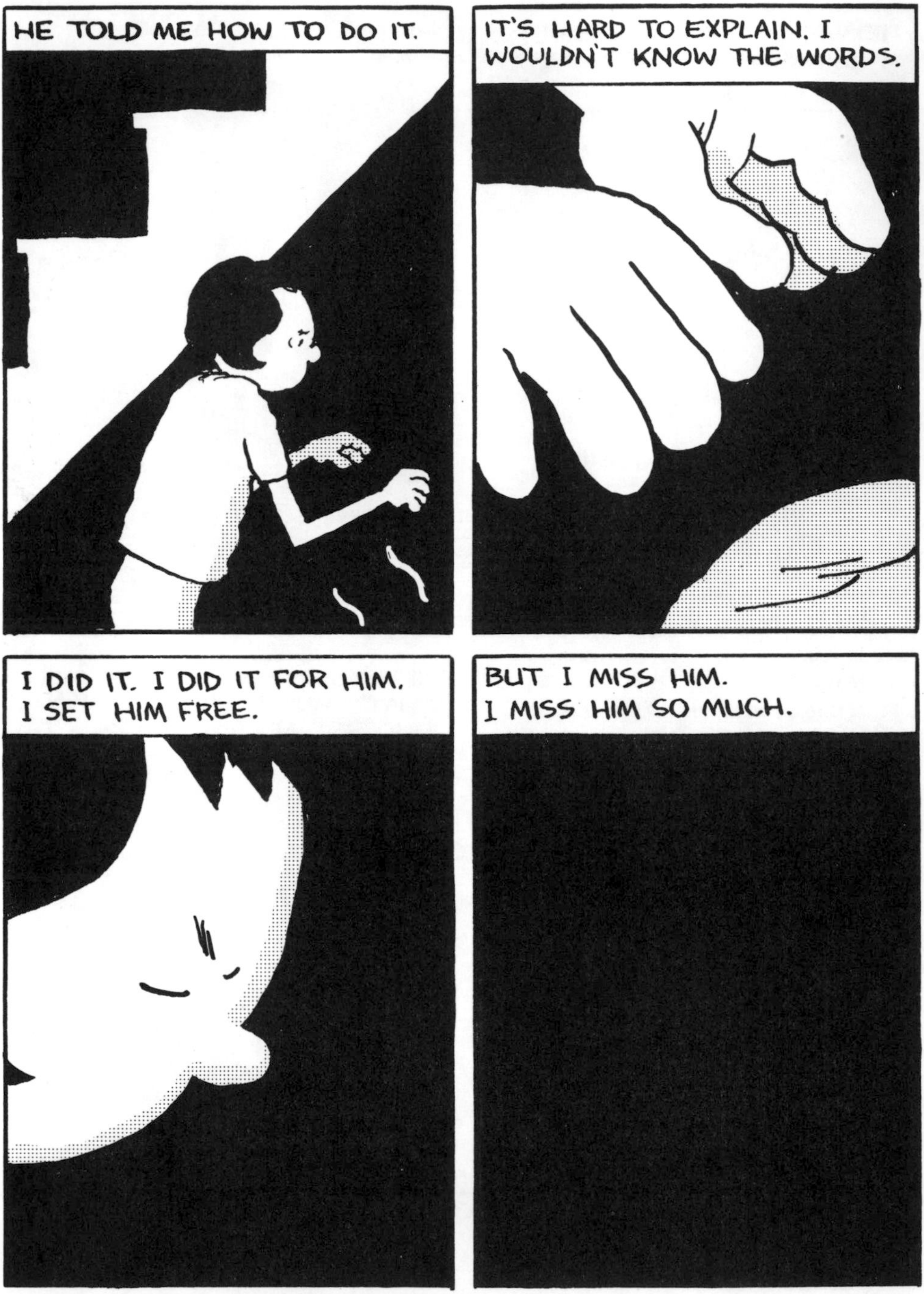
HE TOLD ME HOW TO DO IT.
IT'S HARD TO EXPLAIN. I WOULDN'T KNOW THE WORDS.
I DID IT. I DID IT FOR HIM. I SET HIM FREE.
BUT I MISS HIM. I MISS HIM SO MUCH.

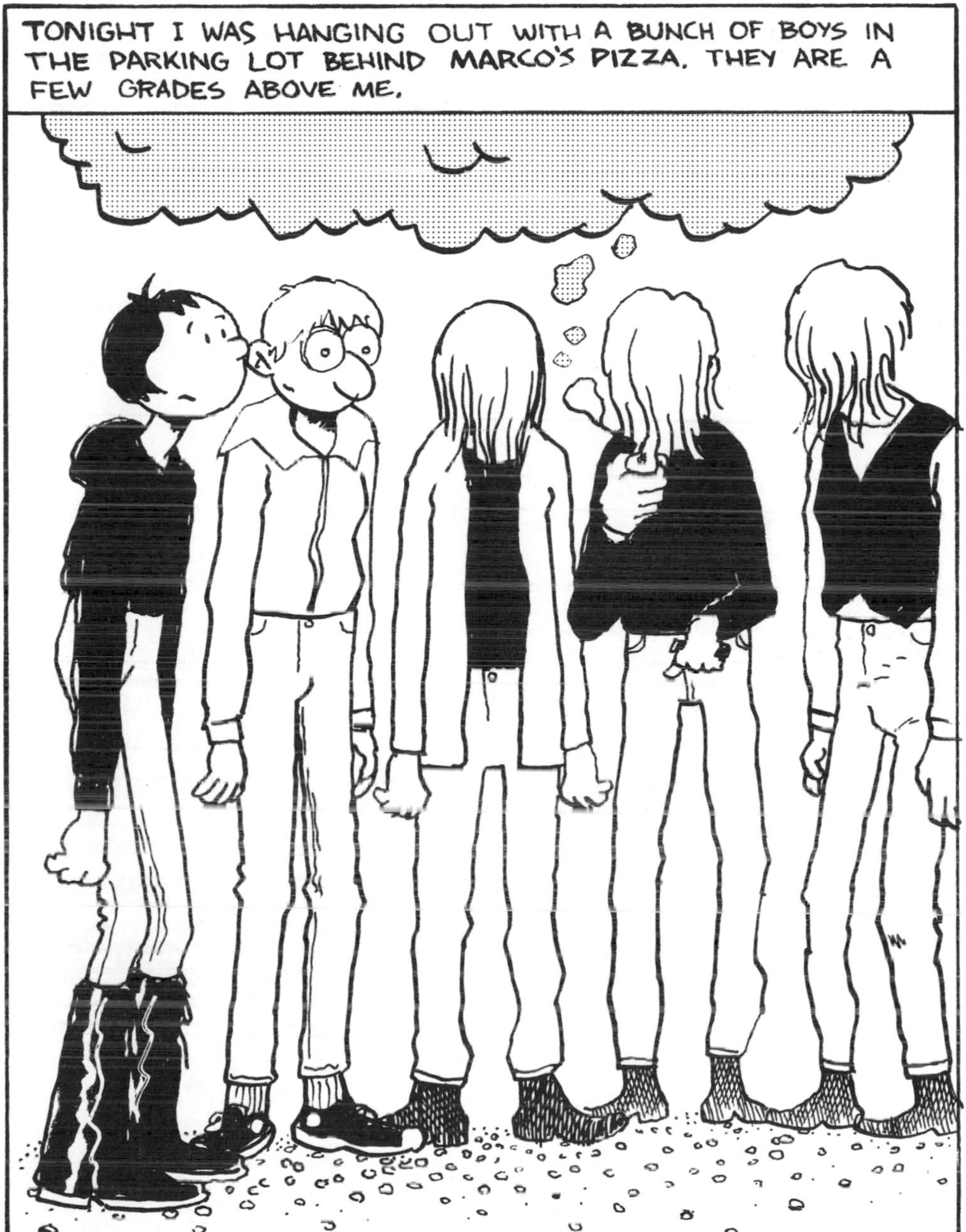
TONIGHT I WAS HANGING OUT WITH A BUNCH OF BOYS IN THE PARKING LOT BEHIND MARCO'S PIZZA. THEY ARE A FEW GRADES ABOVE ME.

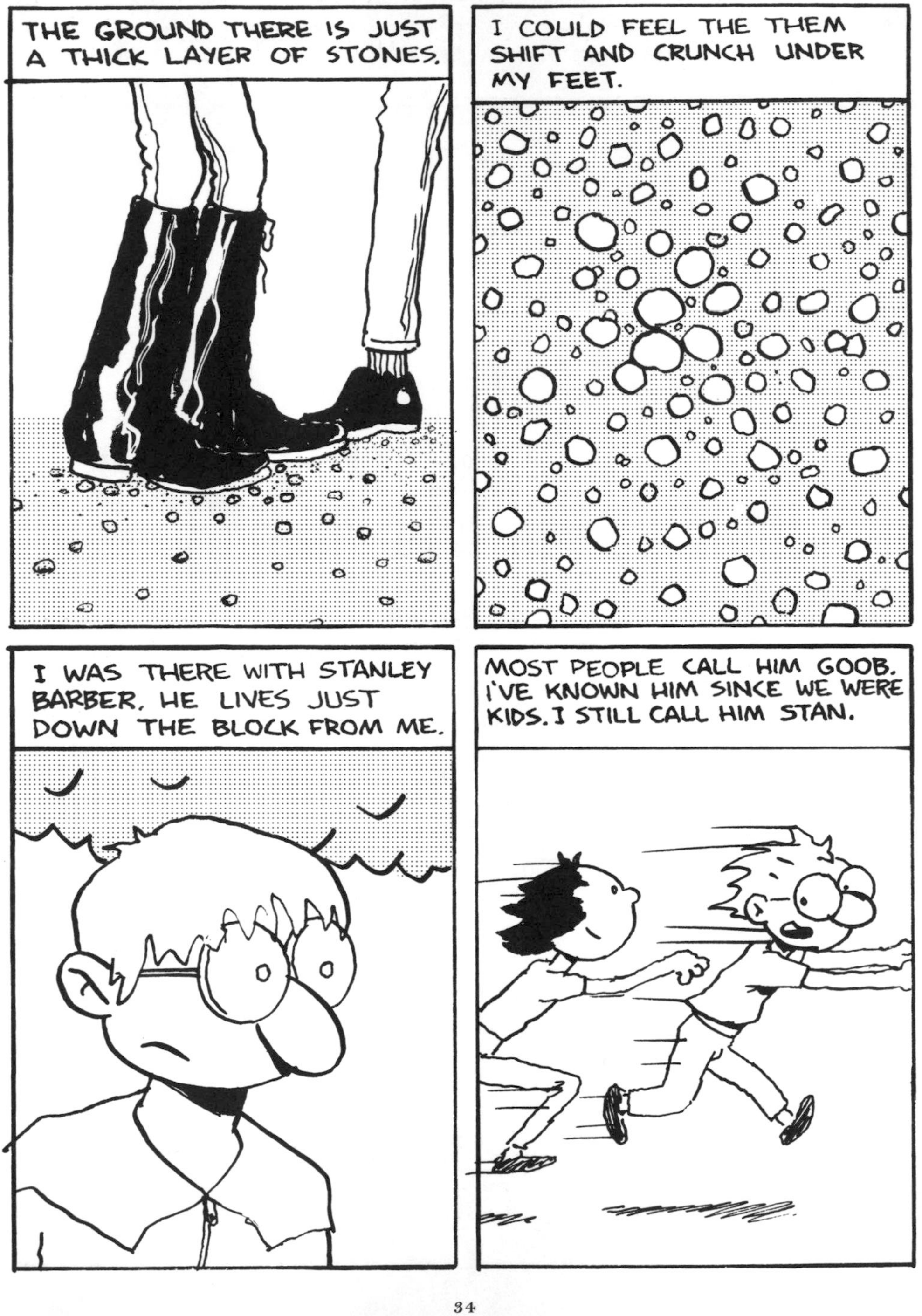
THE GROUND THERE IS JUST A THICK LAYER OF STONES.
I COULD FEEL THE THEM SHIFT AND CRUNCH UNDER MY FEET.
I WAS THERE WITH STANLEY BARBER, HE LIVES JUST DOWN THE BLOCK FROM ME.
MOST PEOPLE CALL HIM GOOB. I'VE KNOWN HIM SINCE WE WERE KIDS. I STILL CALL HIM STAN.

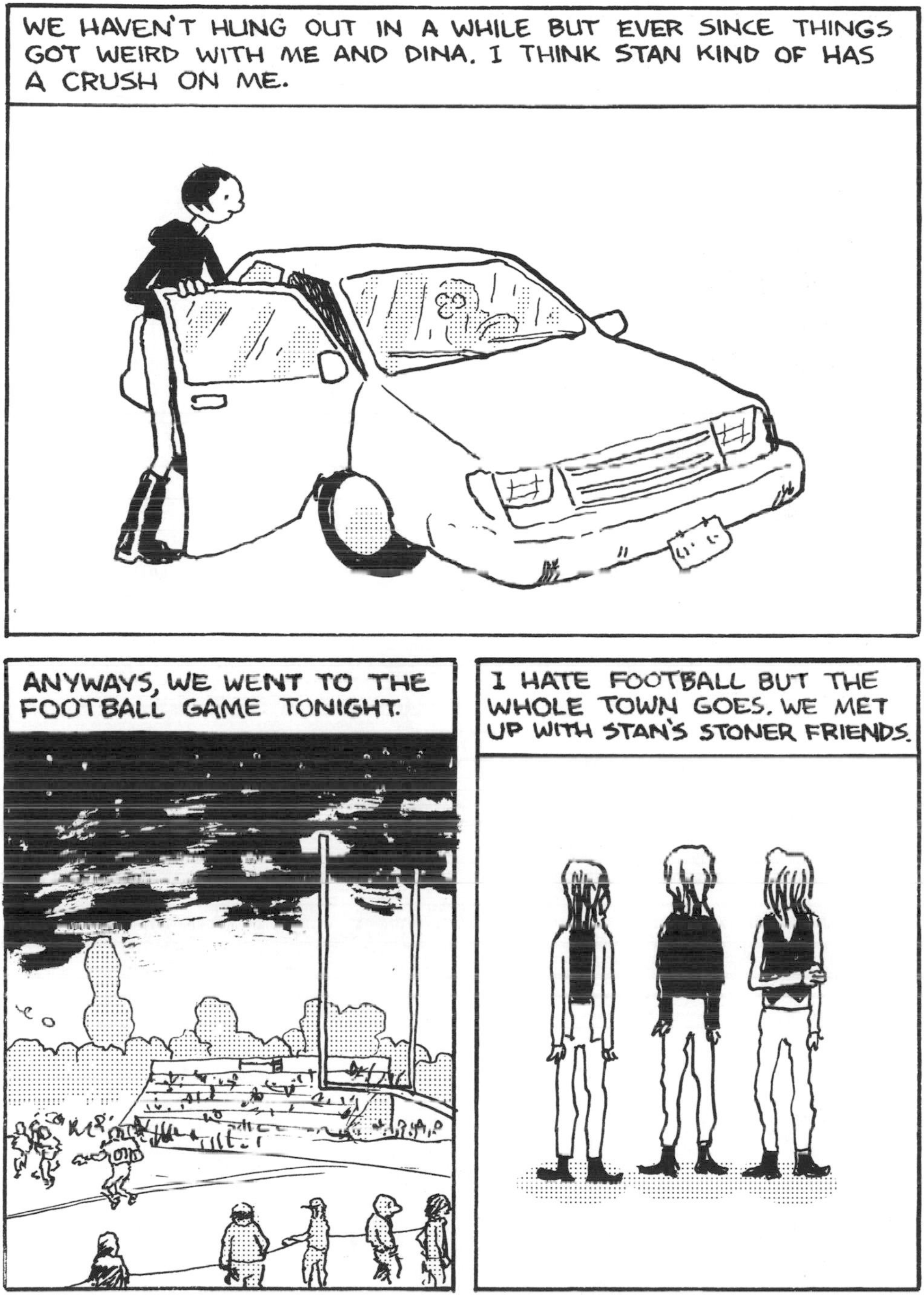
WE HAVEN'T HUNG OUT IN A WHILE BUT EVER SINCE THINGS GOT WEIRD WITH ME AND DINA. I THINK STAN KIND OF HAS A CRUSH ON ME.
ANYWAYS, WE WENT TO THE FOOTBALL GAME TONIGHT.
I HATE FOOTBALL BUT THE WHOLE TOWN GOES. WE MET UP WITH STAN'S STONER FRIENDS.

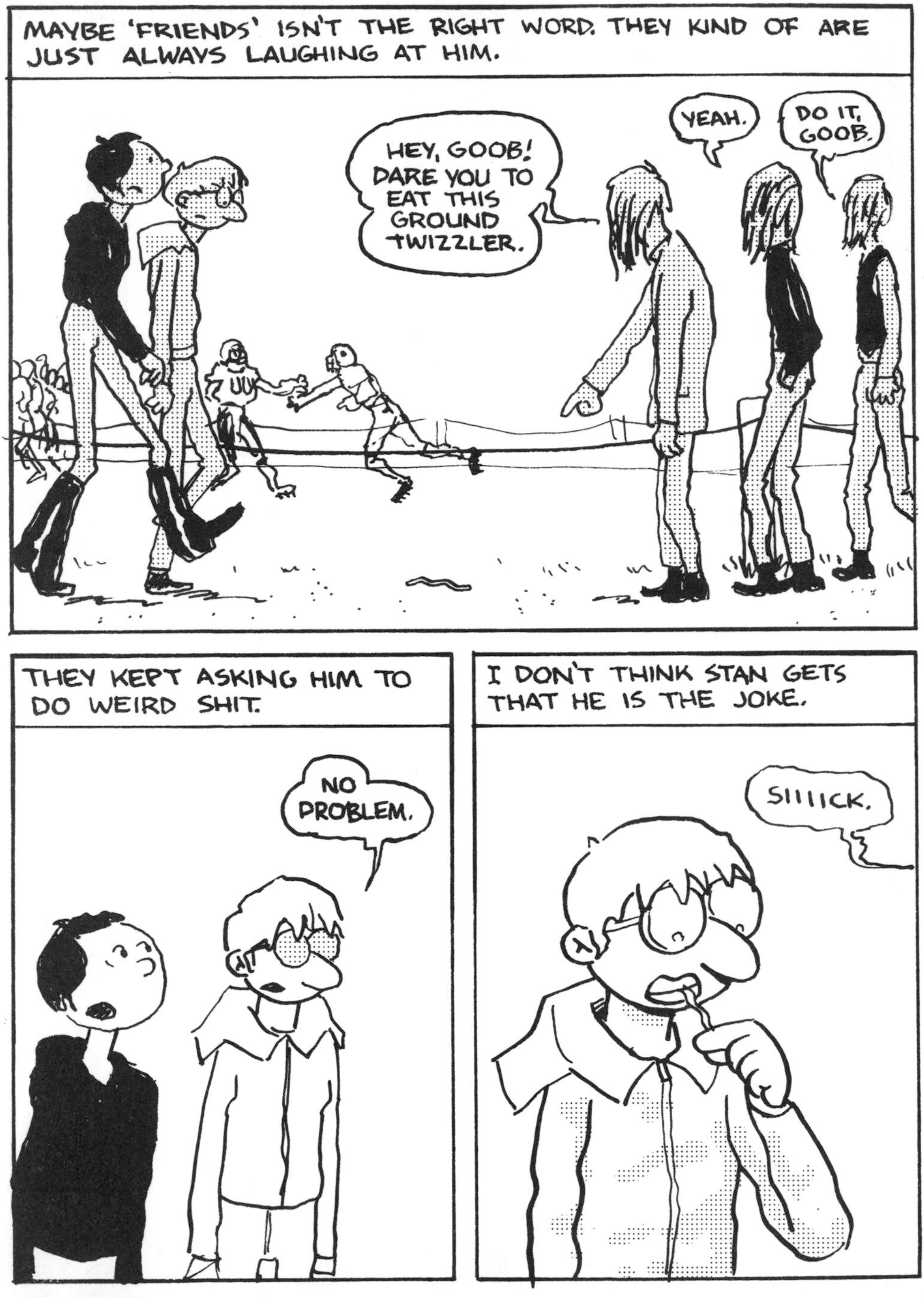
MAYBE 'FRIENDS' ISN'T THE RIGHT WORD. THEY KIND OF ARE JUST ALWAYS LAUGHING AT HIM.
HEY, GOOB! DARE YOU TO EAT THIS GROUND TWIZZLER.
YEAH.
DO IT, GOOB.
THEY KEPT ASKING HIM TO DO WEIRD SHIT.
NO PROBLEM.
I DON'T THINK STAN GETS THAT HE IS THE JOKE.
SIIIICK.

THE SHAGS FOUND OUT STANLEY HAD SOME POT SO THAT'S HOW WE ENDED UP IN THE PARKING LOT. I'D NEVER DONE IT BEFORE. I GUESS I WAS AFRAID OF MYSELF.

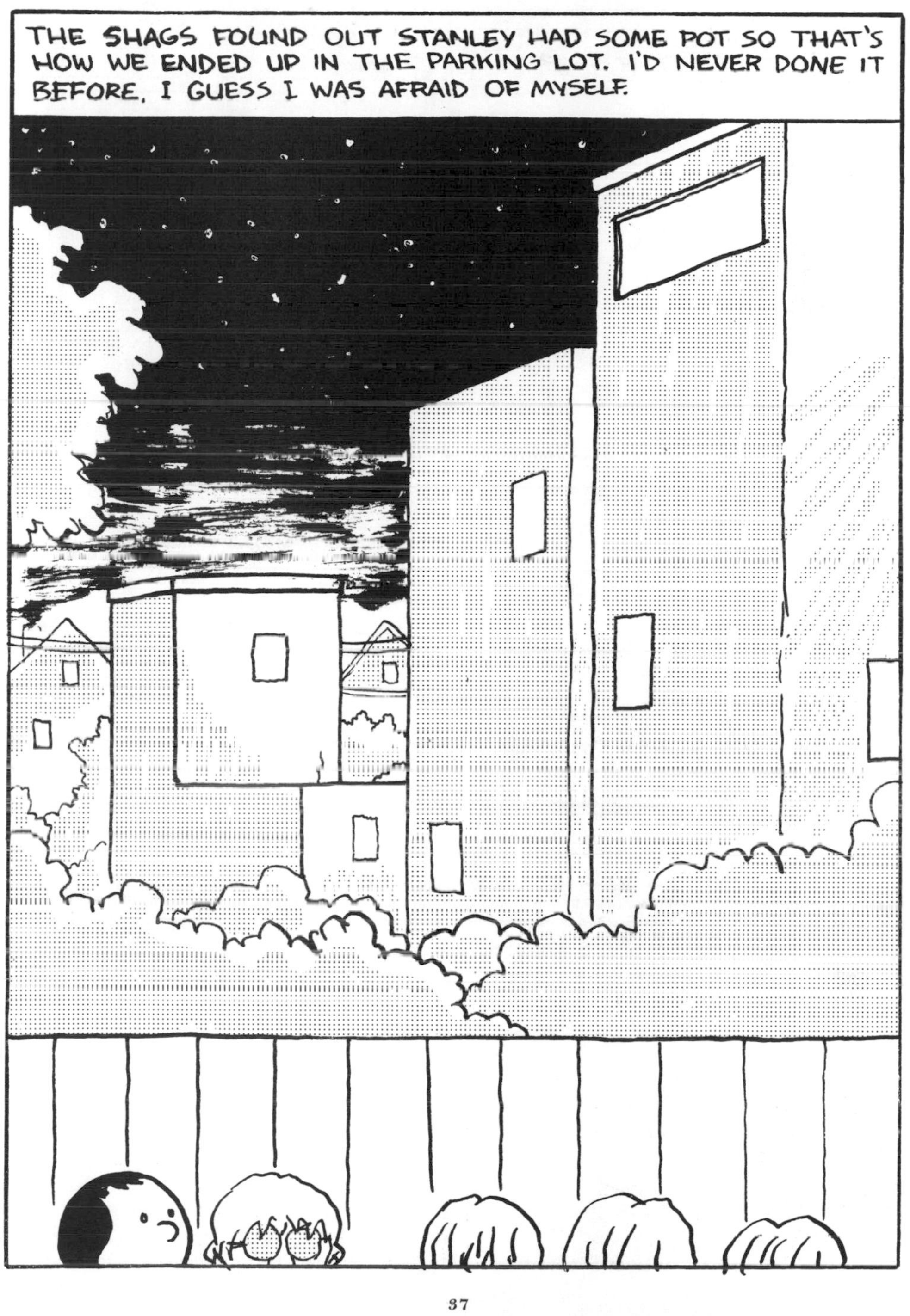

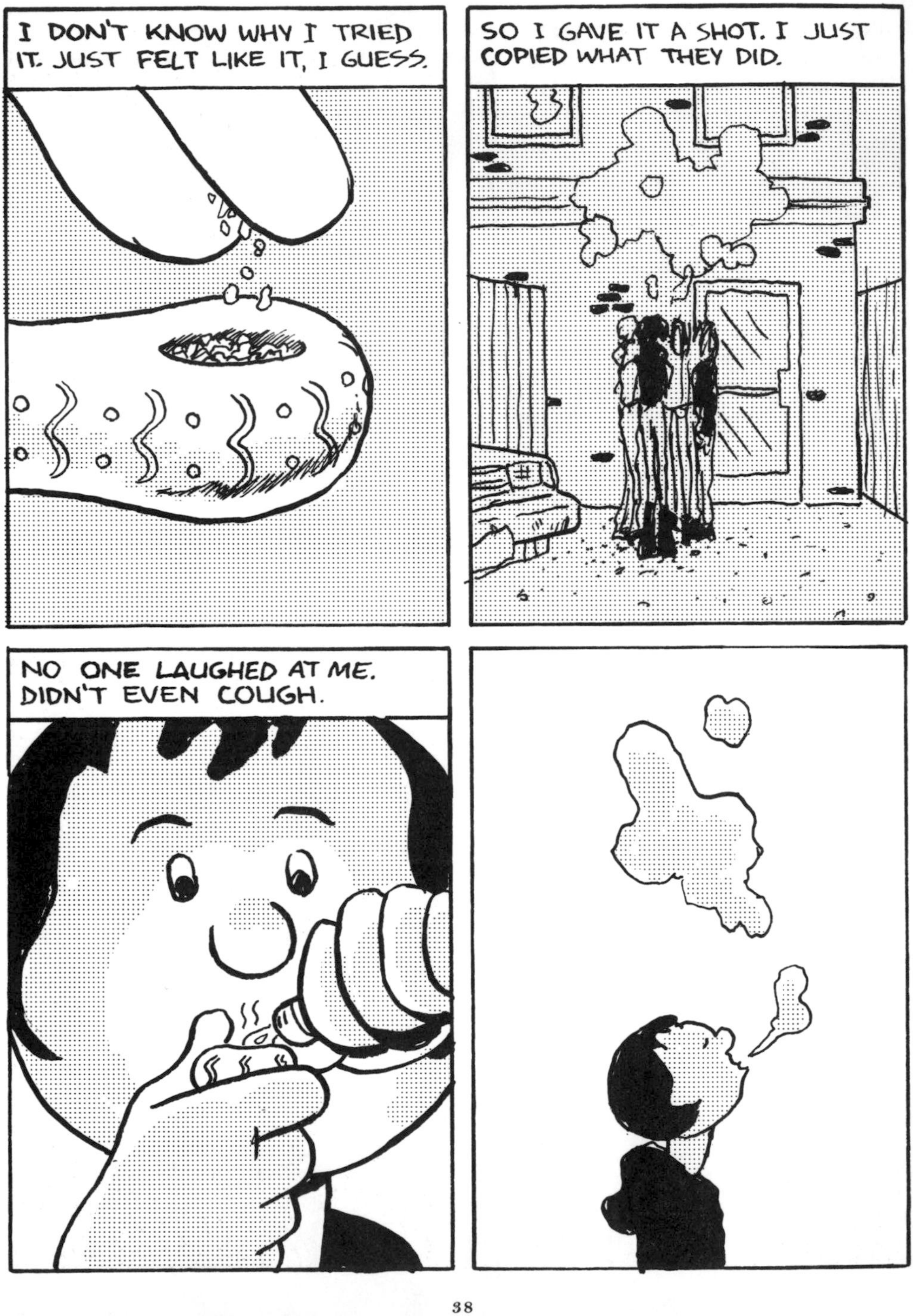
I DON'T KNOW WHY I TRIED IT. JUST FELT LIKE IT, I GUESS.
SO I GAVE IT A SHOT. I JUST COPIED WHAT THEY DID.
NO ONE LAUGHED AT ME. DIDN'T EVEN COUGH.

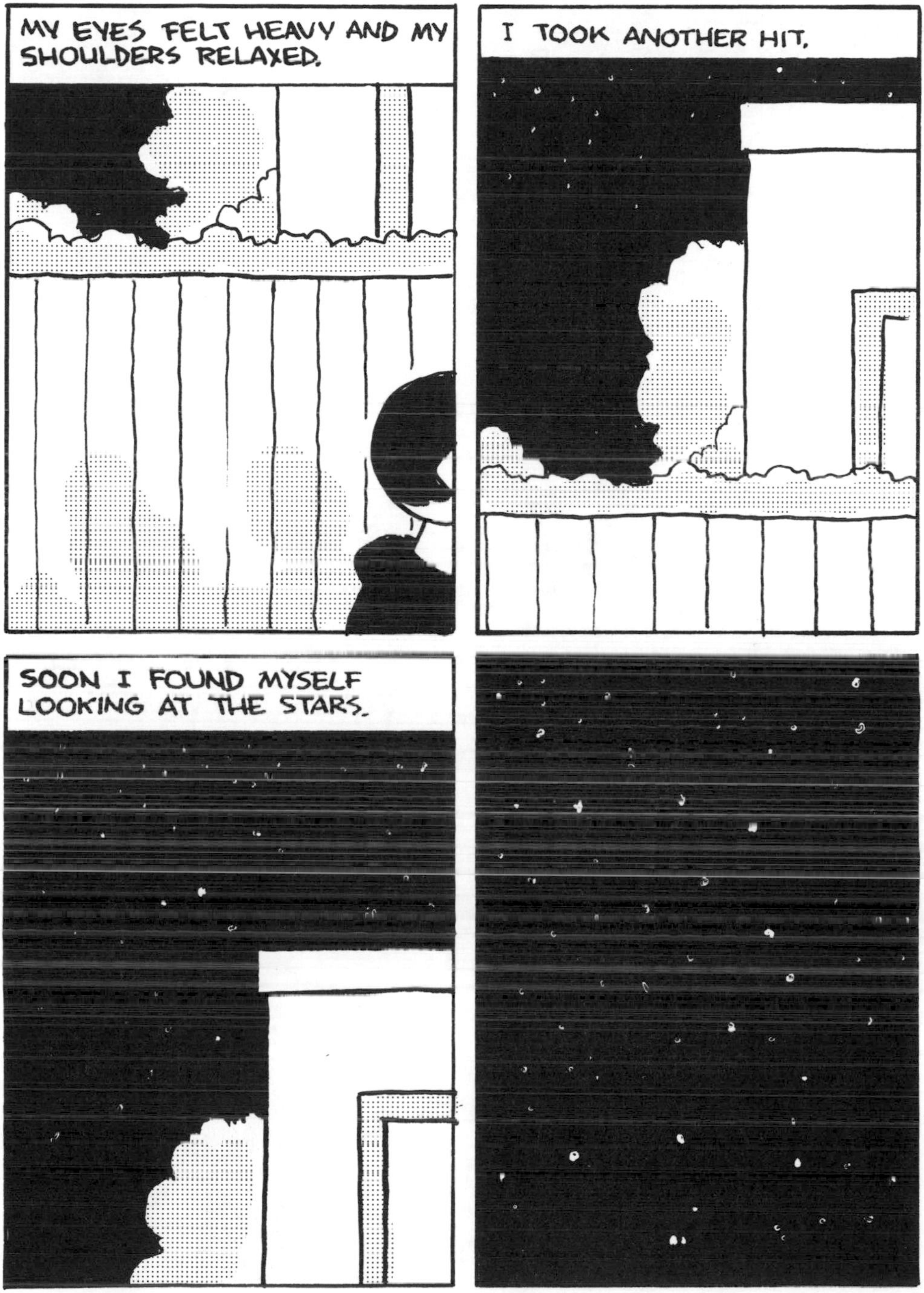
MY EYES FELT HEAVY AND MY SHOULDERS RELAXED.
I TOOK ANOTHER HIT.
SOON I FOUND MYSELF LOOKING AT THE STARS.

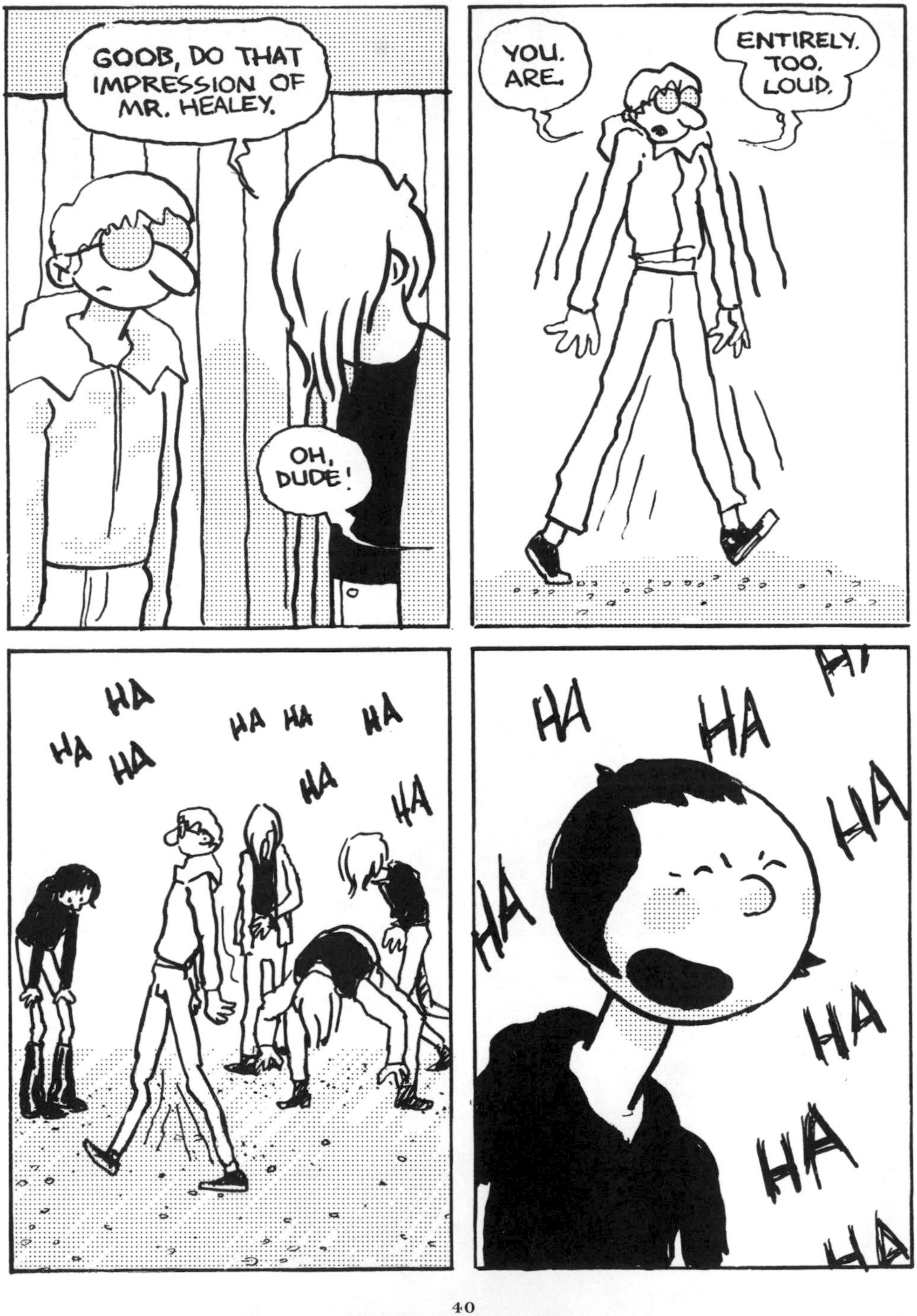
GOOB, DO THAT IMPRESSION OF MR. HEALEY.
OH, DUDE!
YOU. ARE.
ENTIRELY. TOO. LOUD.
HA HA HA HA HA HA HA HA HA
HA HA HA HA HA HA HA HA

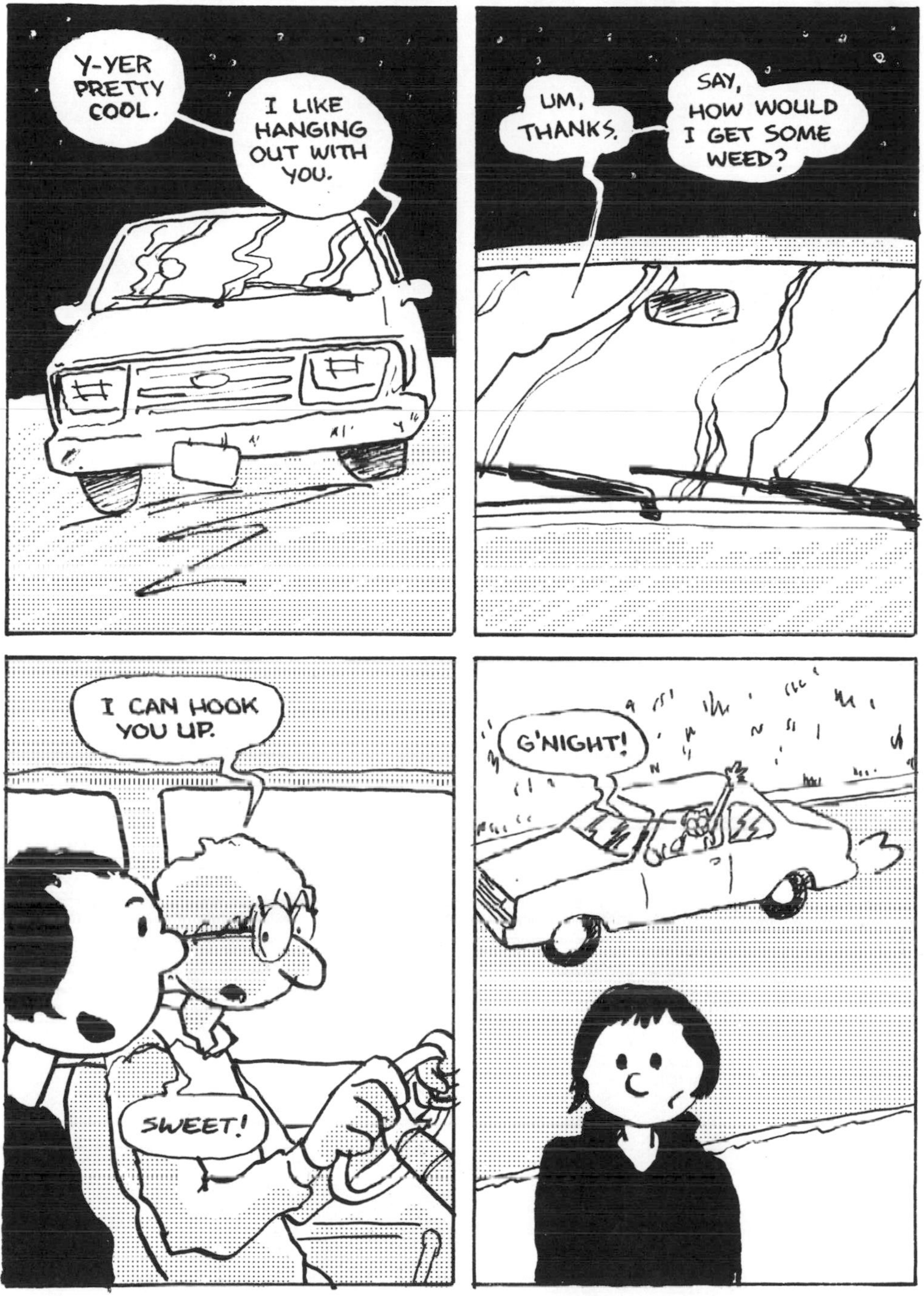
Y-YER PRETTY COOL.
I LIKE HANGING OUT WITH YOU.
UM, THANKS.
SAY, HOW WOULD I GET SOME WEED?
I CAN HOOK YOU UP.
SWEET!
G'NIGHT!

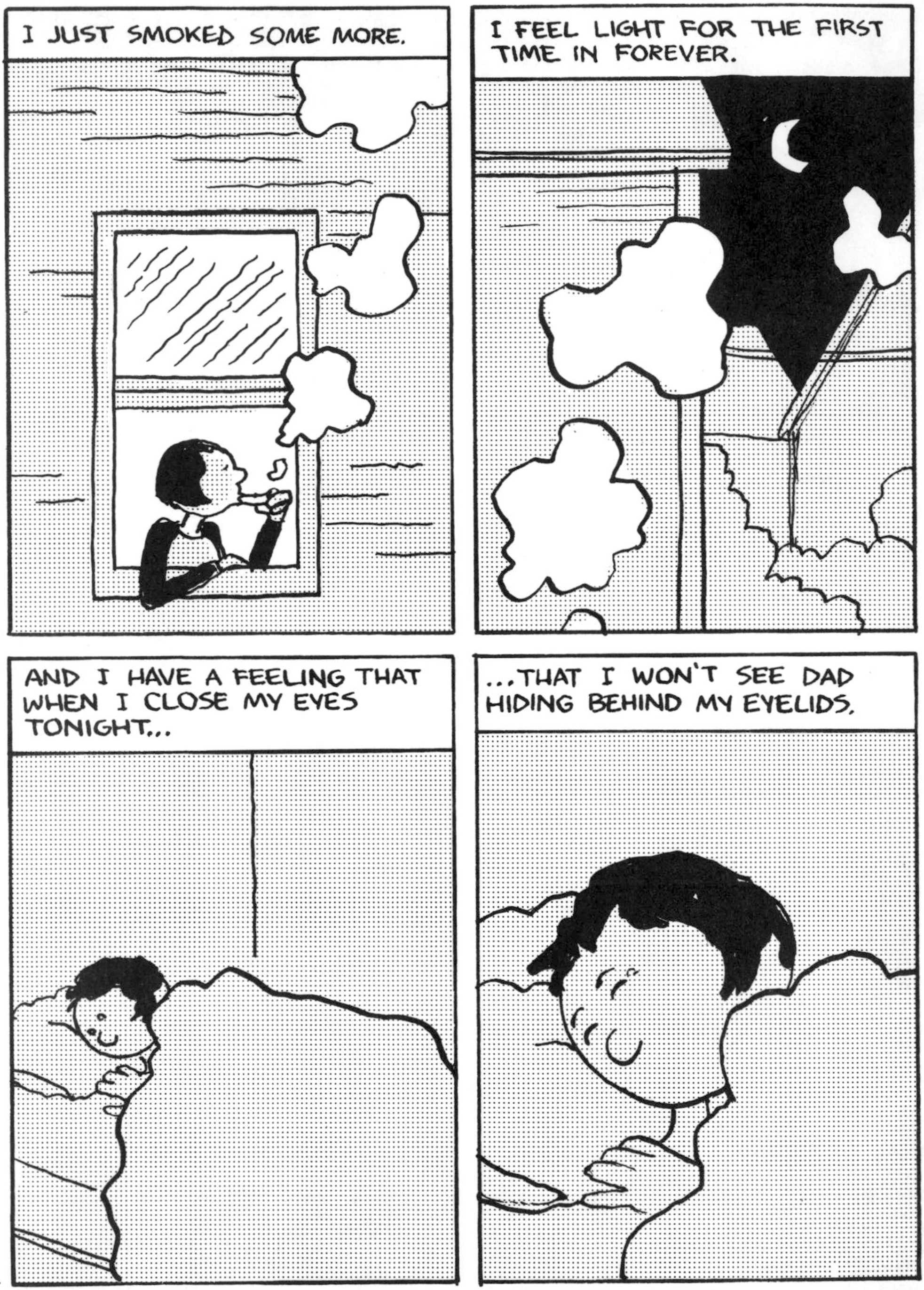
I JUST SMOKED SOME MORE.
I FEEL LIGHT FOR THE FIRST TIME IN FOREVER.
AND I HAVE A FEELING THAT WHEN I CLOSE MY EYES TONIGHT...
...THAT I WON'T SEE DAD HIDING BEHIND MY EYELIDS.

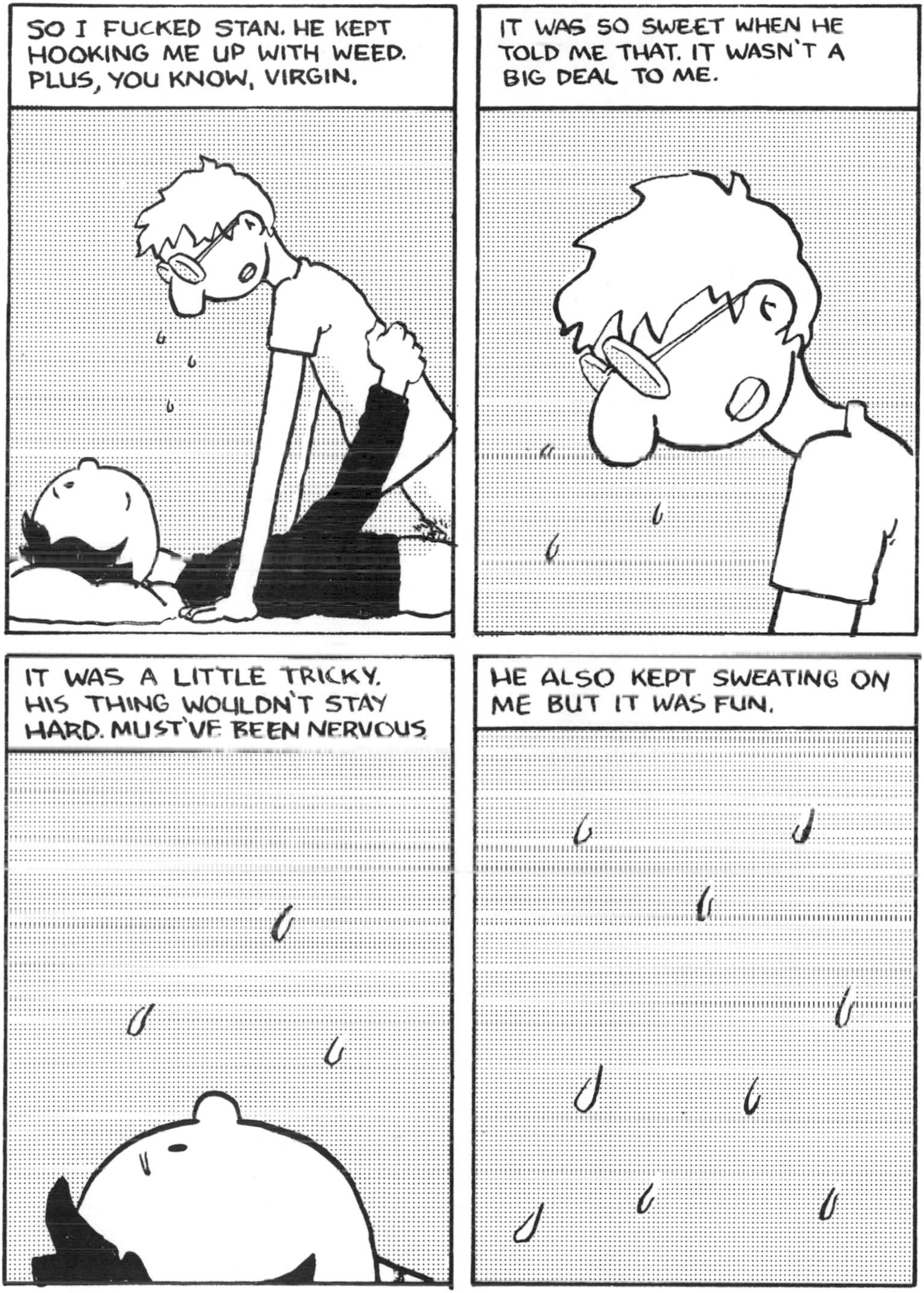
SO I FUCKED STAN. HE KEPT HOOKING ME UP WITH WEED. PLUS, YOU KNOW, VIRGIN.
IT WAS SO SWEET WHEN HE TOLD ME THAT. IT WASN'T A BIG DEAL TO ME.
IT WAS A LITTLE TRICKY. HIS THING WOULDN'T STAY HARD. MUST'VE BEEN NERVOUS.
HE ALSO KEPT SWEATING ON ME BUT IT WAS FUN.

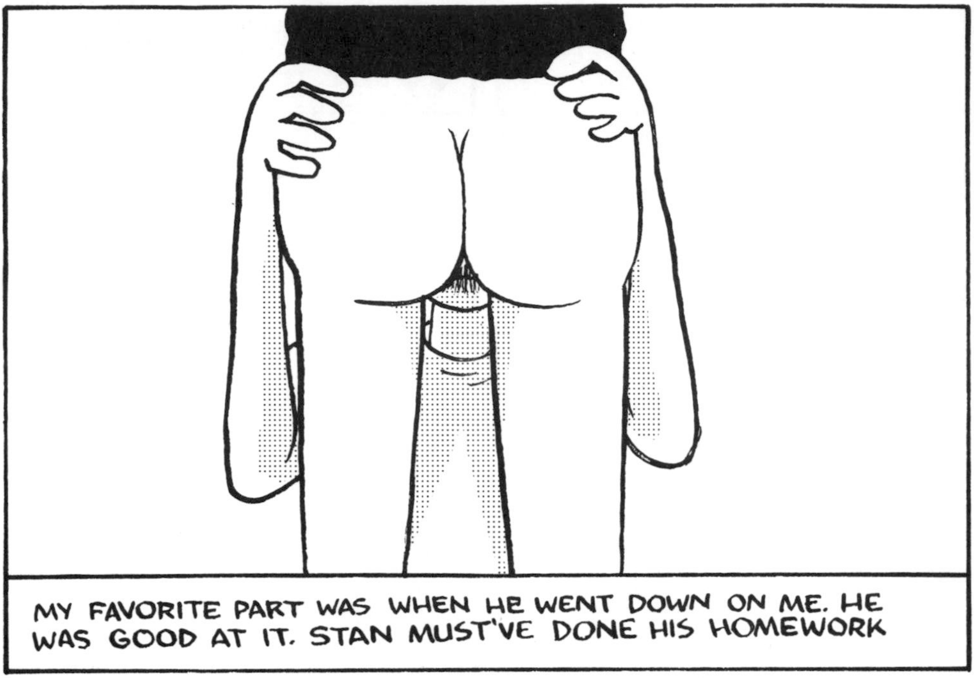
MY FAVORITE PART WAS WHEN HE WENT DOWN ON ME. HE WAS GOOD AT IT. STAN MUST'VE DONE HIS HOMEWORK

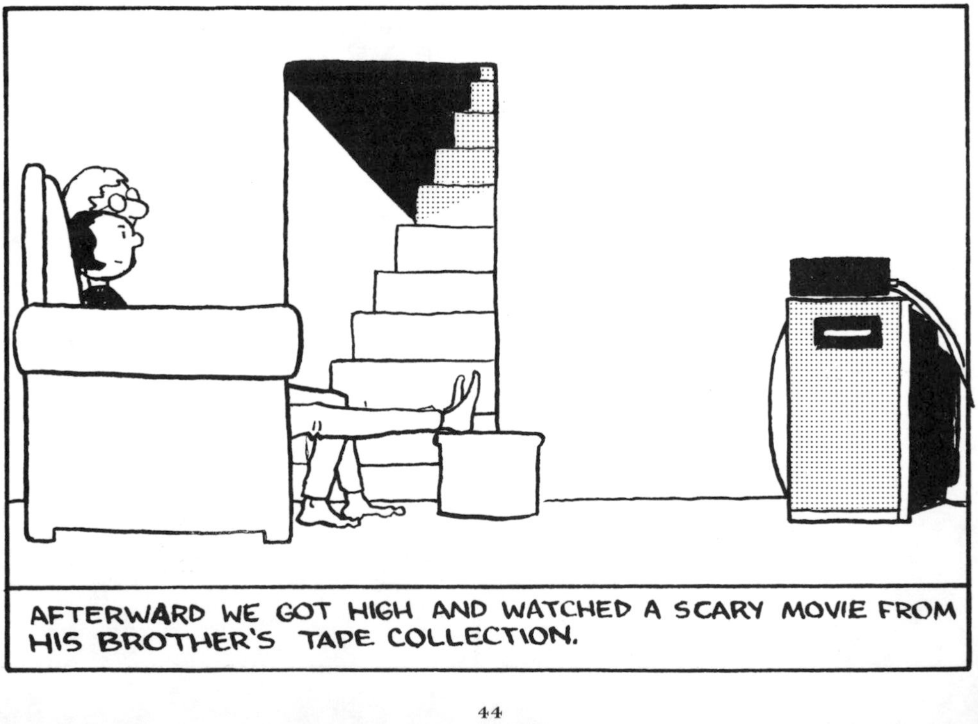
AFTERWARD WE GOT HIGH AND WATCHED A SCARY MOVIE FROM HIS BROTHER'S TAPE COLLECTION.

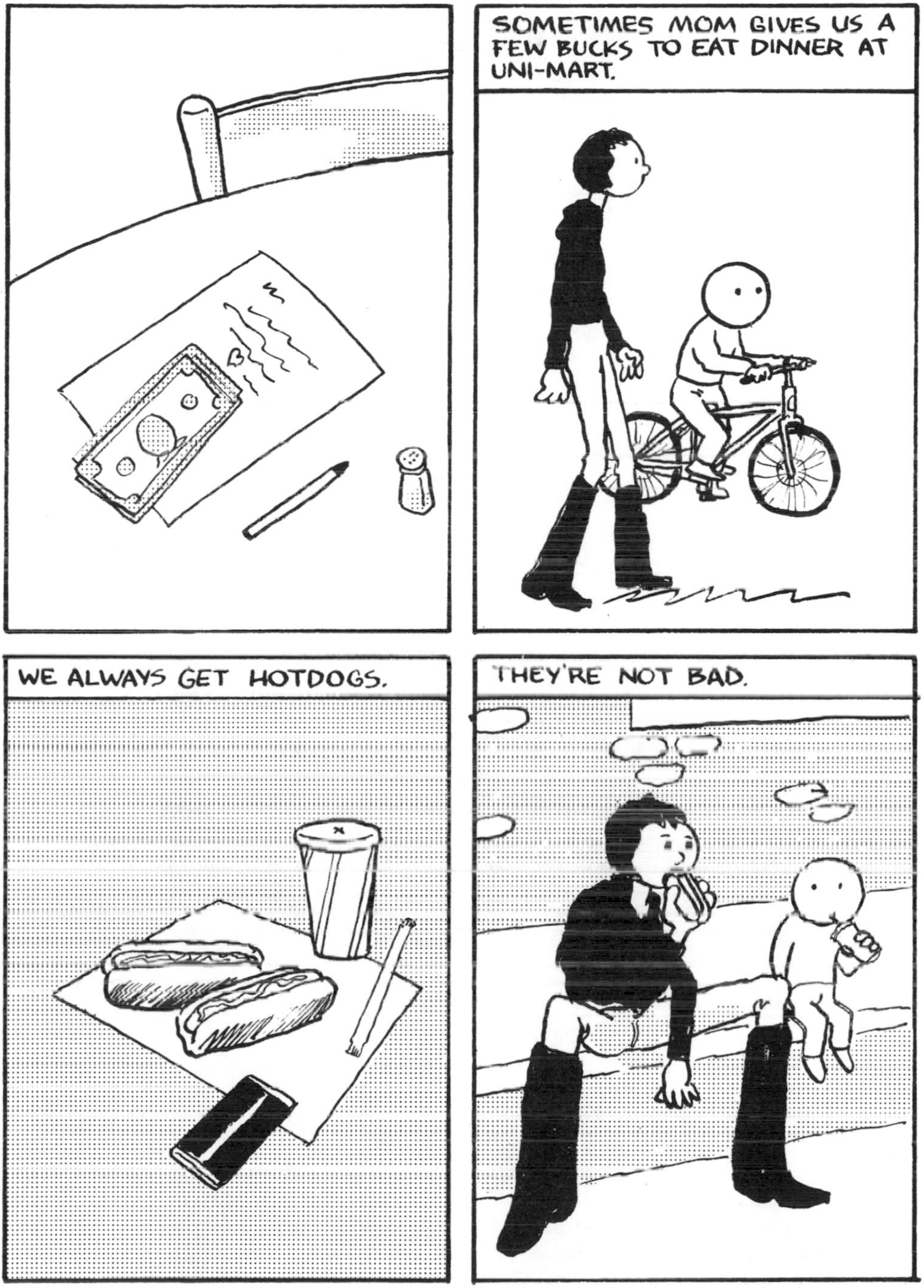
SOMETIMES MOM GIVES US A FEW BUCKS TO EAT DINNER AT UNI-MART.
WE ALWAYS GET HOTDOGS.
THEY'RE NOT BAD.

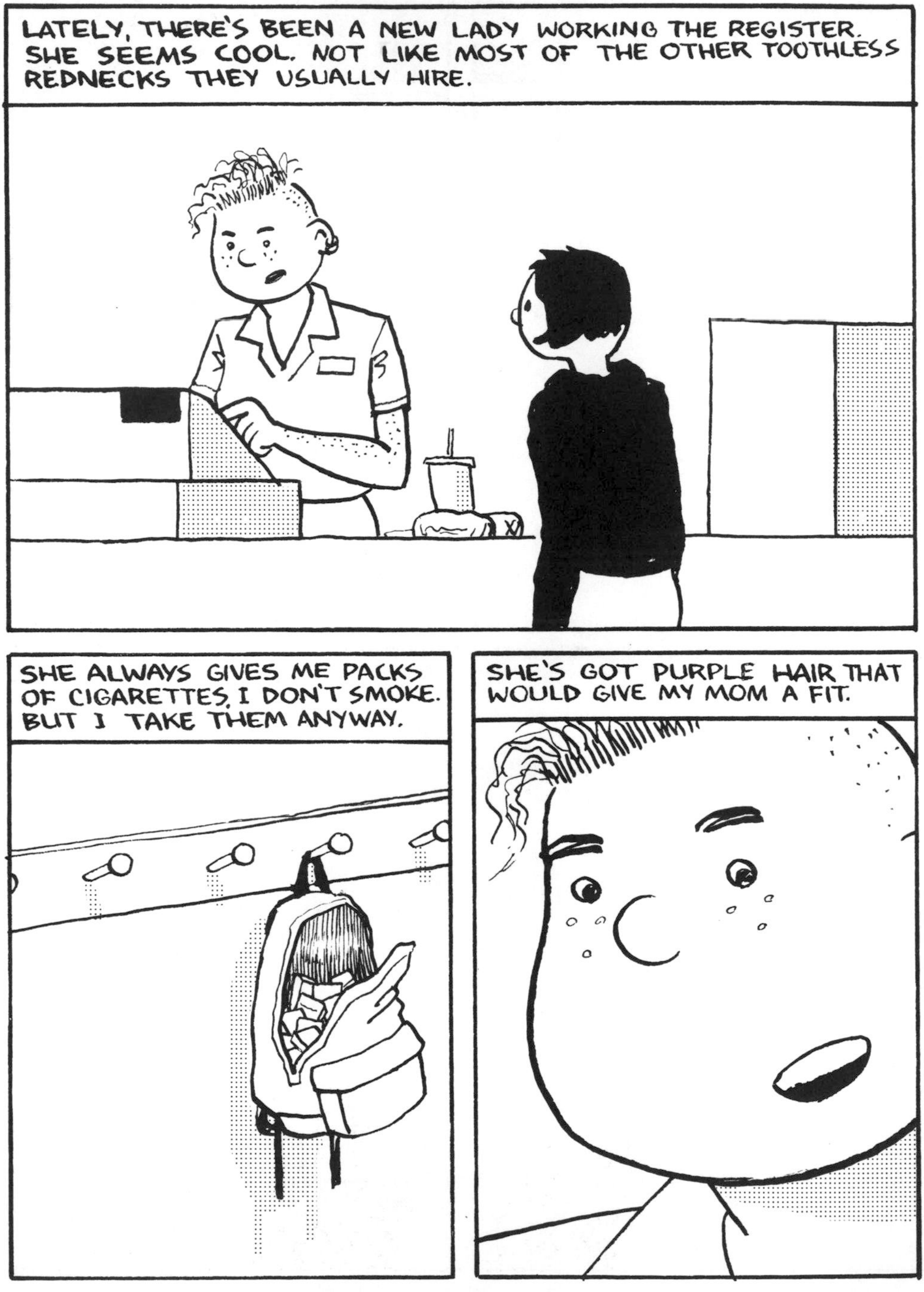
LATELY, THERE'S BEEN A NEW LADY WORKING THE REGISTER. SHE SEEMS COOL. NOT LIKE MOST OF THE OTHER TOOTHLESS REDNECKS THEY USUALLY HIRE.
SHE ALWAYS GIVES ME PACKS OF CIGARETTES. I DON'T SMOKE. BUT I TAKE THEM ANYWAY.
SHE'S GOT PURPLE HAIR THAT WOULD GIVE MY MOM A FIT.

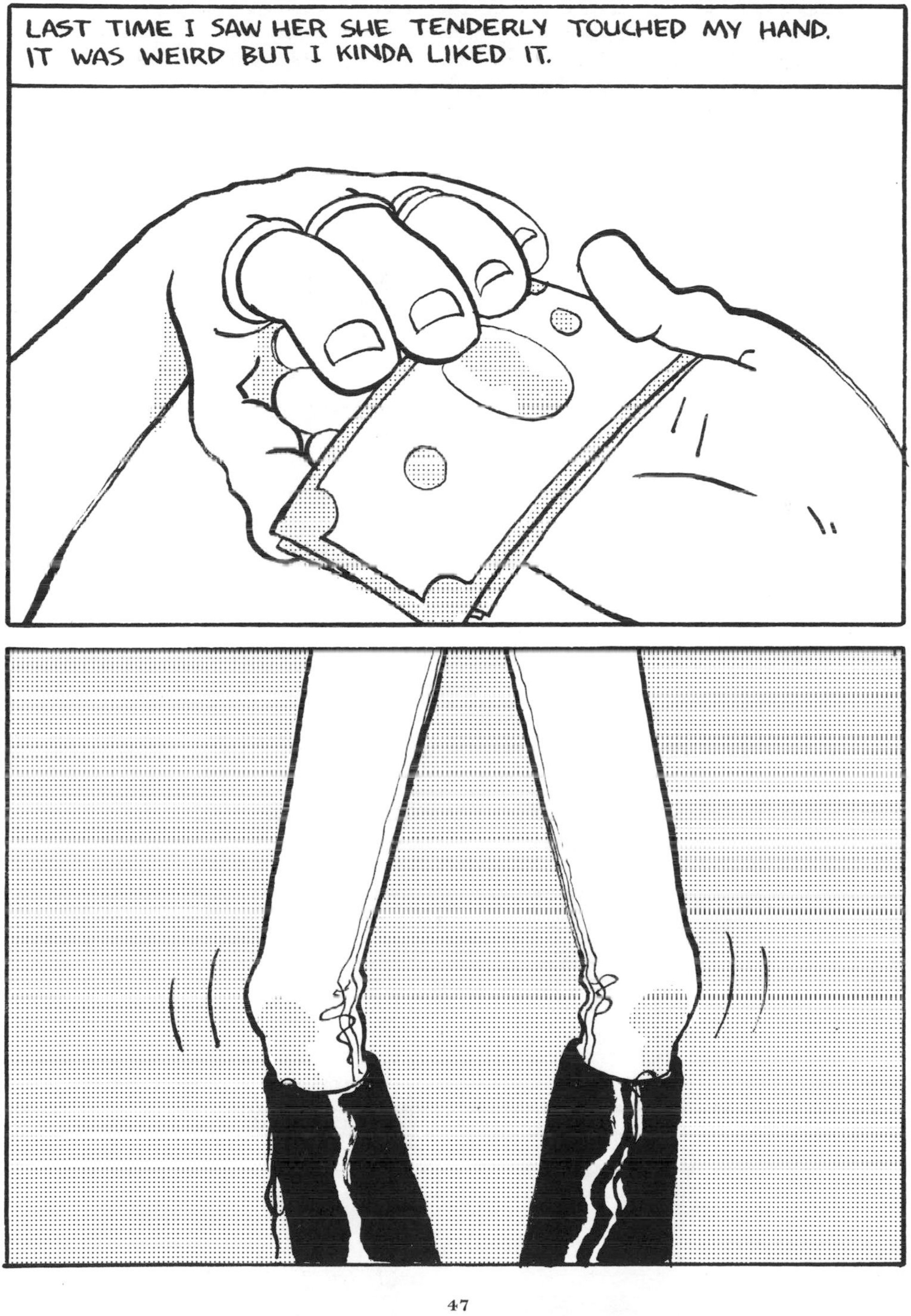
LAST TIME I SAW HER SHE TENDERLY TOUCHED MY HAND.
IT WAS WEIRD BUT I KINDA LIKED IT.

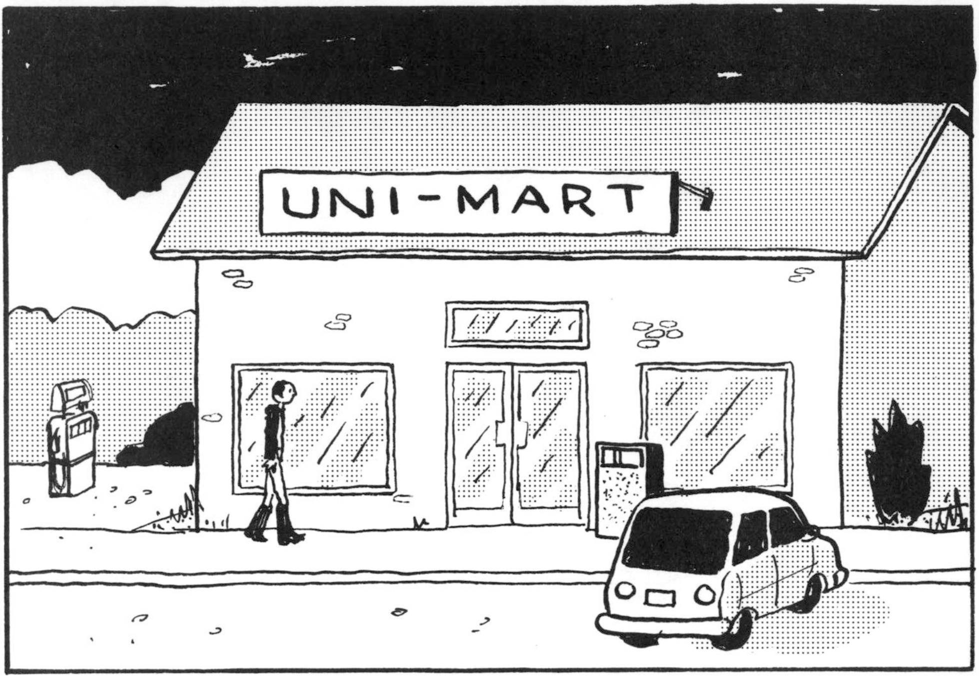
UNI-MART

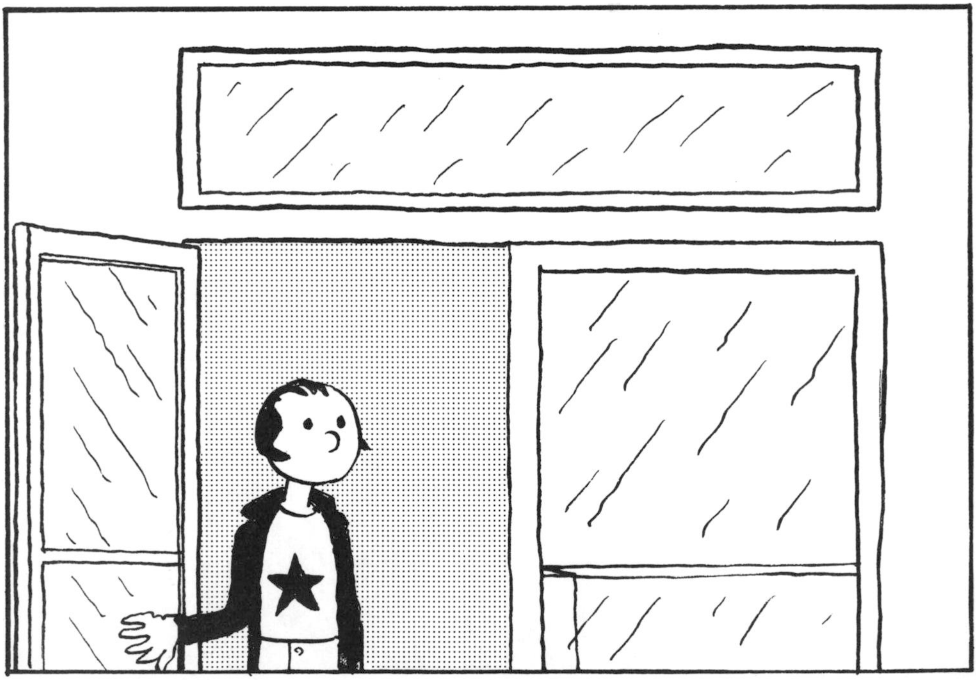

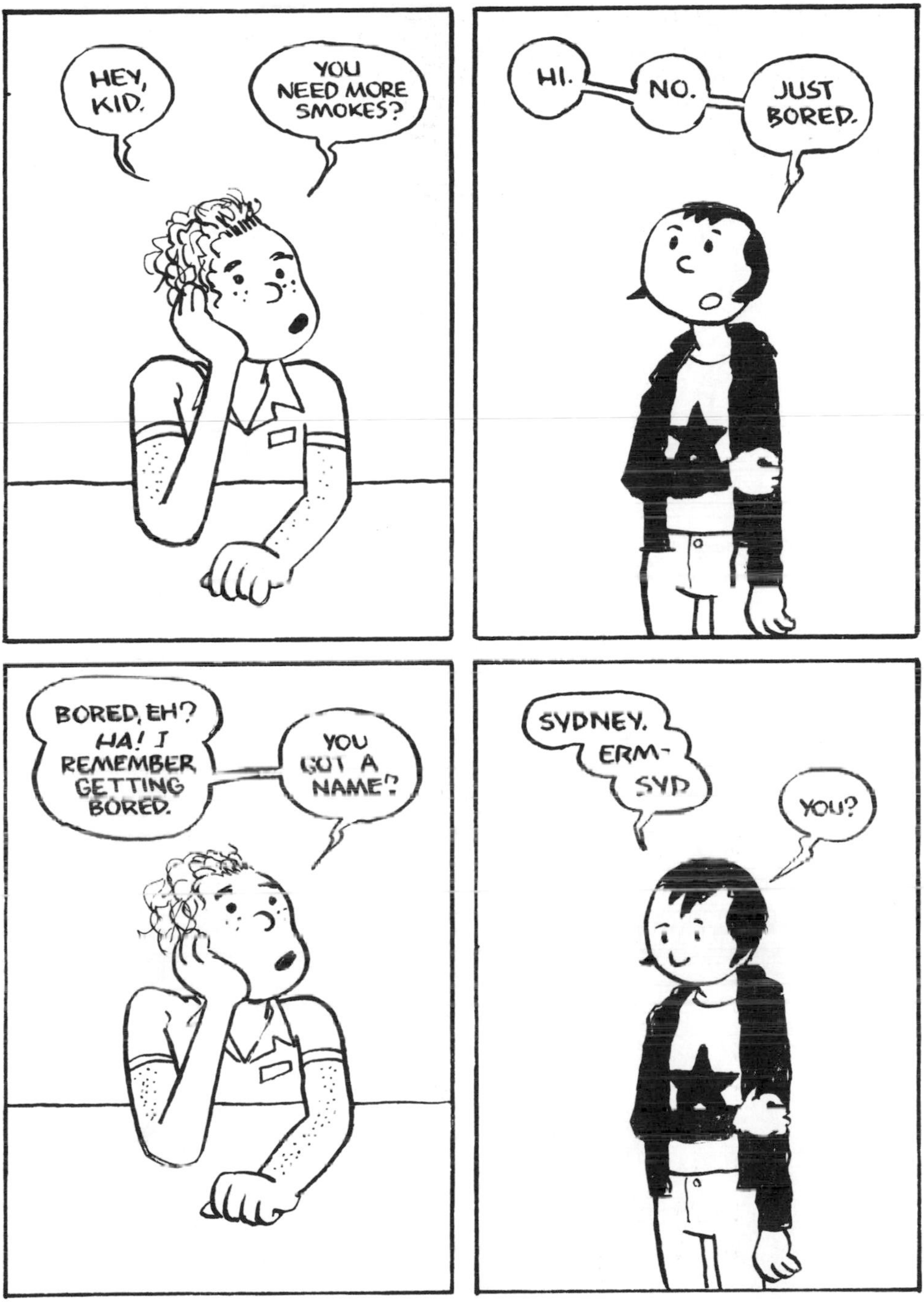
HEY, KID.
YOU NEED MORE SMOKES?
HI.
NO.
JUST BORED.
BORED, EH? HA! I REMEMBER GETTING BORED.
YOU GOT A NAME?
SYDNEY. ERM- SYD
YOU?

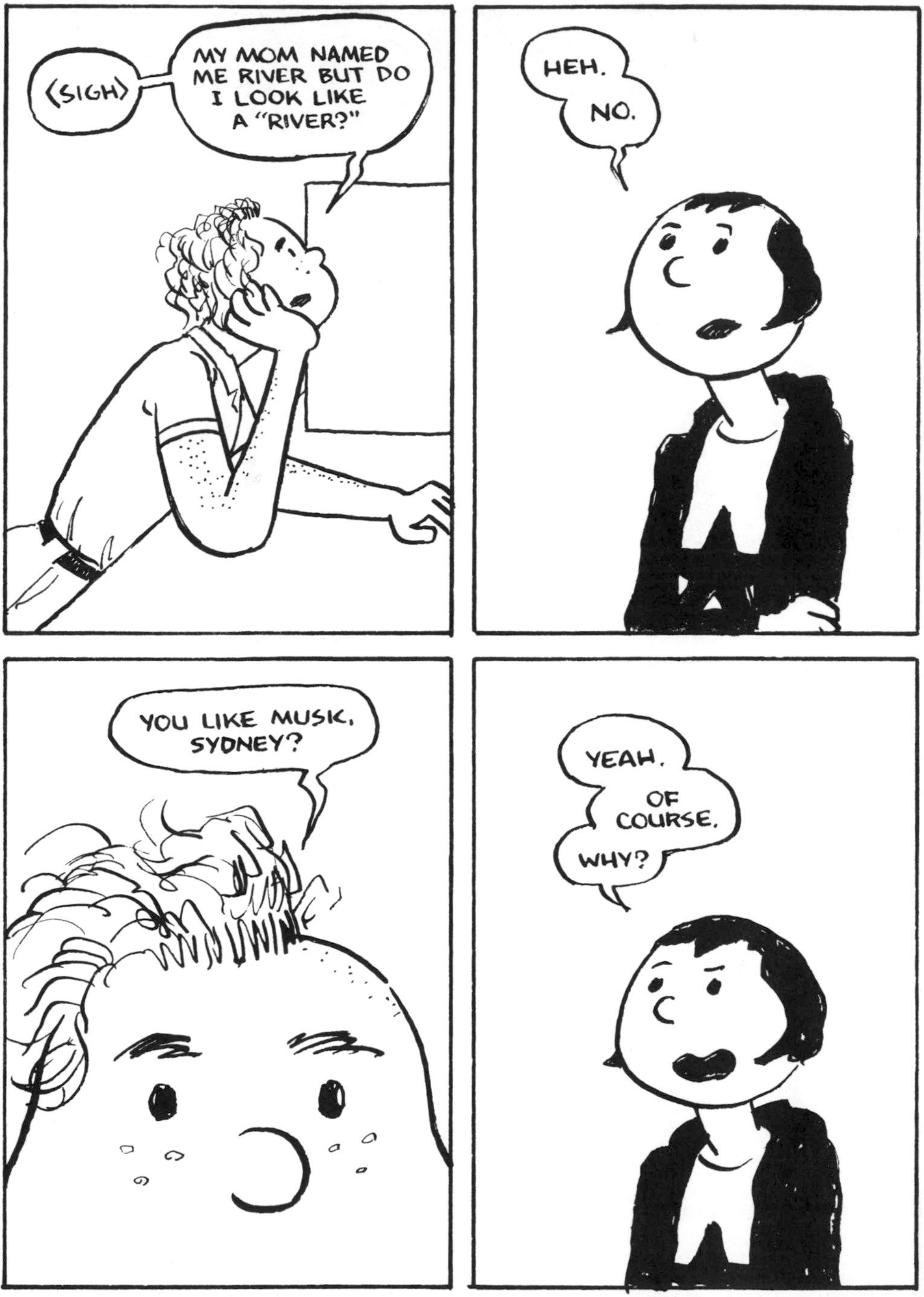
(SIGH)
MY MOM NAMED ME RIVER BUT DO I LOOK LIKE A "RIVER?"
HEH.
NO.
YOU LIKE MUSK, SYDNEY?
YEAH.
OF COURSE.
WHY?

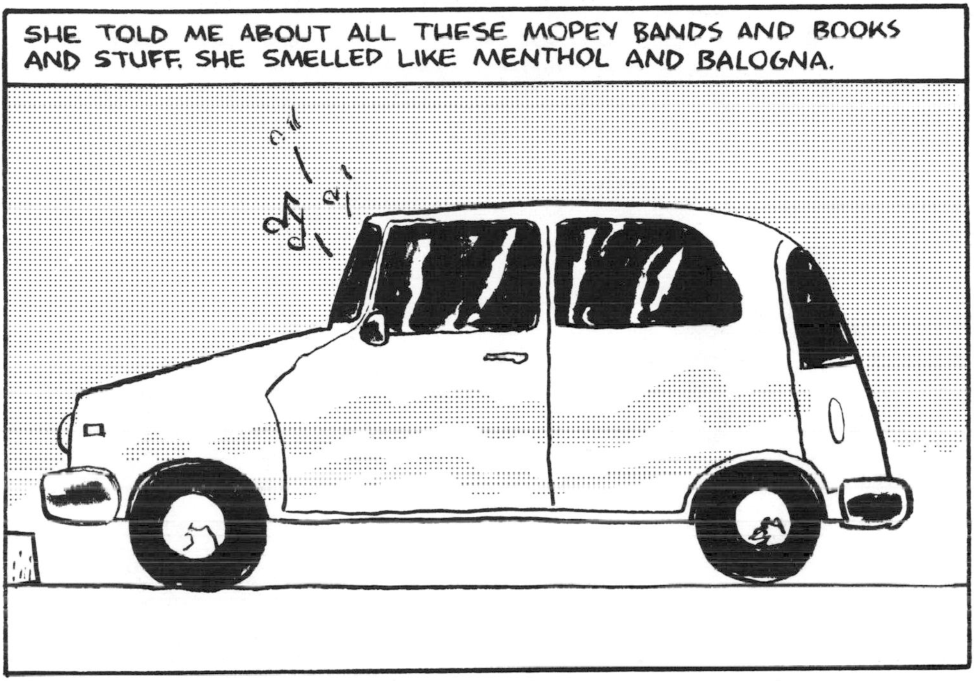
SHE TOLD ME ABOUT ALL THESE MOPEY BANDS AND BOOKS AND STUFF. SHE SMELLED LIKE MENTHOL AND BALOGNA.

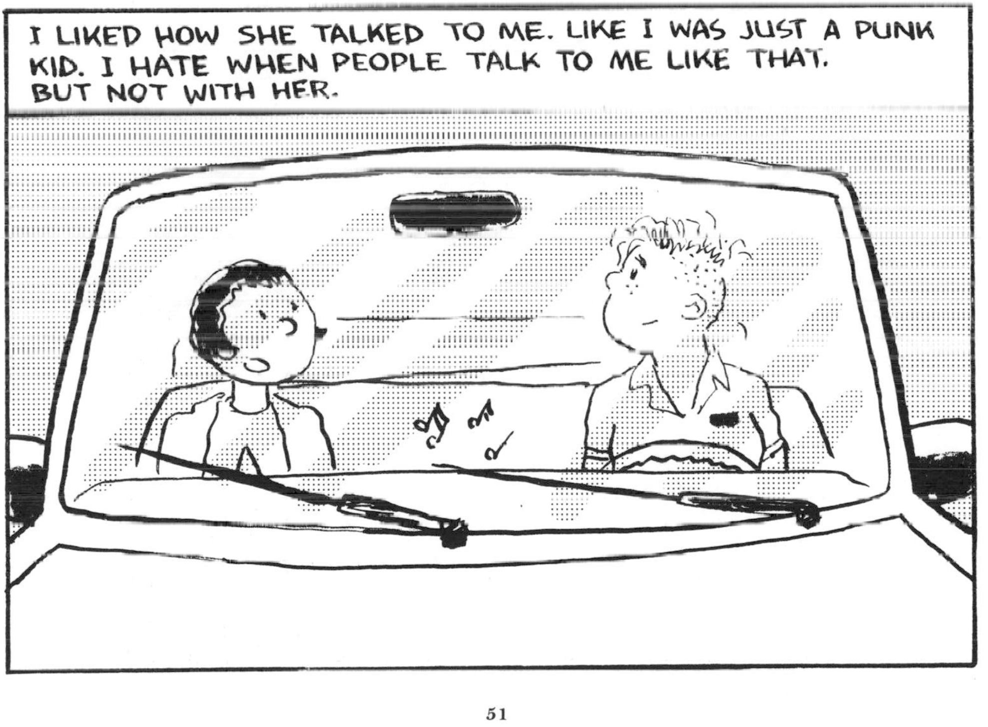
I LIKED HOW SHE TALKED TO ME. LIKE I WAS JUST A PUNK KID. I HATE WHEN PEOPLE TALK TO ME LIKE THAT. BUT NOT WITH HER.

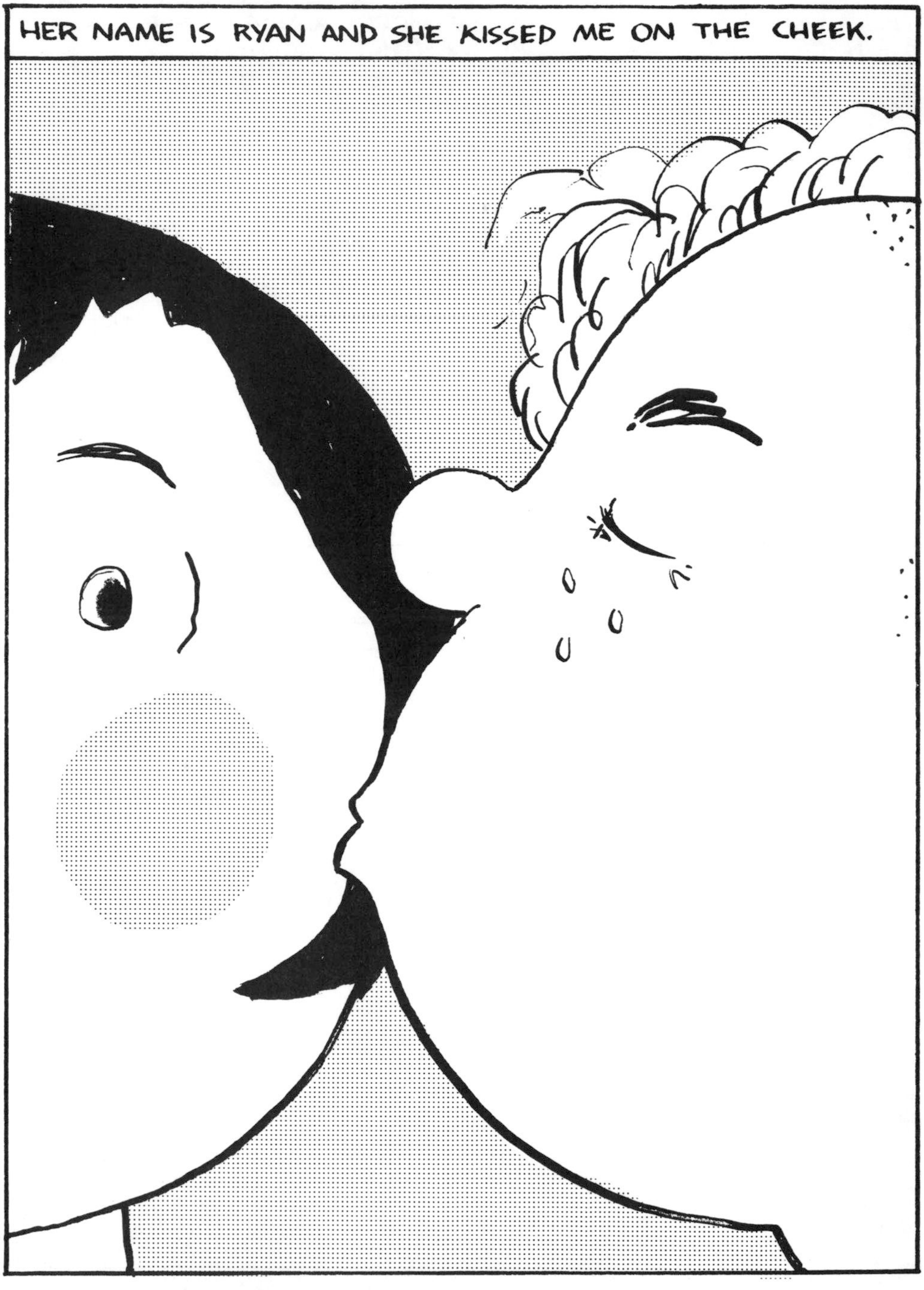
HER NAME IS RYAN AND SHE KISSED ME ON THE CHEEK.

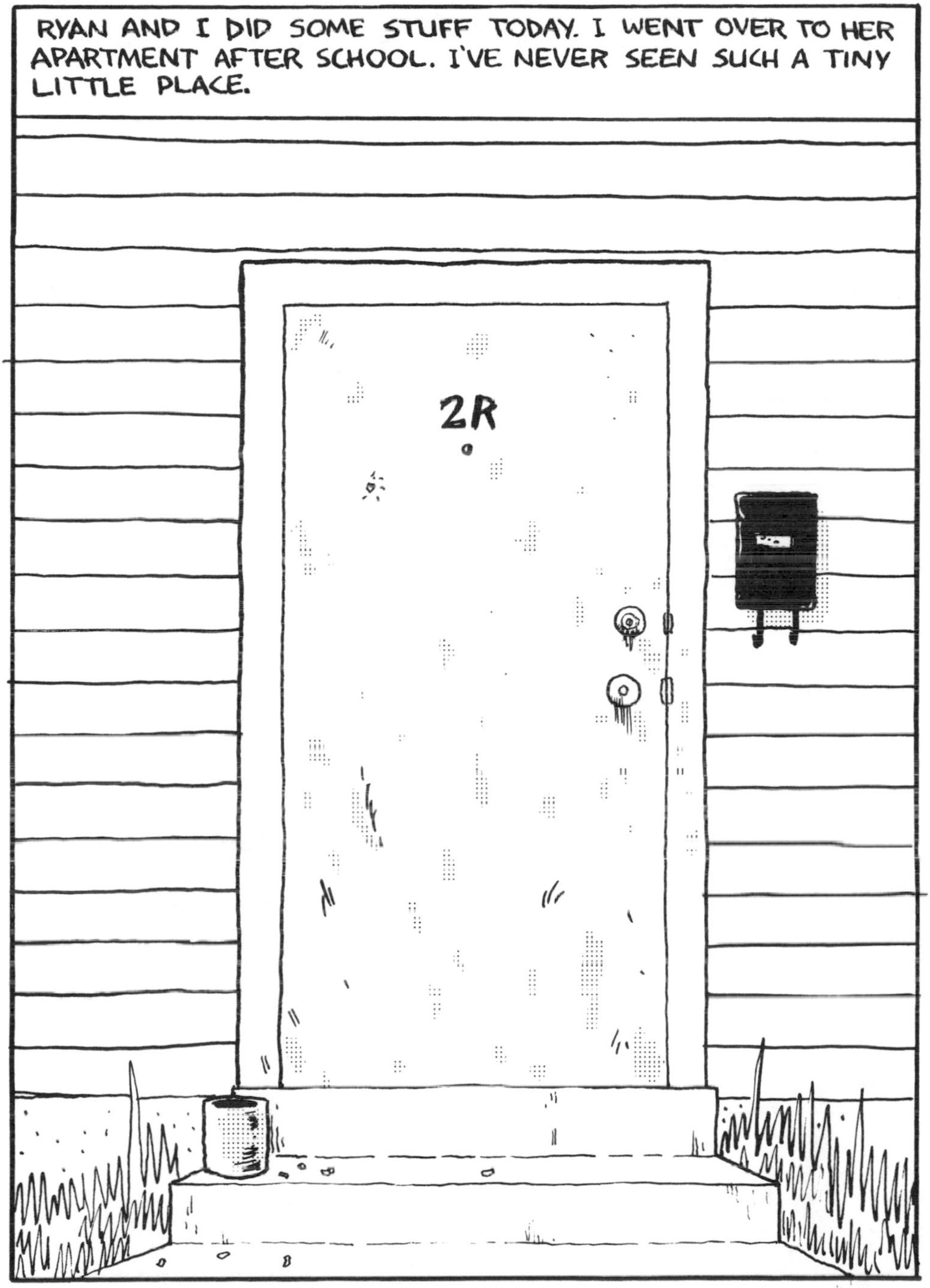
RYAN AND I DID SOME STUFF TODAY. I WENT OVER TO HER APARTMENT AFTER SCHOOL. I'VE NEVER SEEN SUCH A TINY LITTLE PLACE.
2R

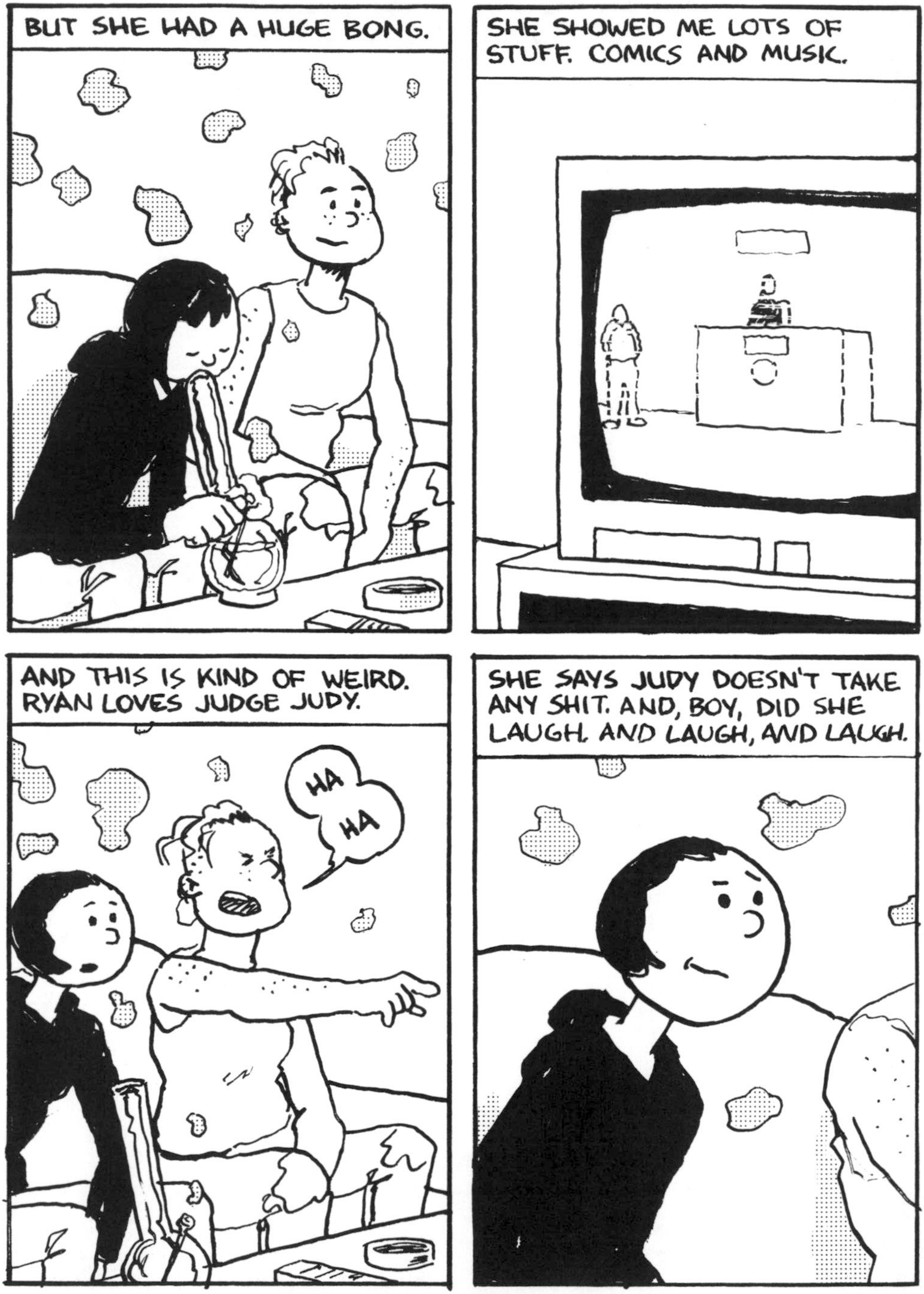
BUT SHE HAD A HUGE BONG.
SHE SHOWED ME LOTS OF STUFF. COMICS AND MUSIC.
AND THIS IS KIND OF WEIRD. RYAN LOVES JUDGE JUDY.
HA HA
SHE SAYS JUDY DOESN'T TAKE ANY SHIT. AND, BOY, DID SHE LAUGH. AND LAUGH, AND LAUGH.

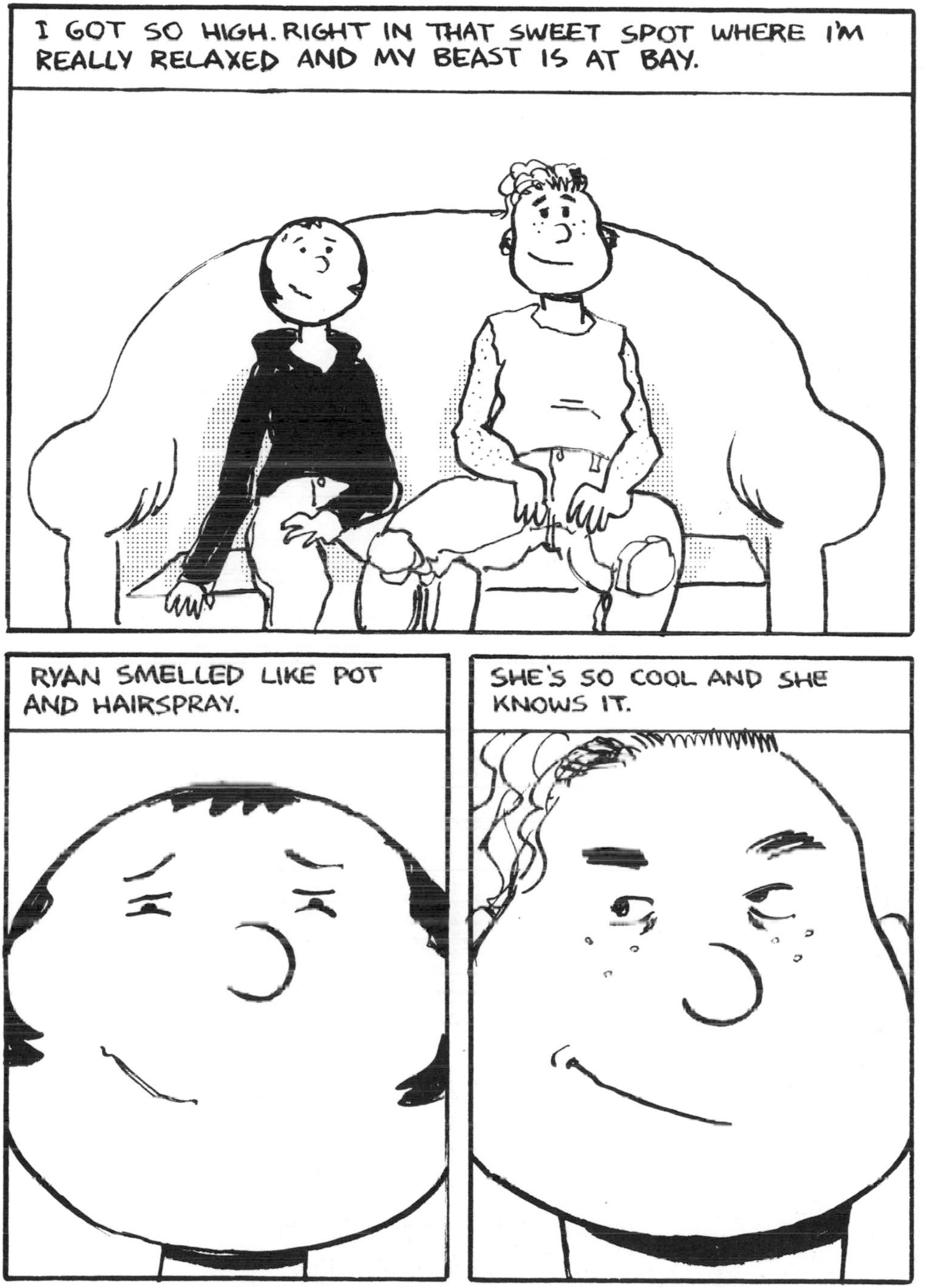
I GOT SO HIGH. RIGHT IN THAT SWEET SPOT WHERE I'M REALLY RELAXED AND MY BEAST IS AT BAY.
RYAN SMELLED LIKE POT AND HAIRSPRAY.
SHE'S SO COOL AND SHE KNOWS IT.

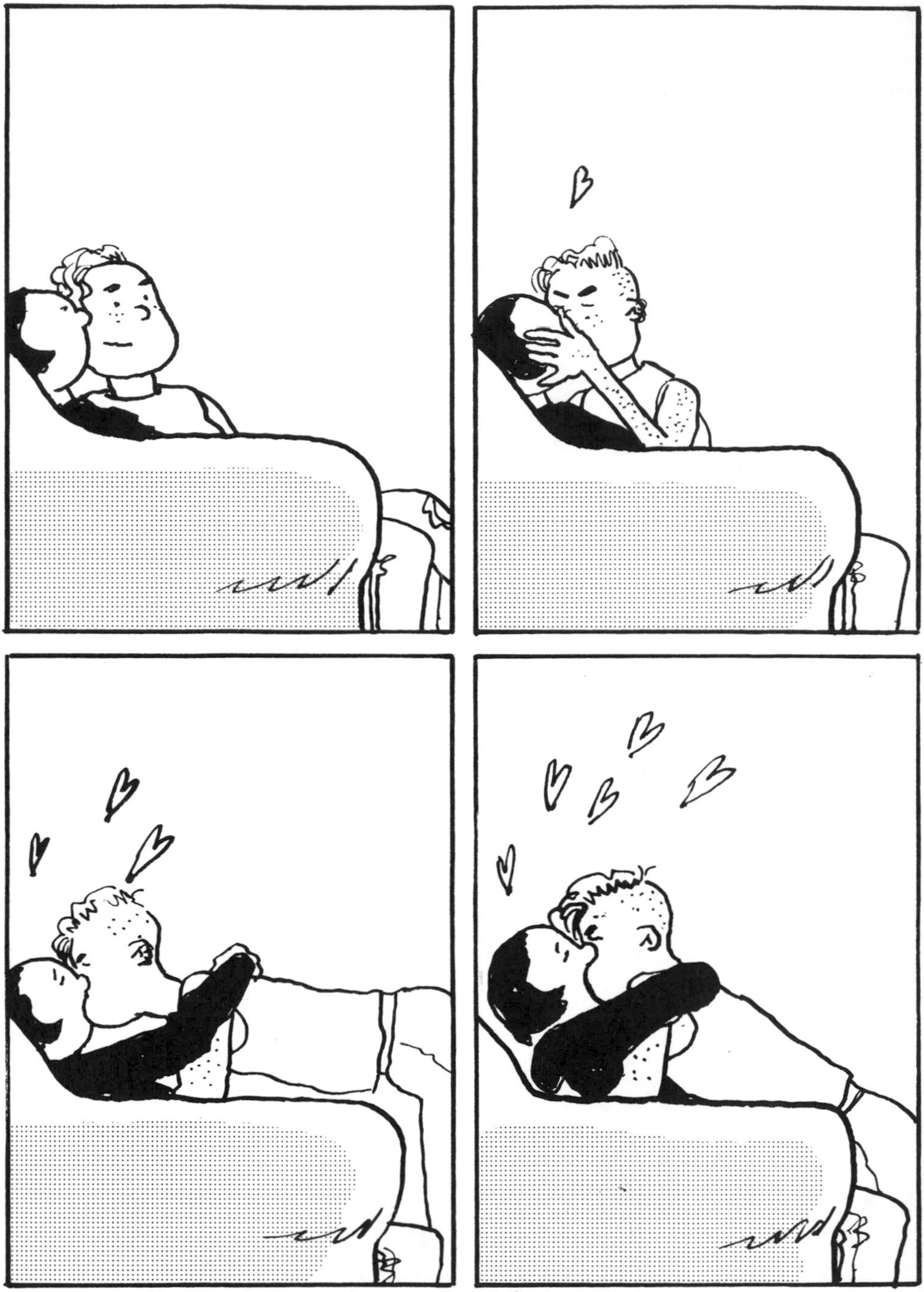

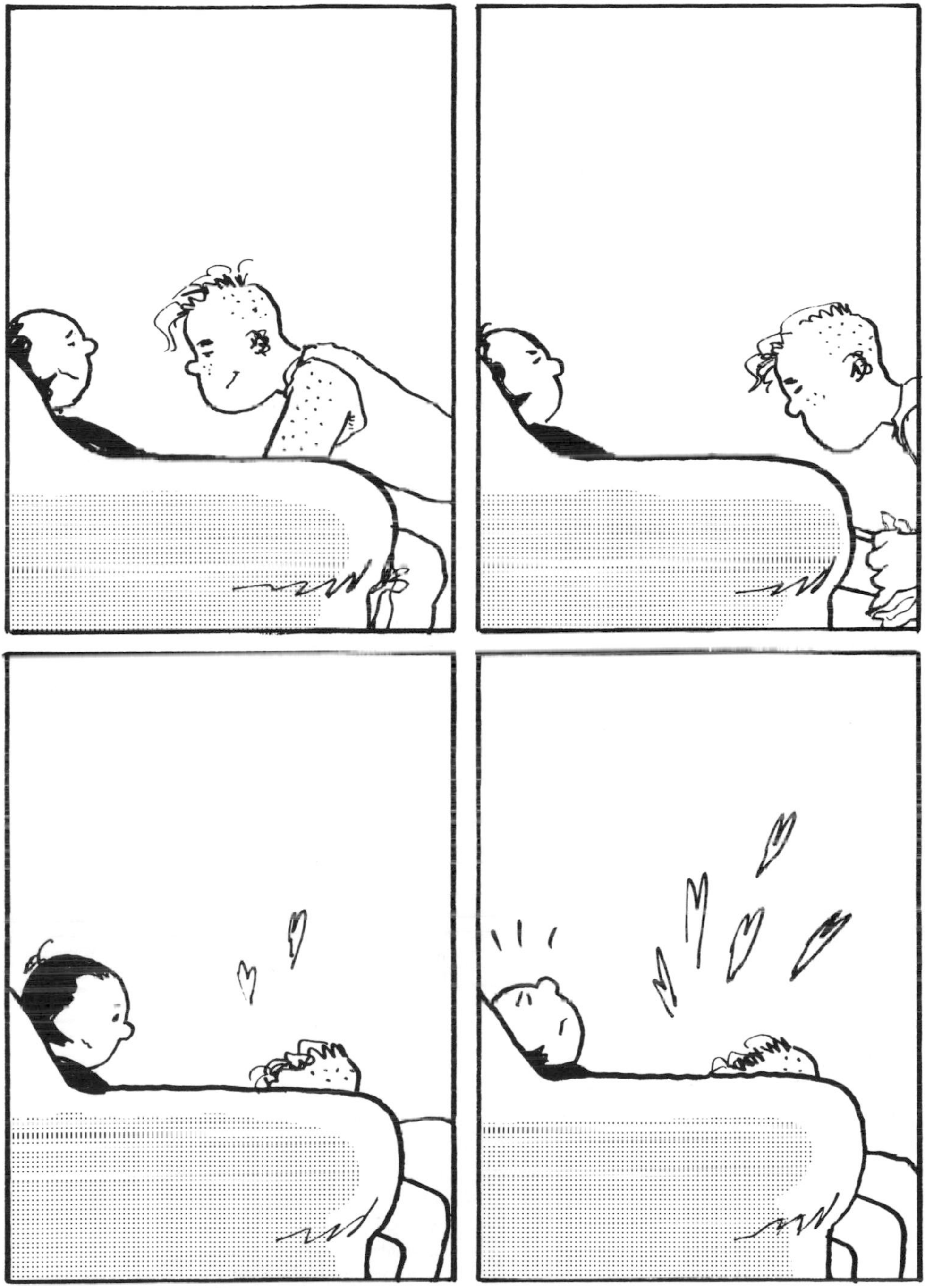

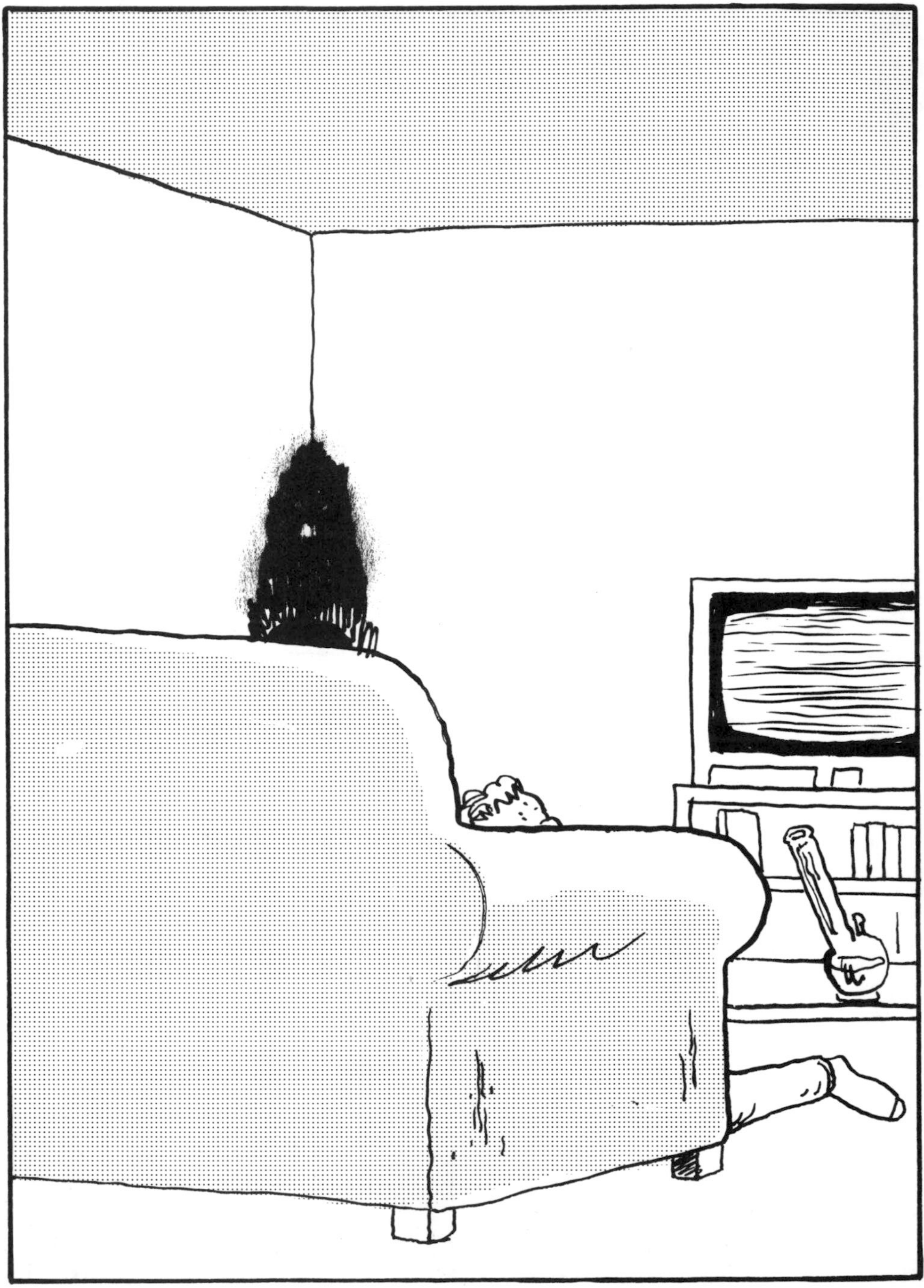

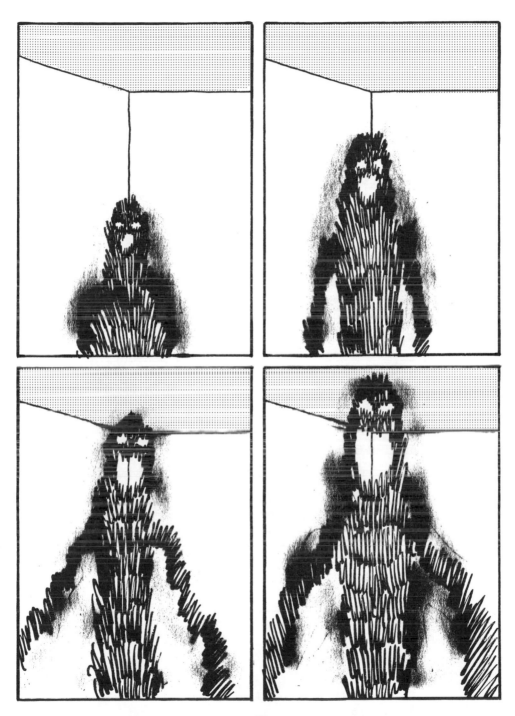

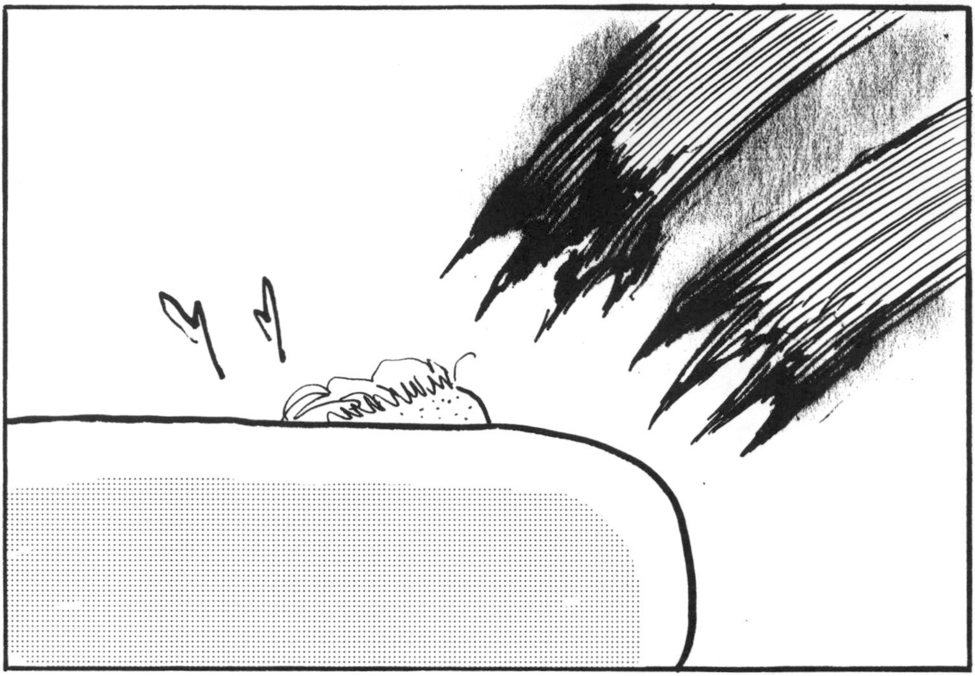

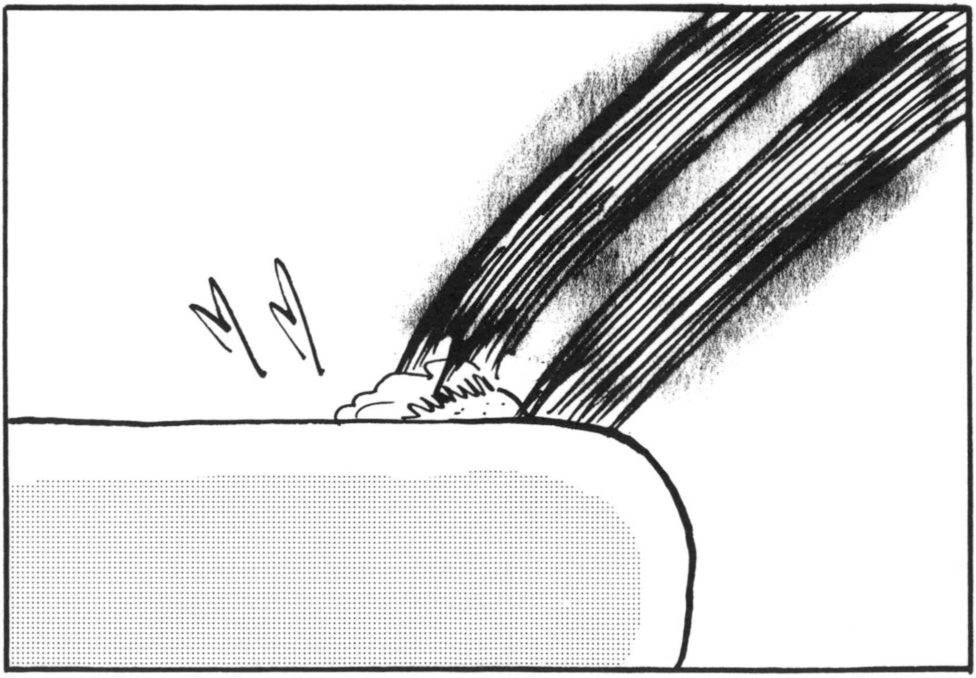

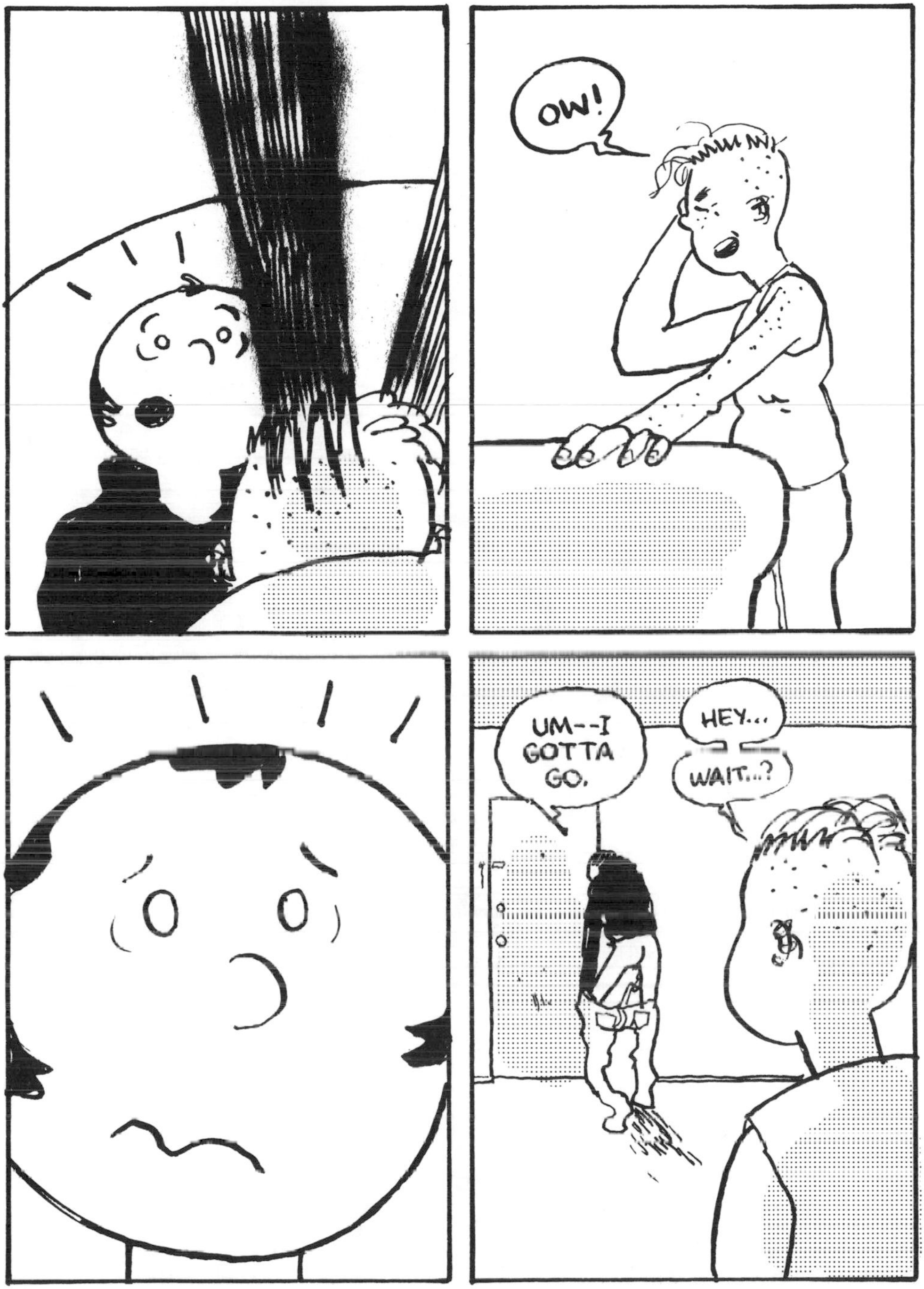
OW!
UM--I GOTTA GO.
HEY...
WAIT...?

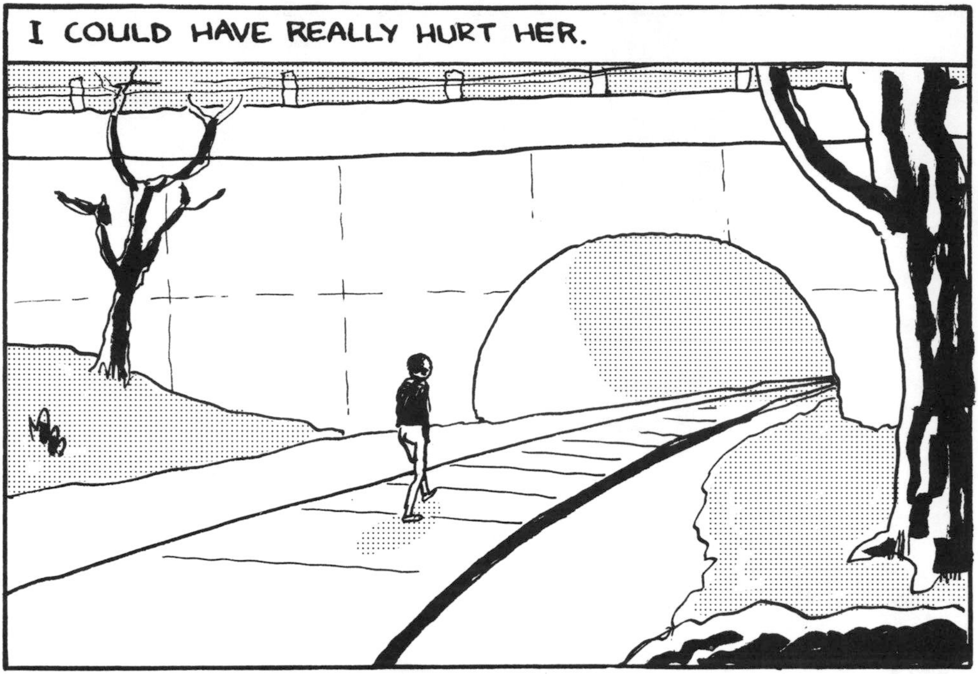
I COULD HAVE REALLY HURT HER.

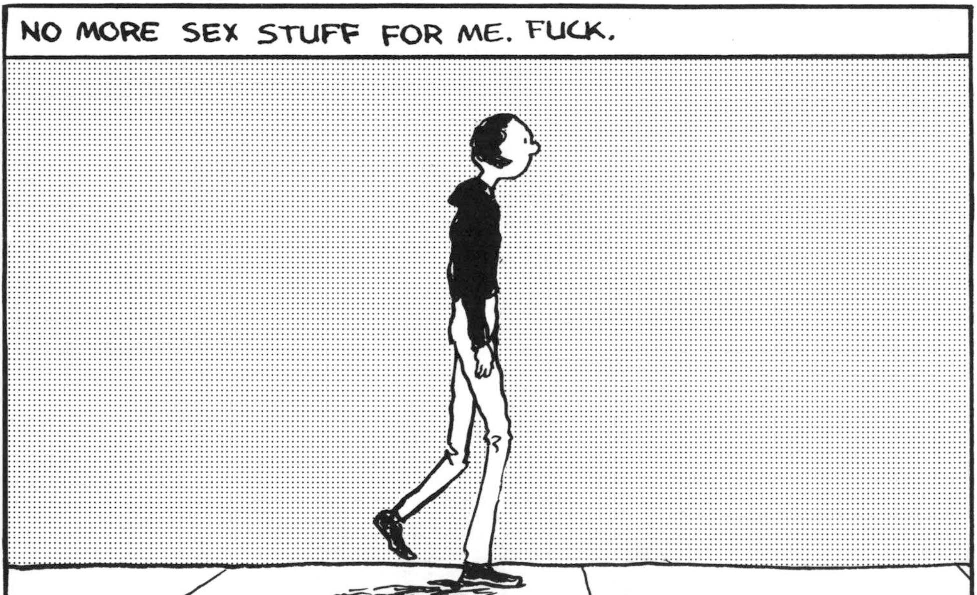
NO MORE SEX STUFF FOR ME. FUCK.

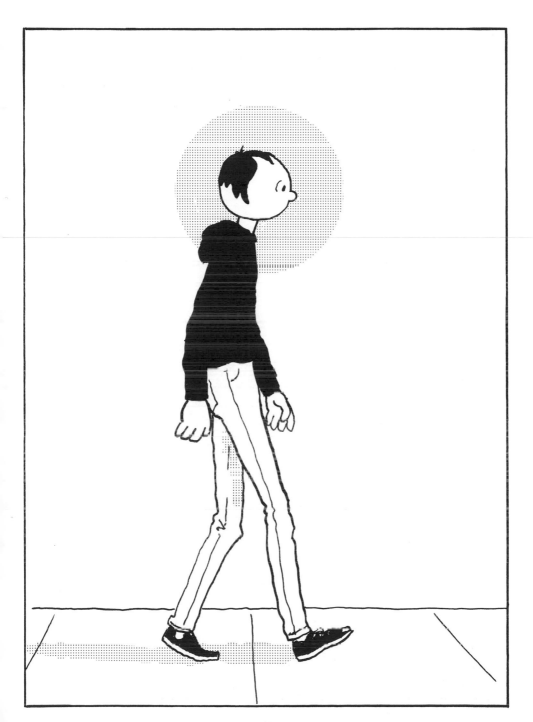

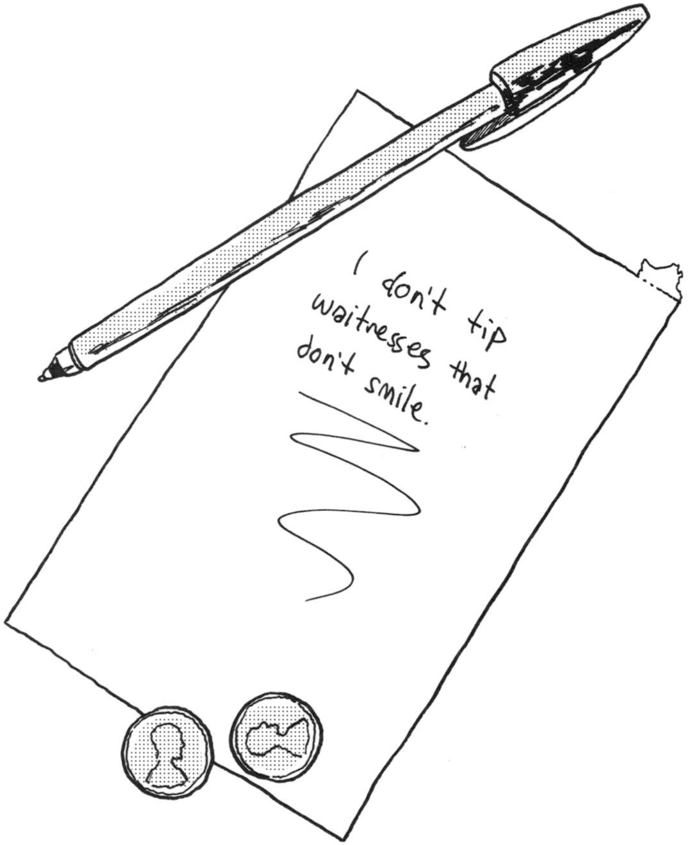
I don't tip
waitresses that
don't smile.

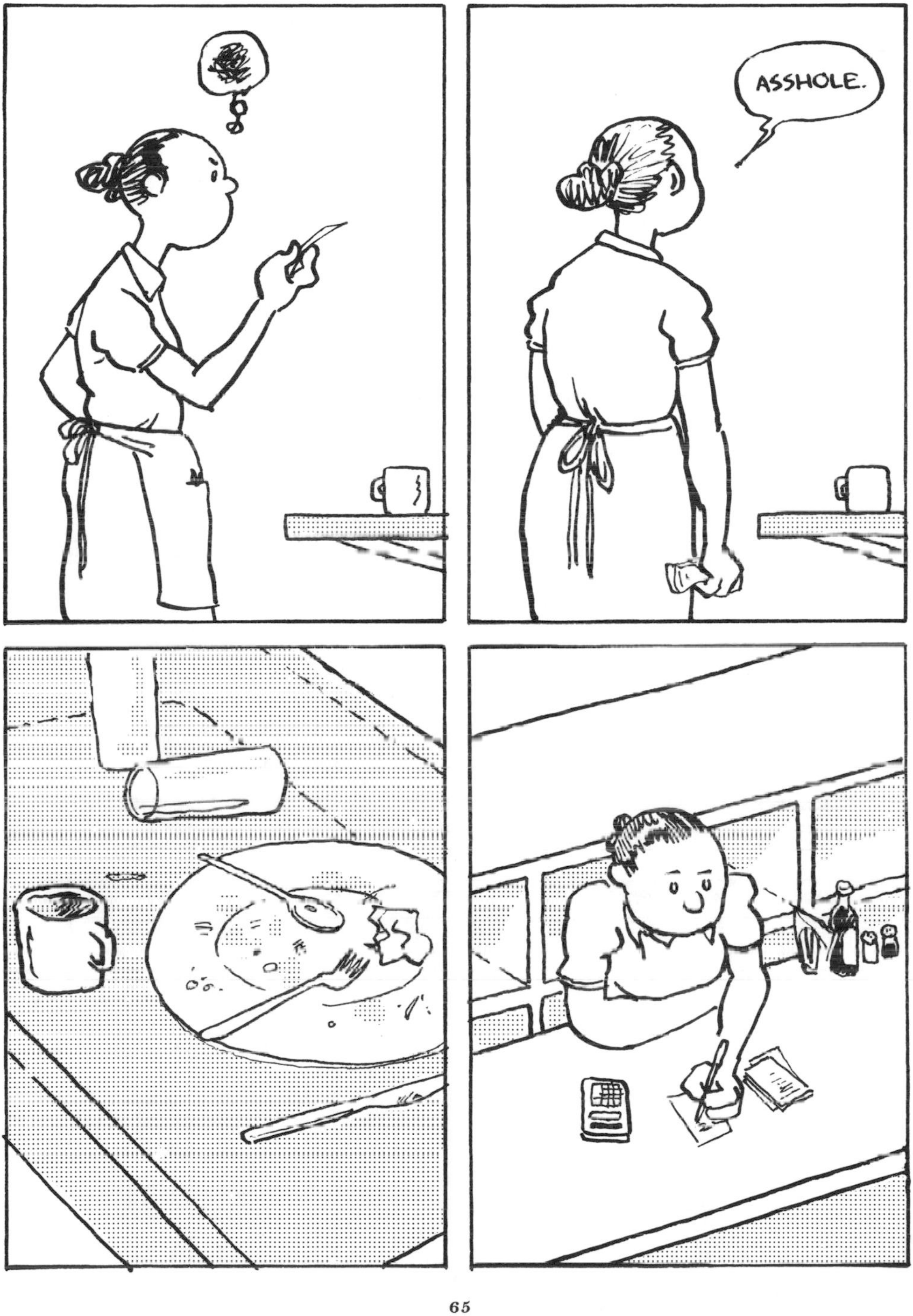
ASSHOLE.

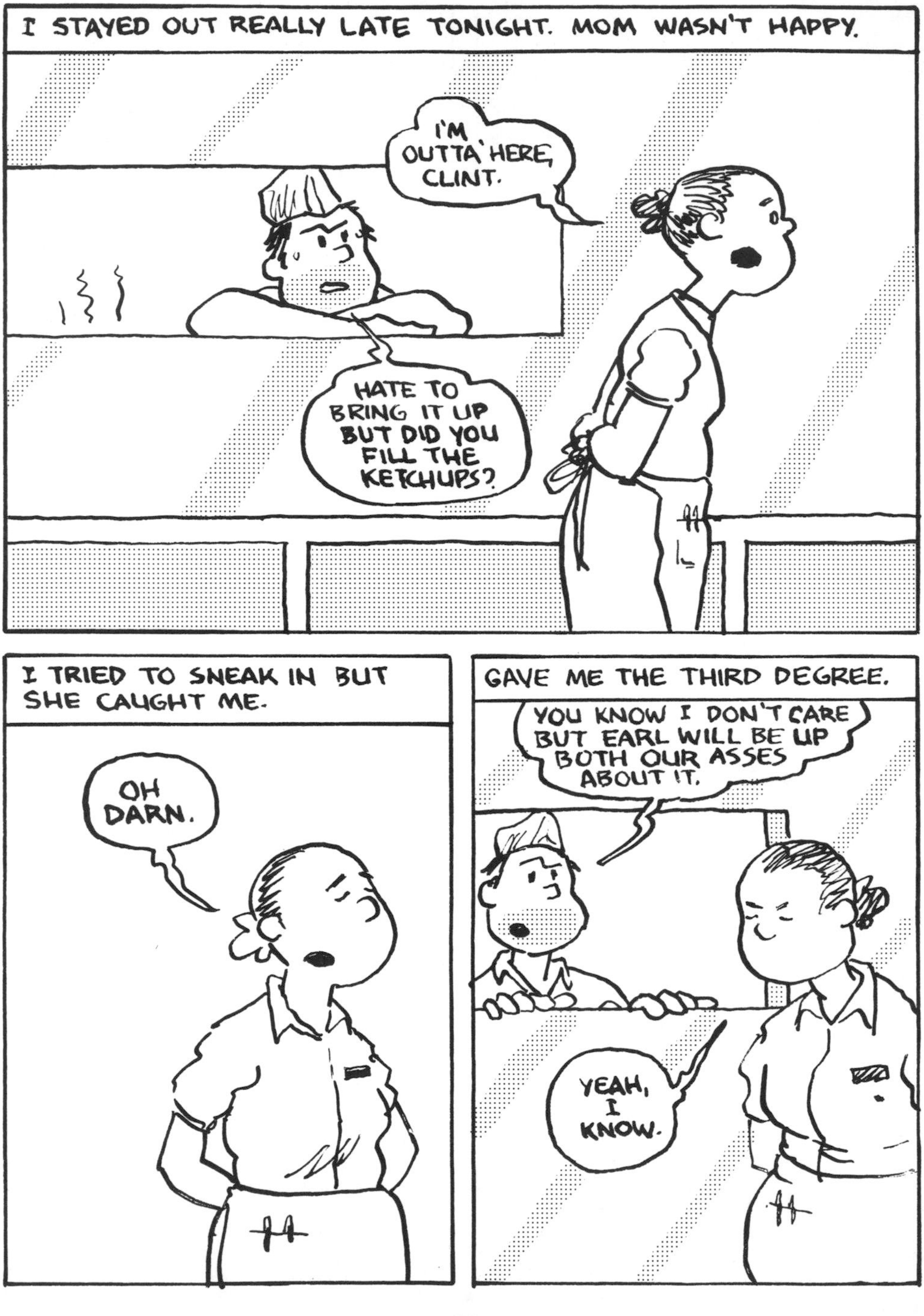
I STAYED OUT REALLY LATE TONIGHT. MOM WASN'T HAPPY.
I'M OUTTA' HERE, CLINT.
HATE TO BRING IT UP BUT DID YOU FILL THE KETCHUPS?
I TRIED TO SNEAK IN BUT SHE CAUGHT ME.
OH DARN.
GAVE ME THE THIRD DEGREE.
YOU KNOW I DON'T CARE BUT EARL WILL BE UP BOTH OUR ASSES ABOUT IT.
YEAH, I KNOW.

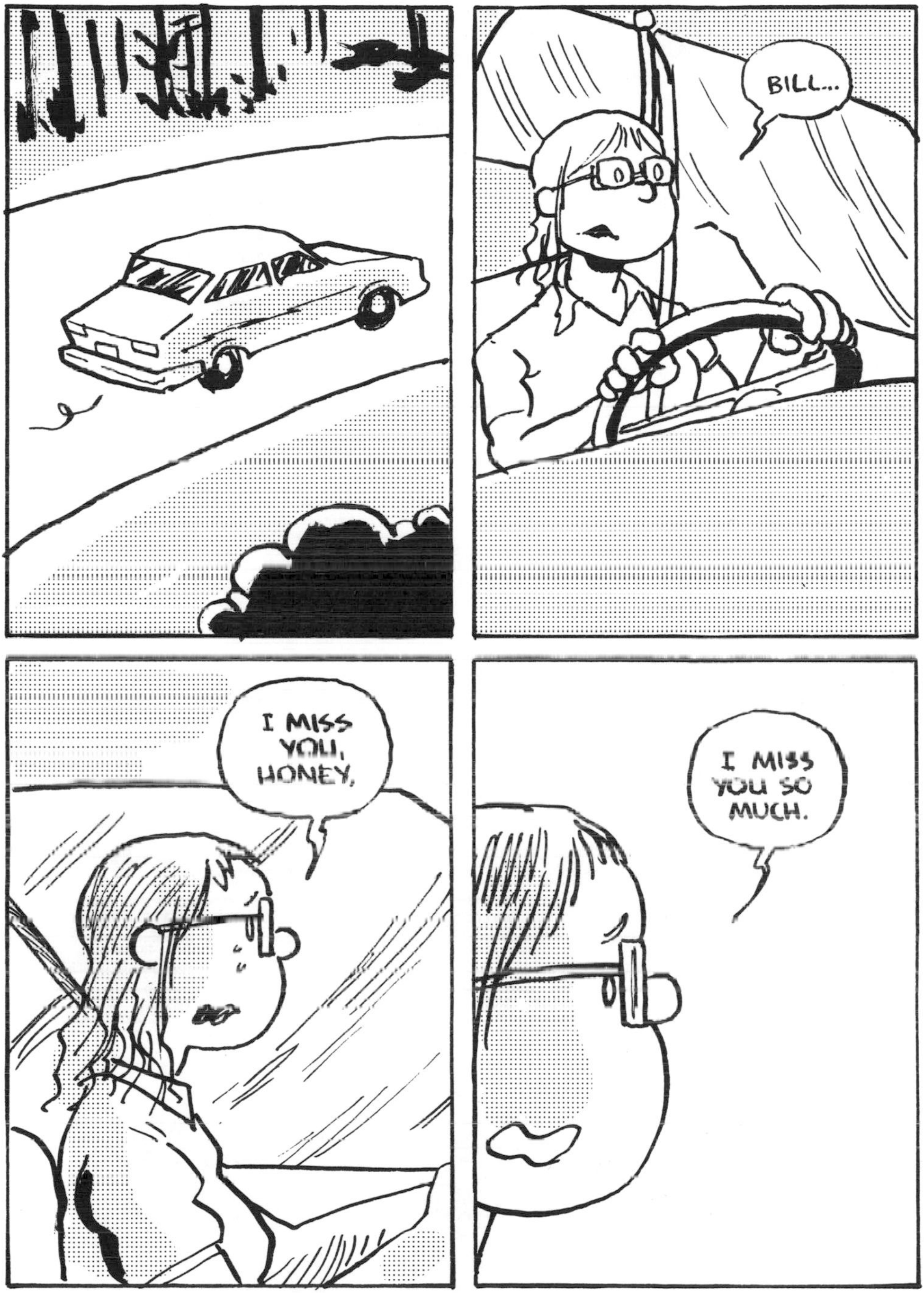
BILL...
I MISS YOU, HONEY,
I MISS YOU SO MUCH.

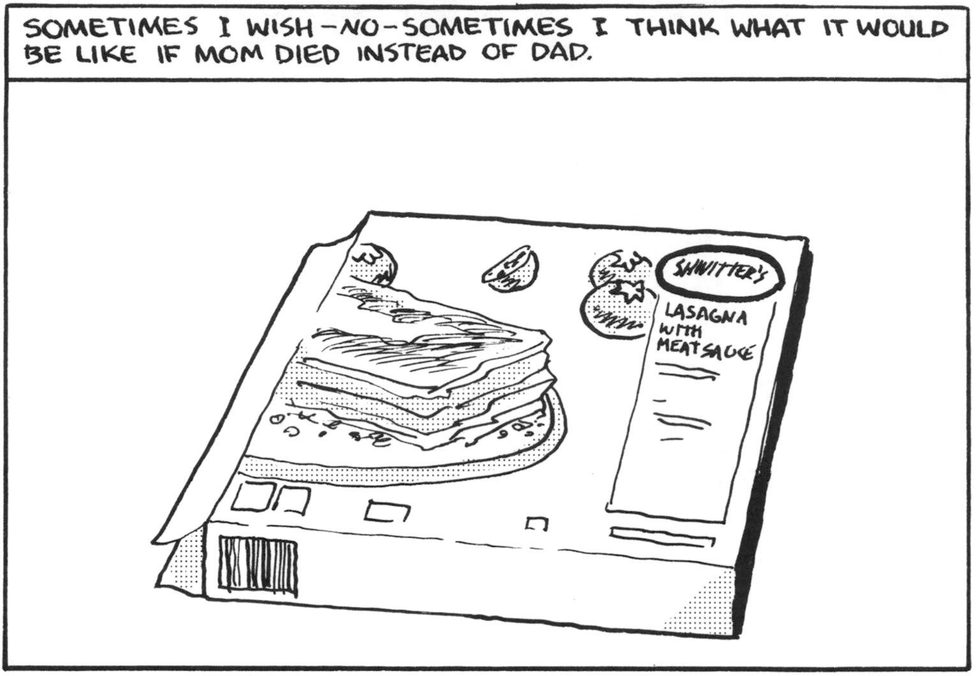
SOMETIMES I WISH—NO—SOMETIMES I THINK WHAT IT WOULD BE LIKE IF MOM DIED INSTEAD OF DAD.
SHWITTER'S
LASAGNA WITH MEAT SAUCE

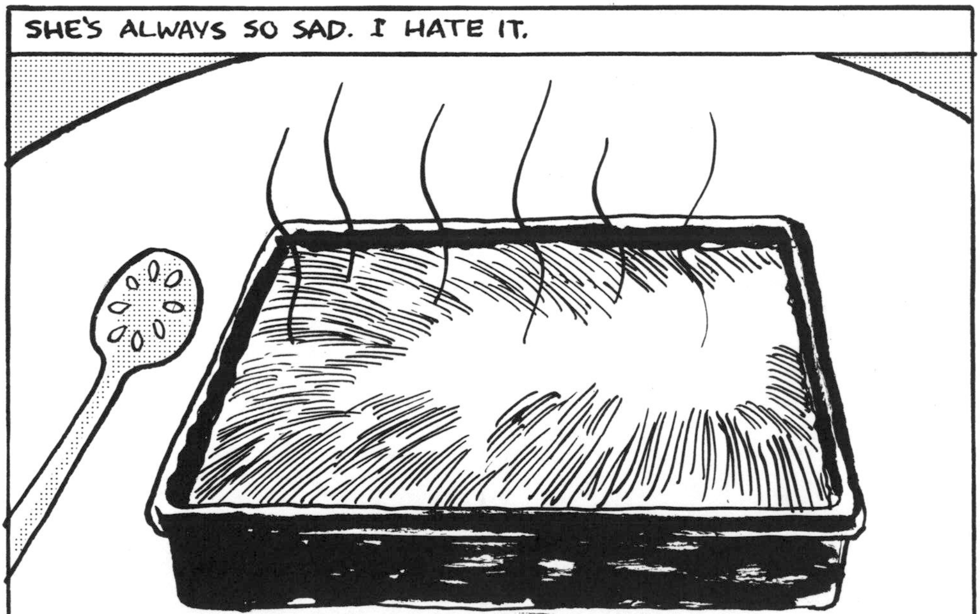
SHE'S ALWAYS SO SAD. I HATE IT.

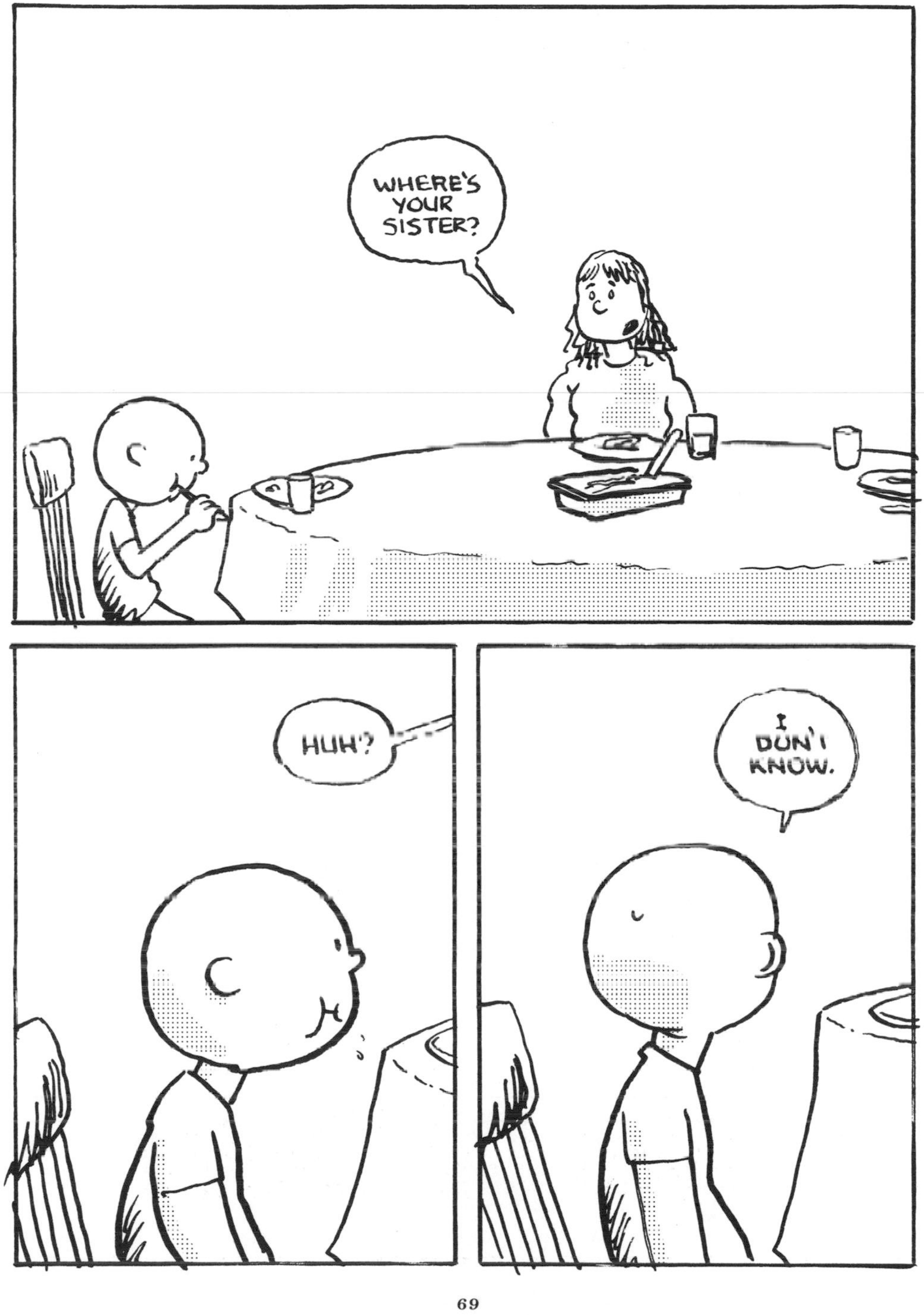
WHERE'S YOUR SISTER?
HUH?
I DON'T KNOW.

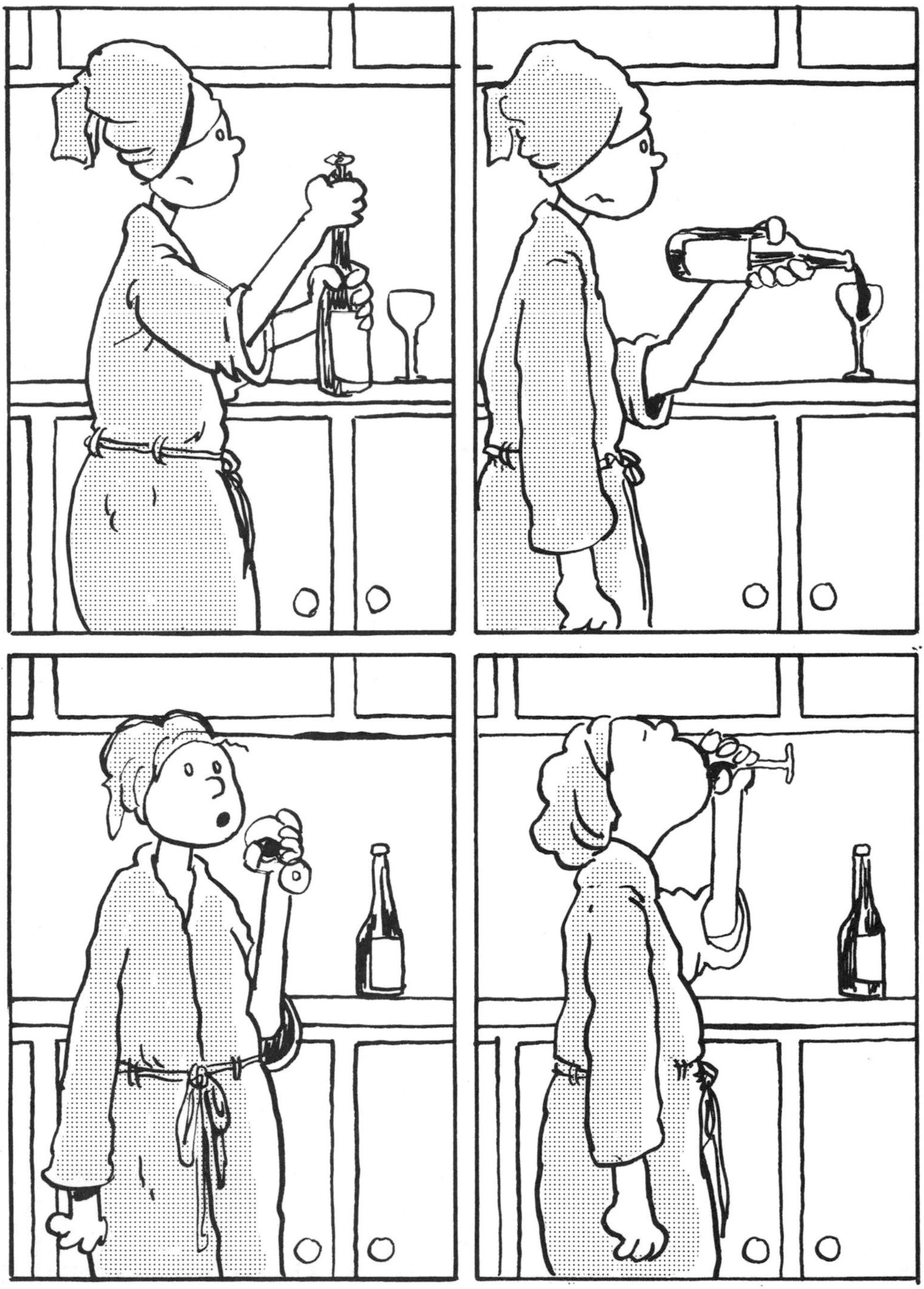

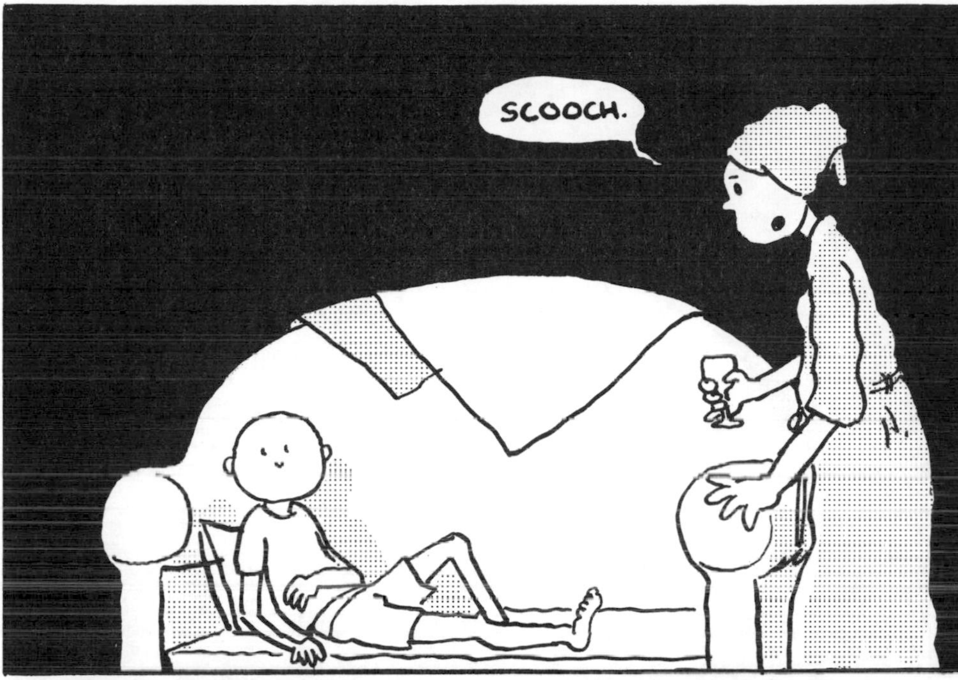
SCOOCH.

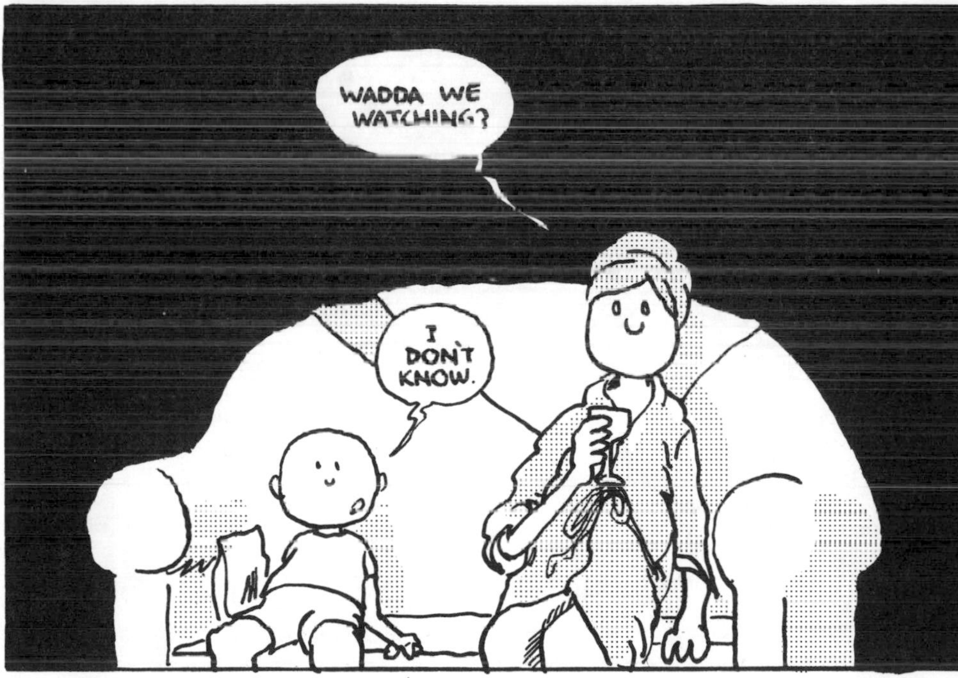
WADDA WE WATCHING?
I DON'T KNOW.

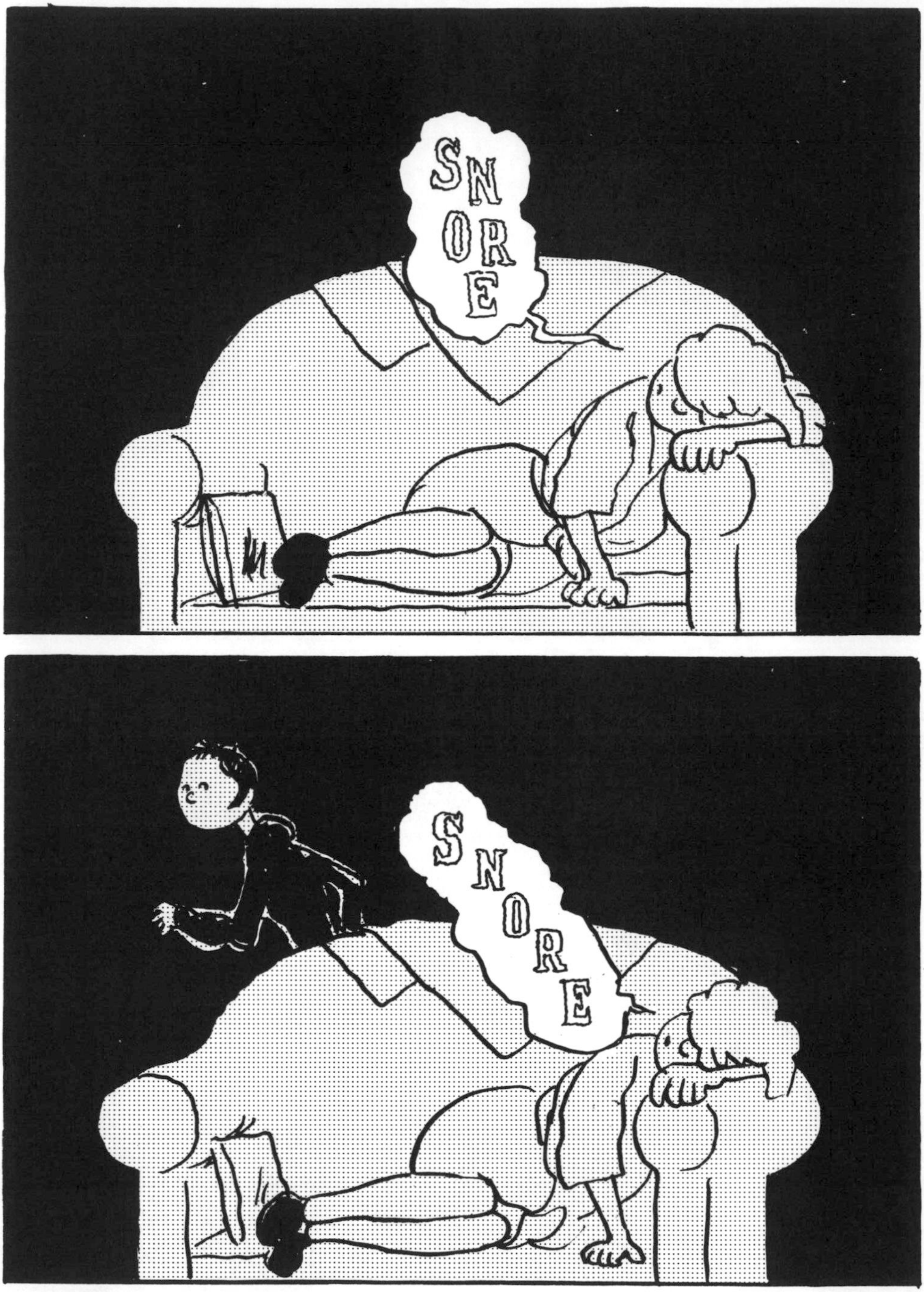
SNORE
SNORE

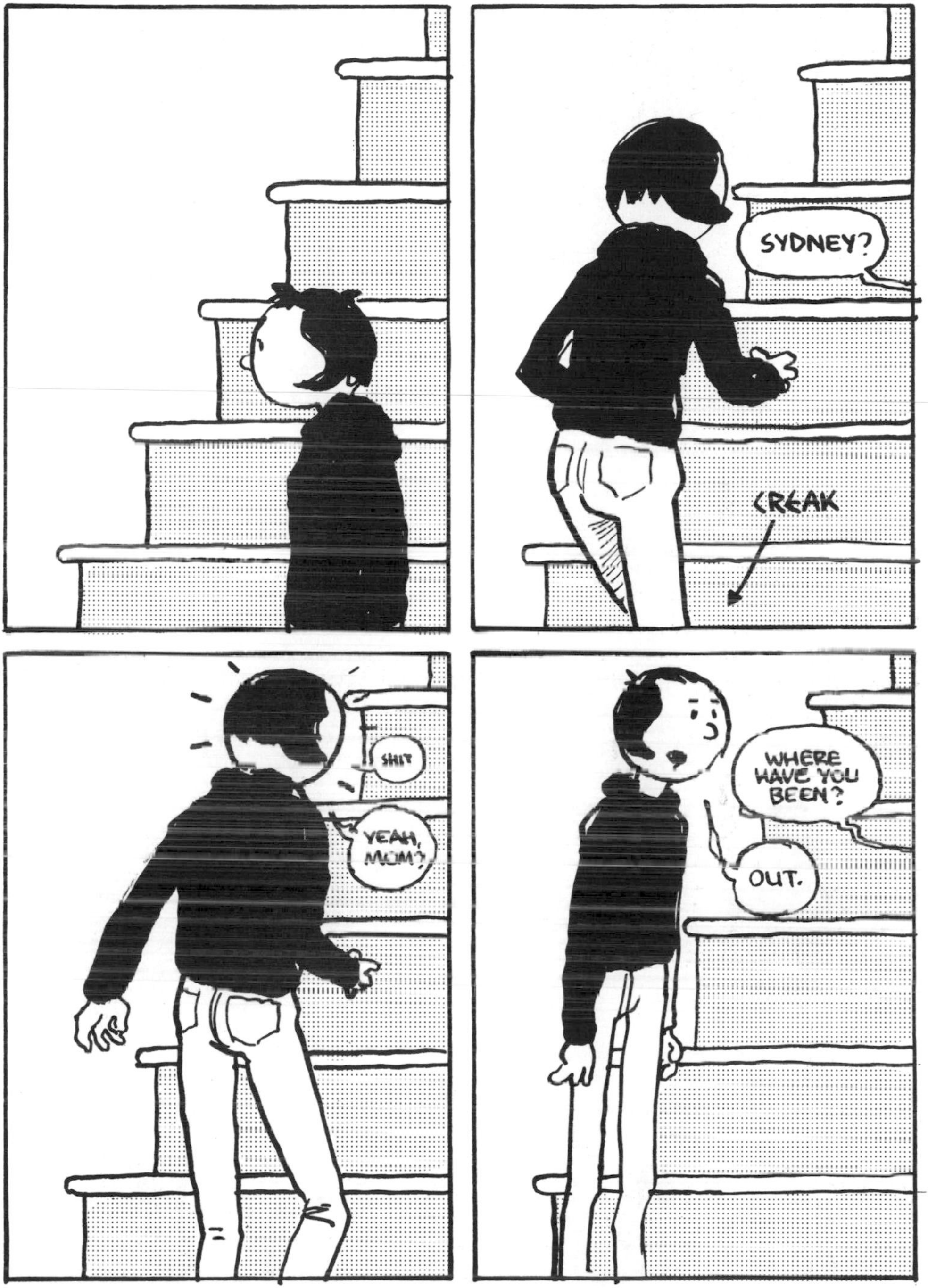
SYDNEY?
CREAK
SHIT
YEAH, MOM?
WHERE HAVE YOU BEEN?
OUT.

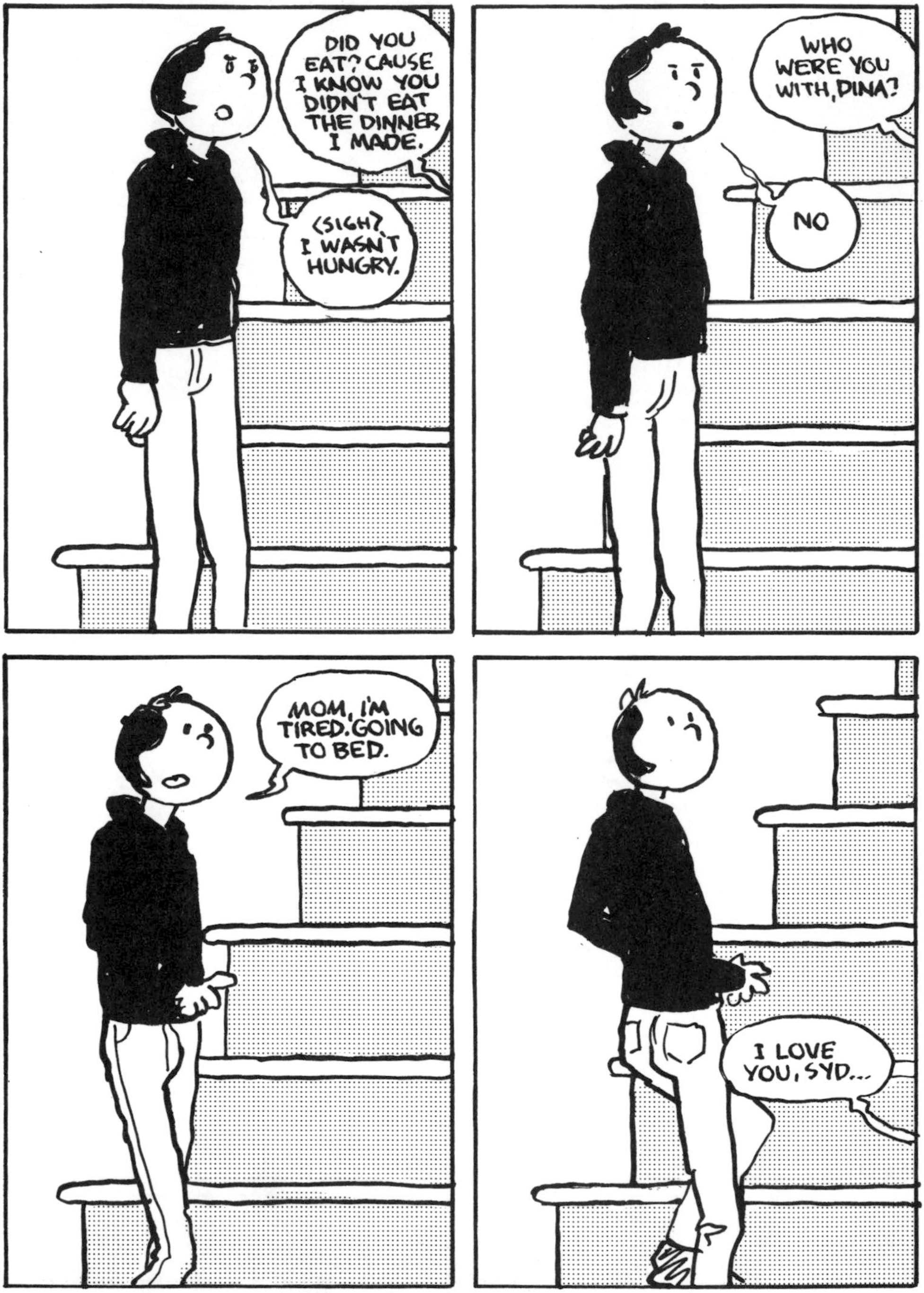
DID YOU EAT? CAUSE I KNOW YOU DIDN'T EAT THE DINNER I MADE.
<SIGH> I WASN'T HUNGRY.
WHO WERE YOU WITH, DINA?
NO
MOM, I'M TIRED. GOING TO BED.
I LOVE YOU, SYD...

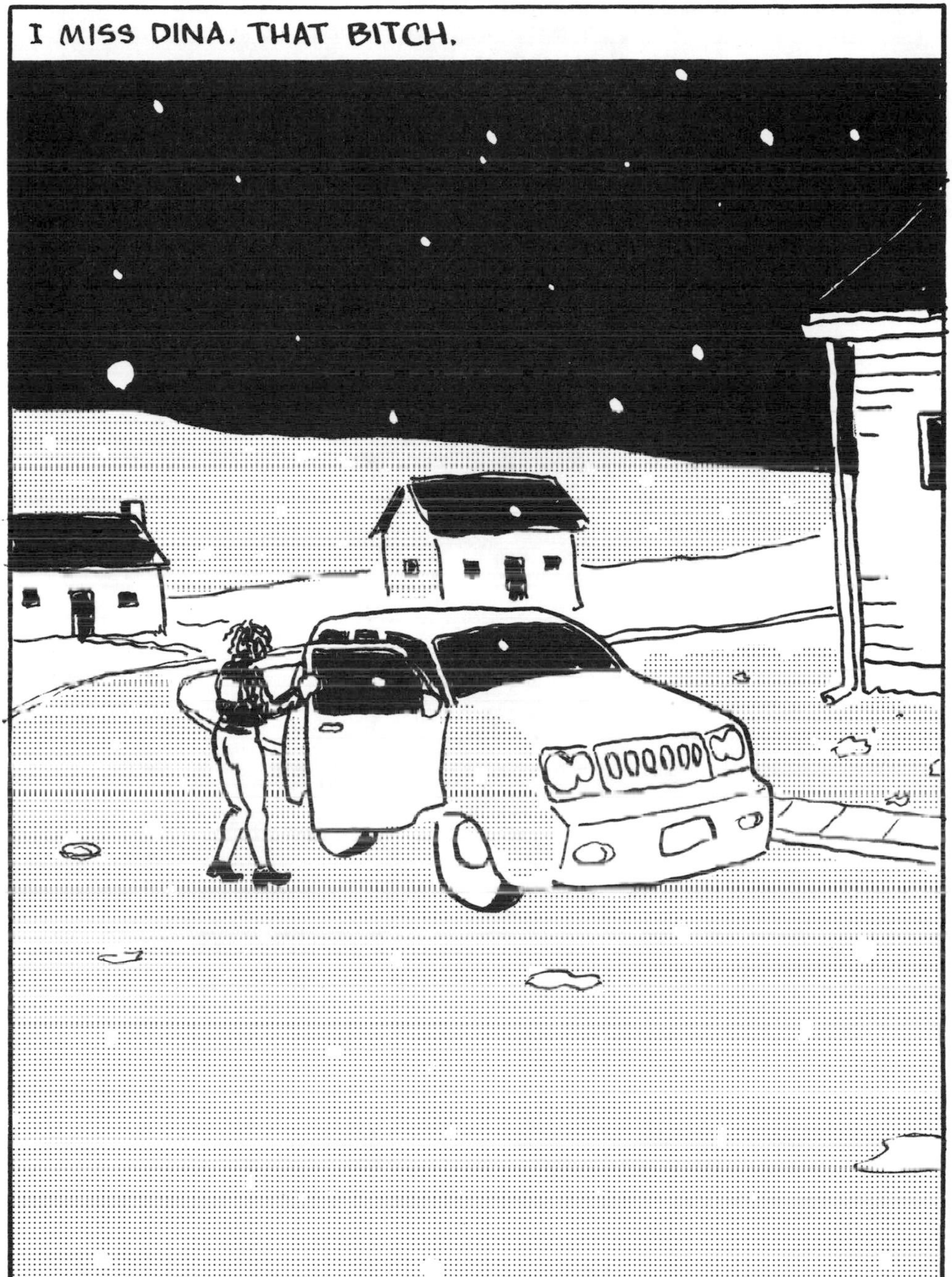
I MISS DINA. THAT BITCH.

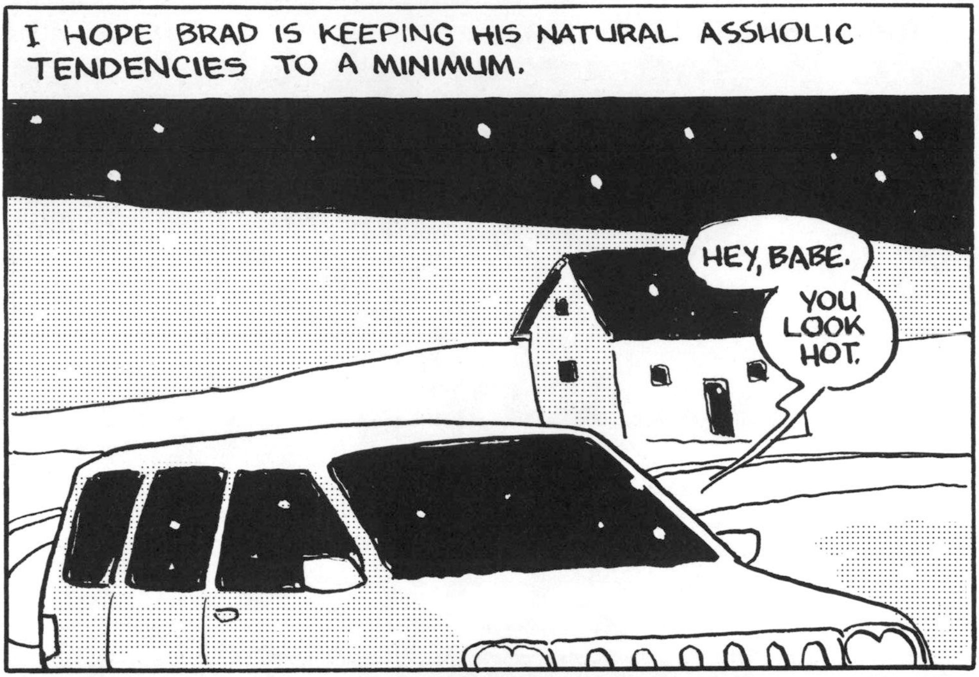
I HOPE BRAD IS KEEPING HIS NATURAL ASSHOLIC TENDENCIES TO A MINIMUM.
HEY, BABE.
YOU LOOK HOT.

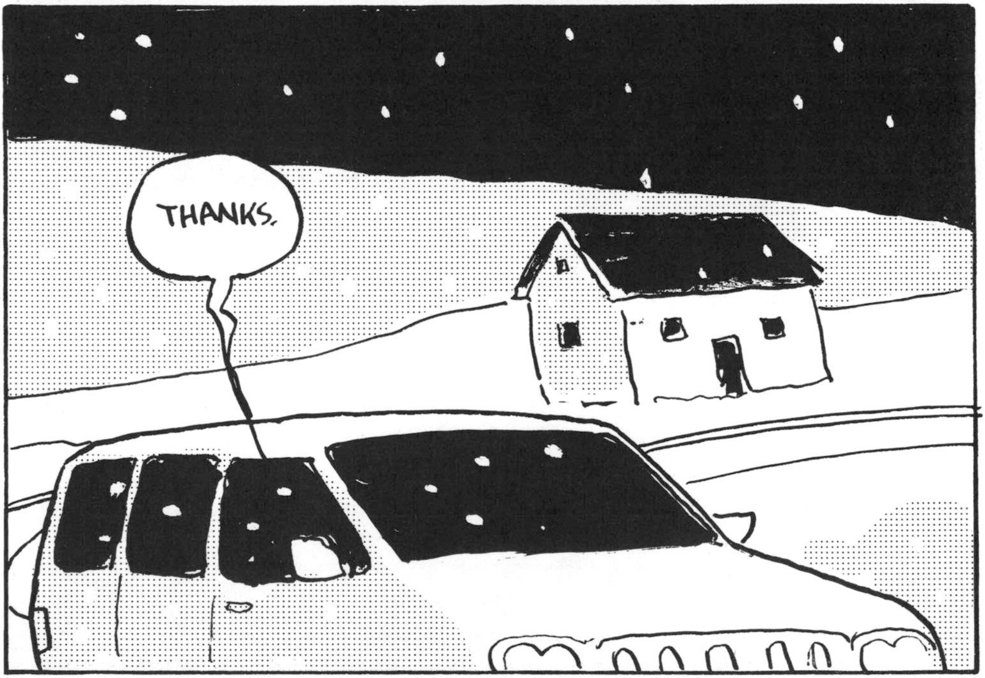
THANKS.

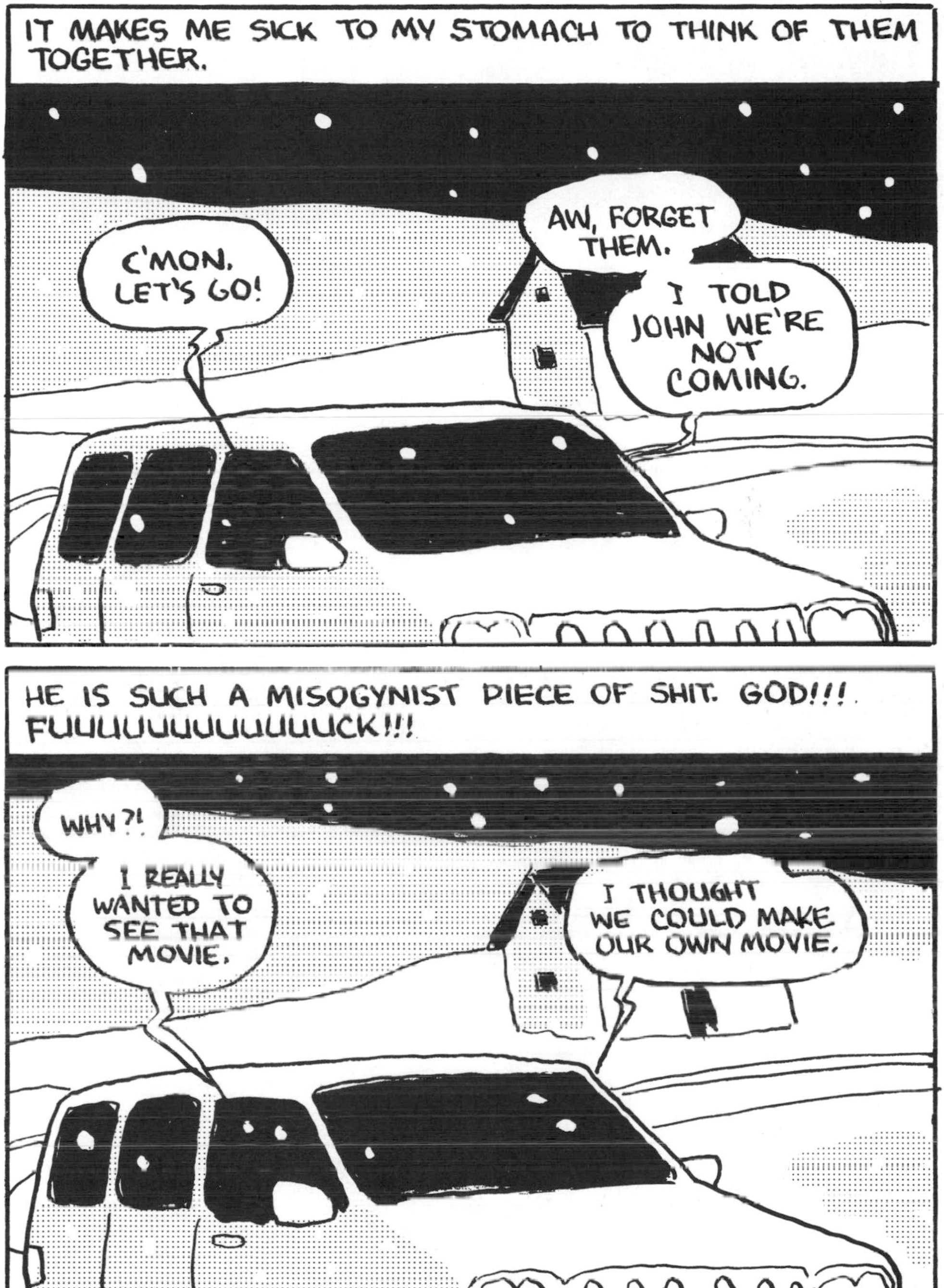
IT MAKES ME SICK TO MY STOMACH TO THINK OF THEM TOGETHER.
C'MON. LET'S GO!
AW, FORGET THEM.
I TOLD JOHN WE'RE NOT COMING.
HE IS SUCH A MISOGYNIST PIECE OF SHIT. GOD!!! FUUUUUUUUUUUUCK!!!
WHY?!
I REALLY WANTED TO SEE THAT MOVIE.
I THOUGHT WE COULD MAKE OUR OWN MOVIE.

SOMETIMES WHEN I WAS WITH RYAN, I WOULD JUST BE THINKING OF DINA.

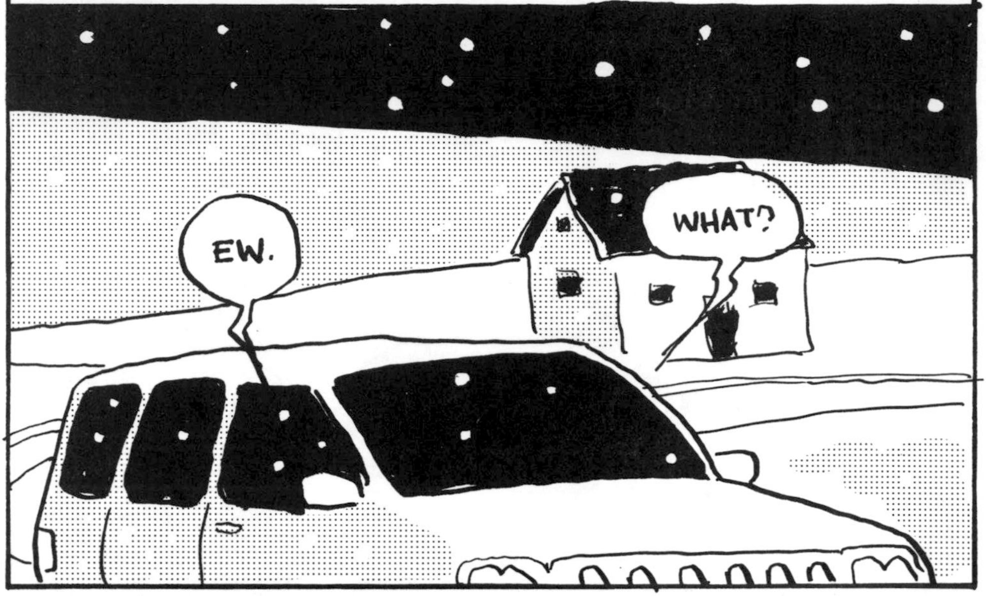
EW.
WHAT?

WHAT THE FUCK DOES THAT MEAN? GUESS I STILL CARE FOR THE JERK.

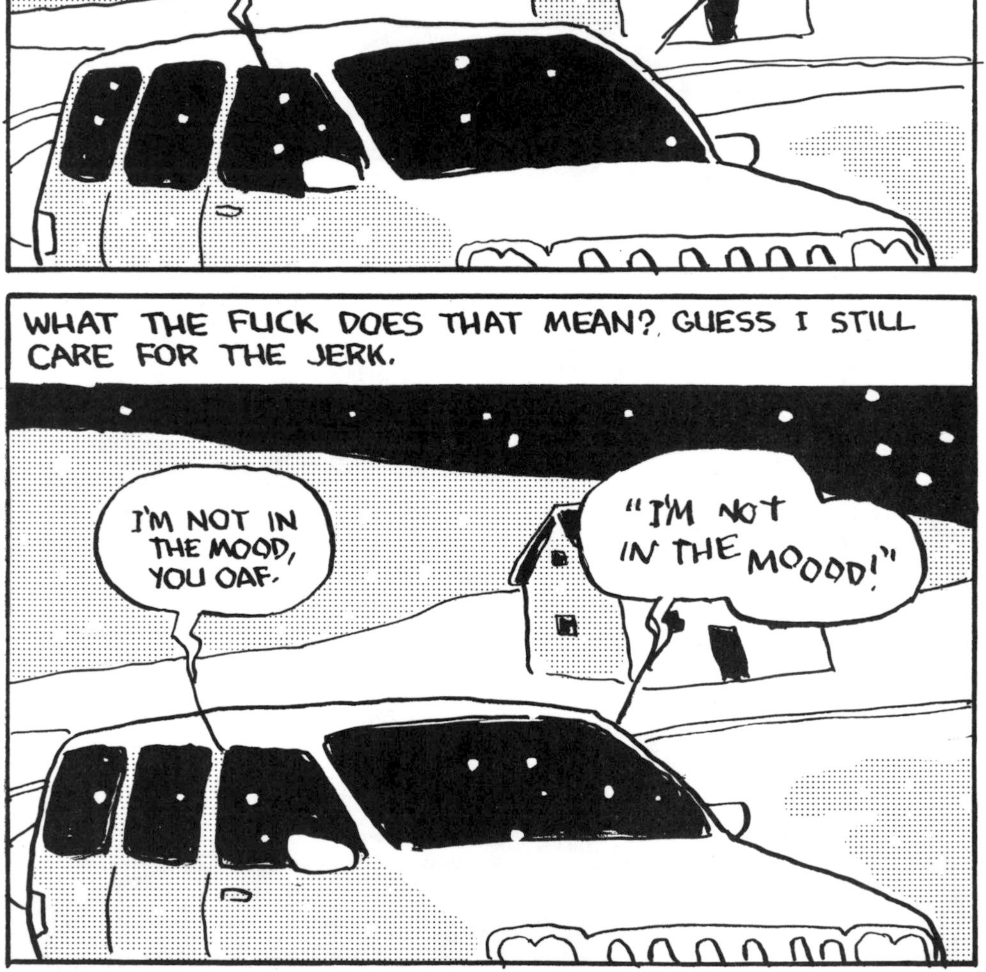
I'M NOT IN THE MOOD, YOU OAF.
"I'M NOT IN THE MOOOD!"

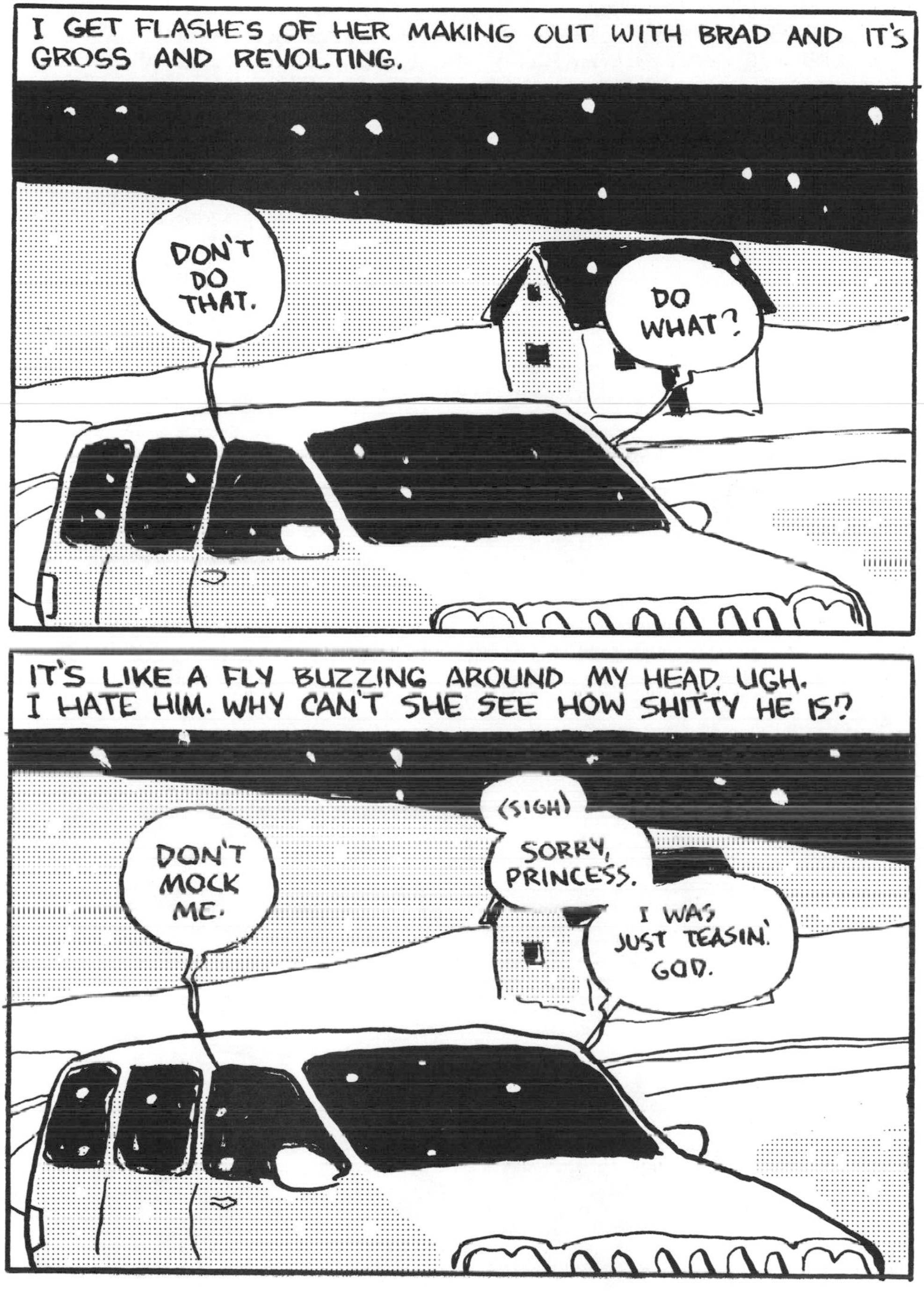
I GET FLASHES OF HER MAKING OUT WITH BRAD AND IT'S GROSS AND REVOLTING.
DON'T DO THAT.
DO WHAT?
IT'S LIKE A FLY BUZZING AROUND MY HEAD. UGH. I HATE HIM. WHY CAN'T SHE SEE HOW SHITTY HE IS?
DON'T MOCK ME.
(SIGH)
SORRY, PRINCESS.
I WAS JUST TEASIN'. GOD.

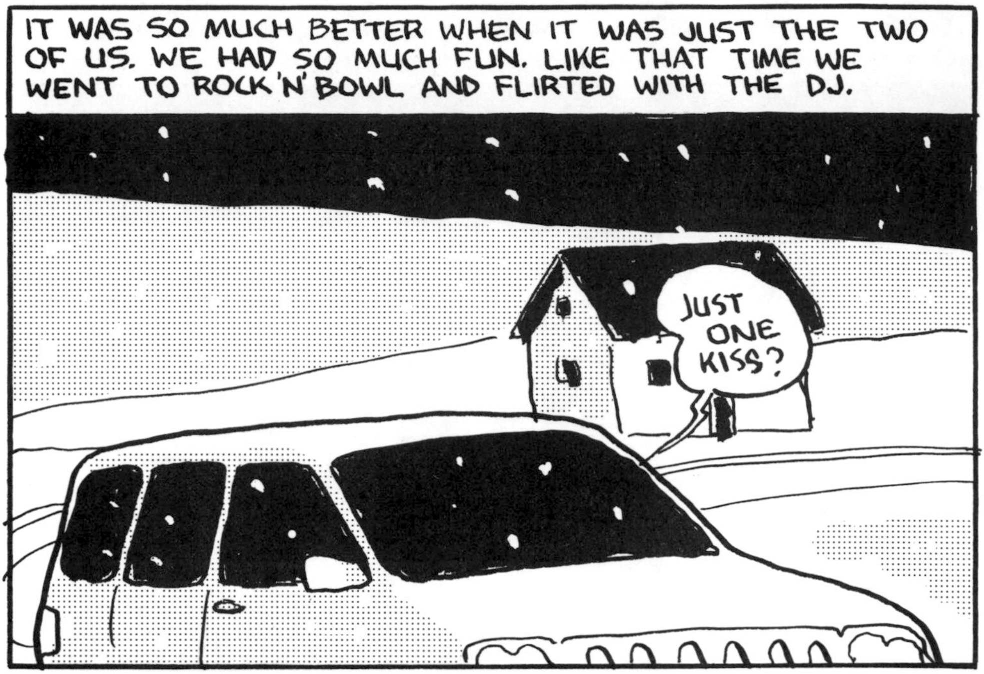
IT WAS SO MUCH BETTER WHEN IT WAS JUST THE TWO OF US. WE HAD SO MUCH FUN. LIKE THAT TIME WE WENT TO ROCK 'N' BOWL AND FLIRTED WITH THE DJ.
JUST ONE KISS?

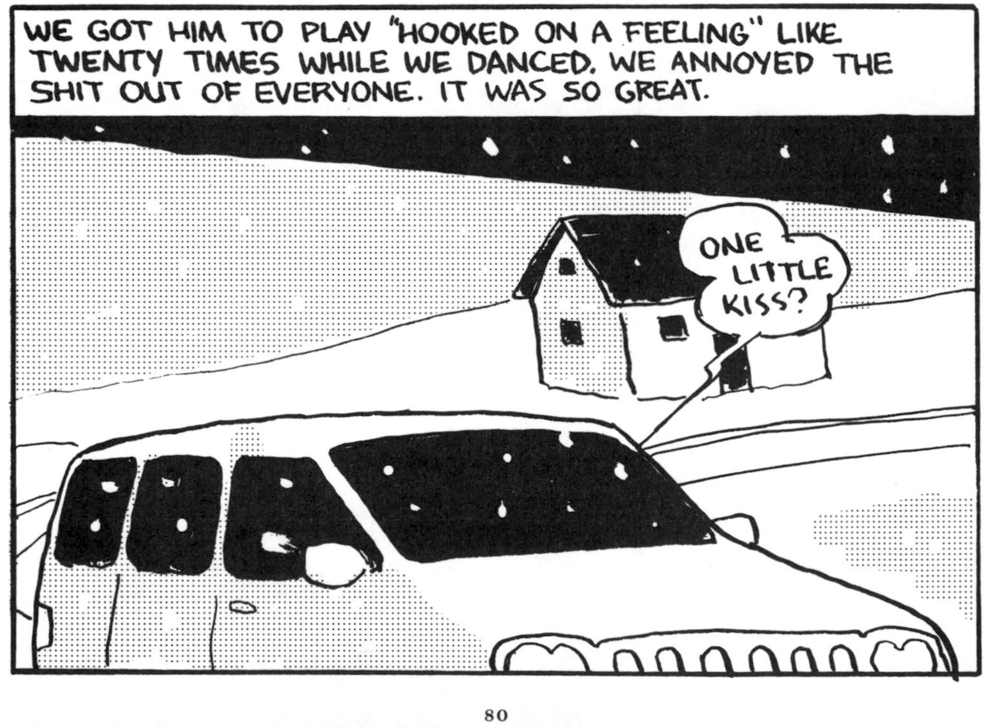
WE GOT HIM TO PLAY "HOOKED ON A FEELING" LIKE TWENTY TIMES WHILE WE DANCED. WE ANNOYED THE SHIT OUT OF EVERYONE. IT WAS SO GREAT.
ONE LITTLE KISS?

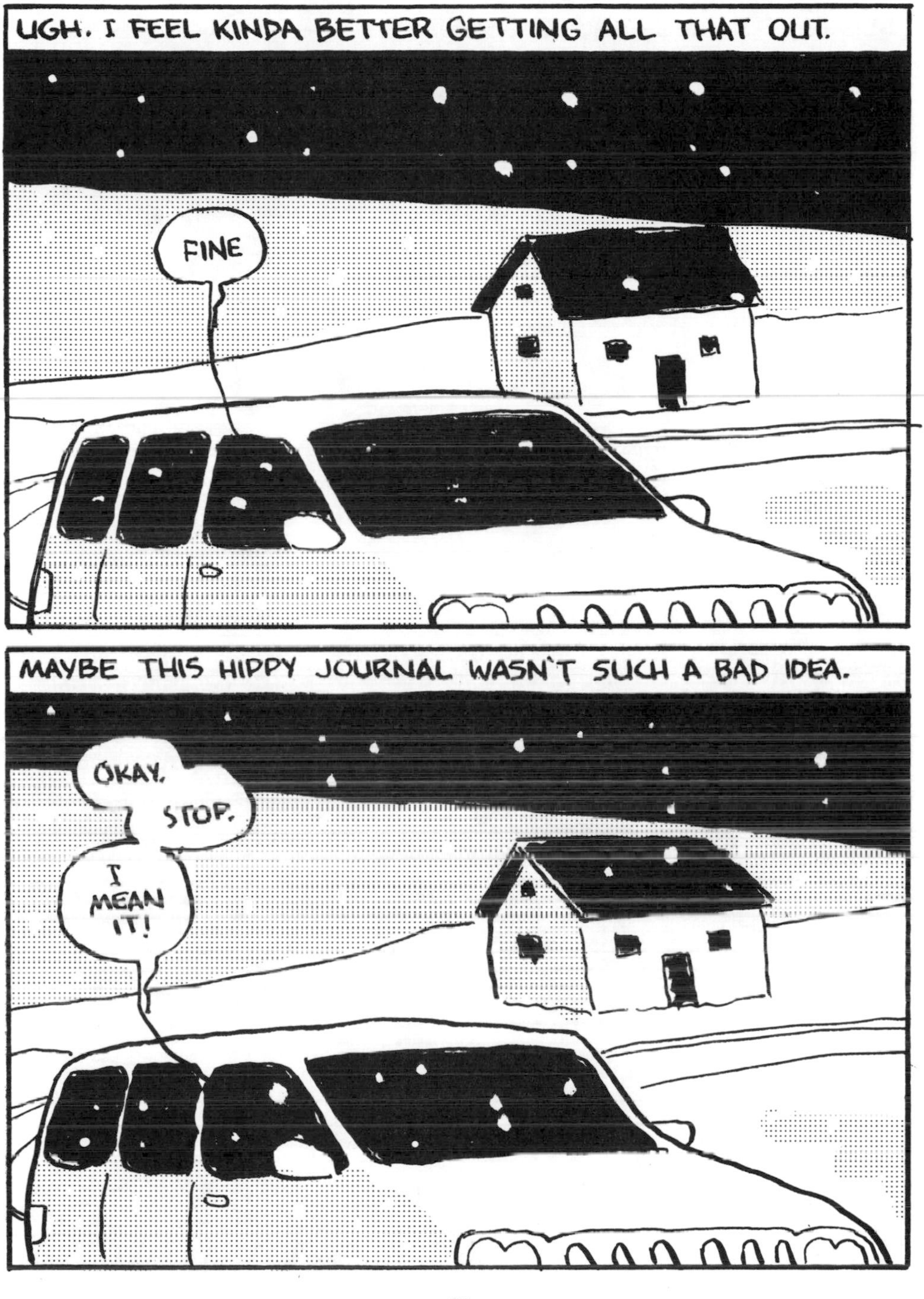
UGH. I FEEL KINDA BETTER GETTING ALL THAT OUT.
FINE
MAYBE THIS HIPPY JOURNAL WASN'T SUCH A BAD IDEA.
OKAY.
STOP.
I MEAN IT!

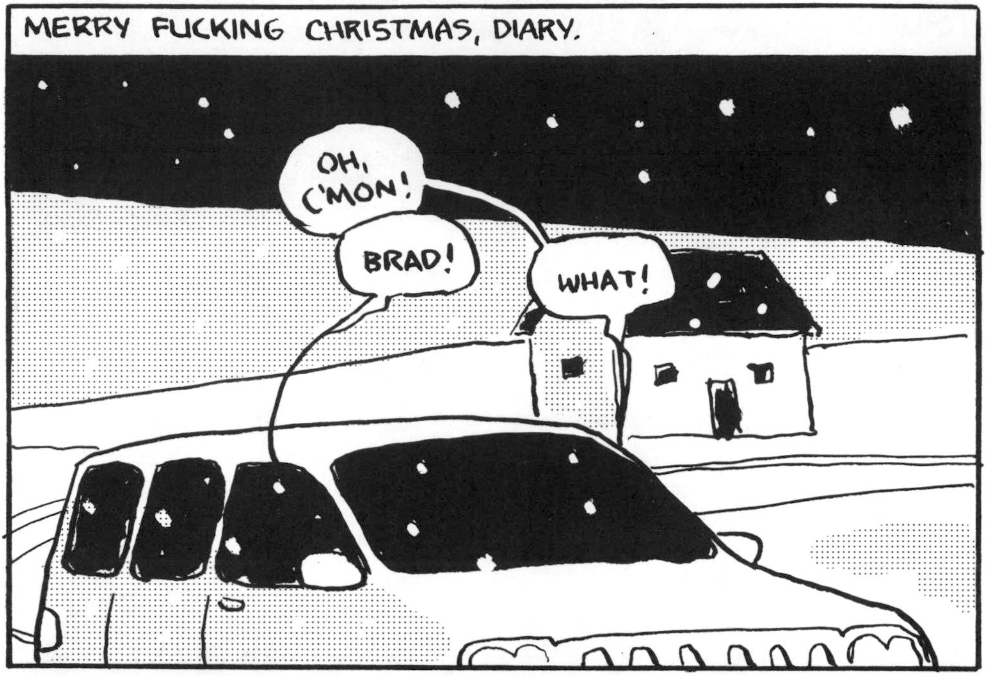
MERRY FUCKING CHRISTMAS, DIARY.
OH, C'MON!
BRAD!
WHAT!

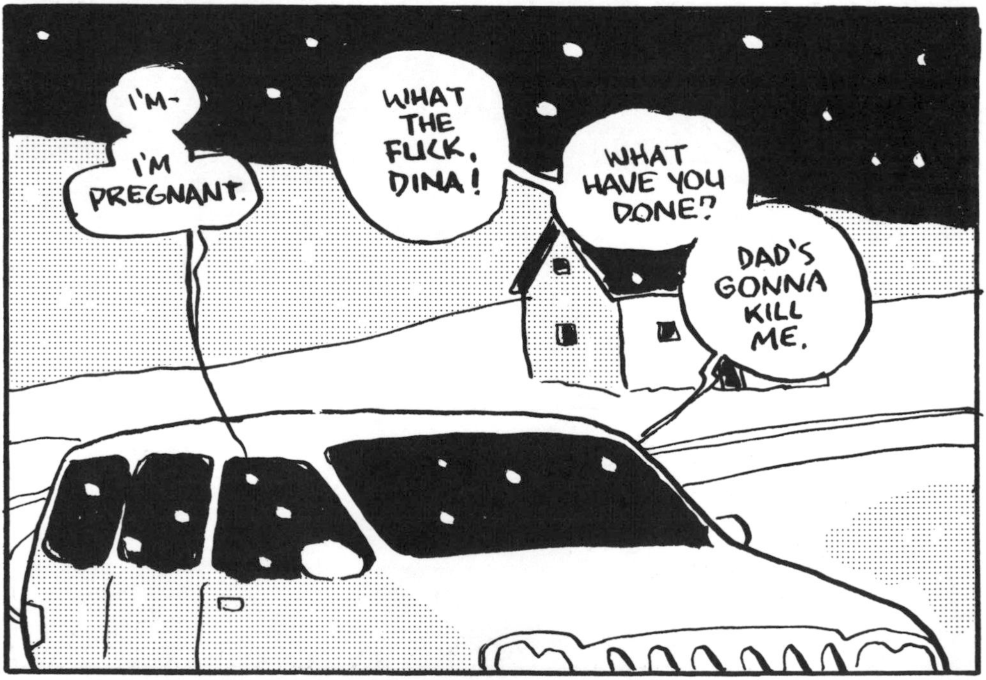
I'M-
I'M PREGNANT.
WHAT THE FUCK, DINA!
WHAT HAVE YOU DONE?
DAD'S GONNA KILL ME.

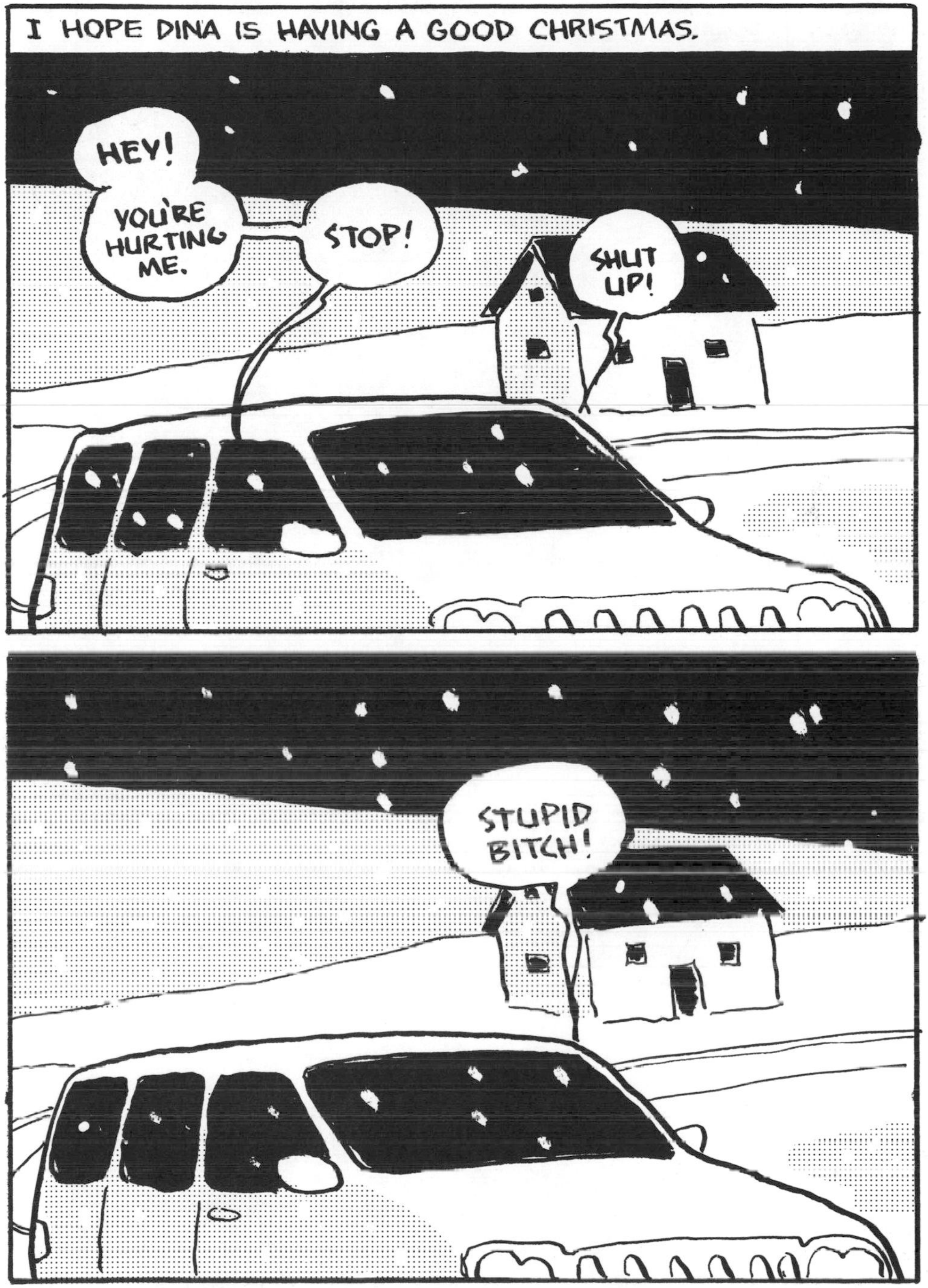
I HOPE DINA IS HAVING A GOOD CHRISTMAS.
HEY!
YOU'RE HURTING ME.
STOP!
SHUT UP!
STUPID BITCH!

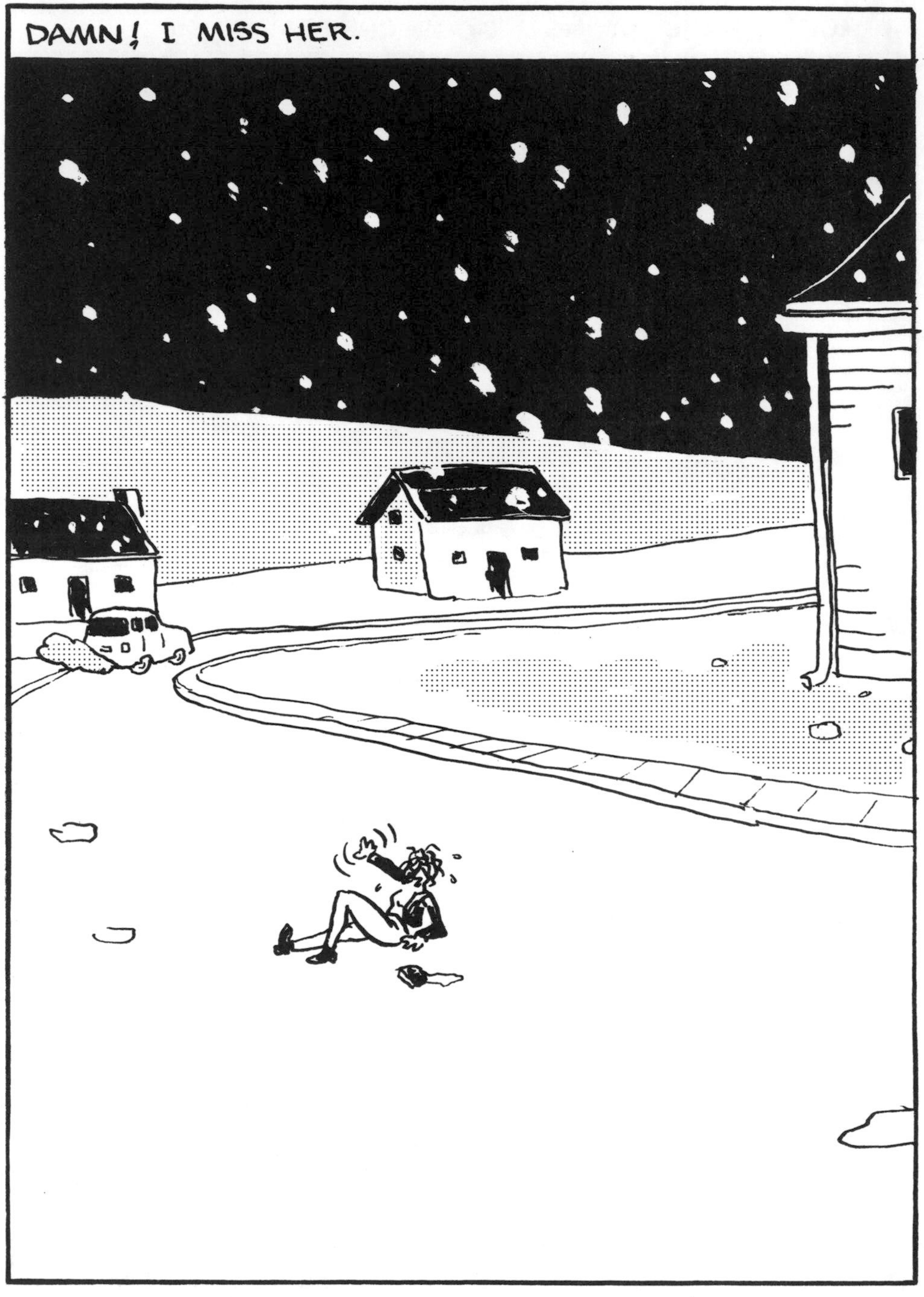
DAMN! I MISS HER.

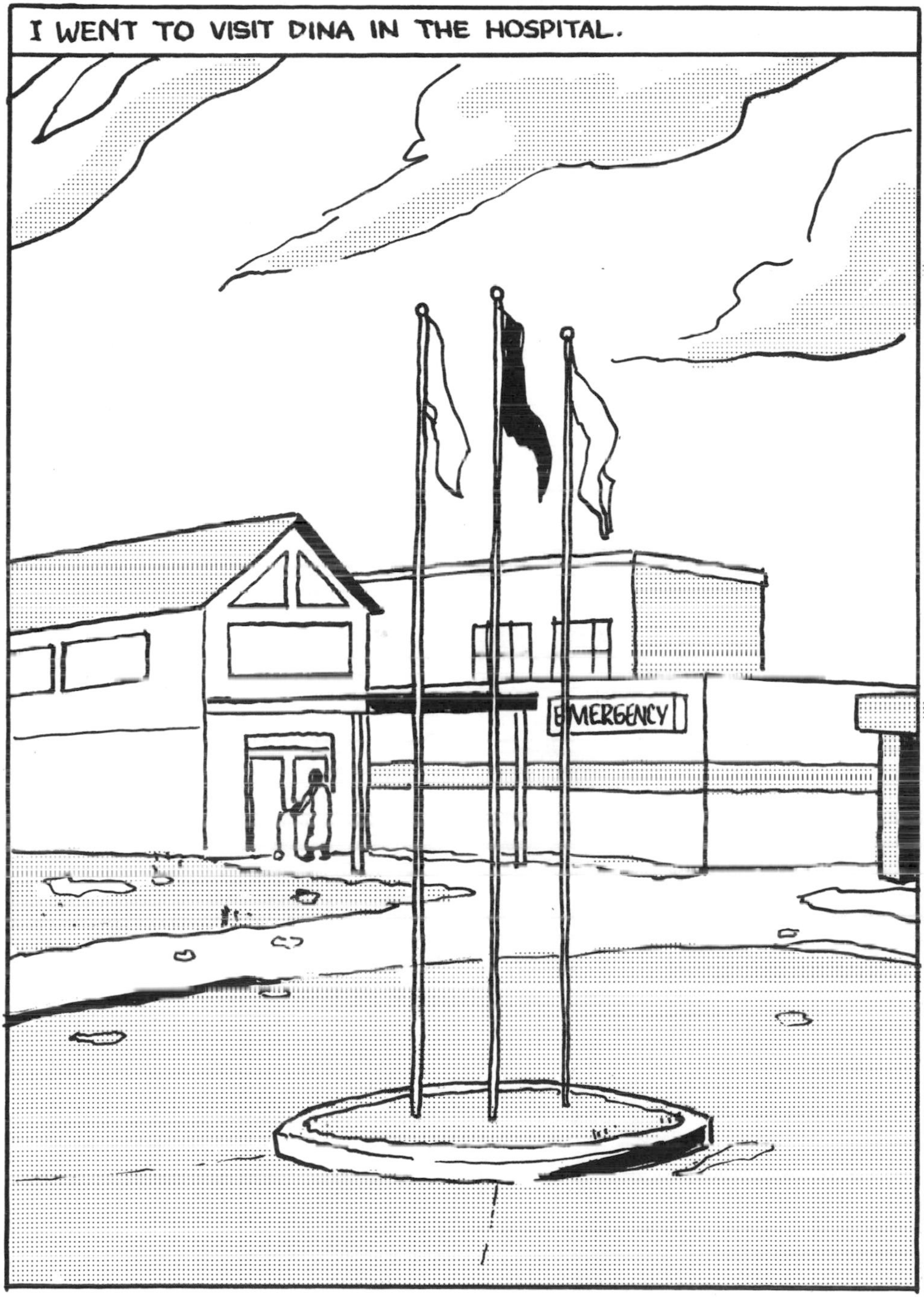
I WENT TO VISIT DINA IN THE HOSPITAL.
EMERGENCY

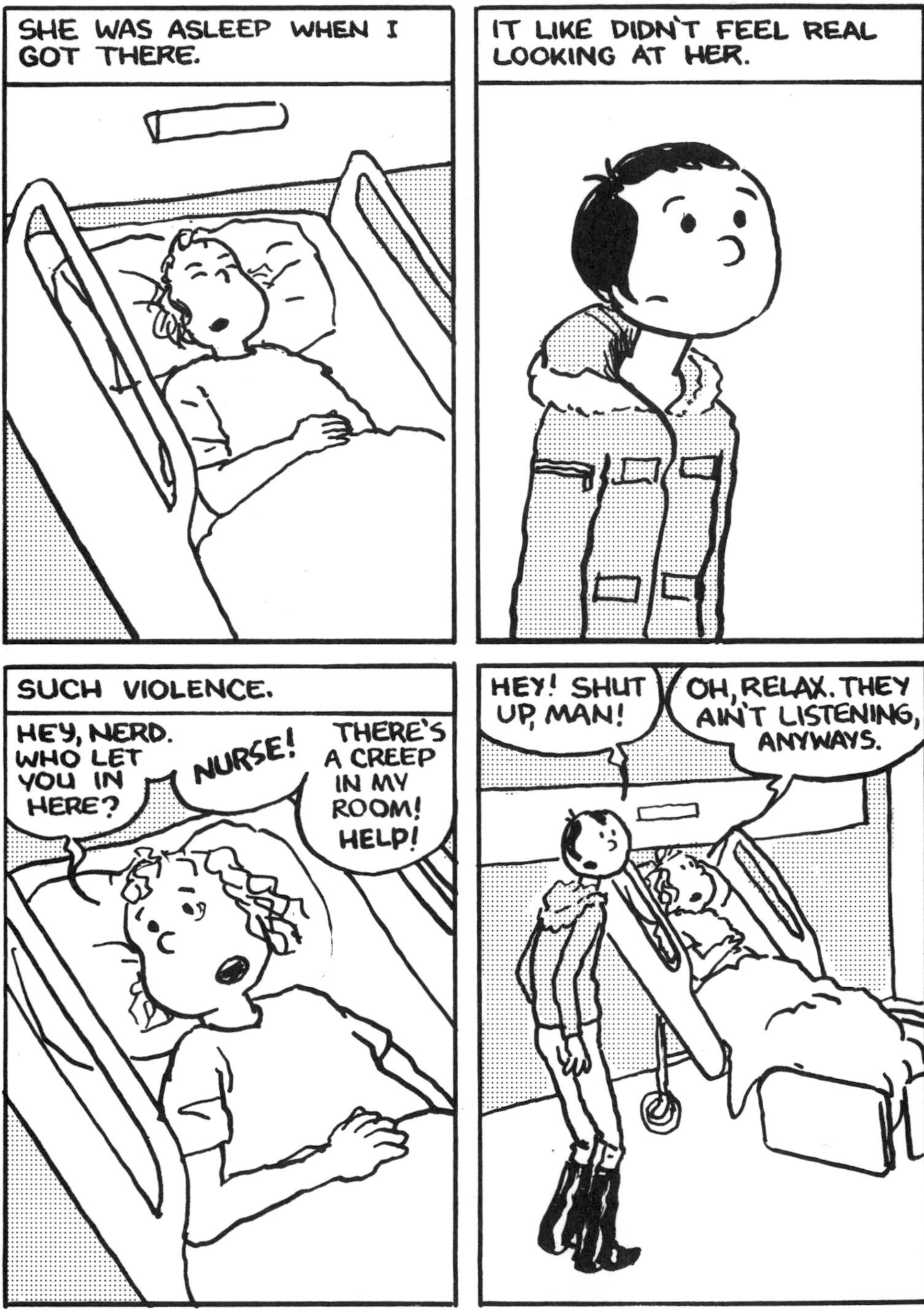
SHE WAS ASLEEP WHEN I GOT THERE.
IT LIKE DIDN'T FEEL REAL LOOKING AT HER.
SUCH VIOLENCE.
HEY, NERD. WHO LET YOU IN HERE?
NURSE!
THERE'S A CREEP IN MY ROOM! HELP!
HEY! SHUT UP, MAN!
OH, RELAX. THEY AIN'T LISTENING, ANYWAYS.

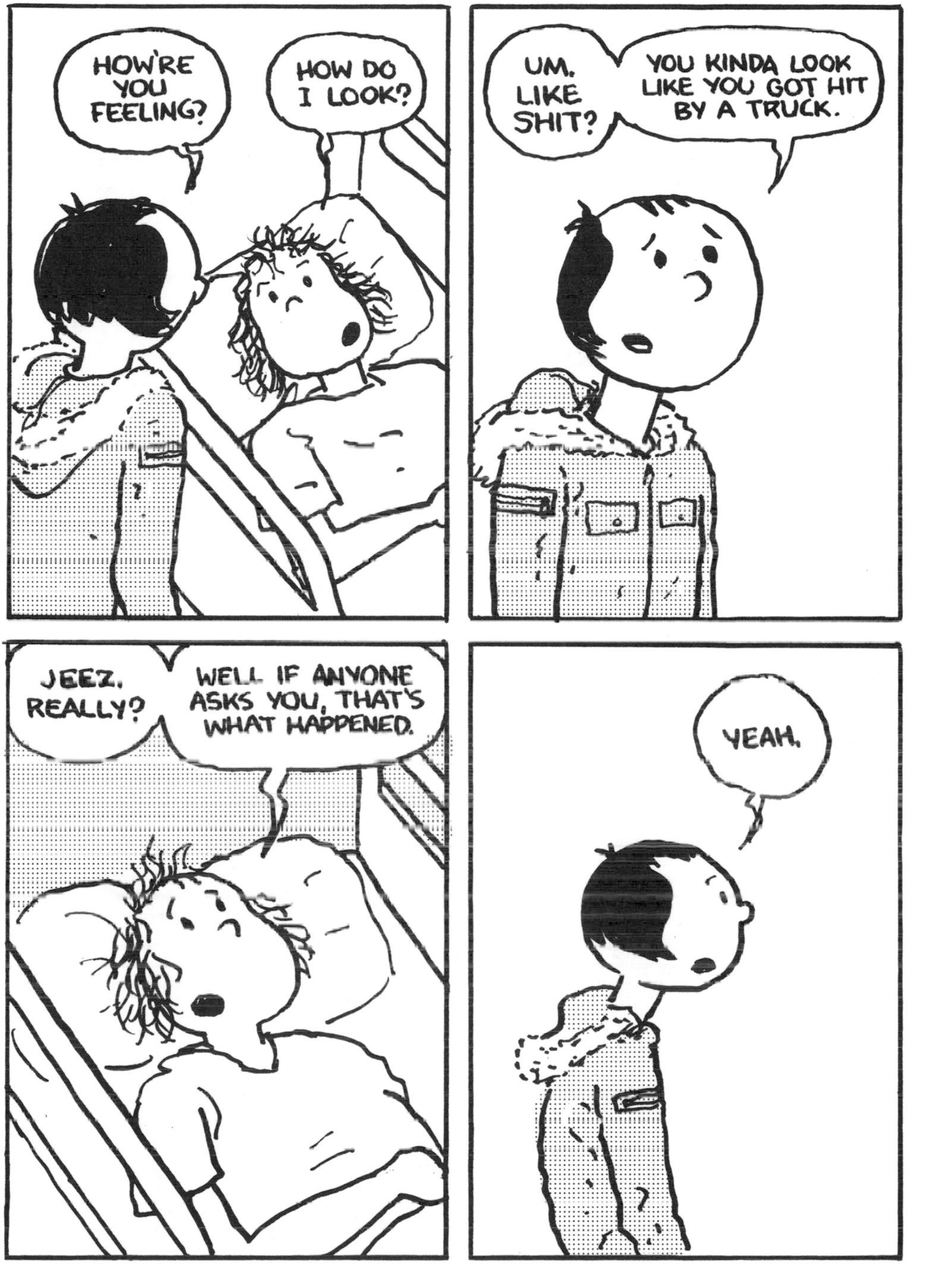
HOW'RE YOU FEELING?
HOW DO I LOOK?
UM. LIKE SHIT?
YOU KINDA LOOK LIKE YOU GOT HIT BY A TRUCK.
JEEZ. REALLY?
WELL IF ANYONE ASKS YOU, THAT'S WHAT HAPPENED.
YEAH.

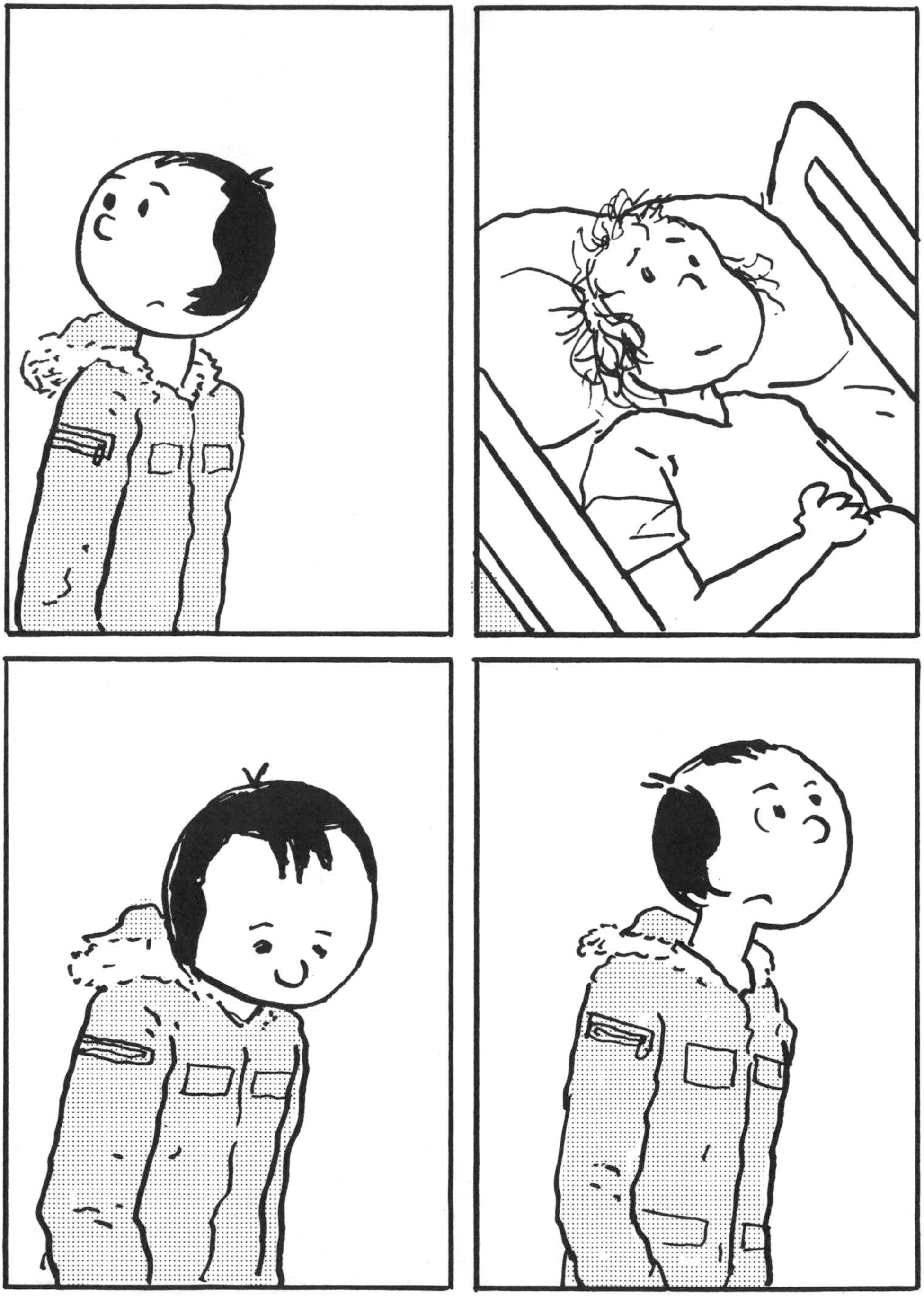

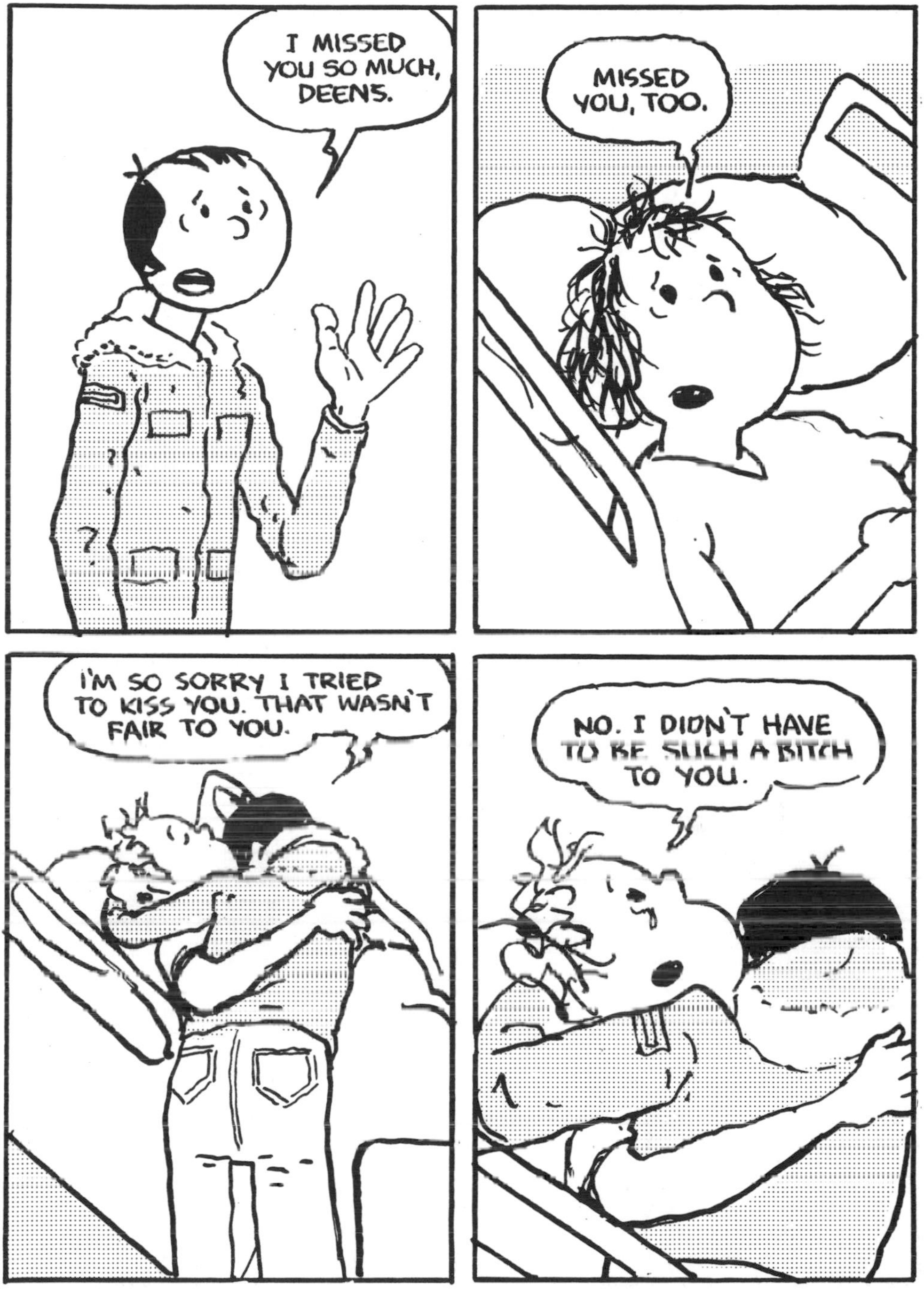
I MISSED YOU SO MUCH, DEENS.
MISSED YOU, TOO.
I'M SO SORRY I TRIED TO KISS YOU. THAT WASN'T FAIR TO YOU.
NO. I DIDN'T HAVE TO BE SUCH A BITCH TO YOU.

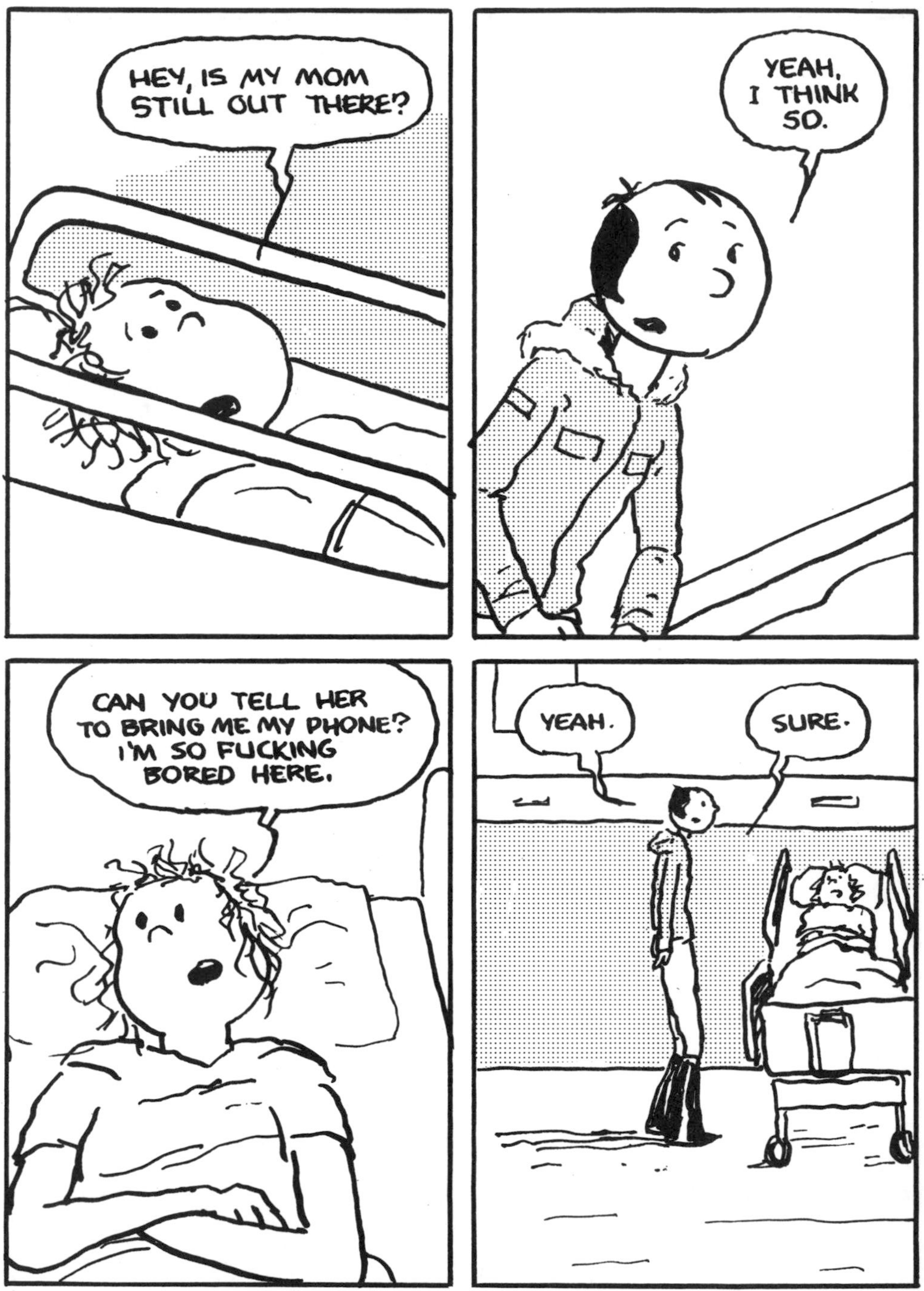
HEY, IS MY MOM STILL OUT THERE?
YEAH, I THINK SO.
CAN YOU TELL HER TO BRING ME MY PHONE? I'M SO FUCKING BORED HERE.
YEAH.
SURE.

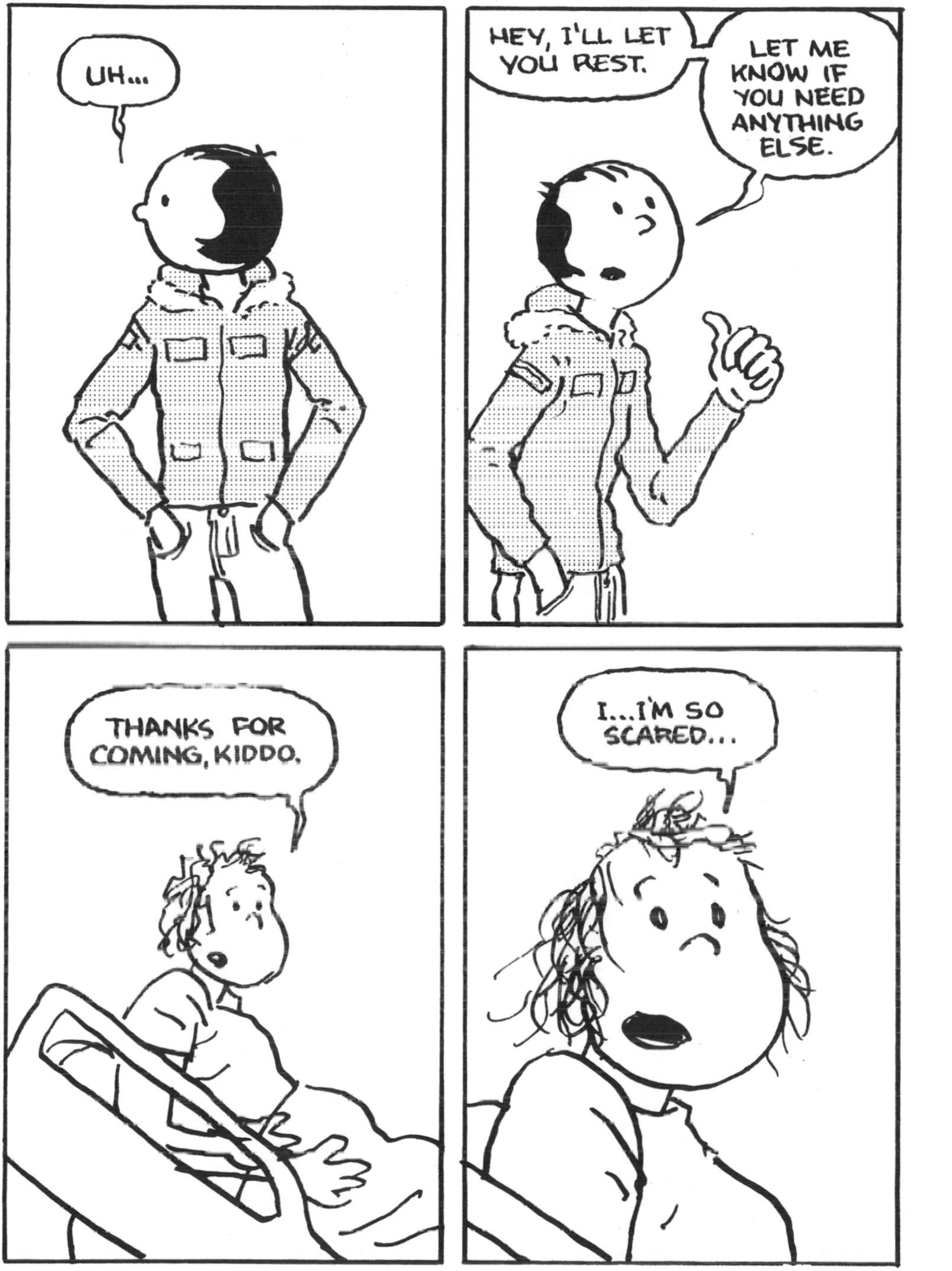
UH...
HEY, I'LL LET YOU REST.
LET ME KNOW IF YOU NEED ANYTHING ELSE.
THANKS FOR COMING, KIDDO.
I...I'M SO SCARED...

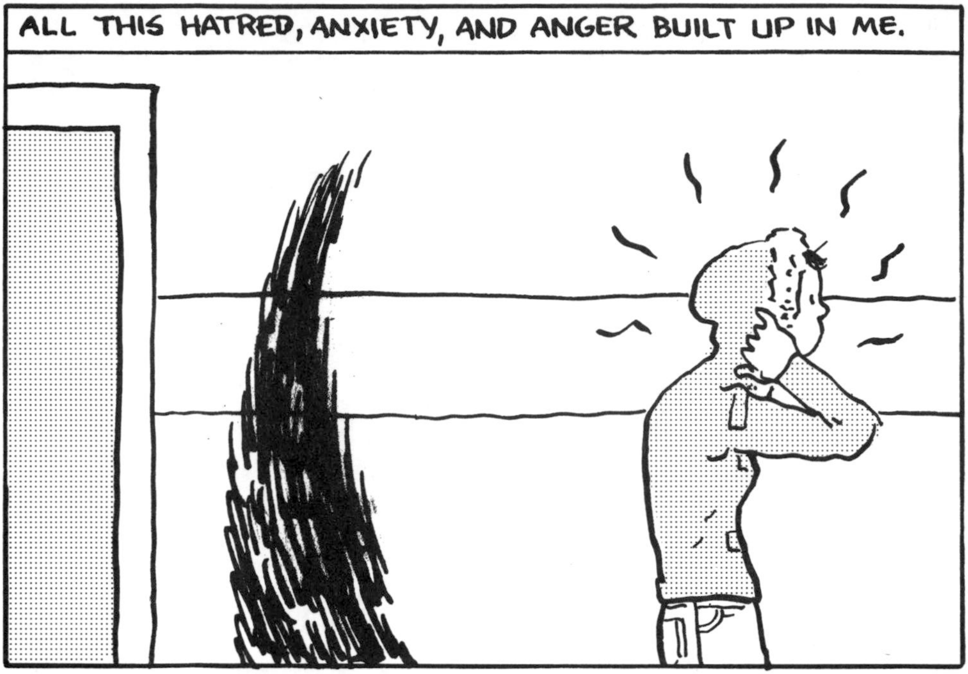
ALL THIS HATRED, ANXIETY, AND ANGER BUILT UP IN ME.

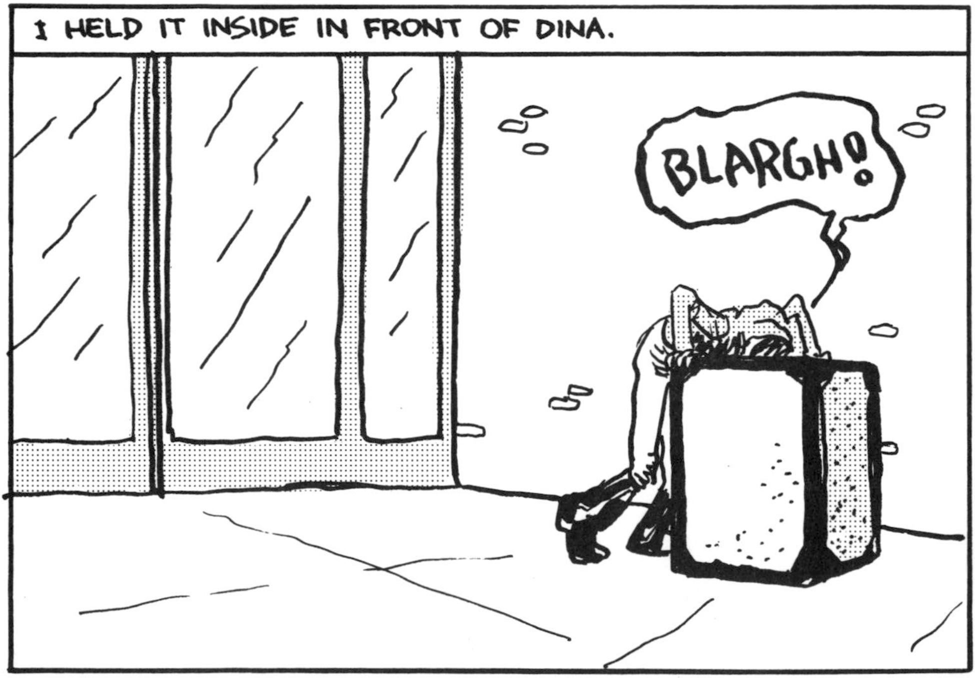
I HELD IT INSIDE IN FRONT OF DINA.
BLARGH!

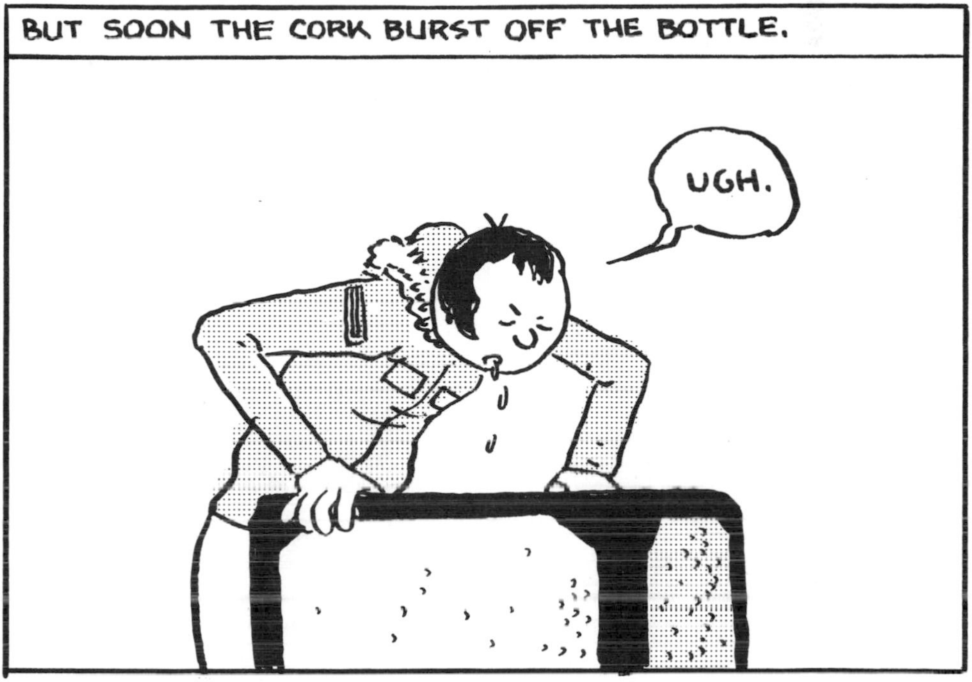
BUT SOON THE CORK BURST OFF THE BOTTLE.
UGH.

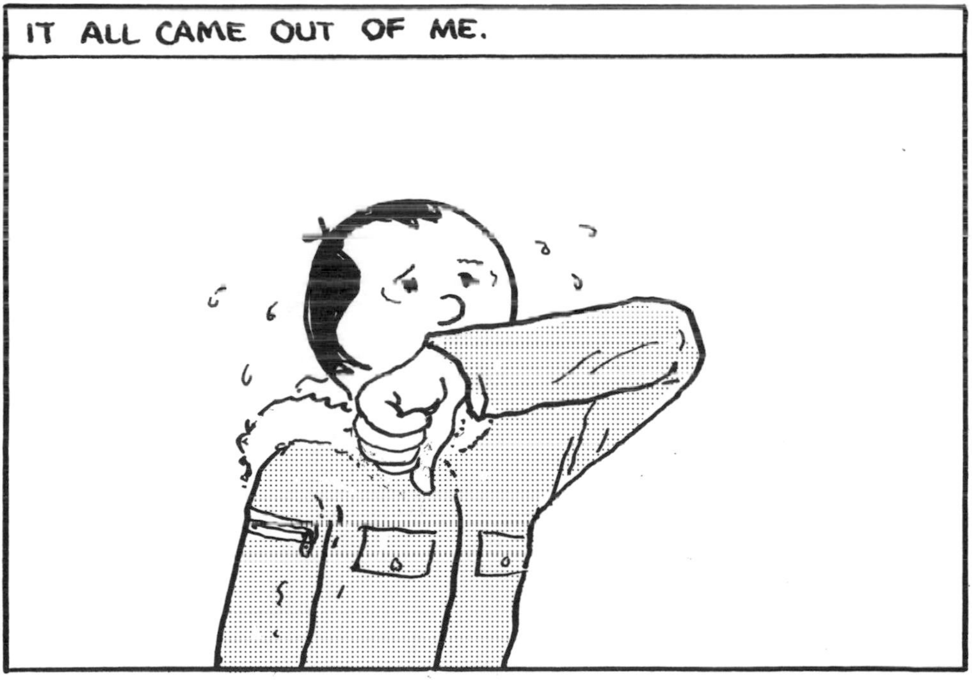
IT ALL CAME OUT OF ME.

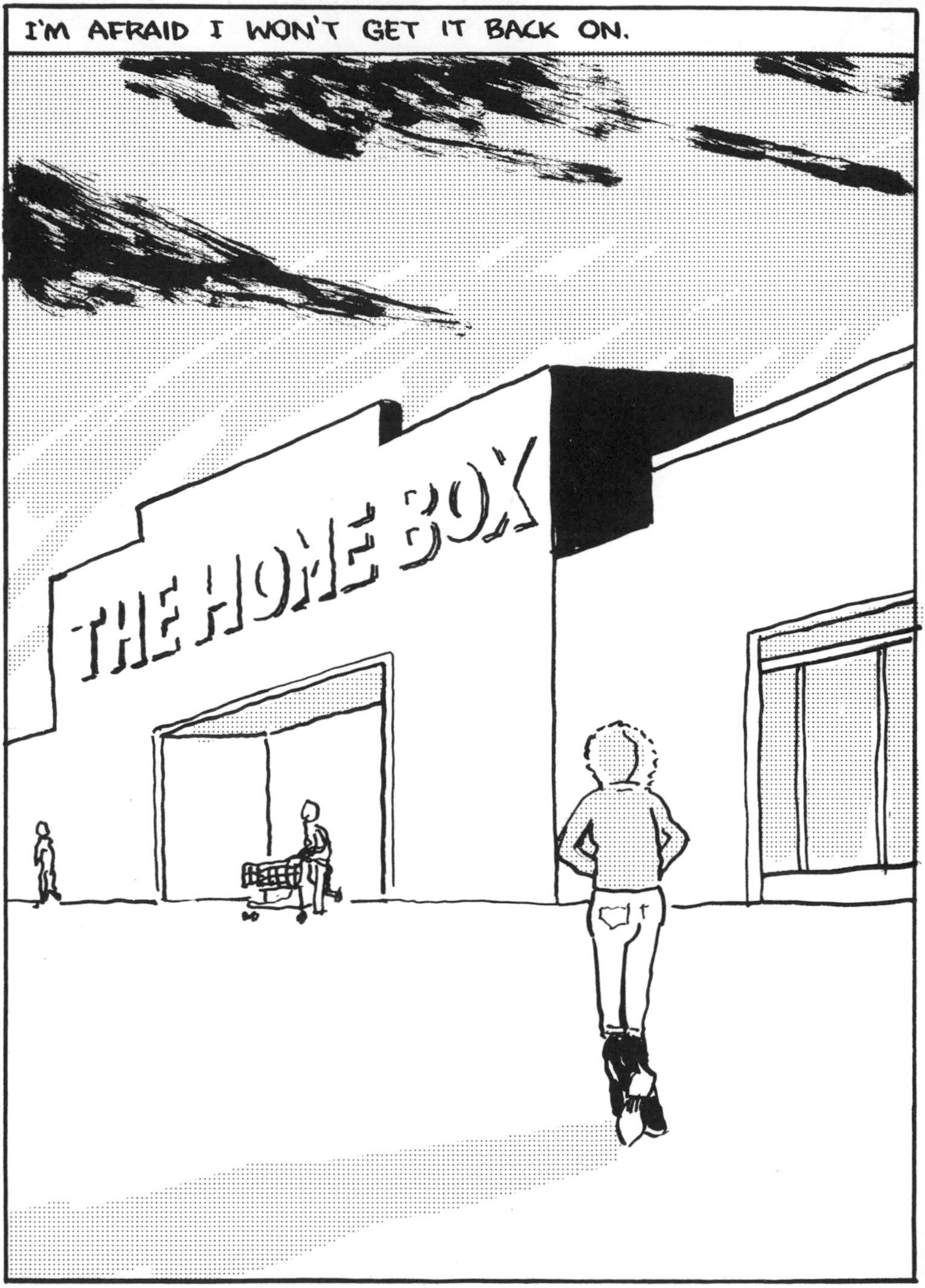
I'M AFRAID I WON'T GET IT BACK ON.
THE HOME BOX

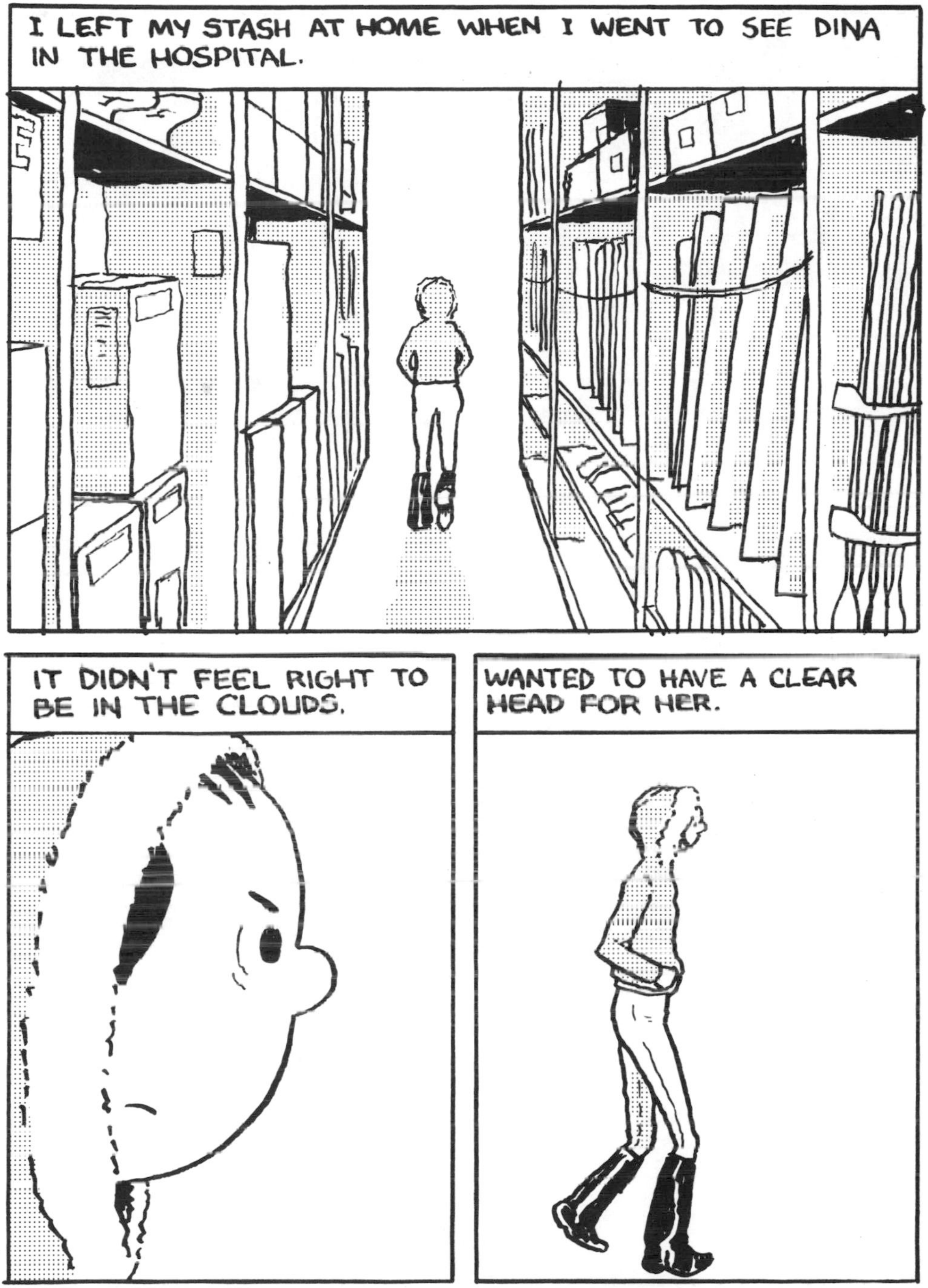
I LEFT MY STASH AT HOME WHEN I WENT TO SEE DINA IN THE HOSPITAL.
IT DIDN'T FEEL RIGHT TO BE IN THE CLOUDS.
WANTED TO HAVE A CLEAR HEAD FOR HER.

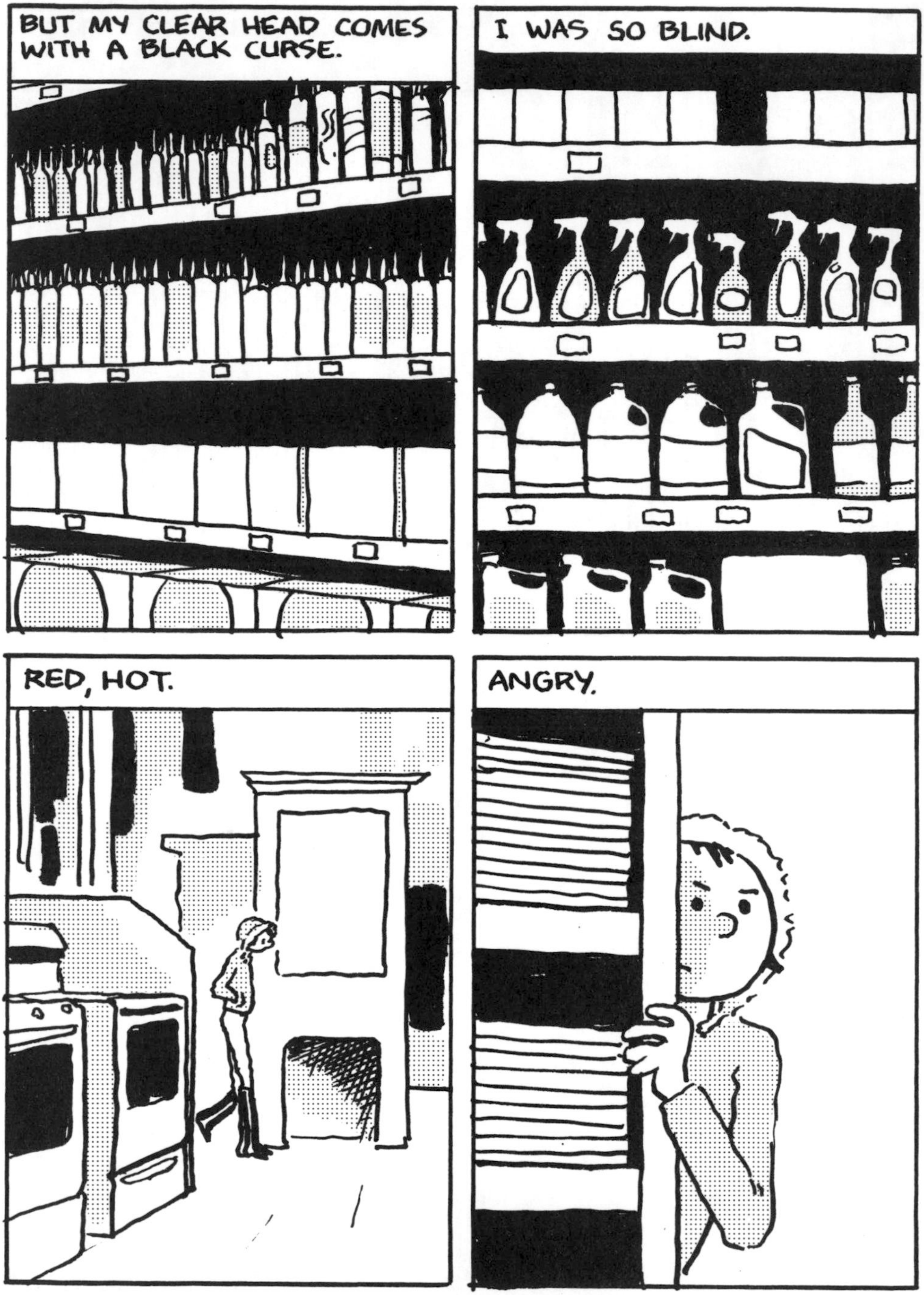
BUT MY CLEAR HEAD COMES WITH A BLACK CURSE.
I WAS SO BLIND.
RED, HOT.
ANGRY.

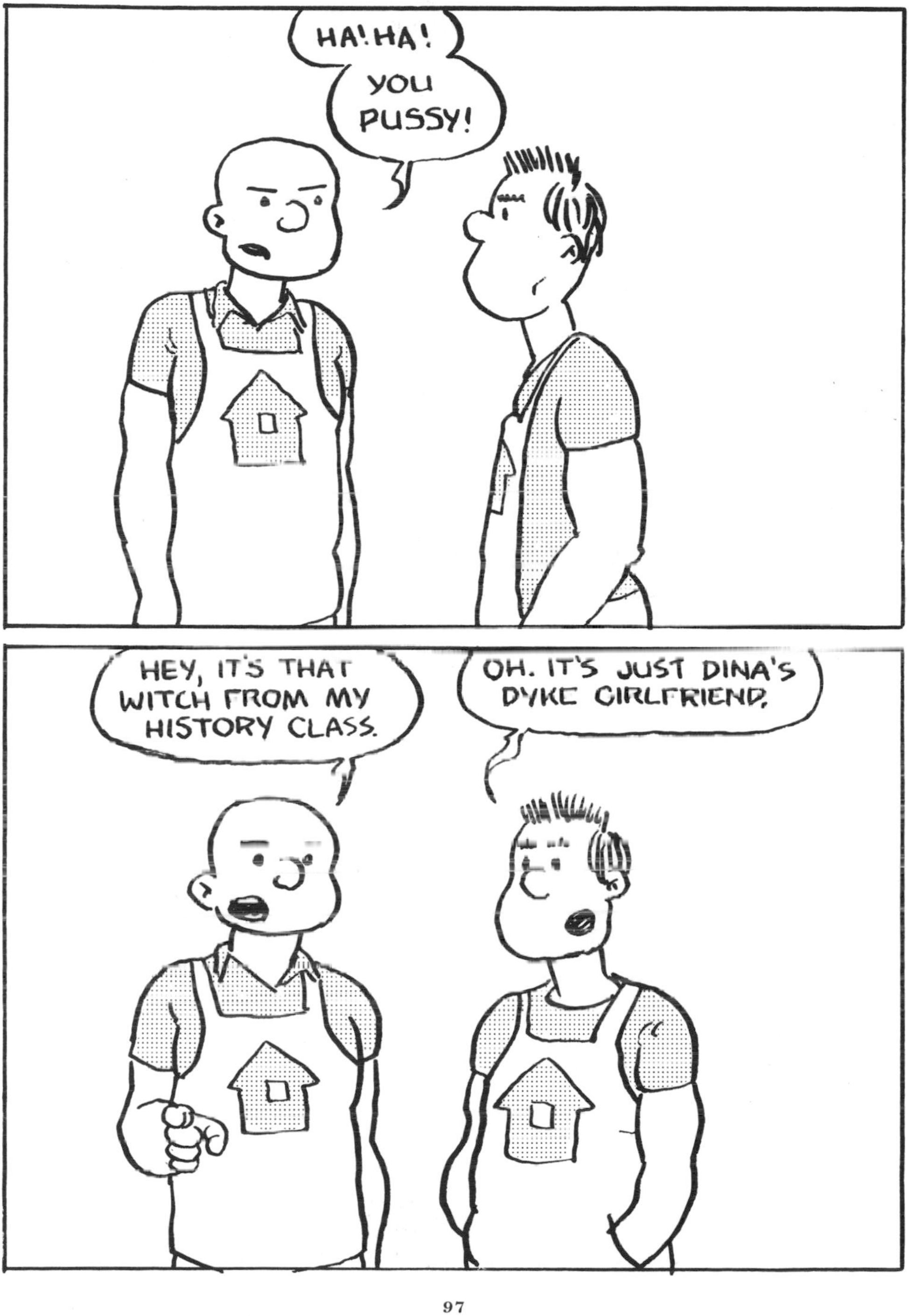
HA! HA!
YOU PUSSY!
HEY, IT'S THAT WITCH FROM MY HISTORY CLASS.
OH. IT'S JUST DINA'S DYKE GIRLFRIEND.

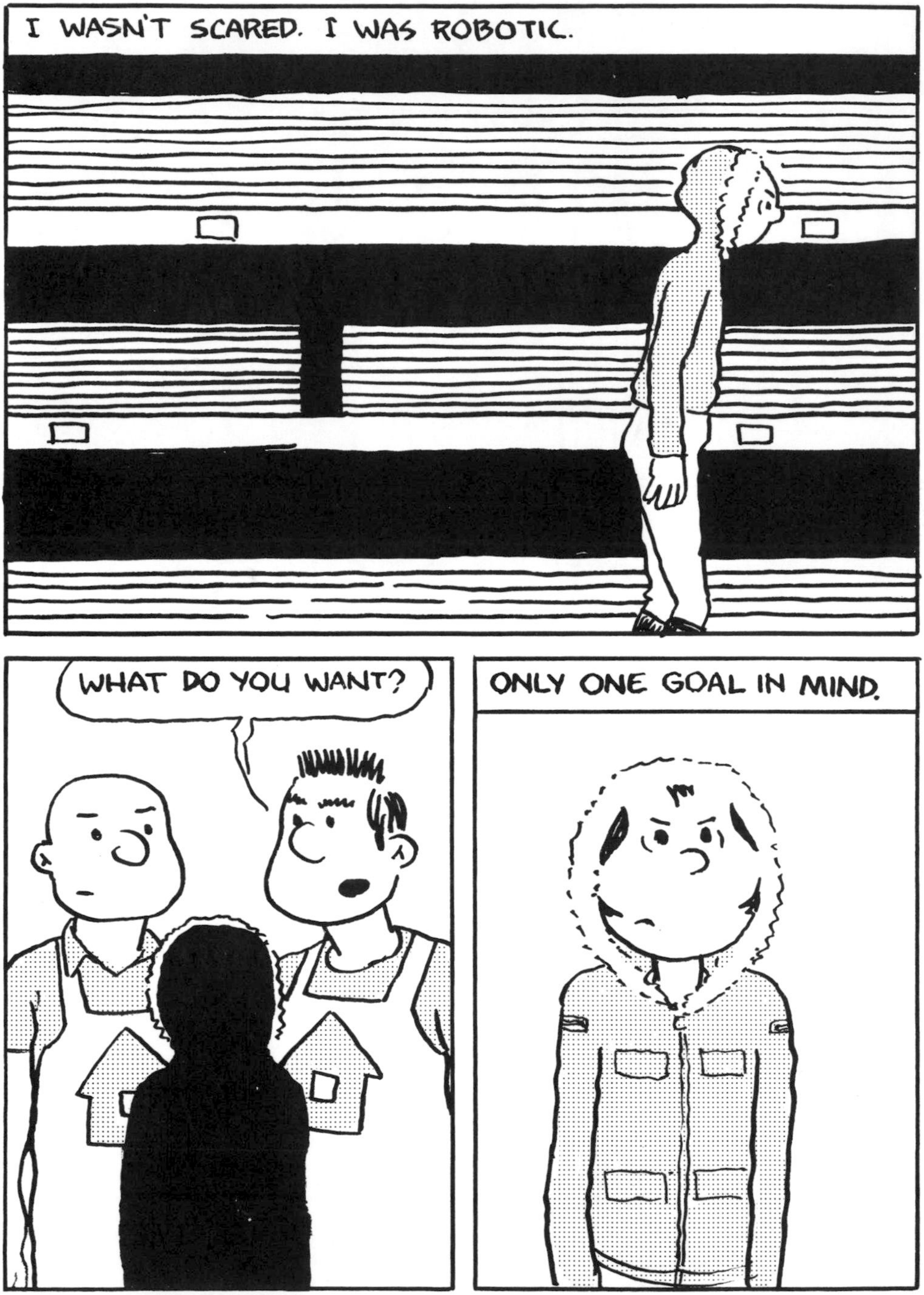
I WASN'T SCARED. I WAS ROBOTIC.
WHAT DO YOU WANT?
ONLY ONE GOAL IN MIND.

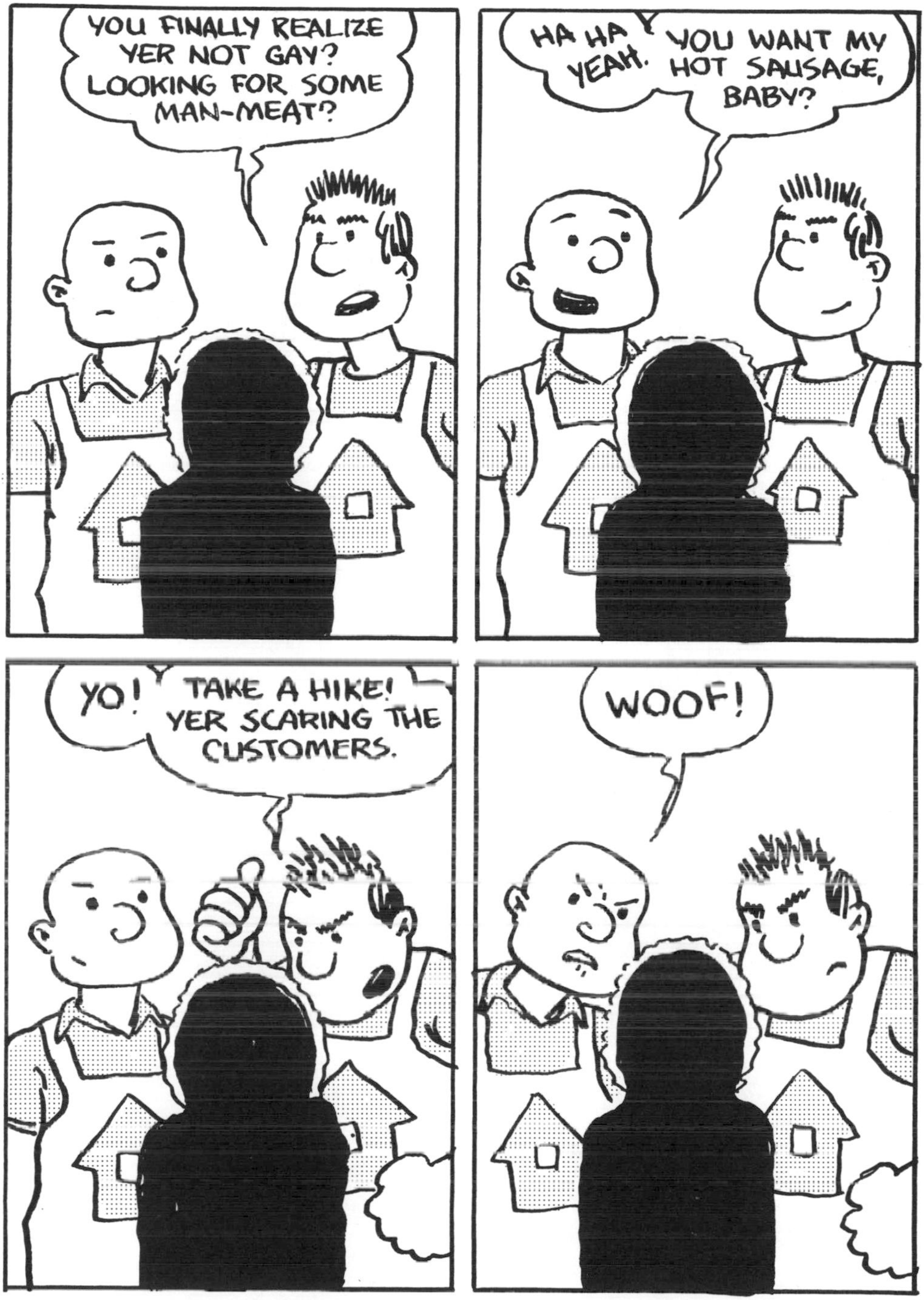
YOU FINALLY REALIZE YER NOT GAY? LOOKING FOR SOME MAN-MEAT?
HA HA YEAH.
YOU WANT MY HOT SAUSAGE, BABY?
YO!
TAKE A HIKE! YER SCARING THE CUSTOMERS.
WOOF!

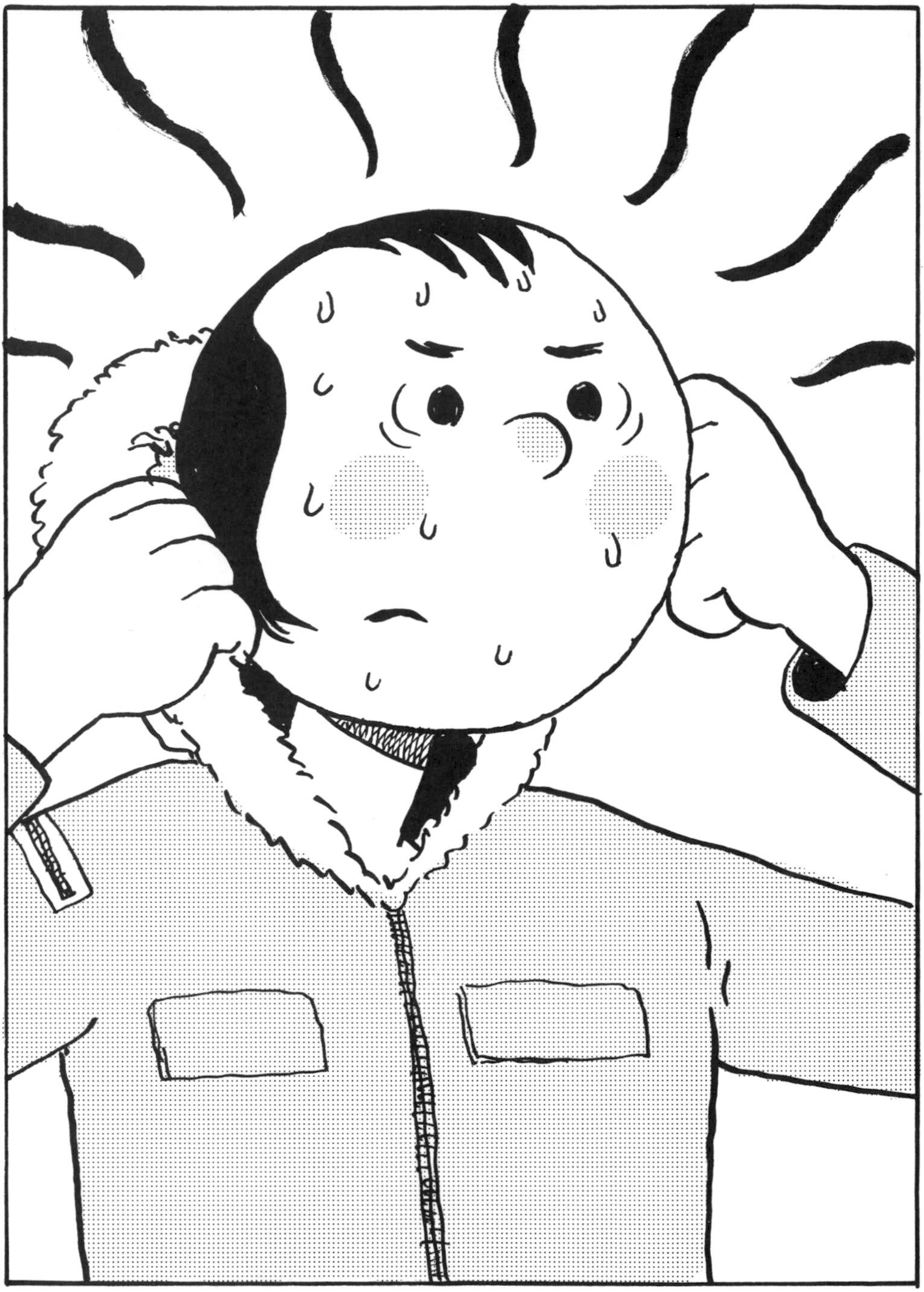

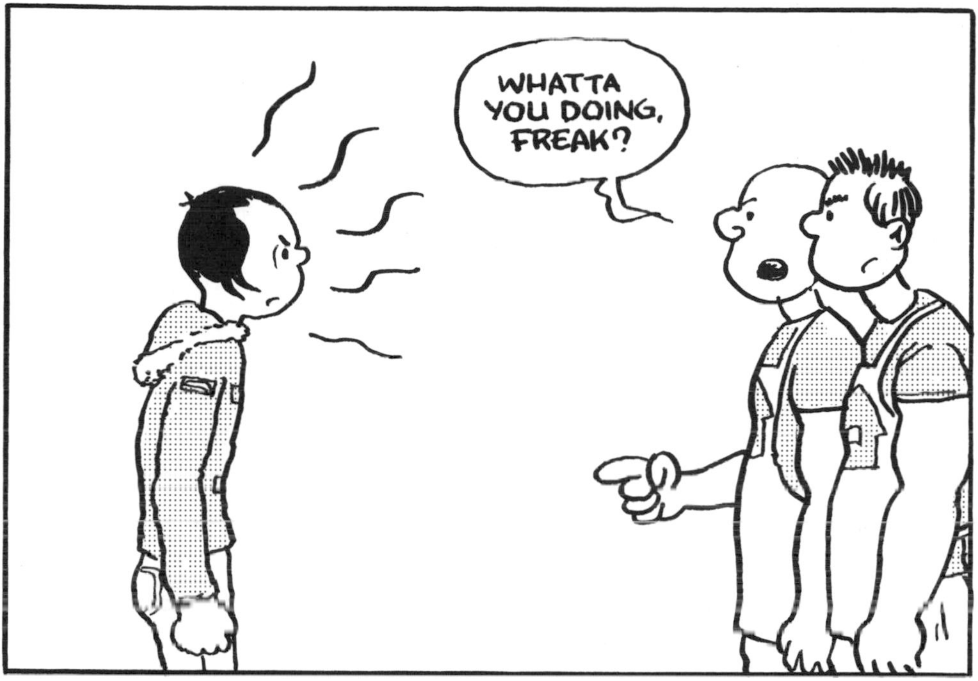
WHATTA YOU DOING, FREAK?

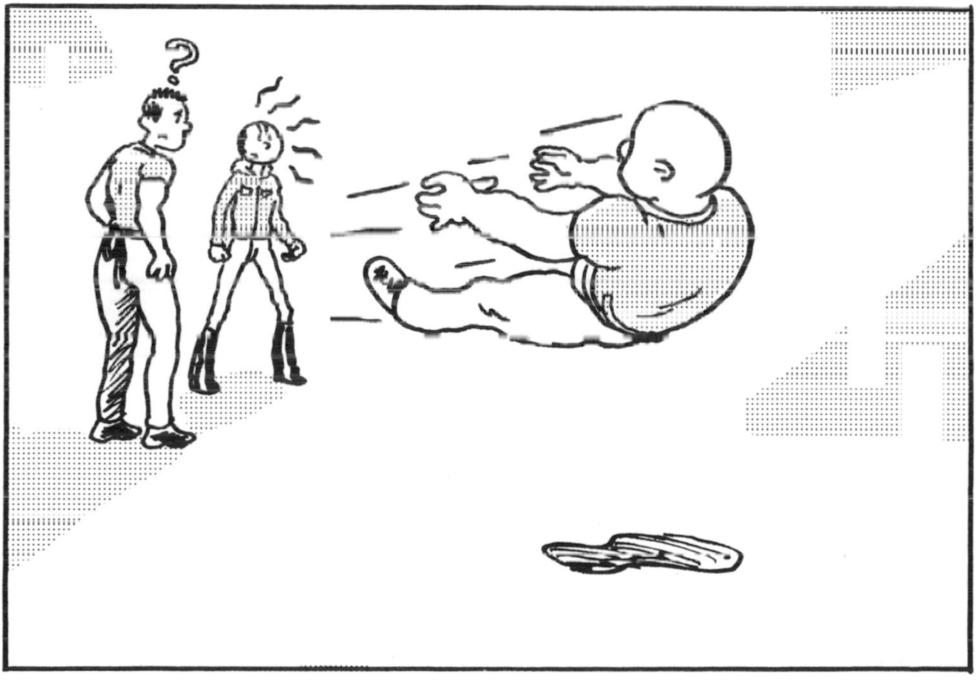

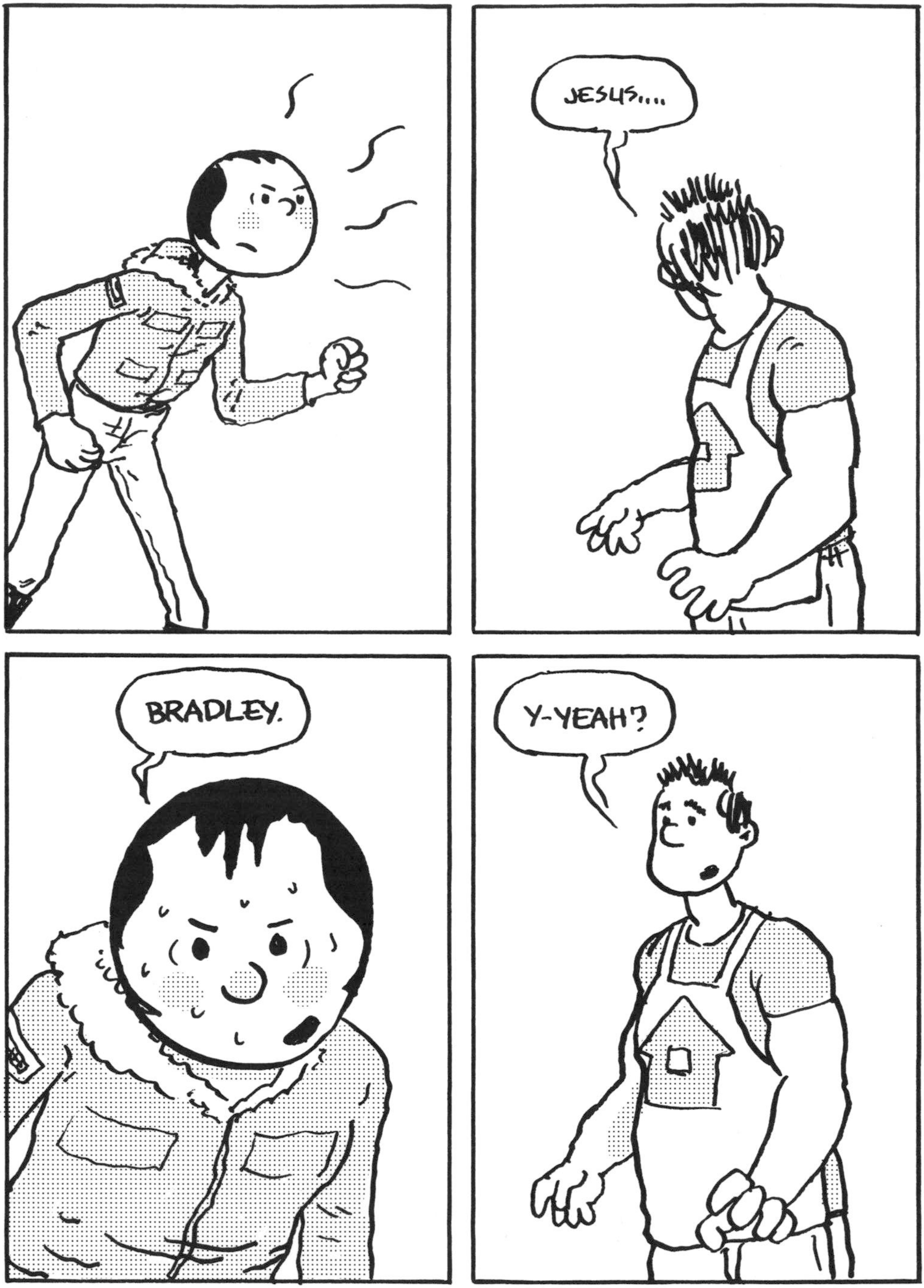
JESUS....
BRADLEY.
Y-YEAH?

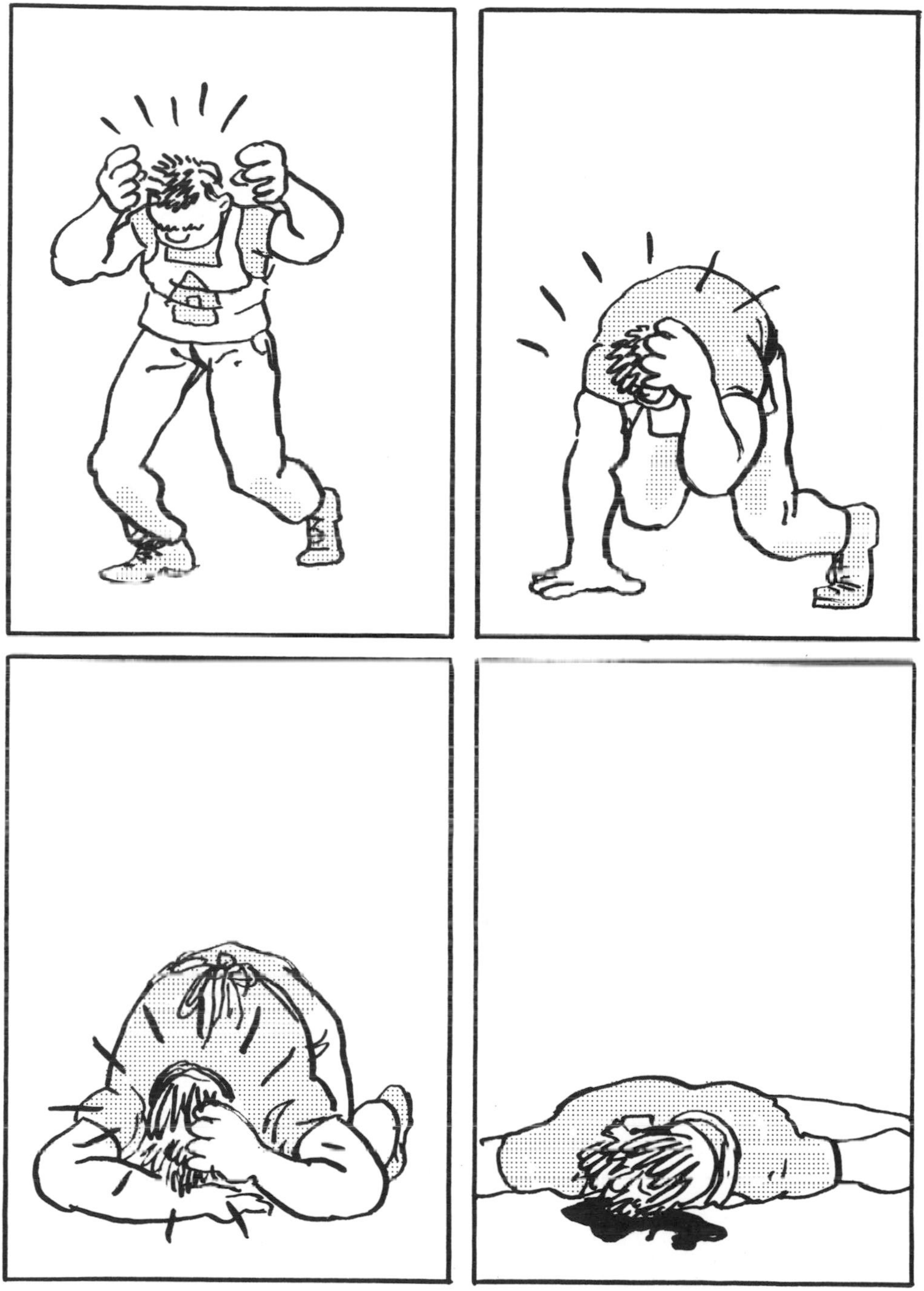

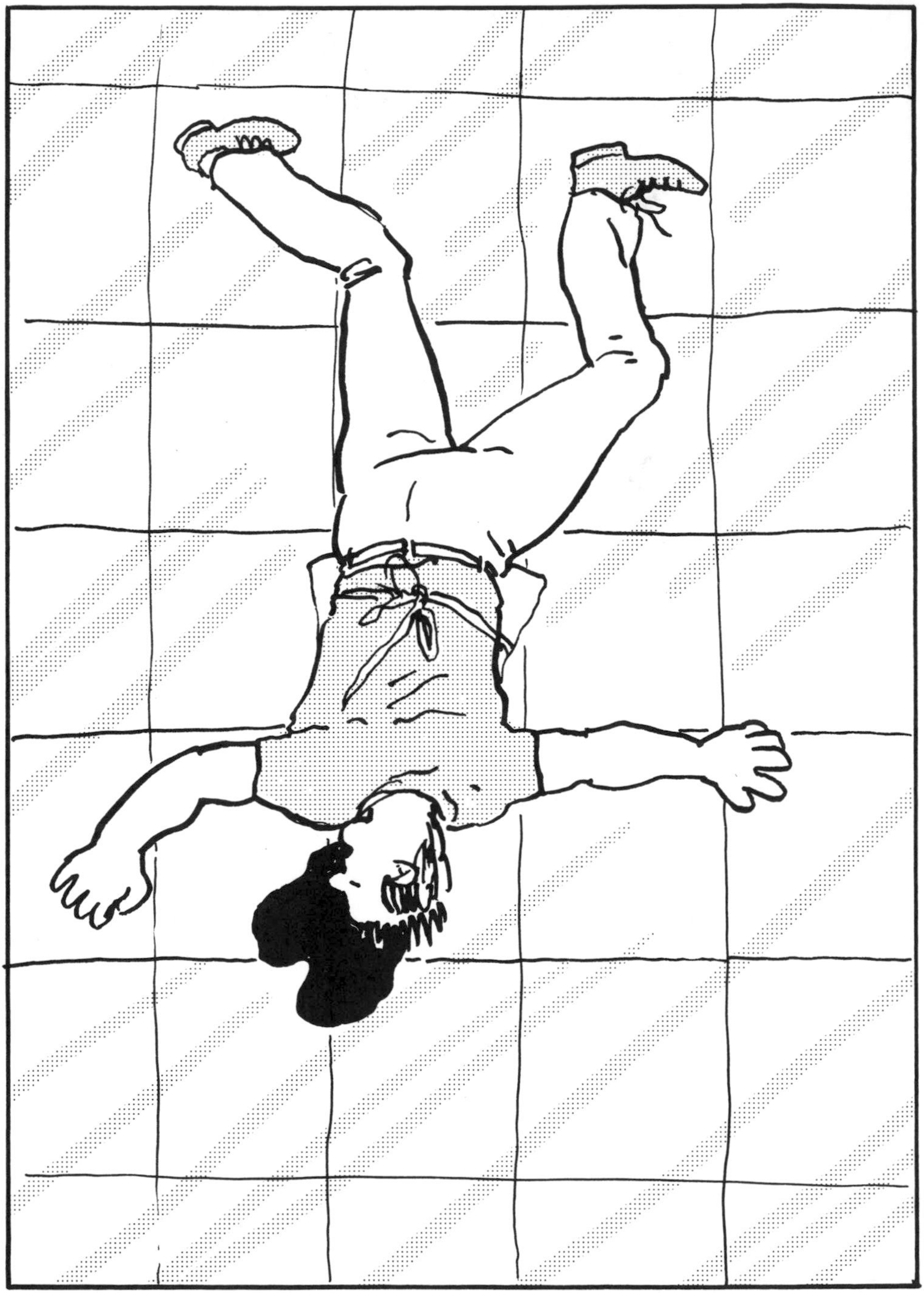

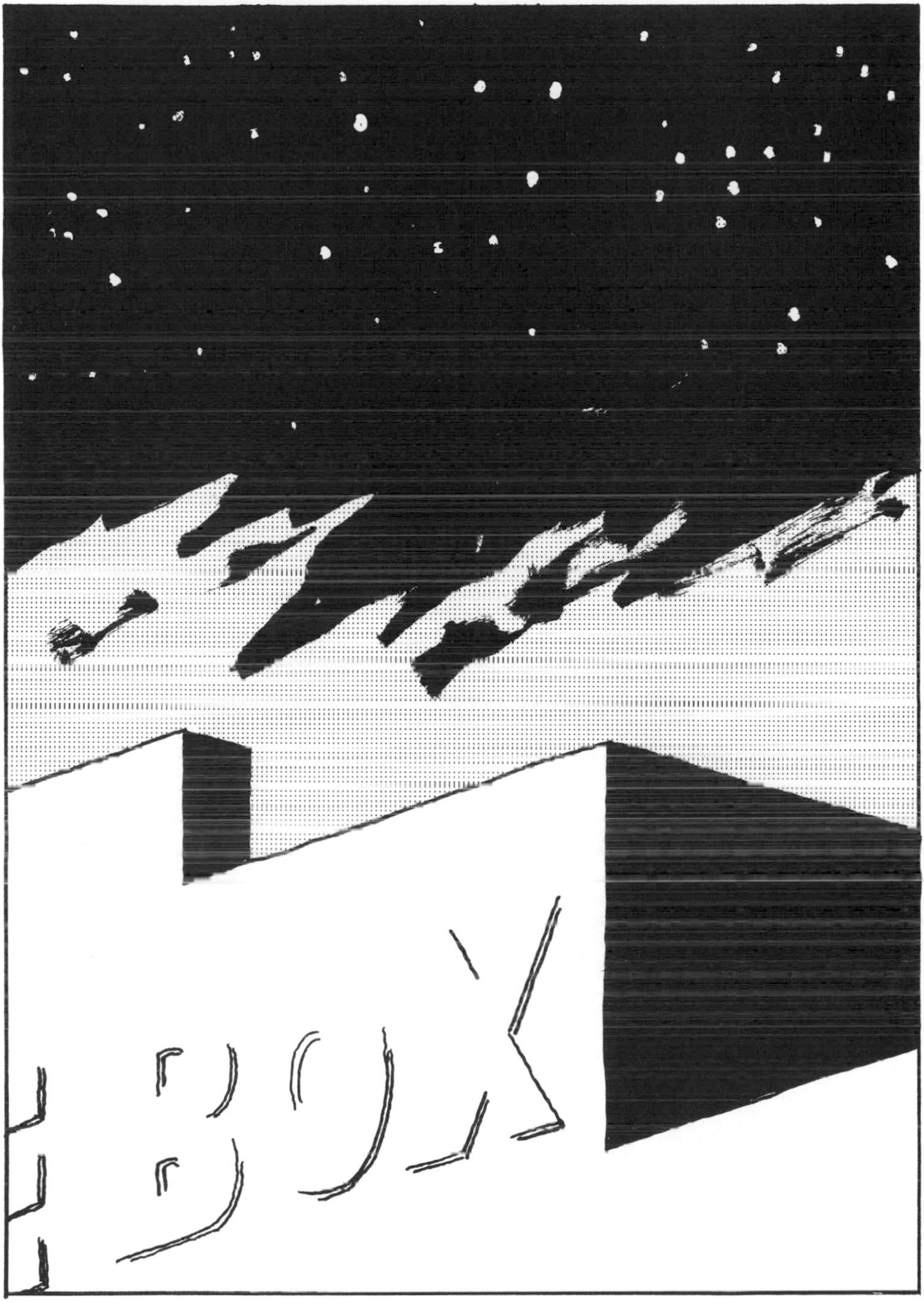
BOX

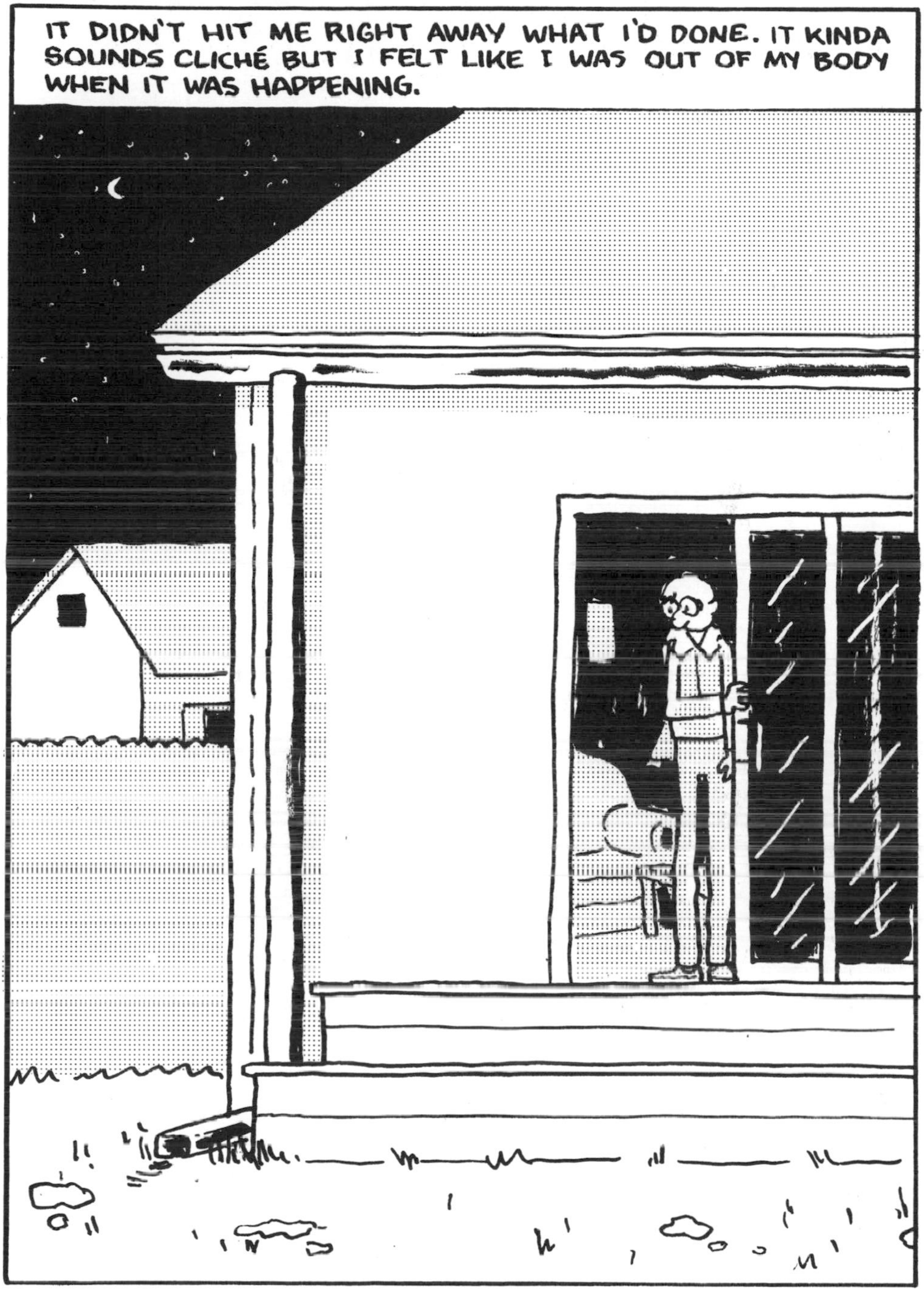
IT DIDN'T HIT ME RIGHT AWAY WHAT I'D DONE. IT KINDA SOUNDS CLICHÉ BUT I FELT LIKE I WAS OUT OF MY BODY WHEN IT WAS HAPPENING.

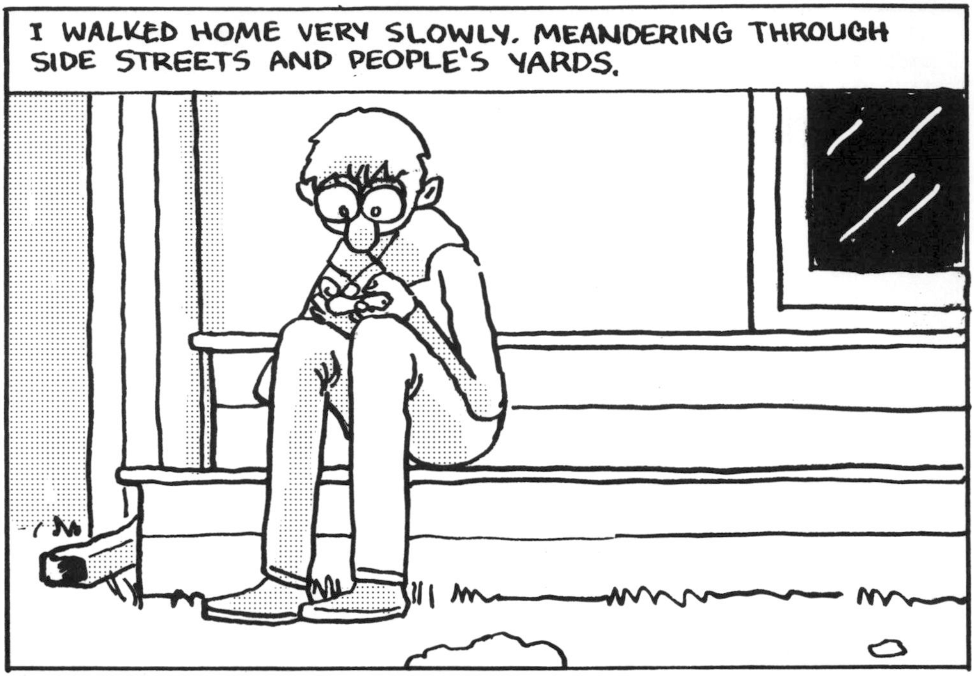
I WALKED HOME VERY SLOWLY. MEANDERING THROUGH SIDE STREETS AND PEOPLE'S YARDS.

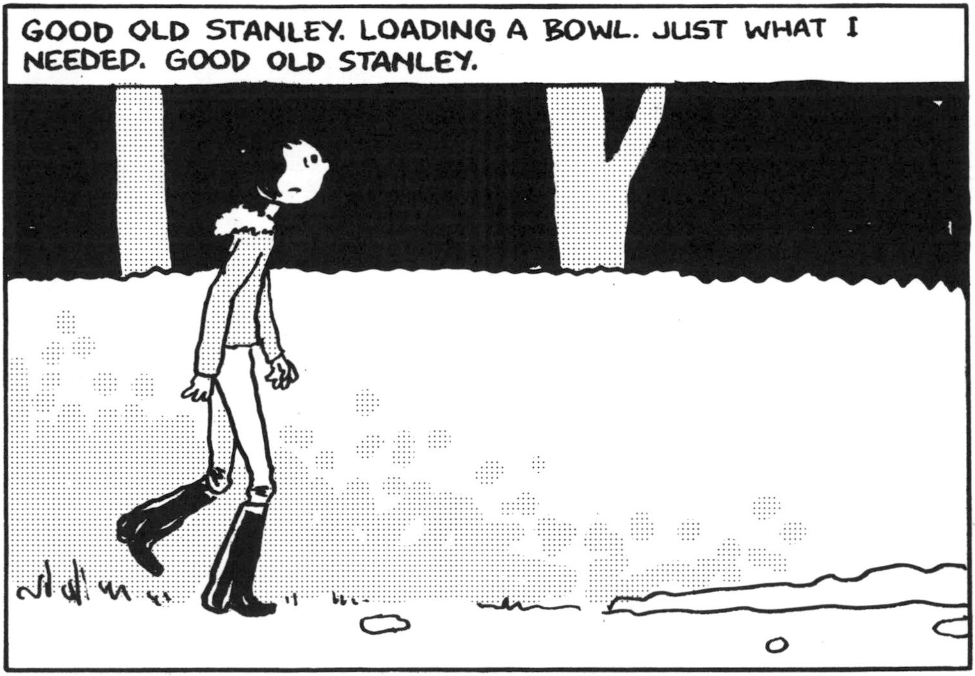
GOOD OLD STANLEY. LOADING A BOWL. JUST WHAT I NEEDED. GOOD OLD STANLEY.

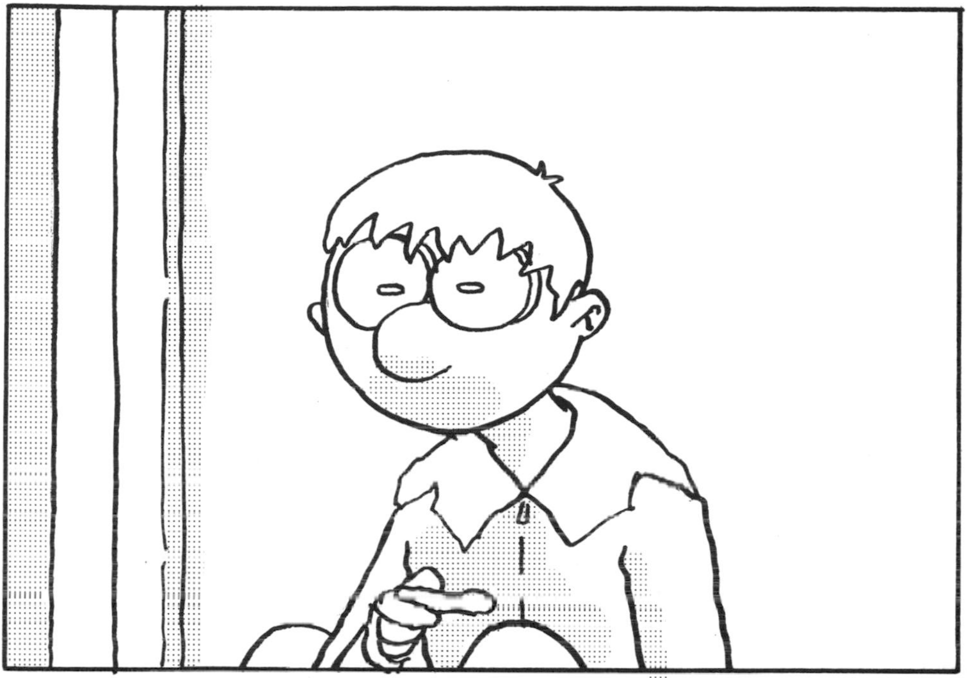

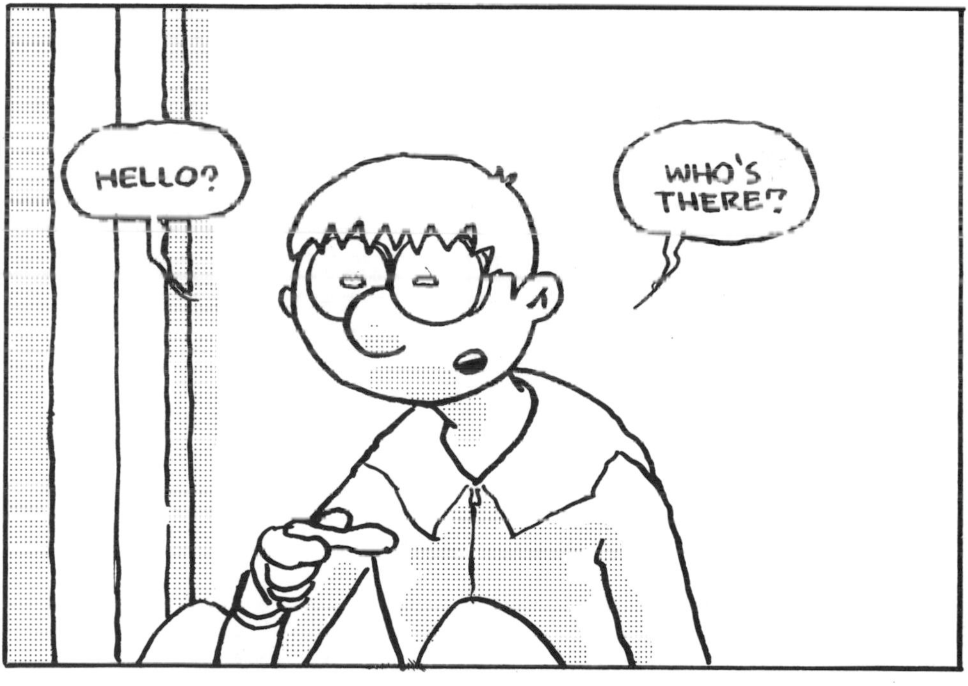
HELLO?
WHO'S THERE?

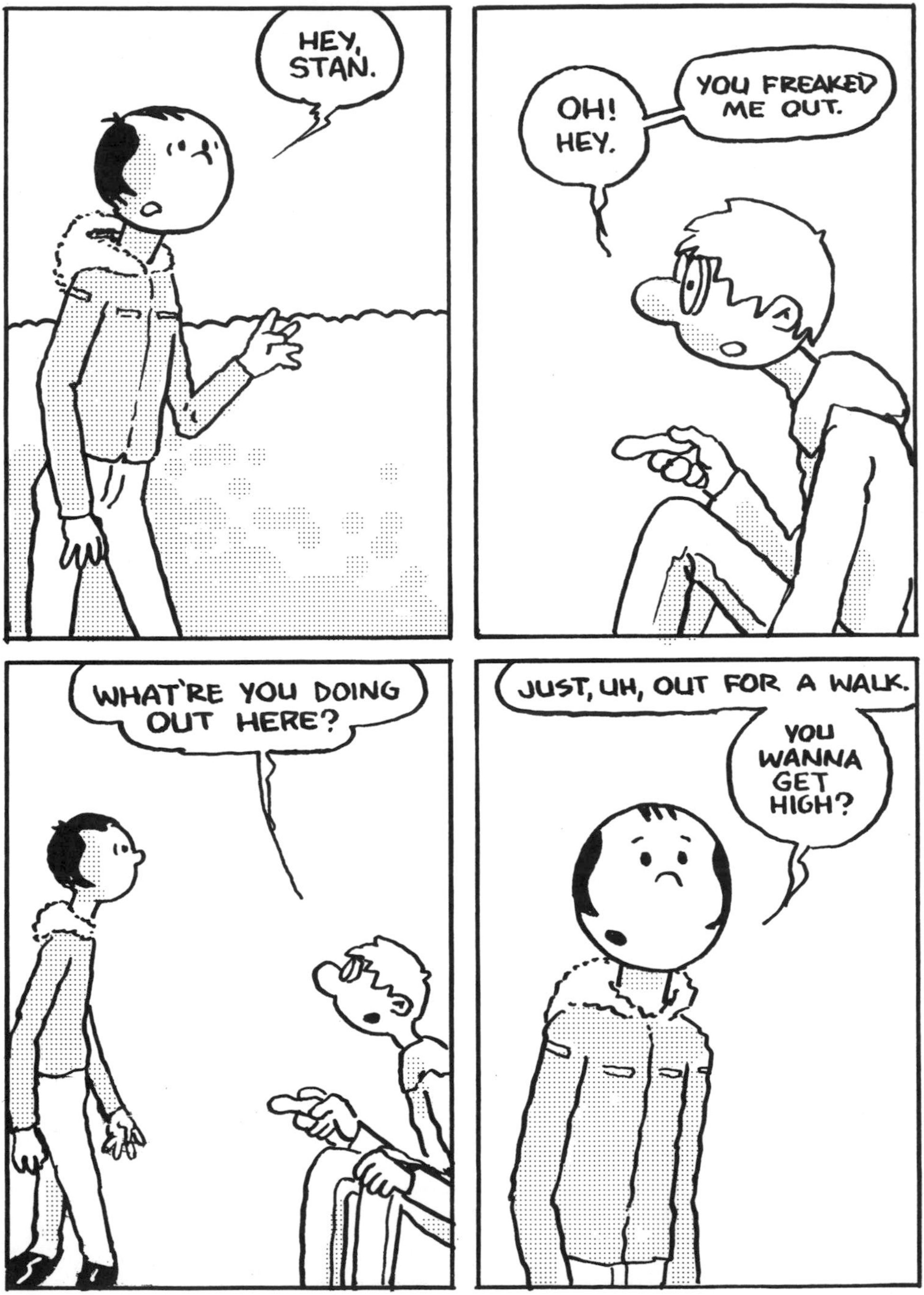
HEY, STAN.
OH! HEY.
YOU FREAKED ME OUT.
WHAT'RE YOU DOING OUT HERE?
JUST, UH, OUT FOR A WALK.
YOU WANNA GET HIGH?

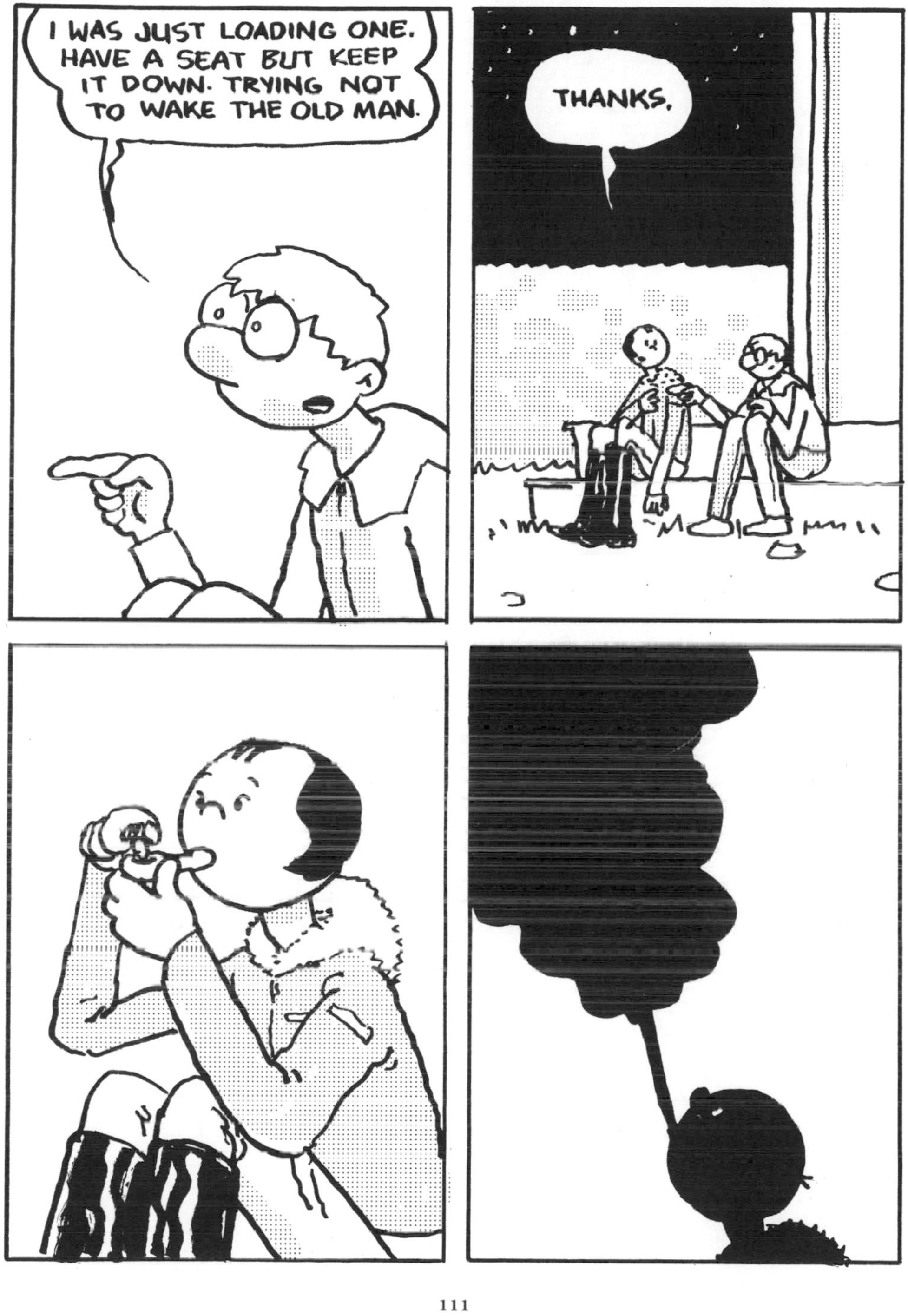
I WAS JUST LOADING ONE. HAVE A SEAT BUT KEEP IT DOWN. TRYING NOT TO WAKE THE OLD MAN.
THANKS.

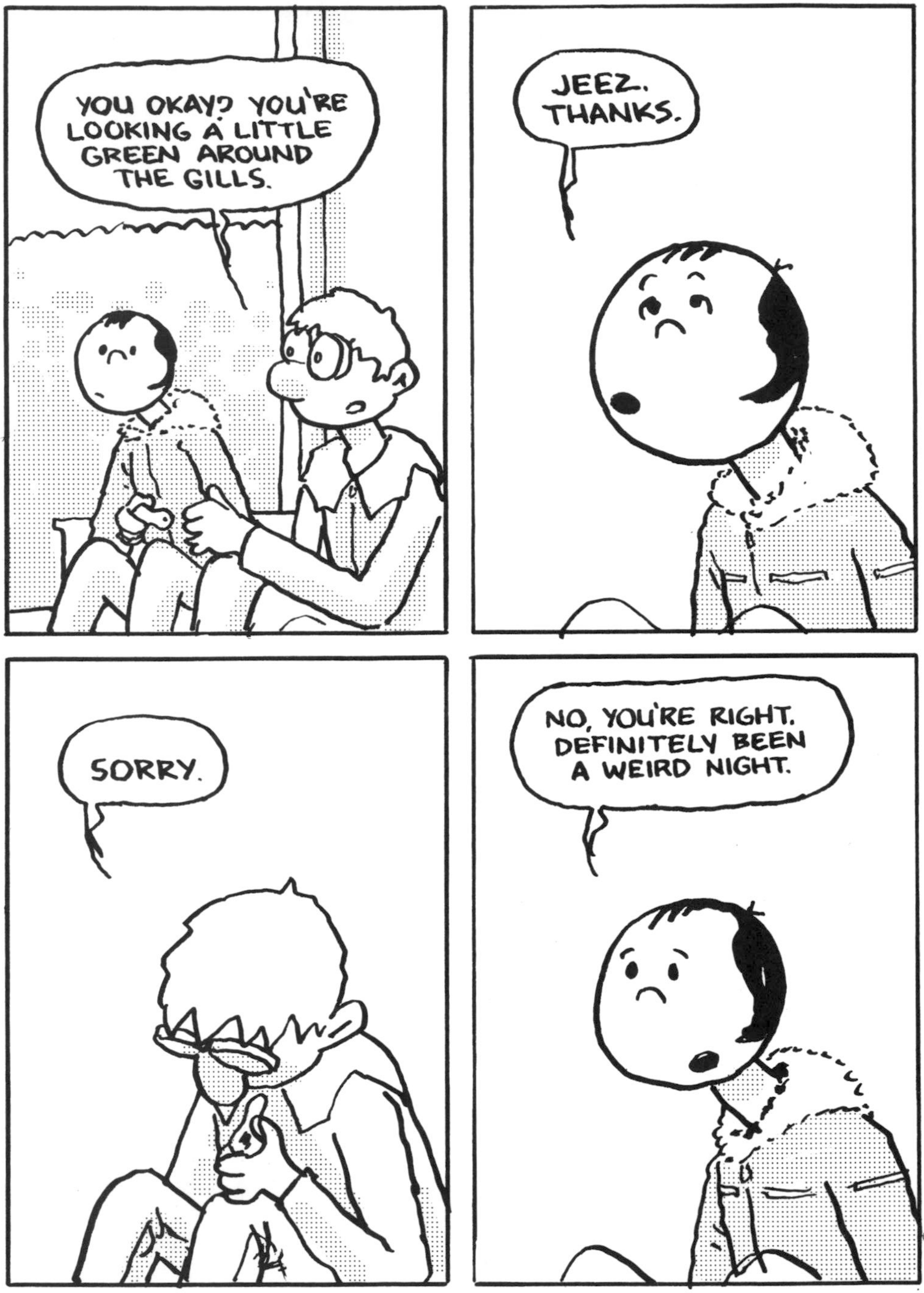
YOU OKAY? YOU'RE LOOKING A LITTLE GREEN AROUND THE GILLS.
JEEZ. THANKS.
SORRY.
NO, YOU'RE RIGHT. DEFINITELY BEEN A WEIRD NIGHT.

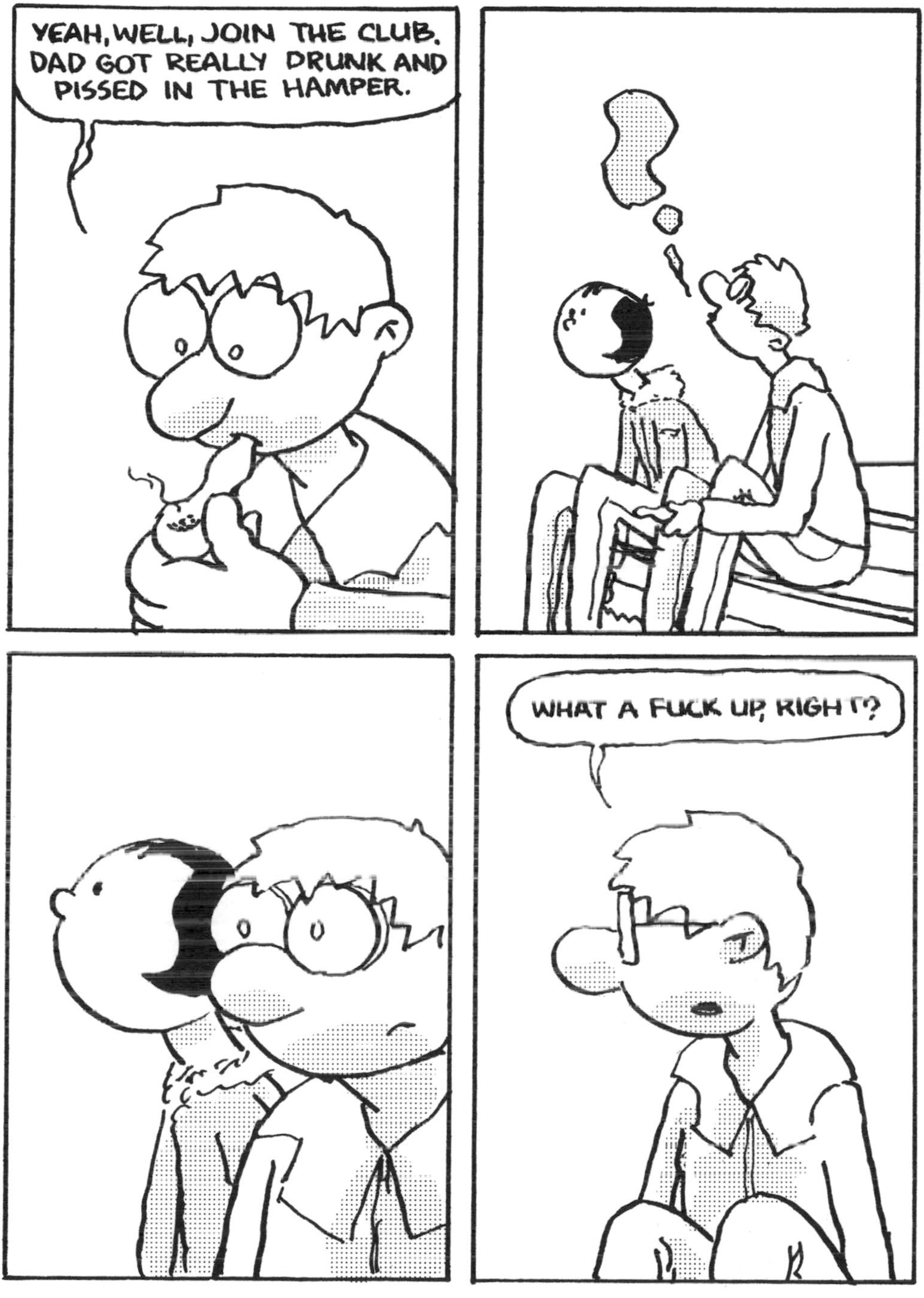
YEAH, WELL, JOIN THE CLUB. DAD GOT REALLY DRUNK AND PISSED IN THE HAMPER.
WHAT A FUCK UP, RIGHT?

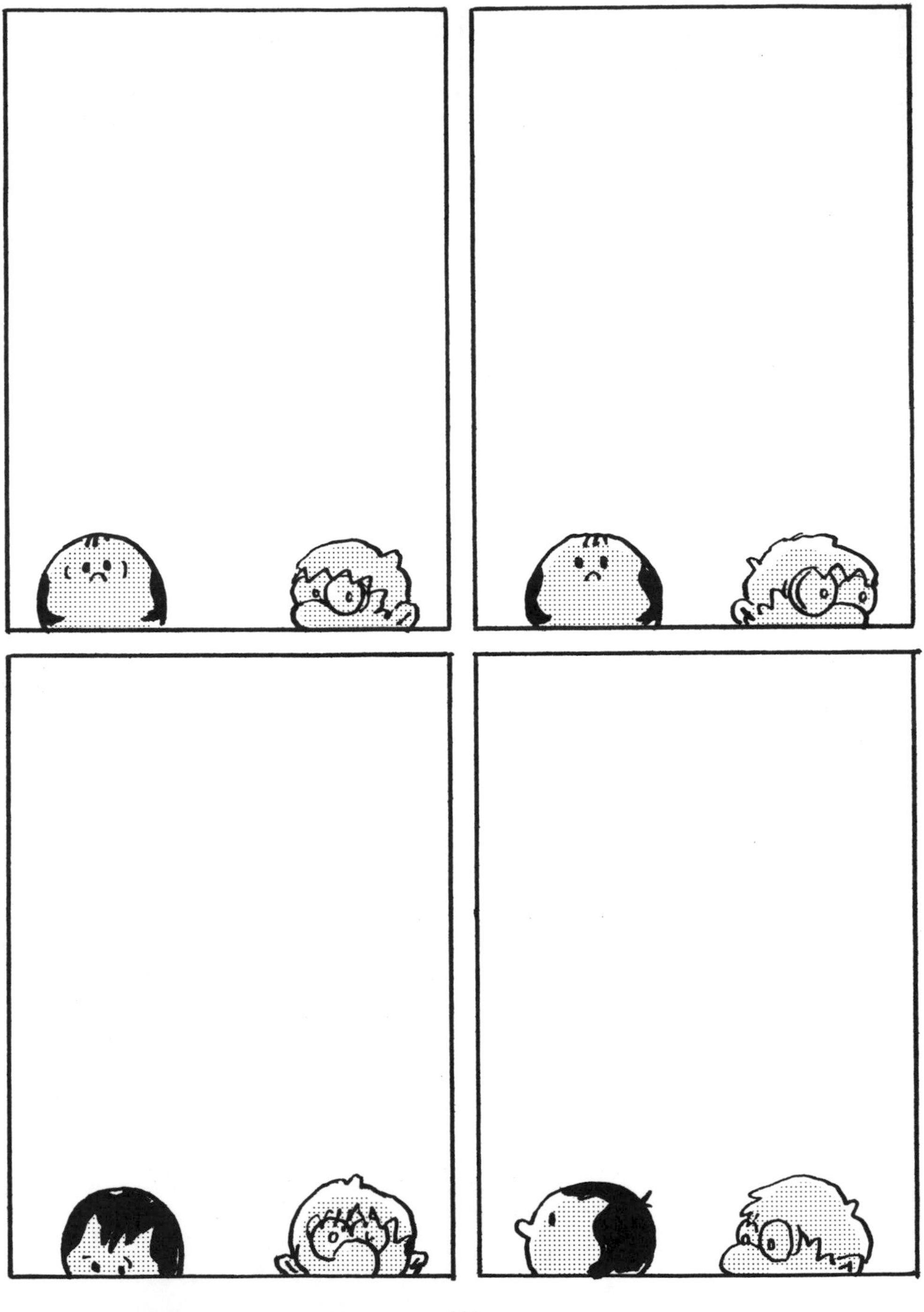

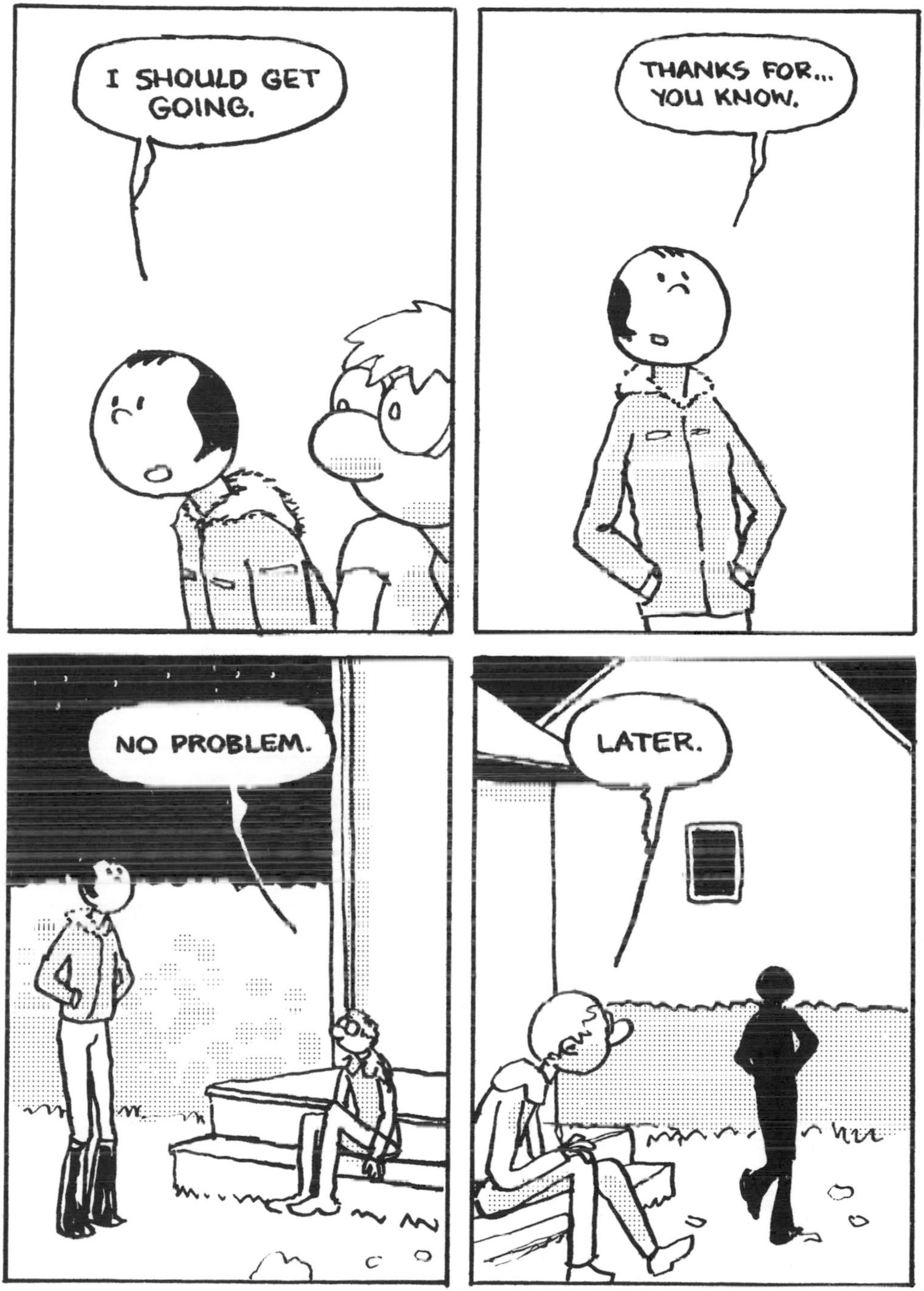
I SHOULD GET GOING.
THANKS FOR... YOU KNOW.
NO PROBLEM.
LATER.

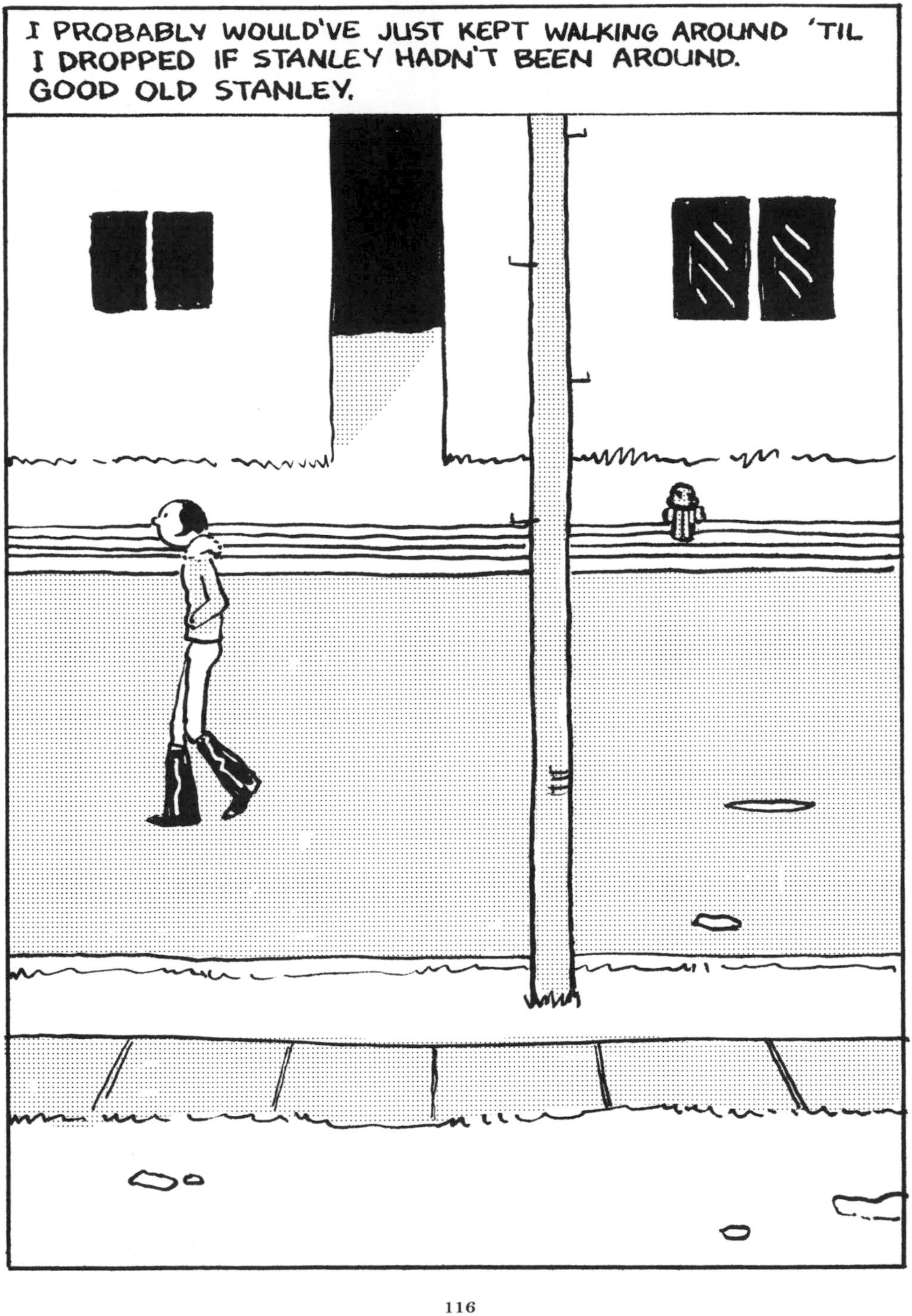
I PROBABLY WOULD'VE JUST KEPT WALKING AROUND 'TIL I DROPPED IF STANLEY HADN'T BEEN AROUND. GOOD OLD STANLEY.

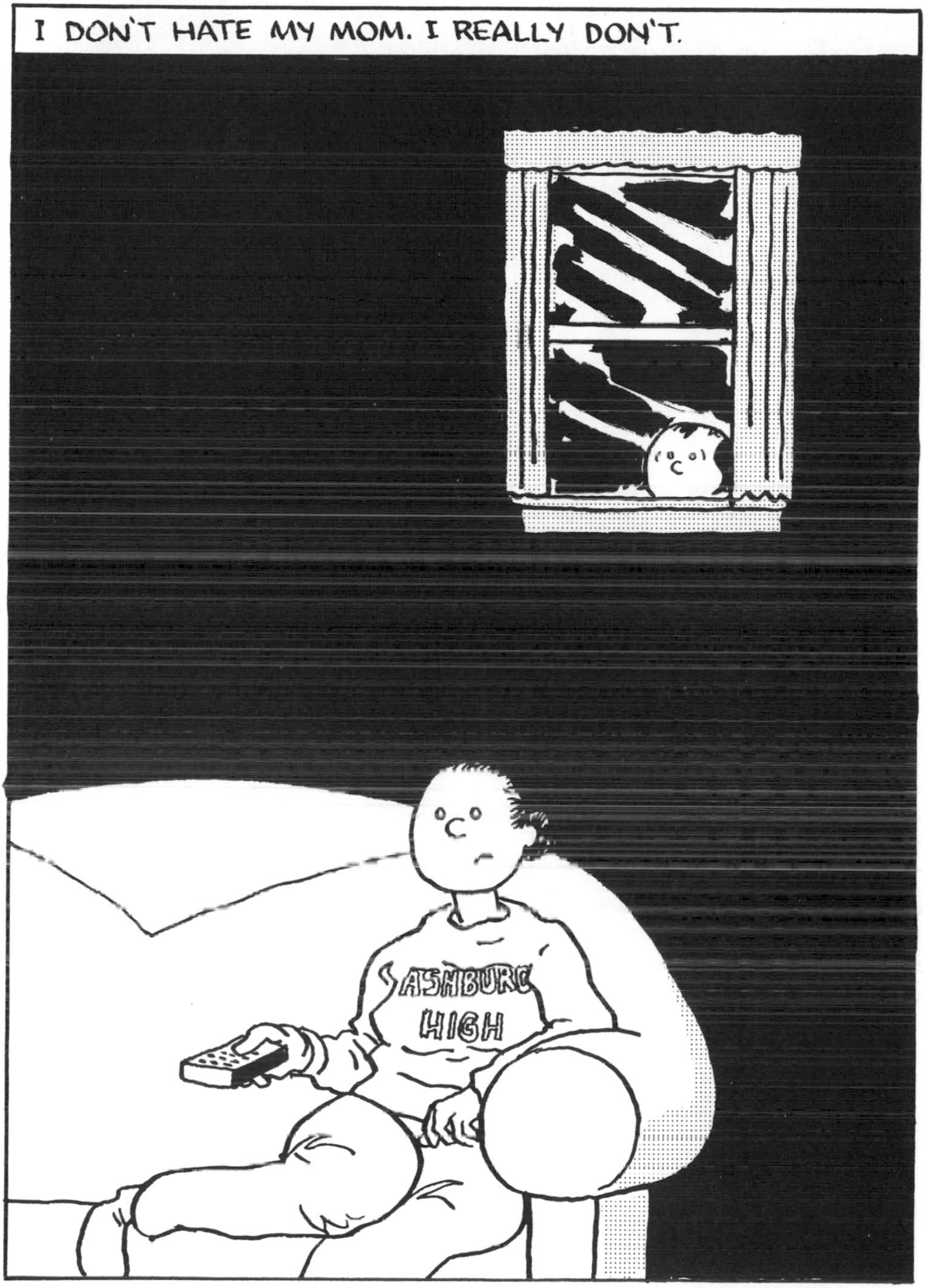
I DON'T HATE MY MOM. I REALLY DON'T.
ASHBURG
HIGH

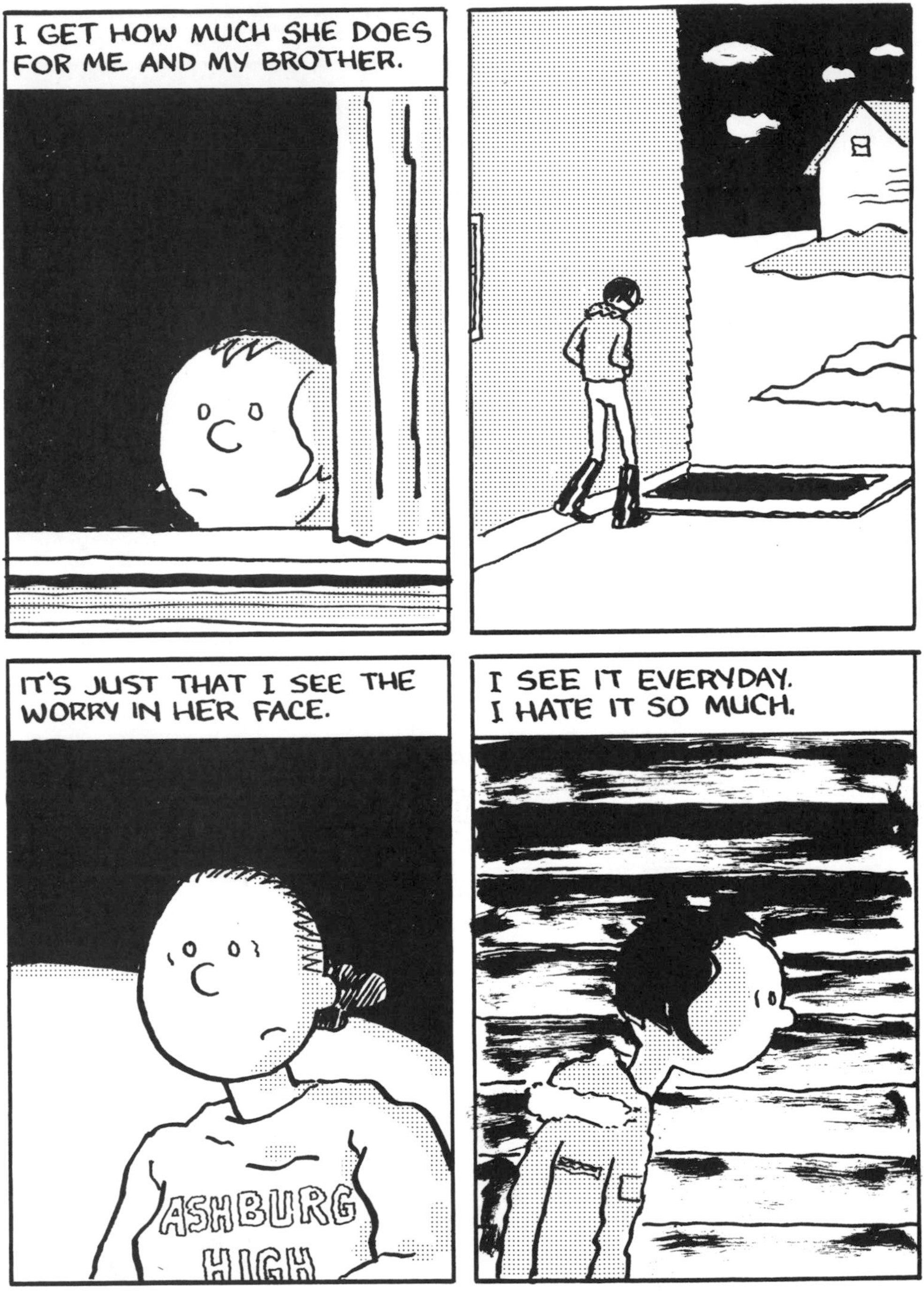
I GET HOW MUCH SHE DOES FOR ME AND MY BROTHER.
IT'S JUST THAT I SEE THE WORRY IN HER FACE.
ASHBURG HIGH
I SEE IT EVERYDAY. I HATE IT SO MUCH.

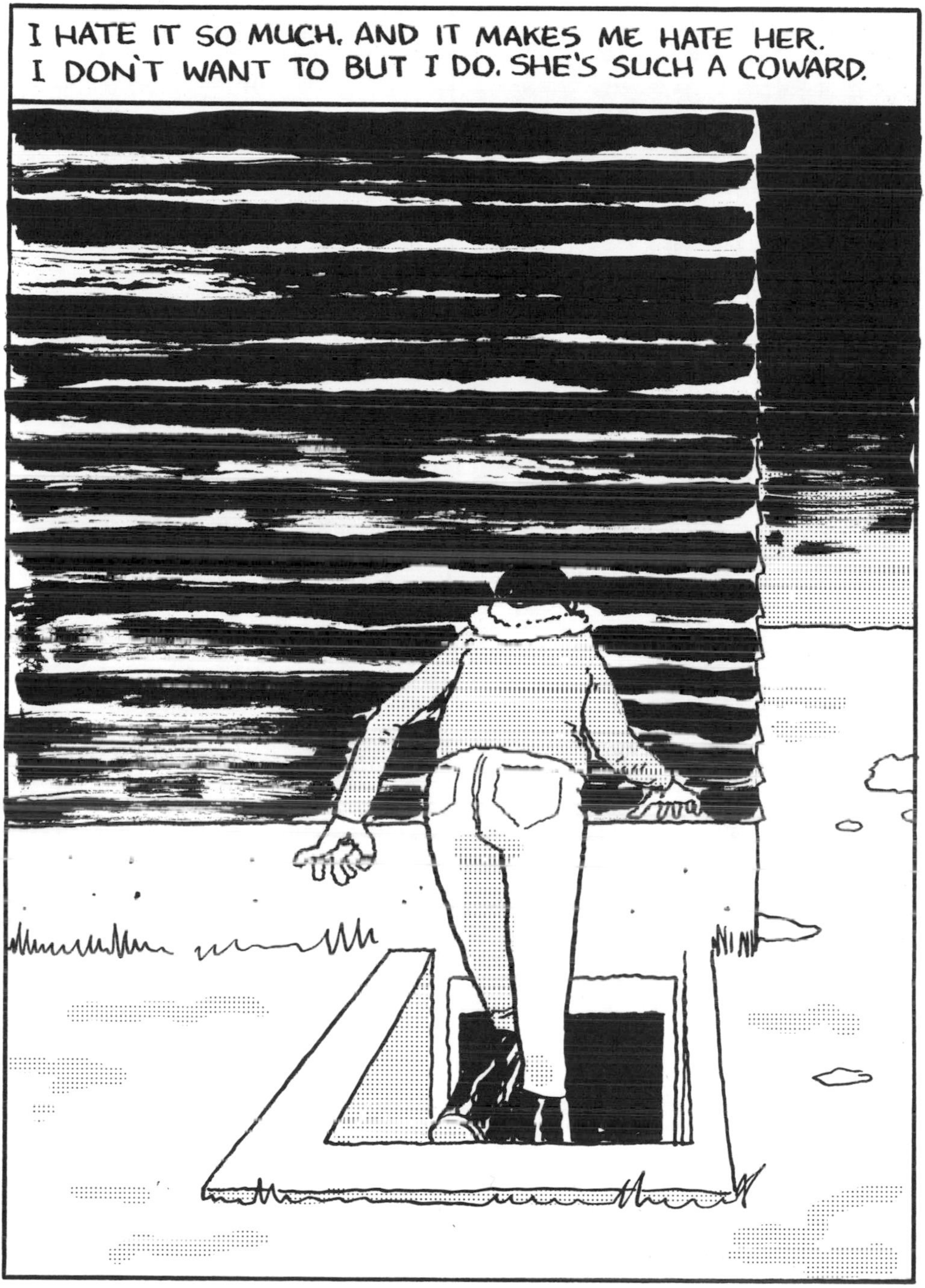
I HATE IT SO MUCH. AND IT MAKES ME HATE HER.
I DON'T WANT TO BUT I DO. SHE'S SUCH A COWARD.

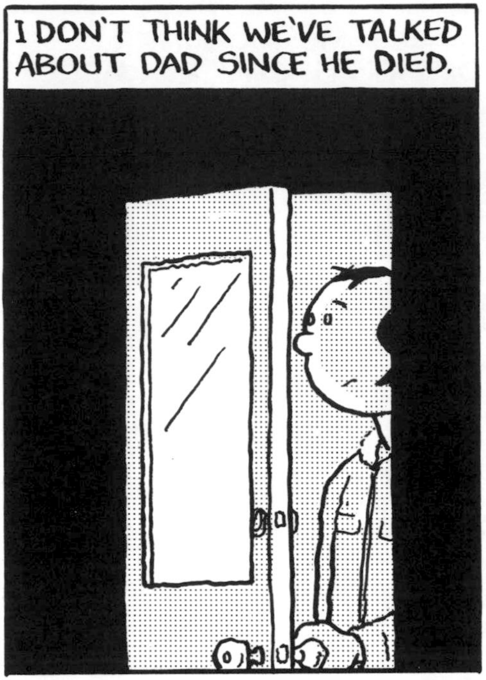
I DON'T THINK WE'VE TALKED ABOUT DAD SINCE HE DIED.

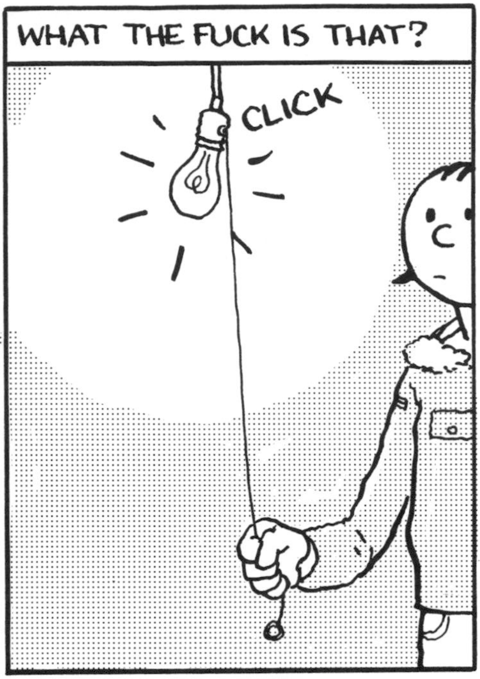
WHAT THE FUCK IS THAT?
CLICK

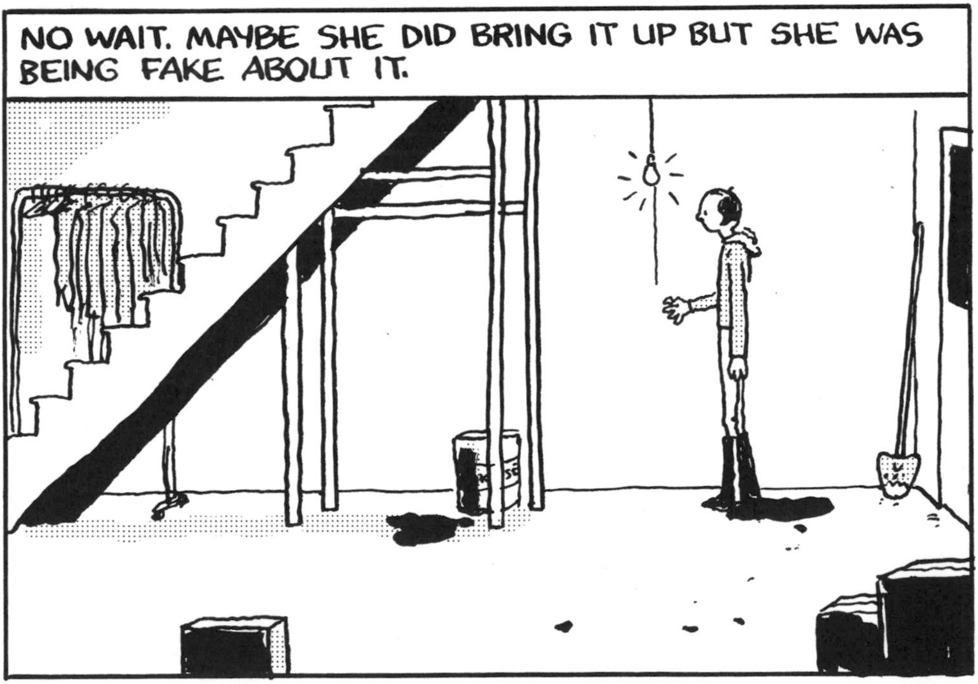
NO WAIT. MAYBE SHE DID BRING IT UP BUT SHE WAS BEING FAKE ABOUT IT.

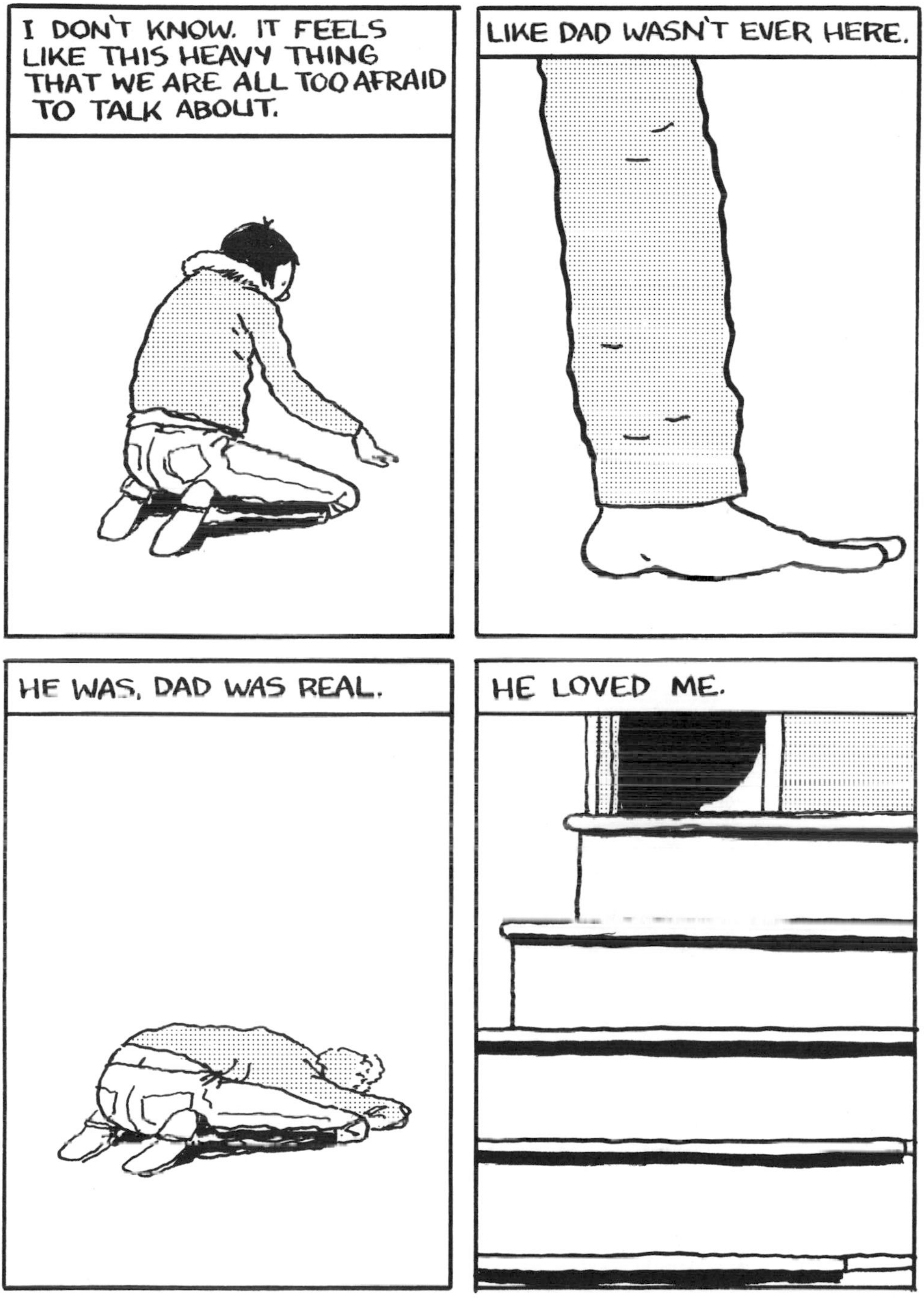
I DON'T KNOW. IT FEELS LIKE THIS HEAVY THING THAT WE ARE ALL TOO AFRAID TO TALK ABOUT.
LIKE DAD WASN'T EVER HERE.
HE WAS. DAD WAS REAL.
HE LOVED ME.

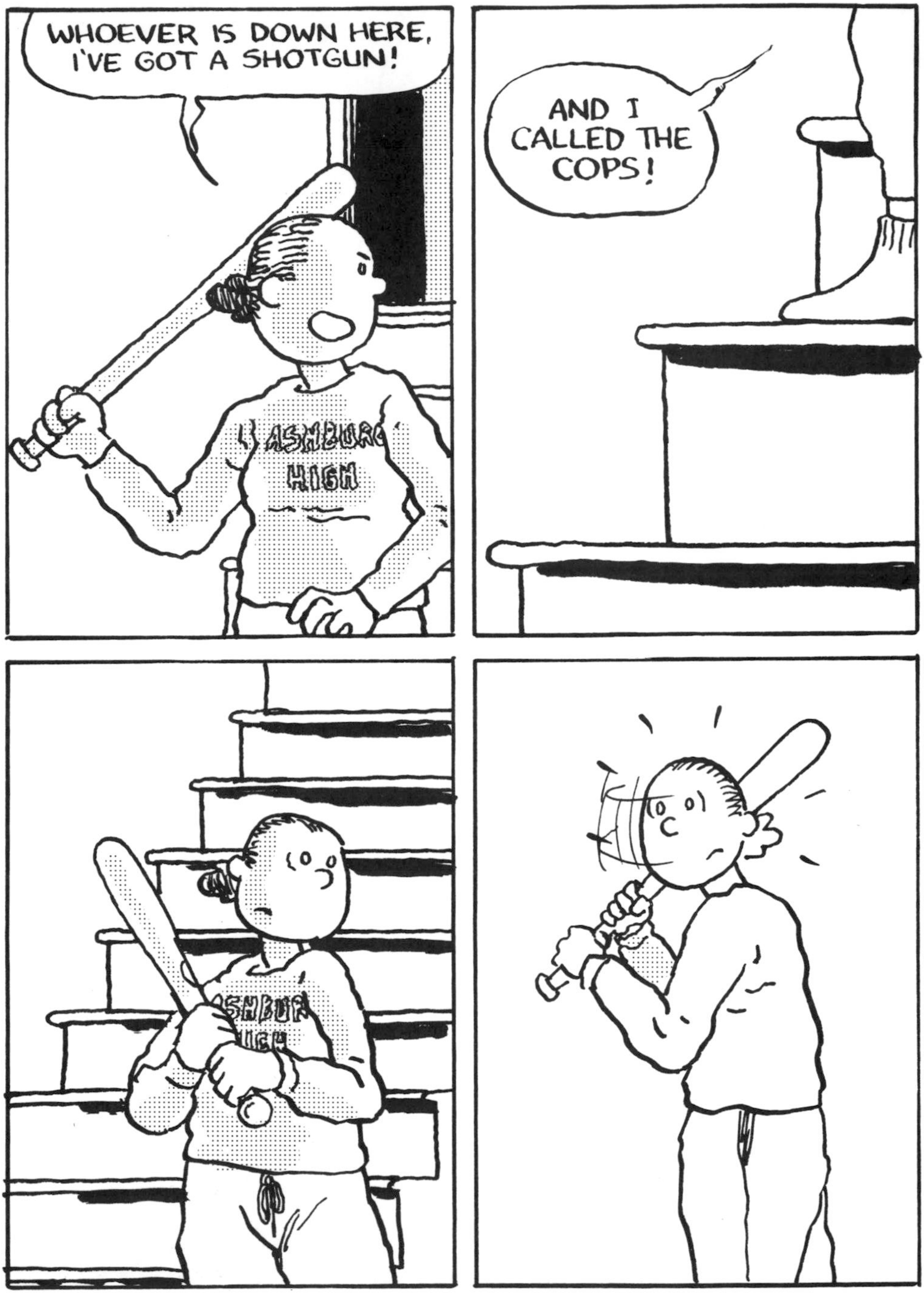
WHOEVER IS DOWN HERE, I'VE GOT A SHOTGUN!
ASHBURG HIGH
AND I CALLED THE COPS!

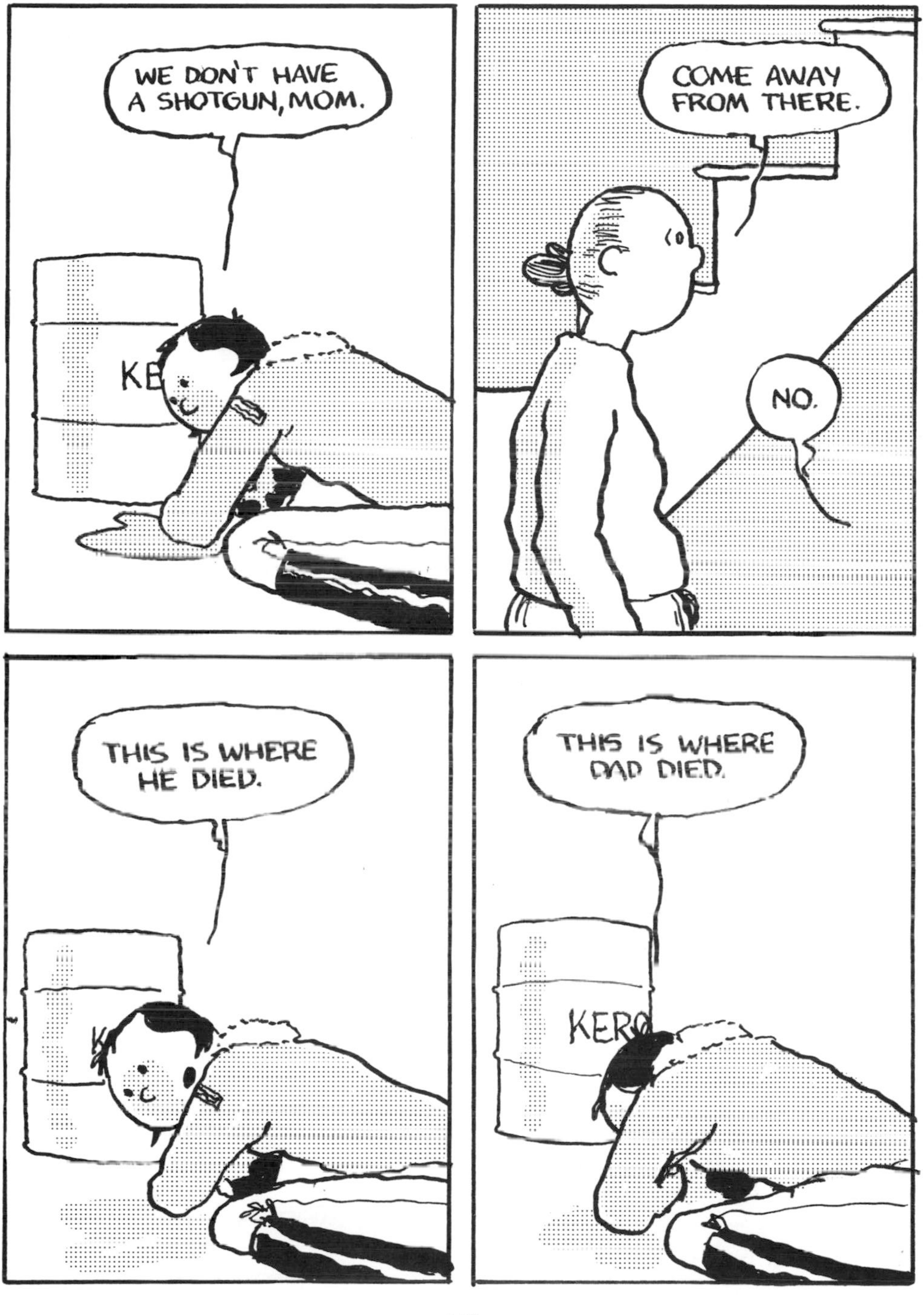
WE DON'T HAVE A SHOTGUN, MOM.
COME AWAY FROM THERE.
NO.
THIS IS WHERE HE DIED.
THIS IS WHERE DAD DIED.

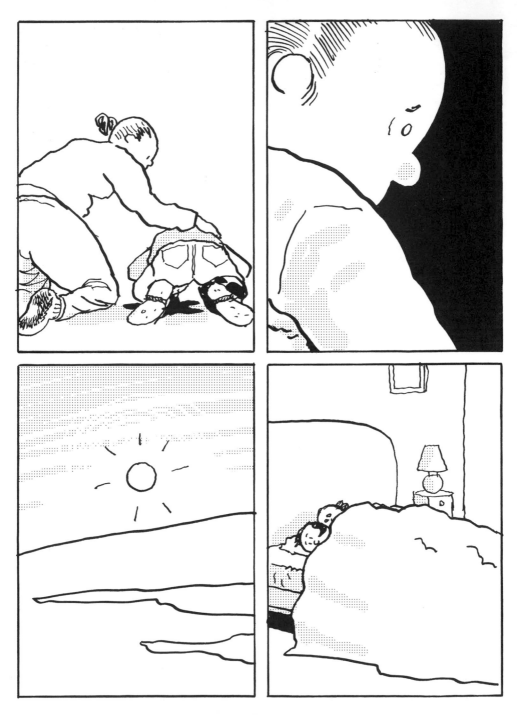

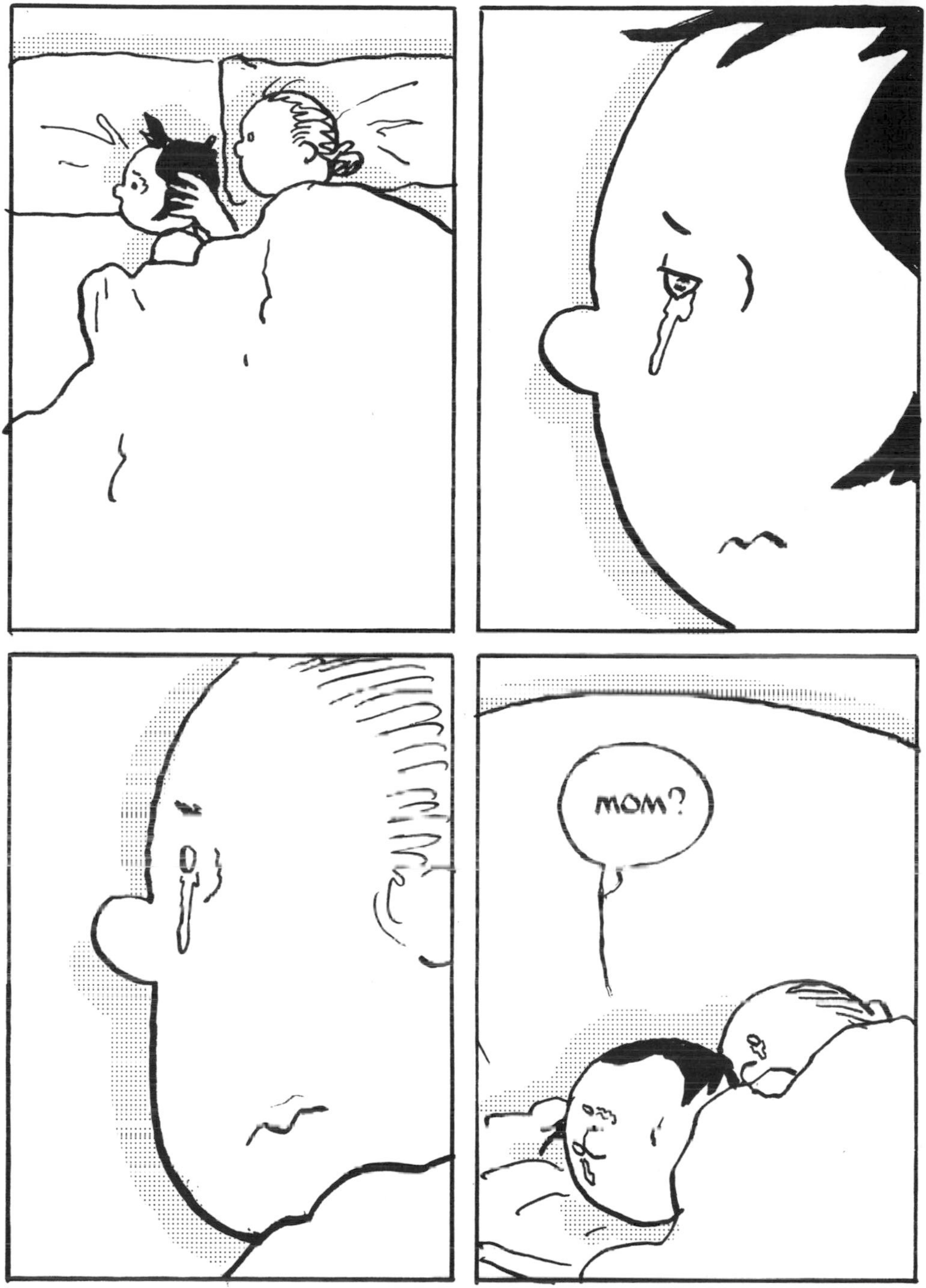
MOM?

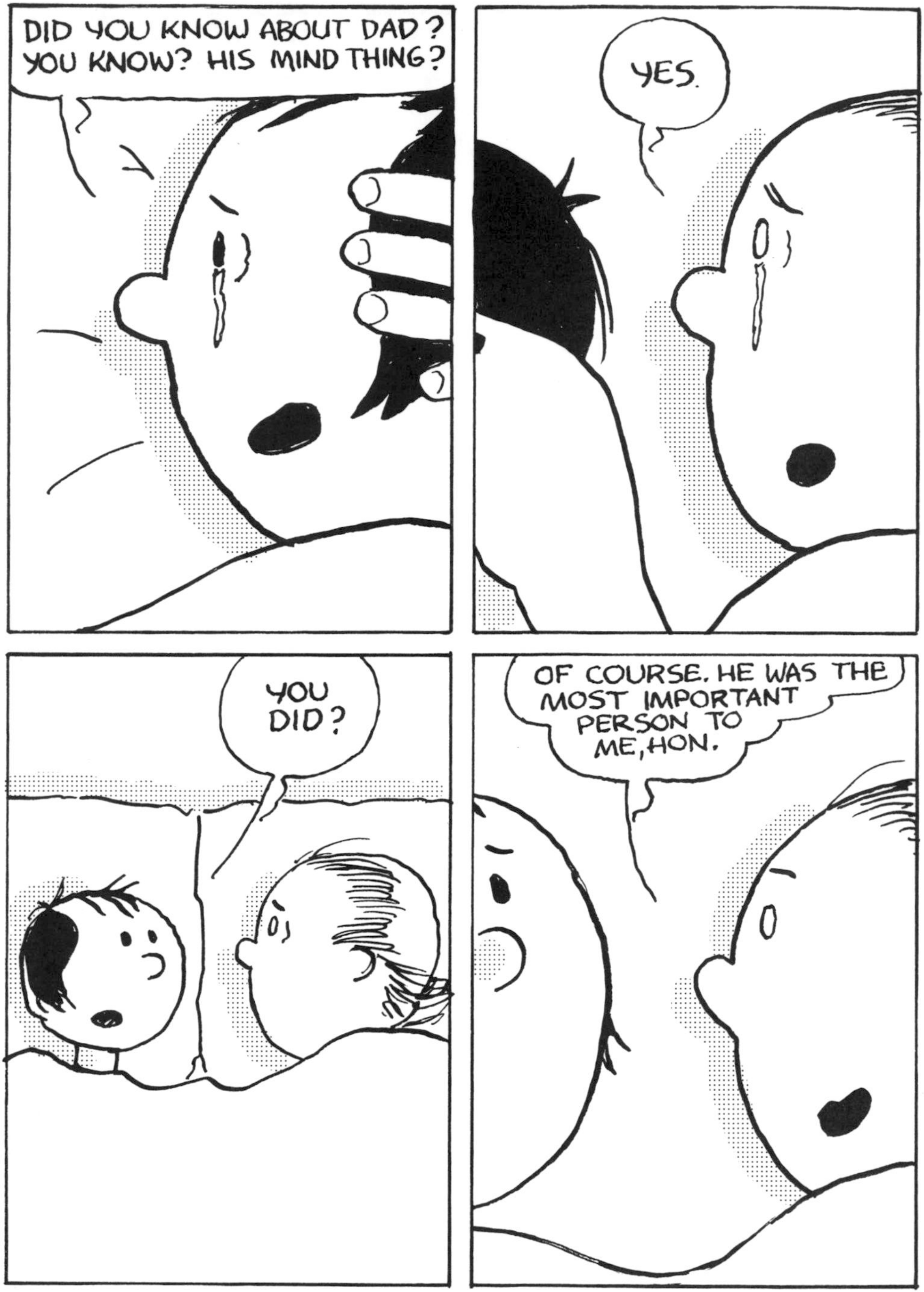
DID YOU KNOW ABOUT DAD? YOU KNOW? HIS MIND THING?
YES.
YOU DID?
OF COURSE. HE WAS THE MOST IMPORTANT PERSON TO ME, HON.

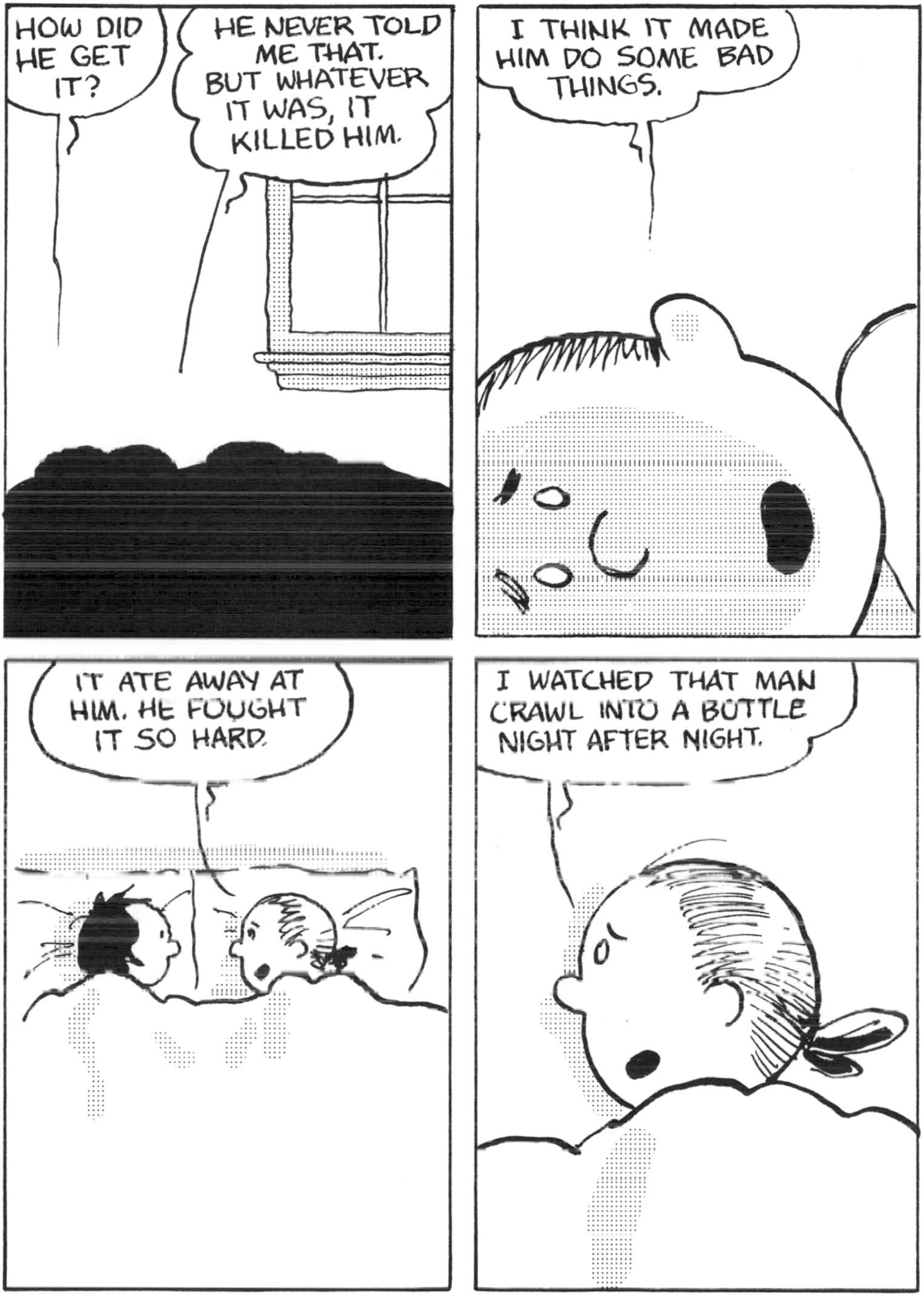
HOW DID HE GET IT?
HE NEVER TOLD ME THAT. BUT WHATEVER IT WAS, IT KILLED HIM.
I THINK IT MADE HIM DO SOME BAD THINGS.
IT ATE AWAY AT HIM. HE FOUGHT IT SO HARD.
I WATCHED THAT MAN CRAWL INTO A BOTTLE NIGHT AFTER NIGHT.

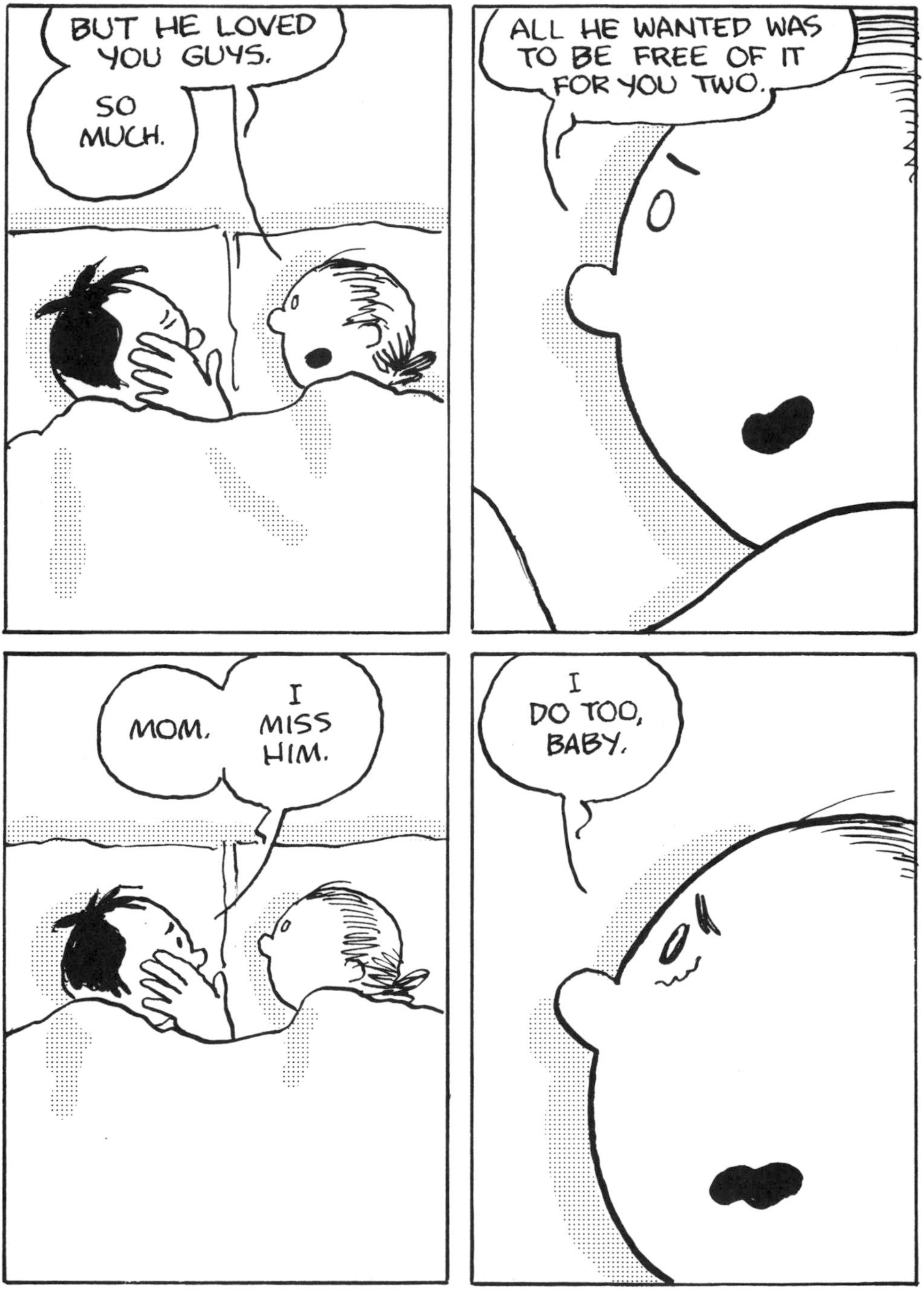
BUT HE LOVED YOU GUYS.
SO MUCH.
ALL HE WANTED WAS TO BE FREE OF IT FOR YOU TWO.
MOM.
I MISS HIM.
I DO TOO, BABY.

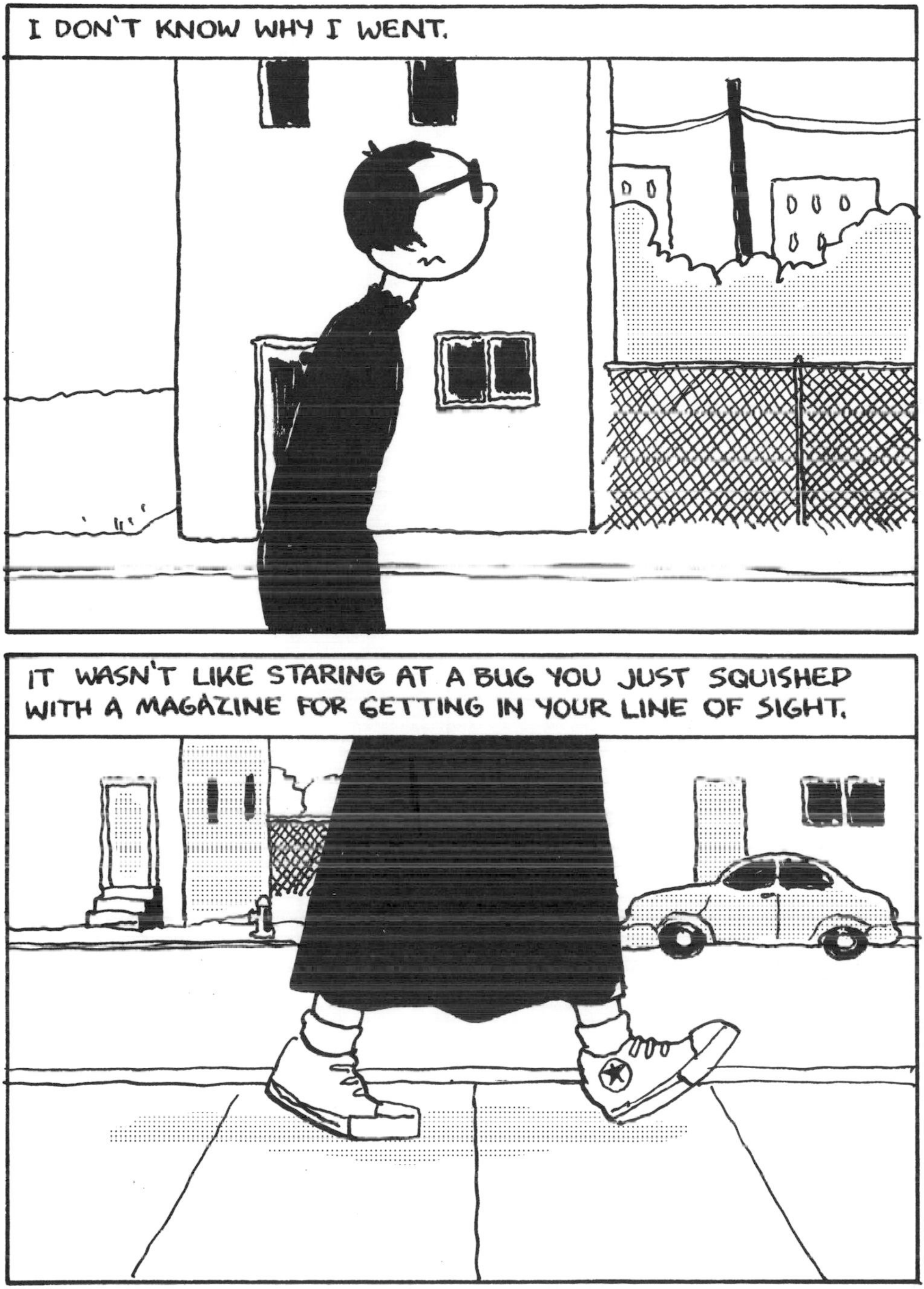
I DON'T KNOW WHY I WENT.
IT WASN'T LIKE STARING AT A BUG YOU JUST SQUISHED WITH A MAGAZINE FOR GETTING IN YOUR LINE OF SIGHT.

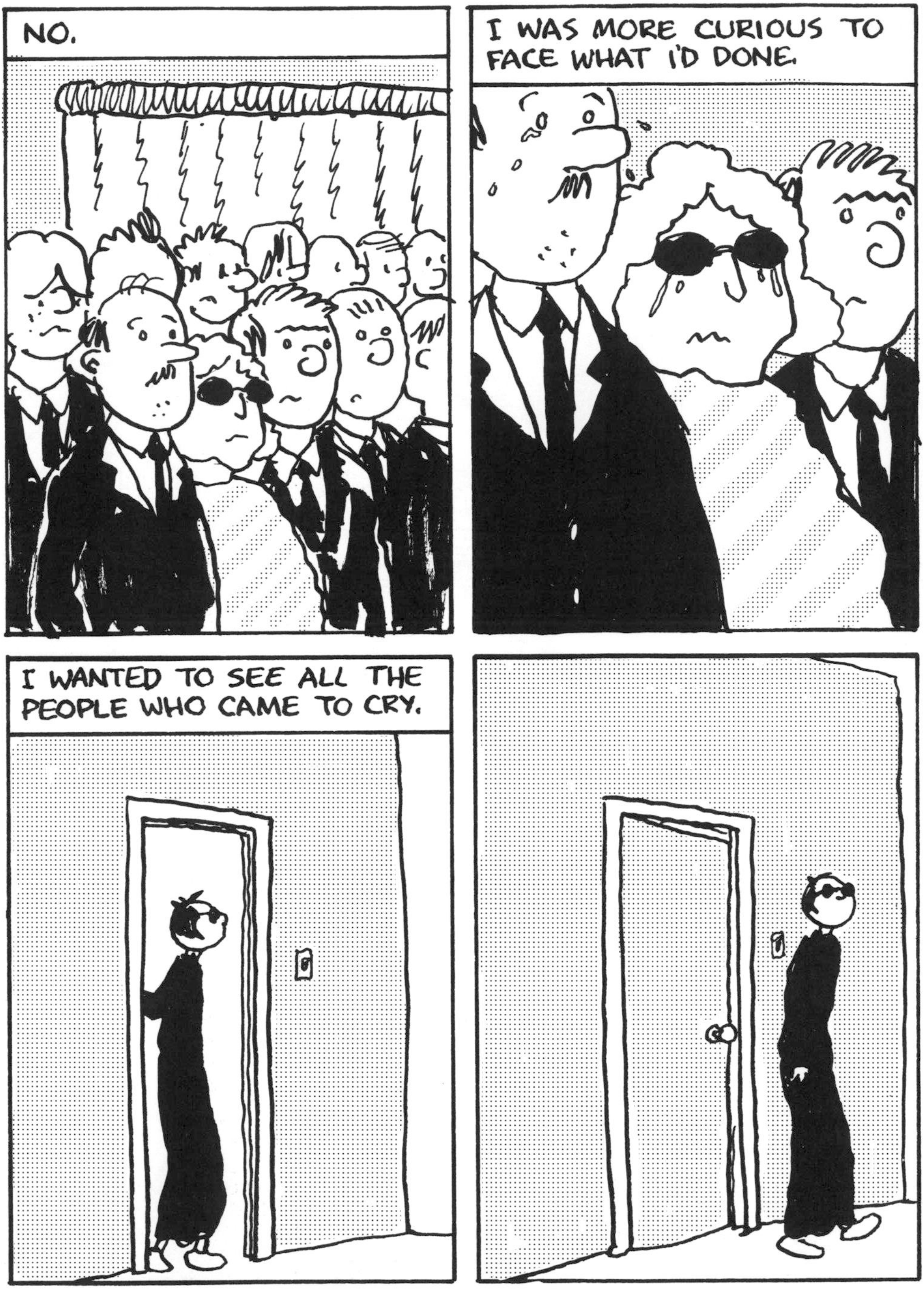
NO.
I WAS MORE CURIOUS TO FACE WHAT I'D DONE.
I WANTED TO SEE ALL THE PEOPLE WHO CAME TO CRY.

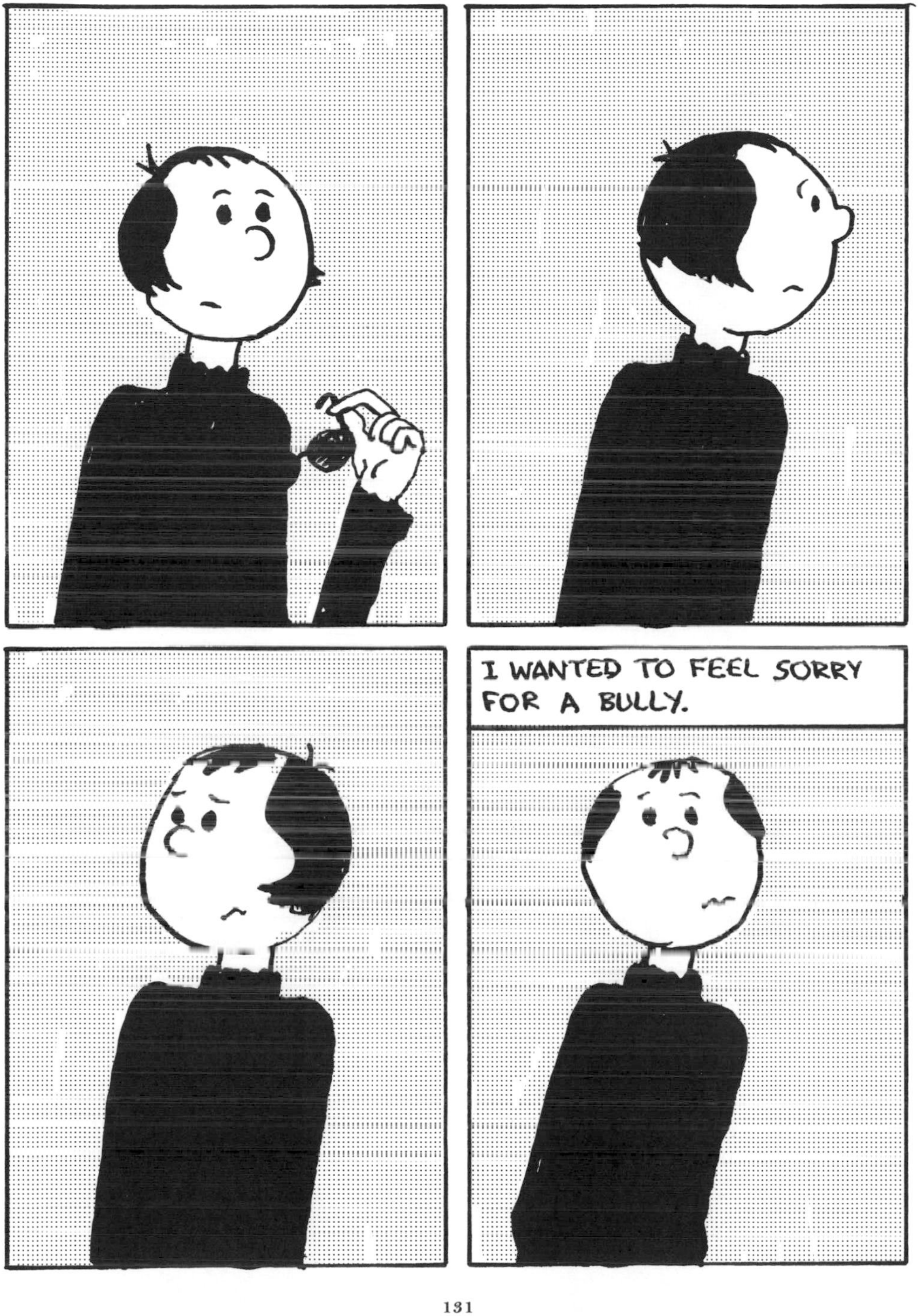
I WANTED TO FEEL SORRY FOR A BULLY.

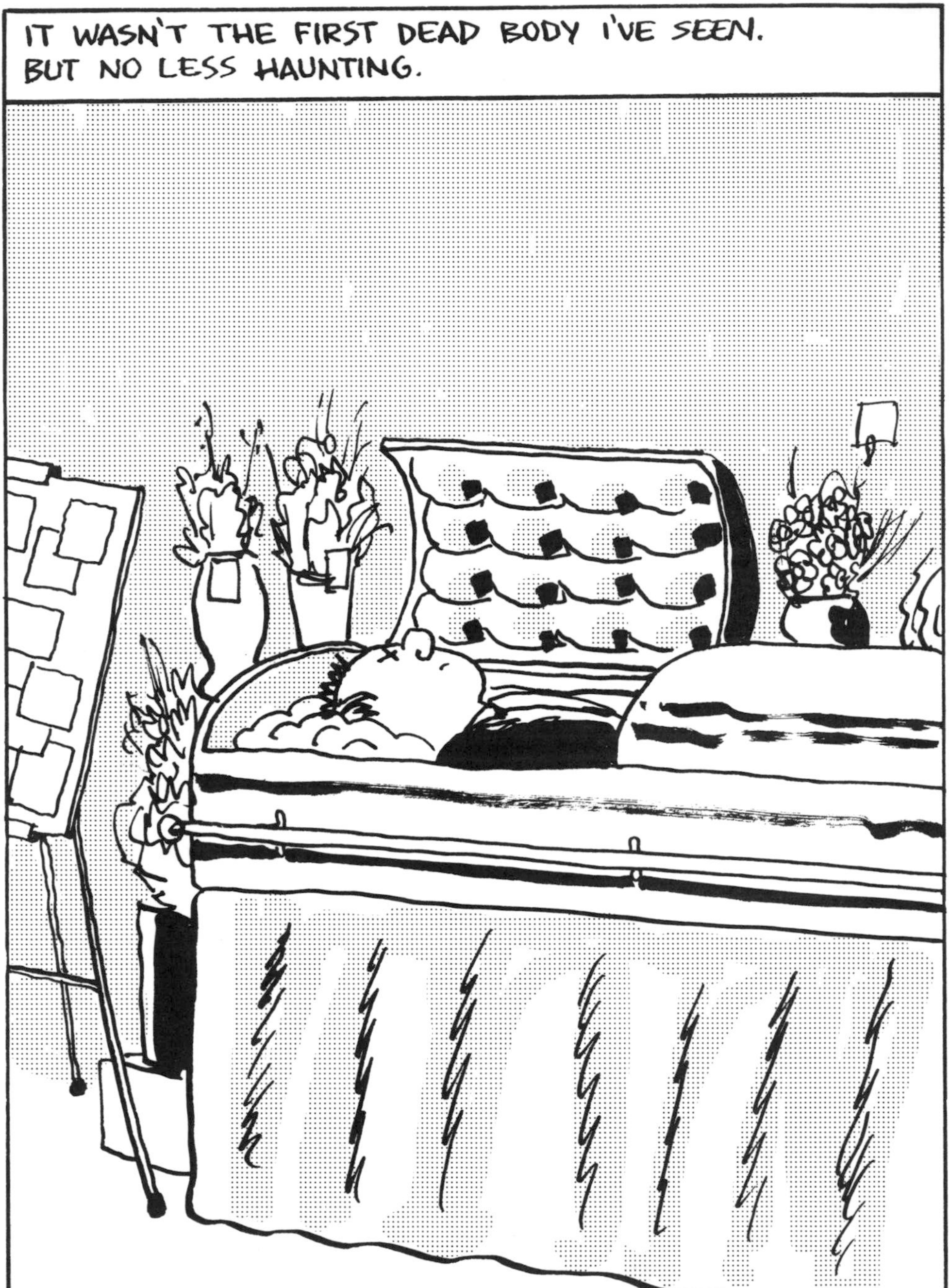
IT WASN'T THE FIRST DEAD BODY I'VE SEEN.
BUT NO LESS HAUNTING.

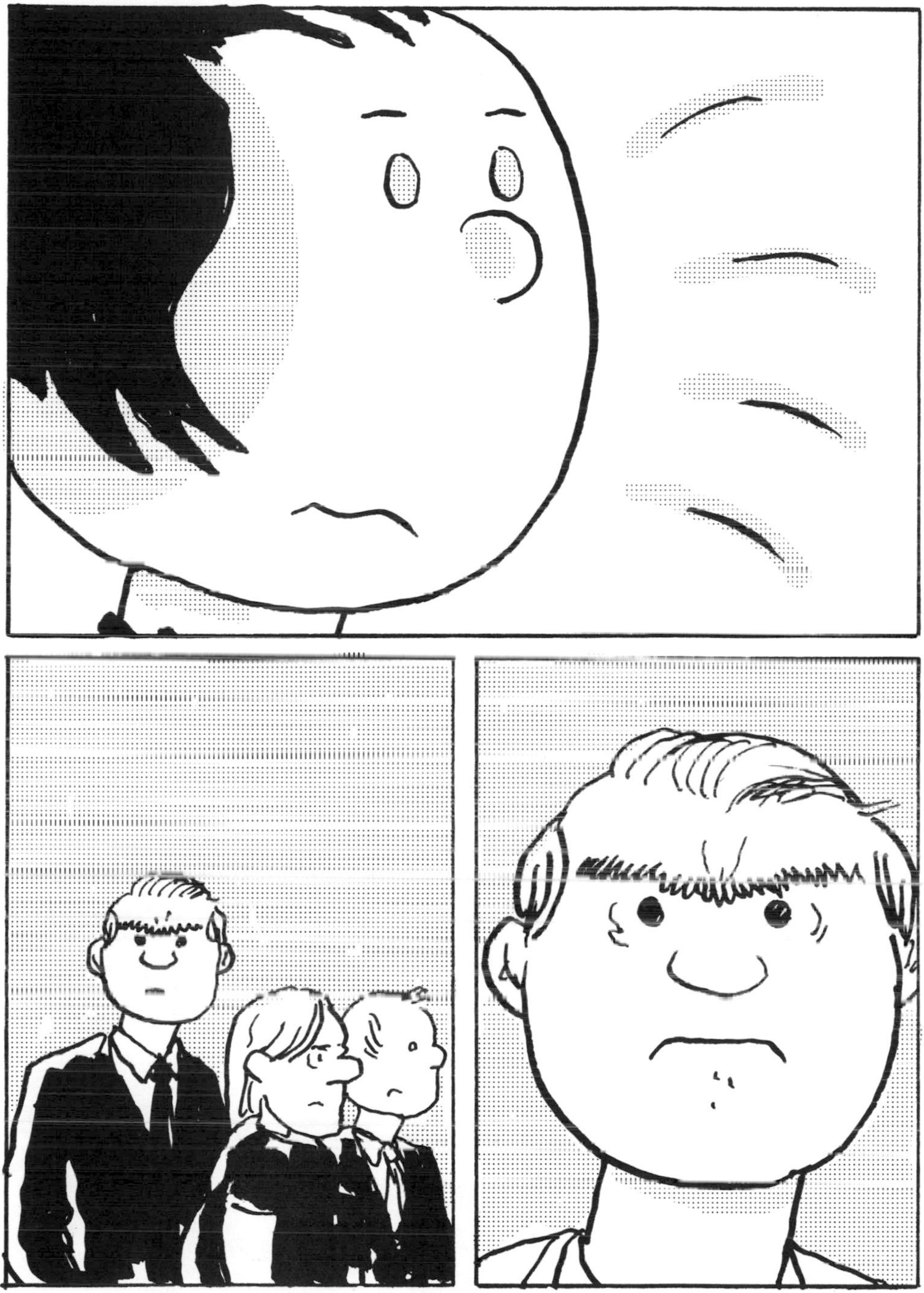

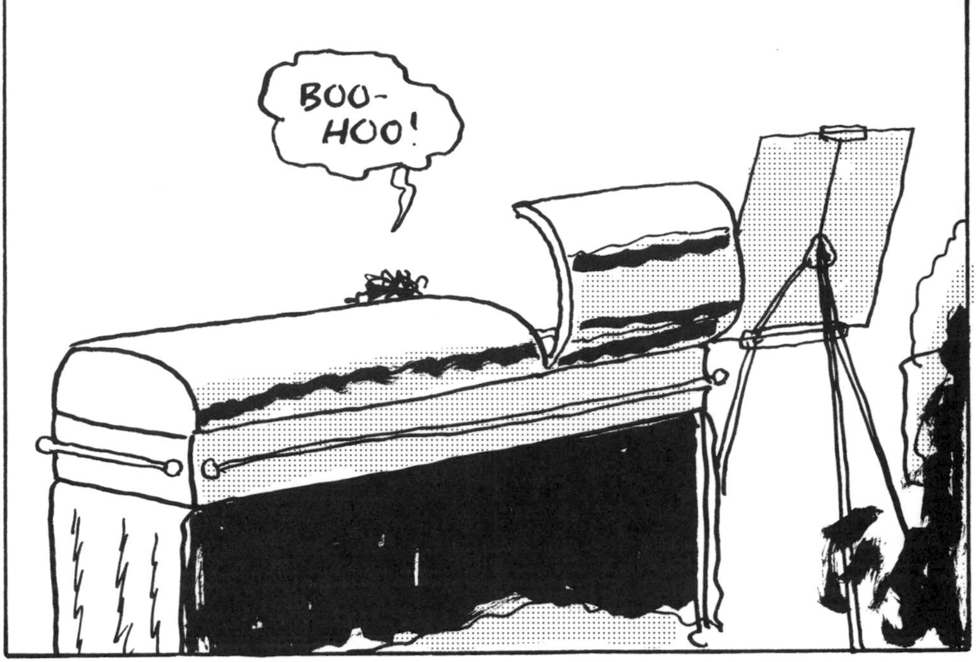
BOO-
HOO!

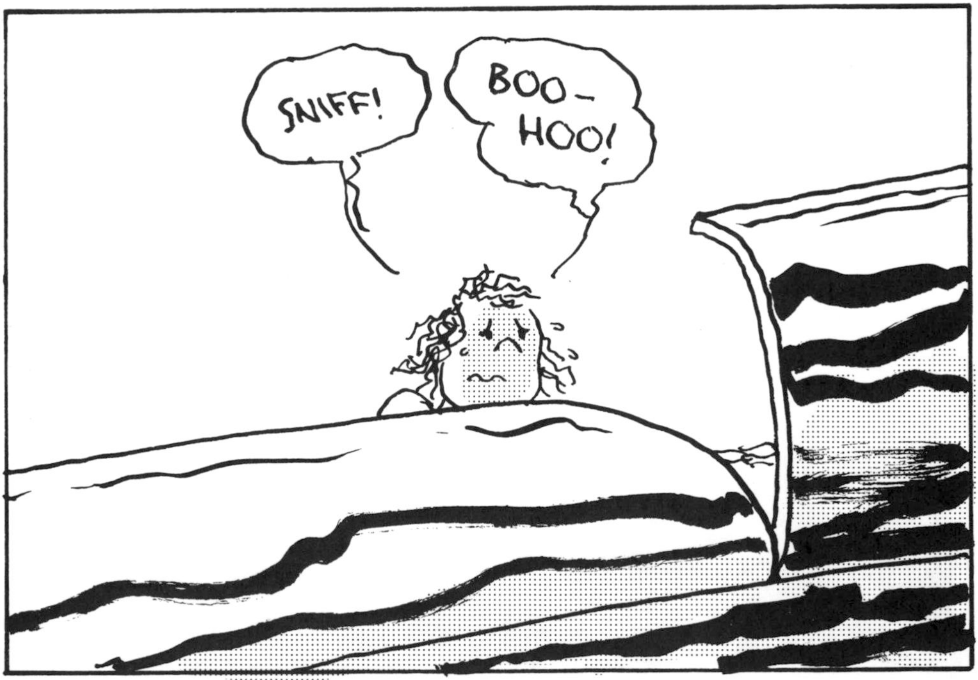
SNIFF!
BOO-
HOO!

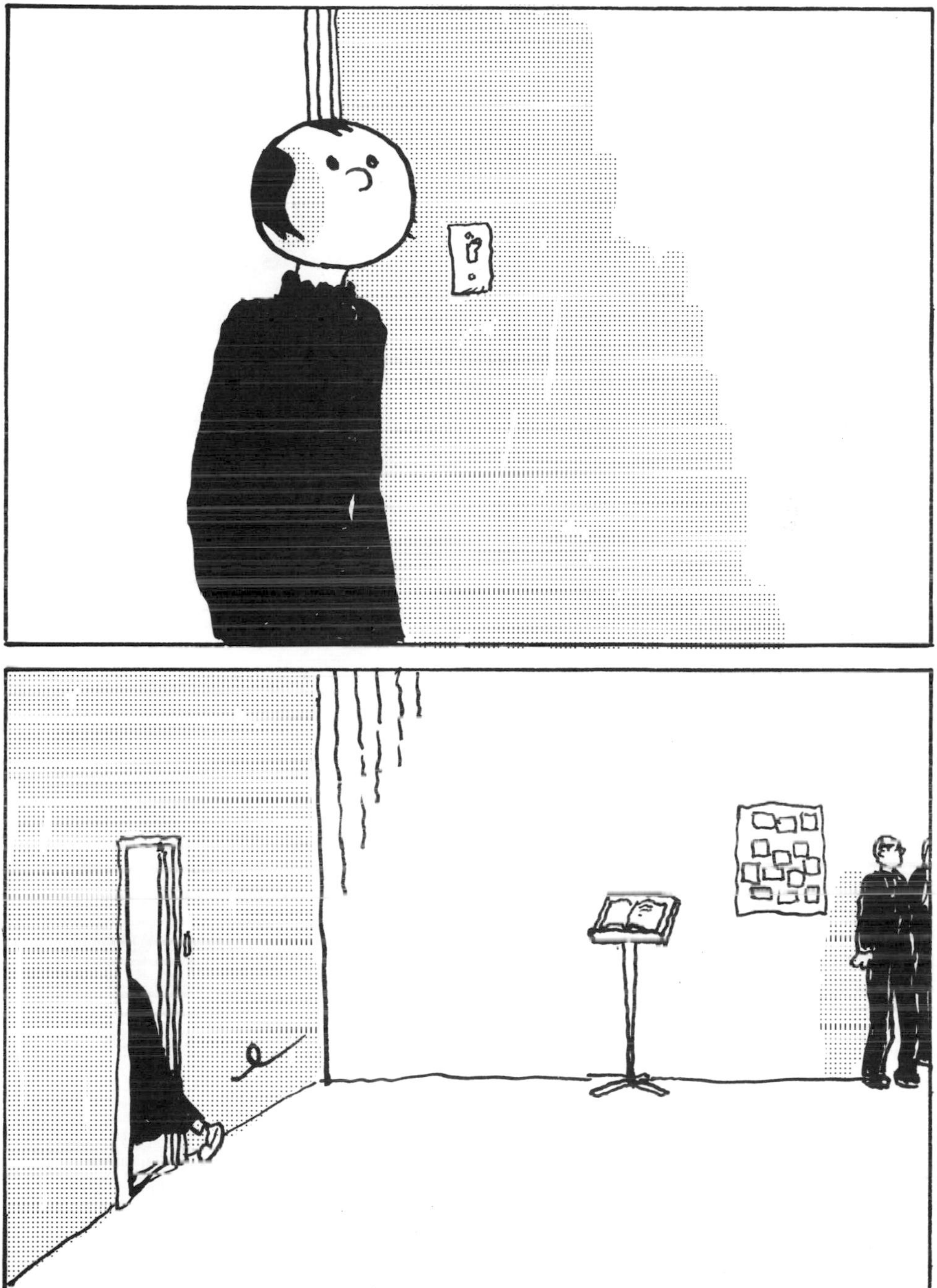

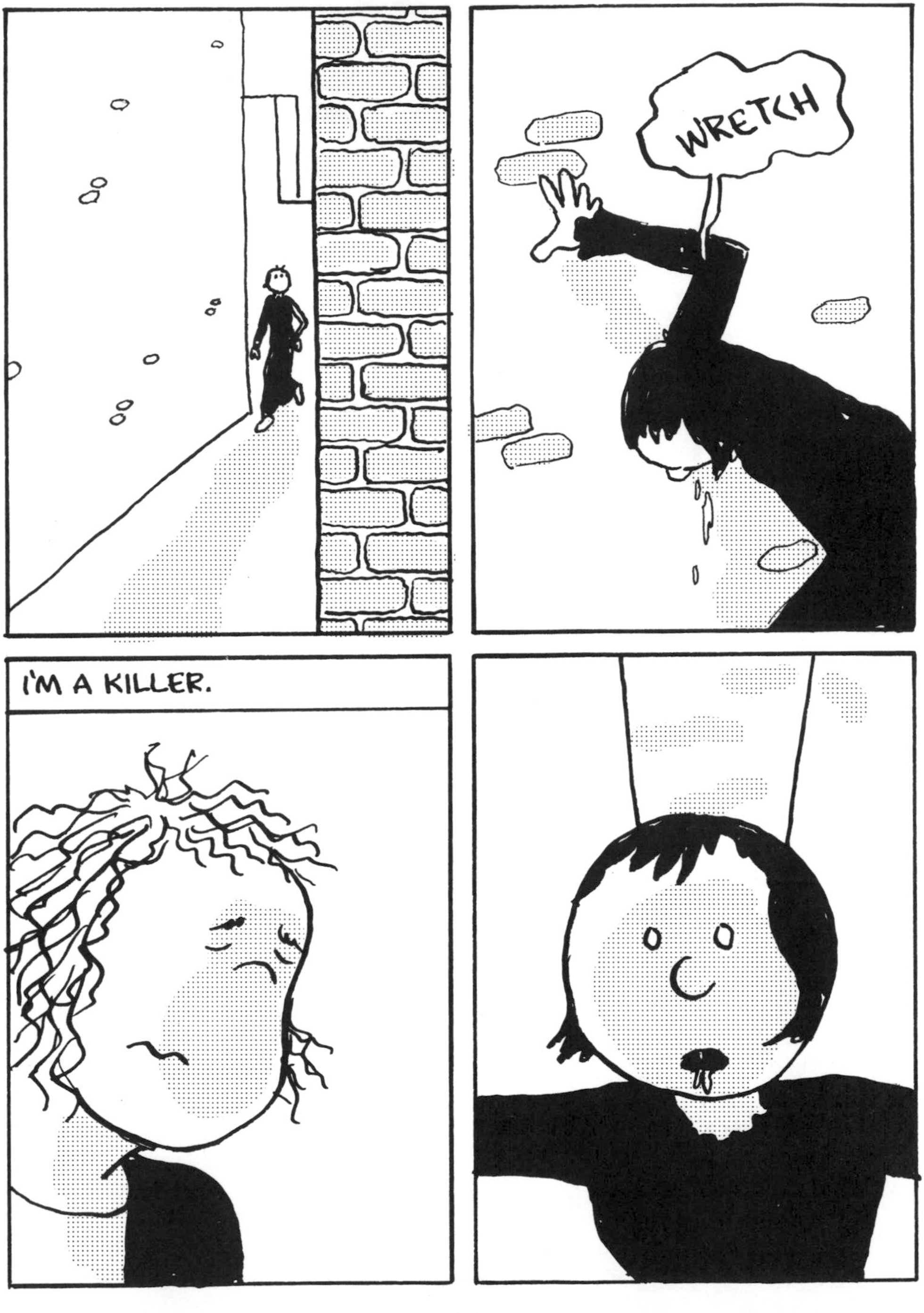
WRETCH
I'M A KILLER.

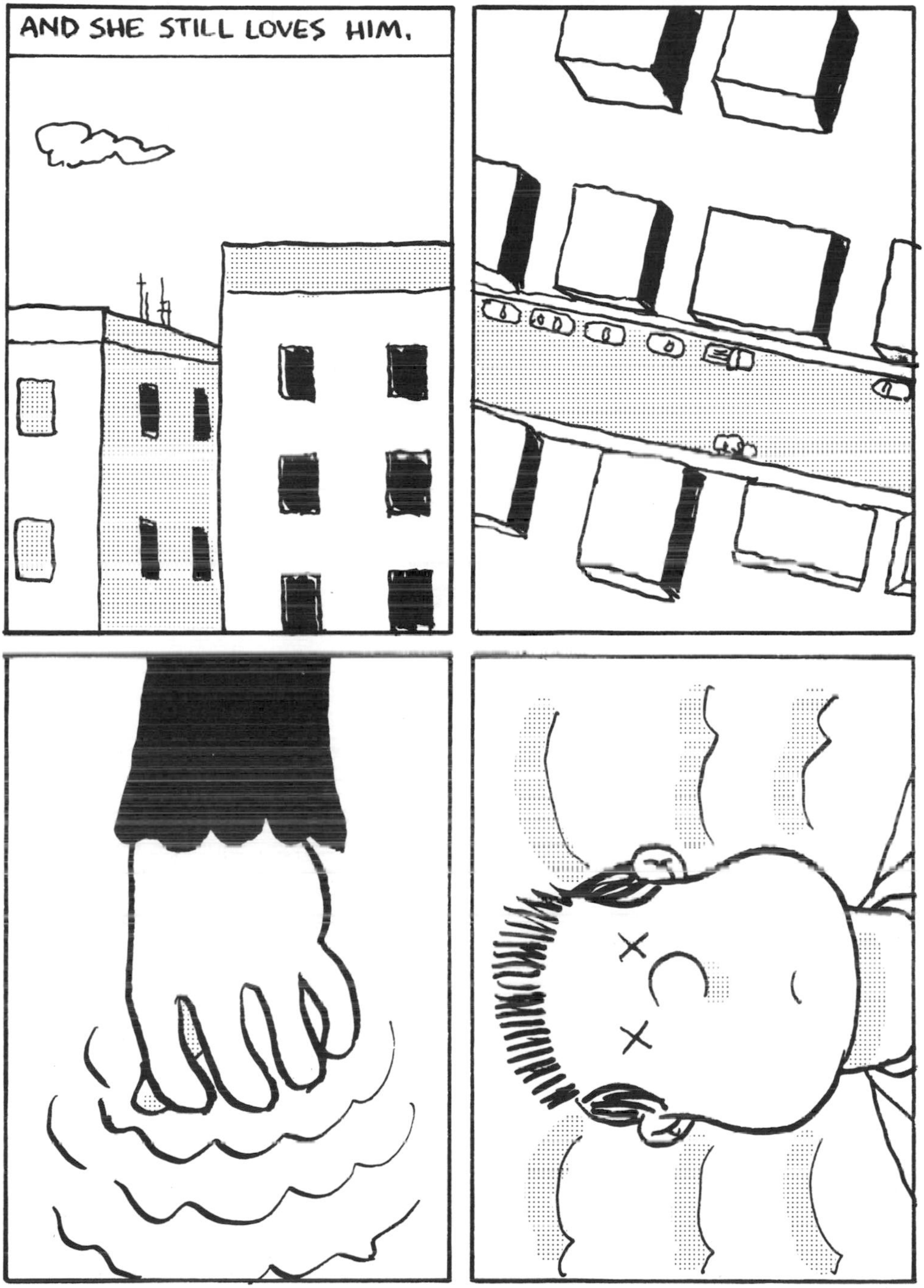
AND SHE STILL LOVES HIM.

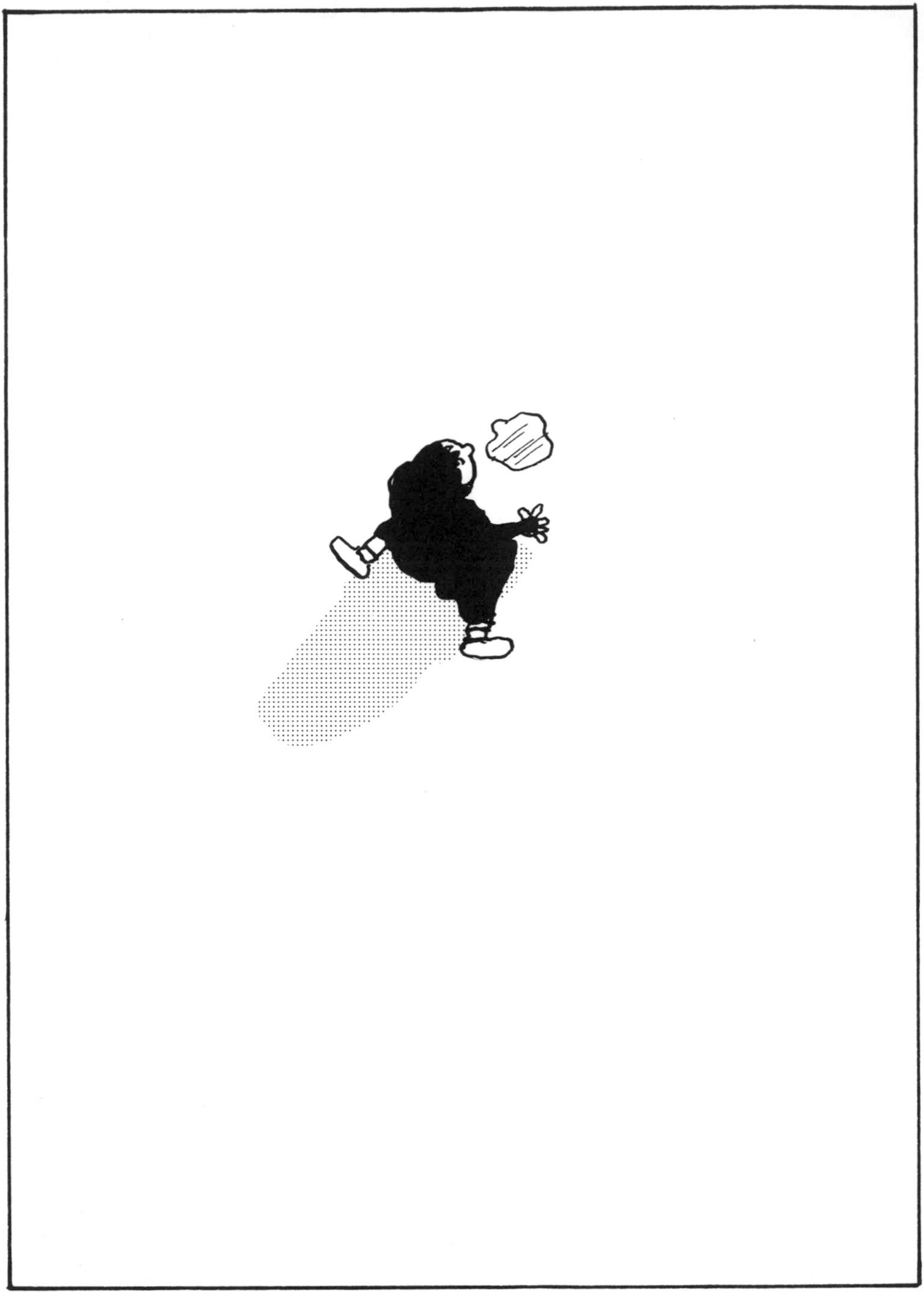

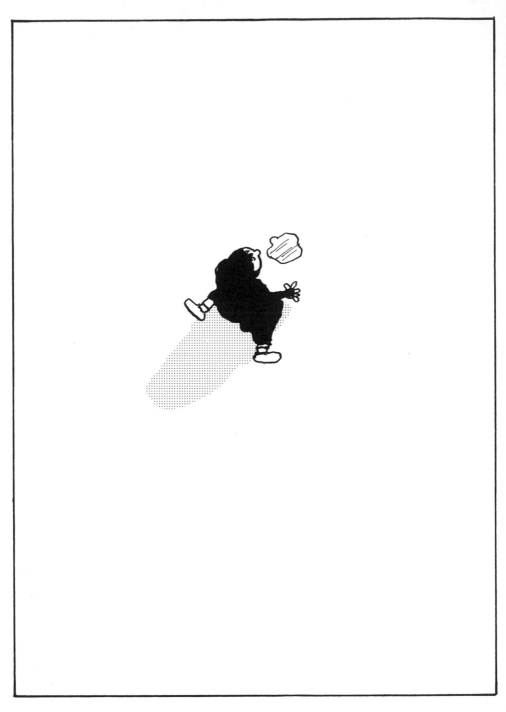

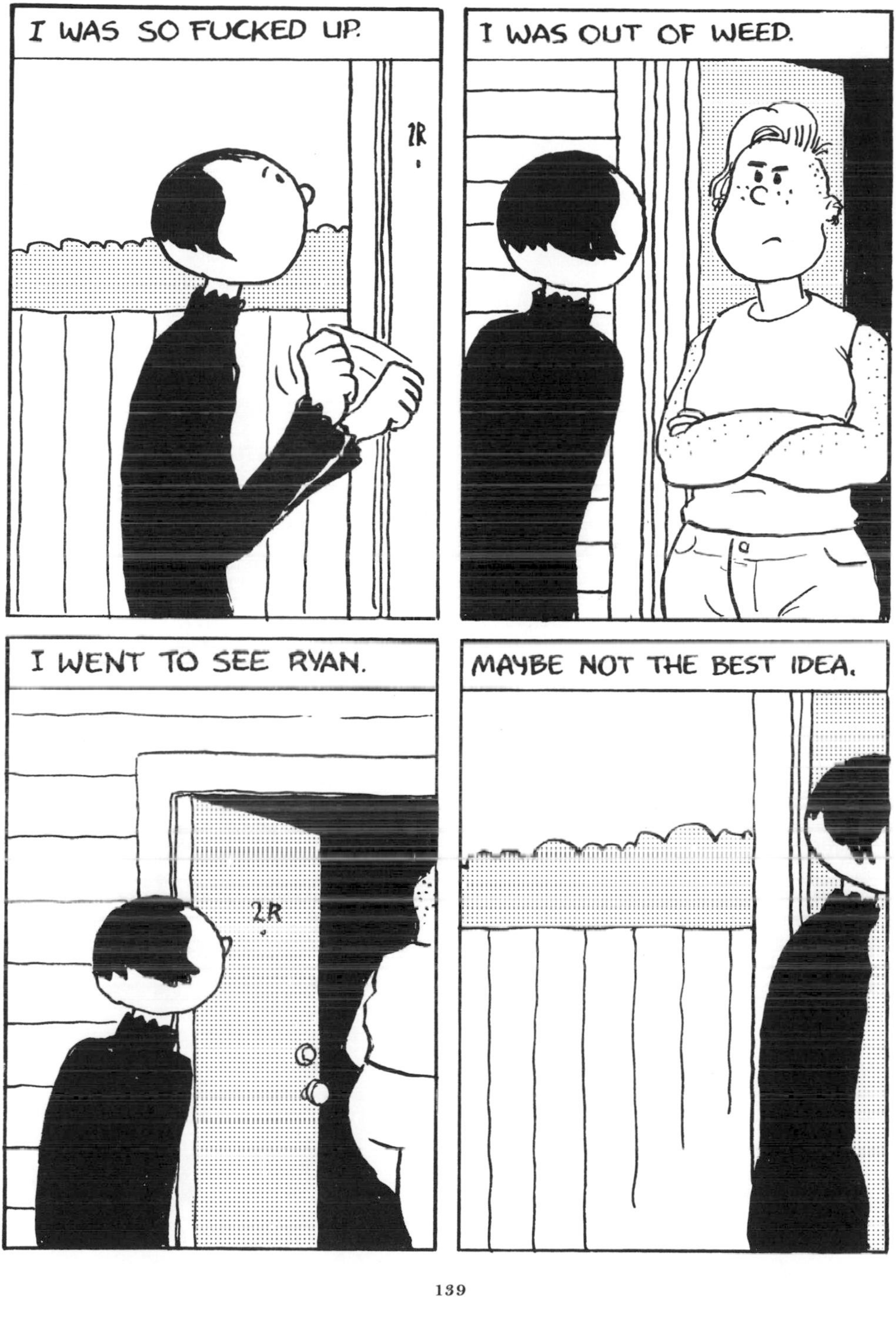
I WAS SO FUCKED UP.
2R
I WAS OUT OF WEED.
I WENT TO SEE RYAN.
2R
MAYBE NOT THE BEST IDEA.

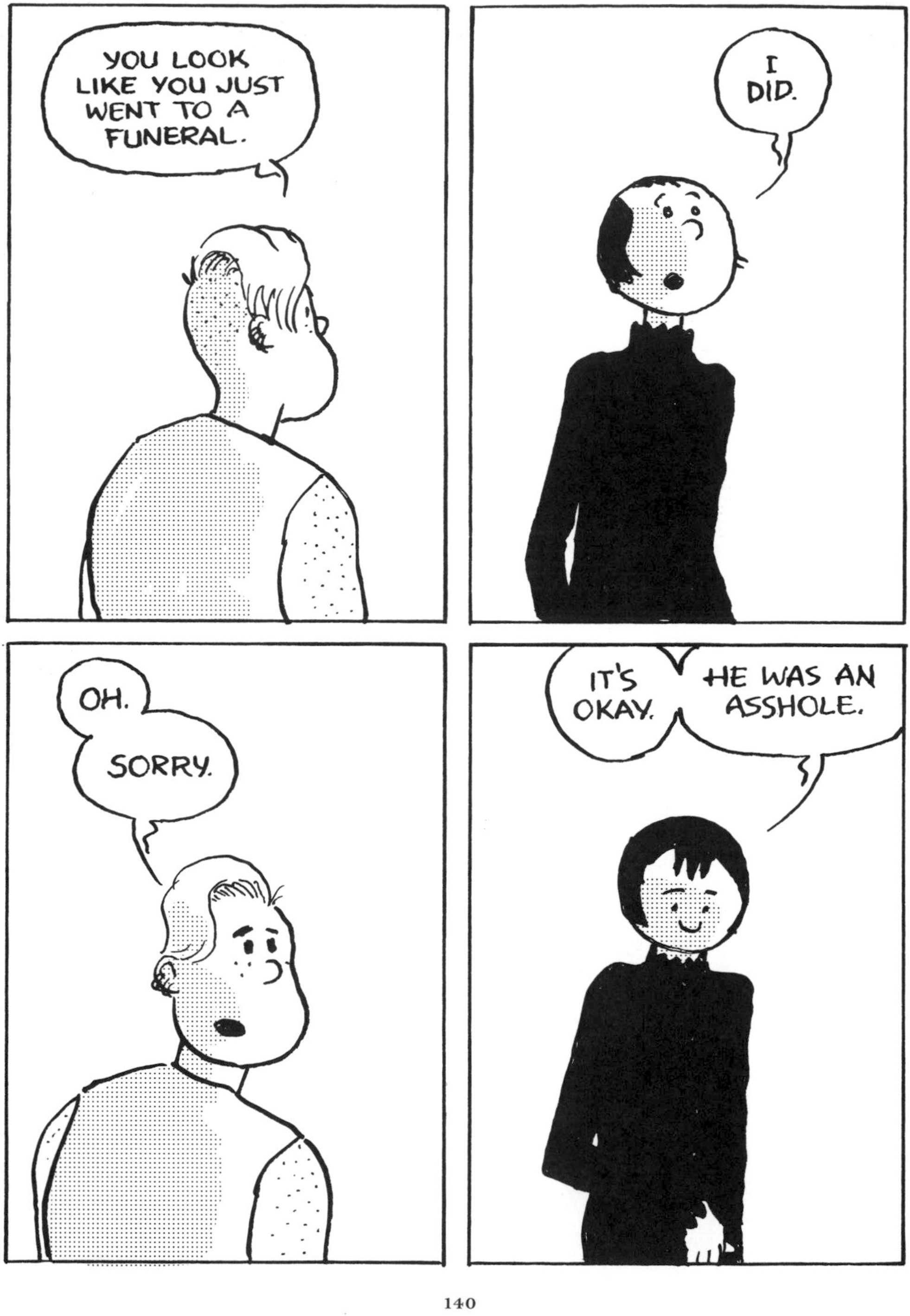
YOU LOOK LIKE YOU JUST WENT TO A FUNERAL.
I DID.
OH.
SORRY.
IT'S OKAY.
HE WAS AN ASSHOLE.

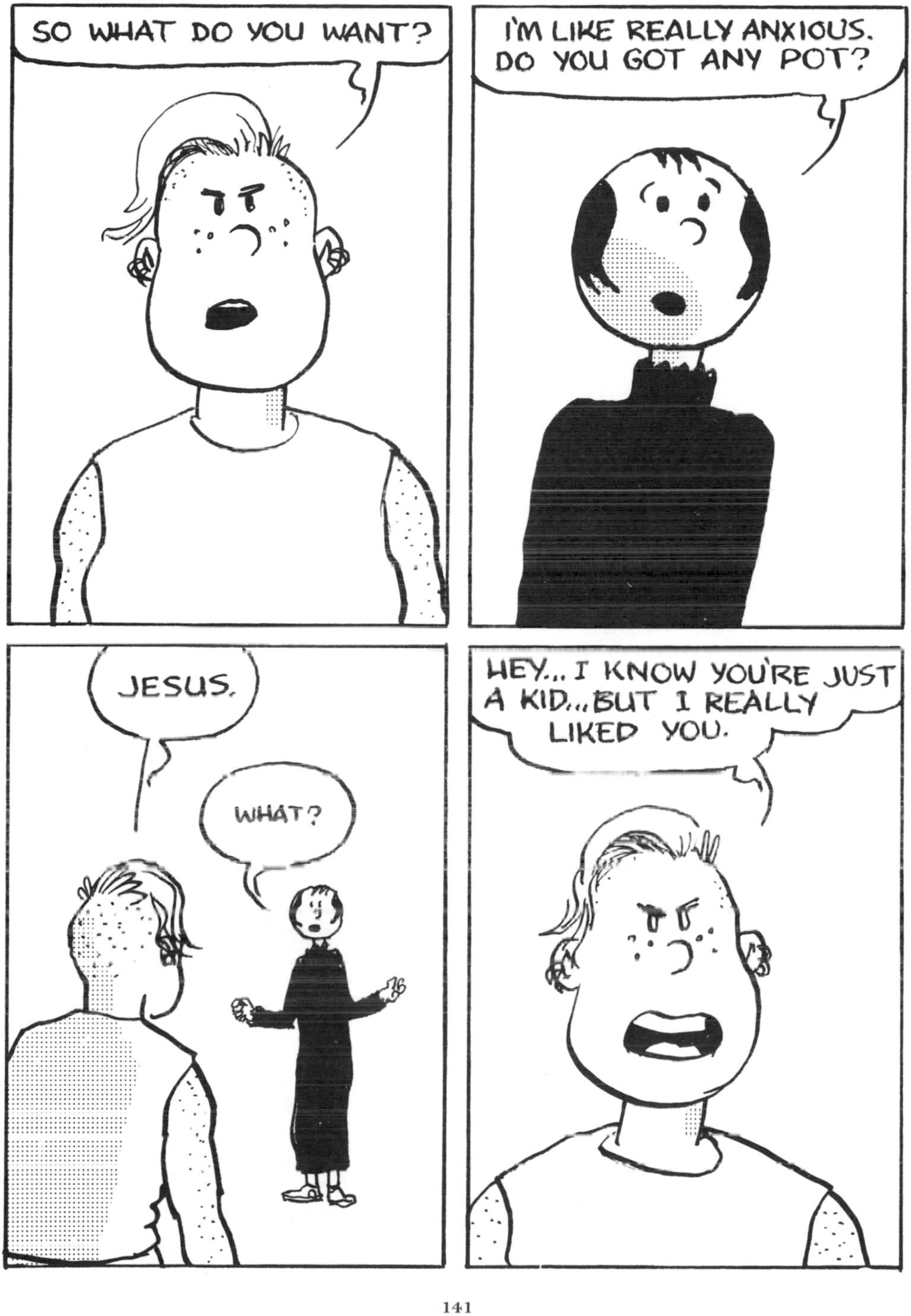
SO WHAT DO YOU WANT?
I'M LIKE REALLY ANXIOUS. DO YOU GOT ANY POT?
JESUS.
WHAT?
HEY... I KNOW YOU'RE JUST A KID...BUT I REALLY LIKED YOU.

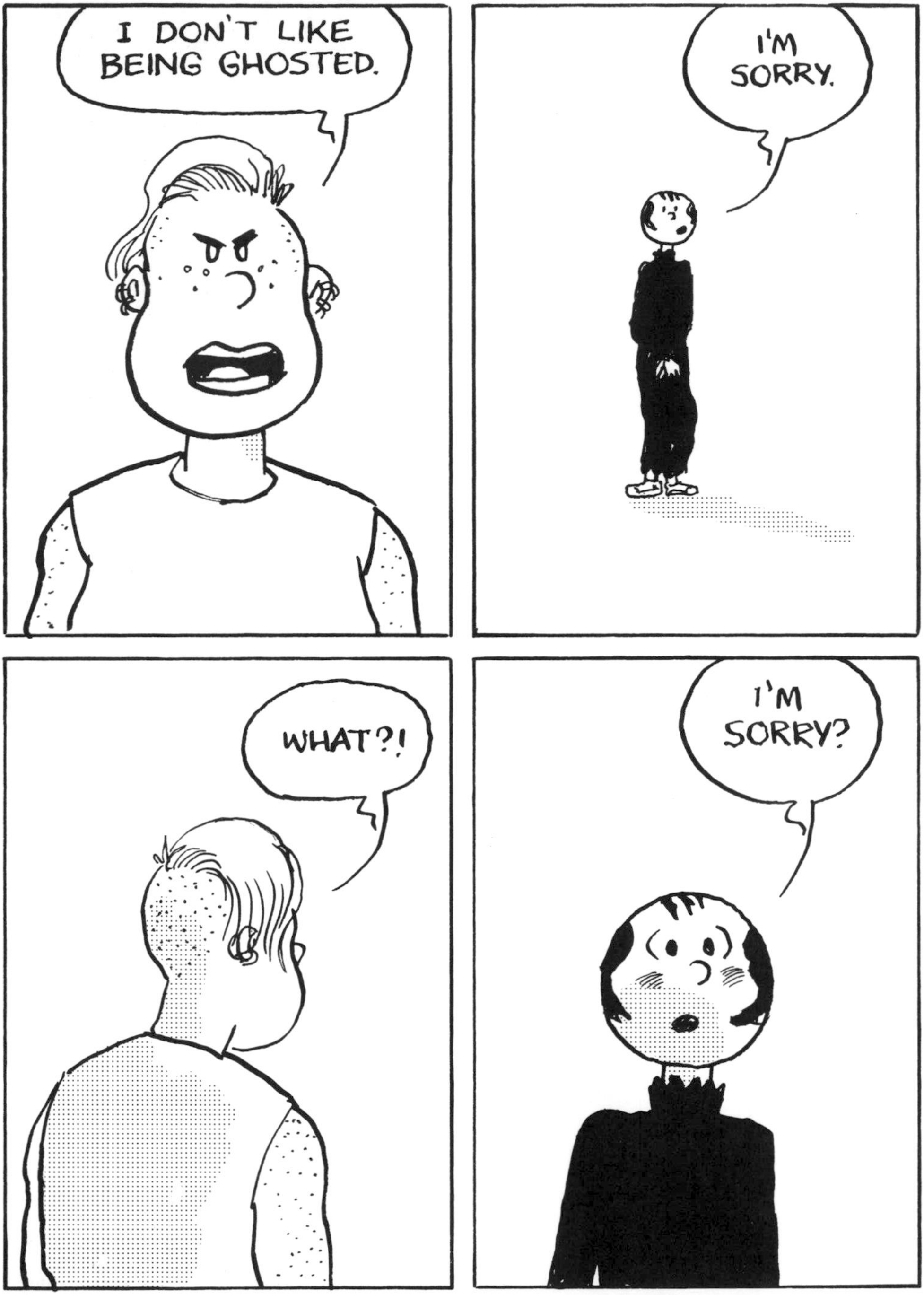
I DON'T LIKE BEING GHOSTED.
I'M SORRY.
WHAT?!
I'M SORRY?

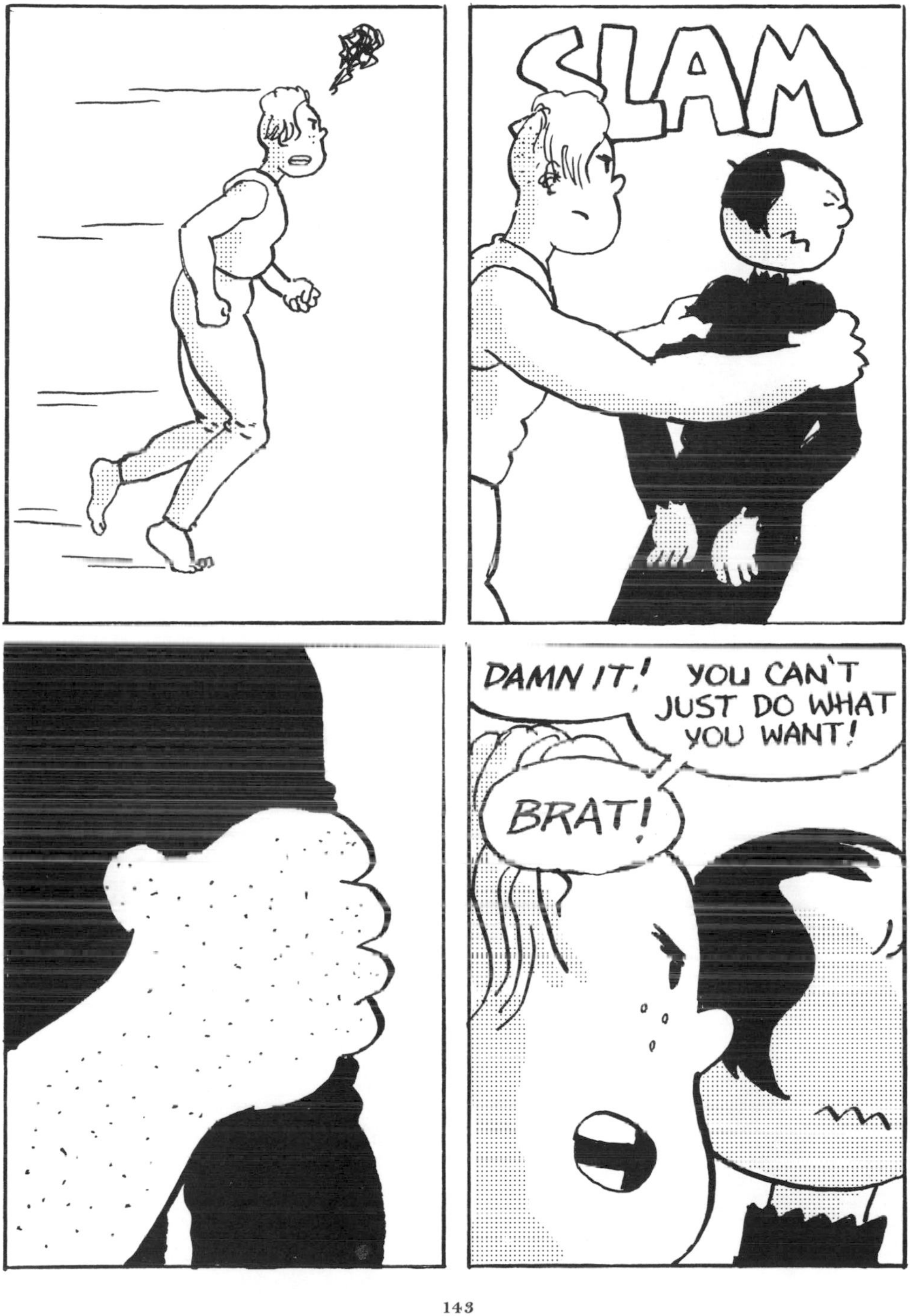
SLAM
DAMN IT! YOU CAN'T JUST DO WHAT YOU WANT!
BRAT!

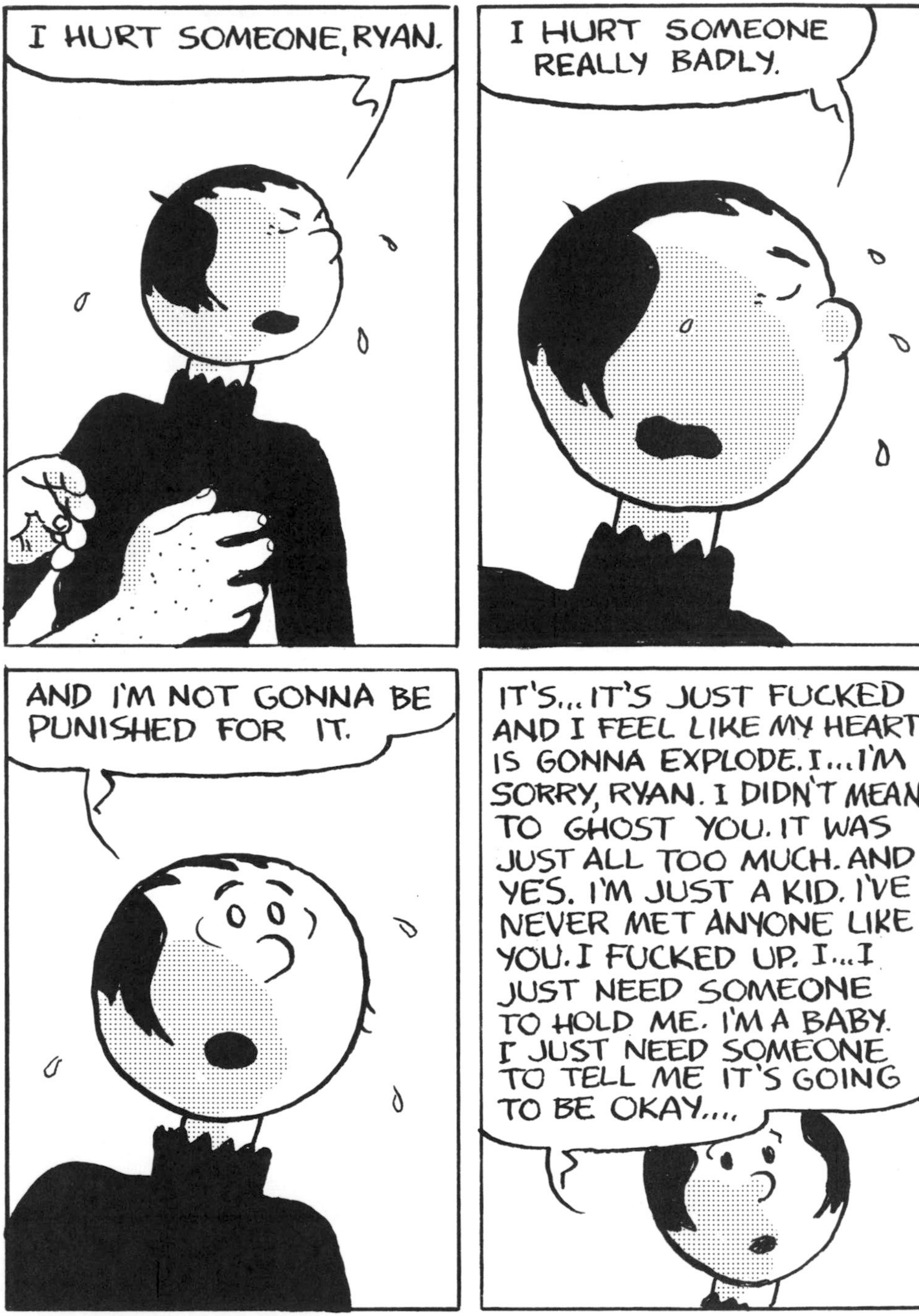
I HURT SOMEONE, RYAN.
I HURT SOMEONE REALLY BADLY.
AND I'M NOT GONNA BE PUNISHED FOR IT.
IT'S... IT'S JUST FUCKED AND I FEEL LIKE MY HEART IS GONNA EXPLODE. I... I'M SORRY, RYAN. I DIDN'T MEAN TO GHOST YOU. IT WAS JUST ALL TOO MUCH. AND YES. I'M JUST A KID. I'VE NEVER MET ANYONE LIKE YOU. I FUCKED UP. I... I JUST NEED SOMEONE TO HOLD ME. I'M A BABY. I JUST NEED SOMEONE TO TELL ME IT'S GOING TO BE OKAY....

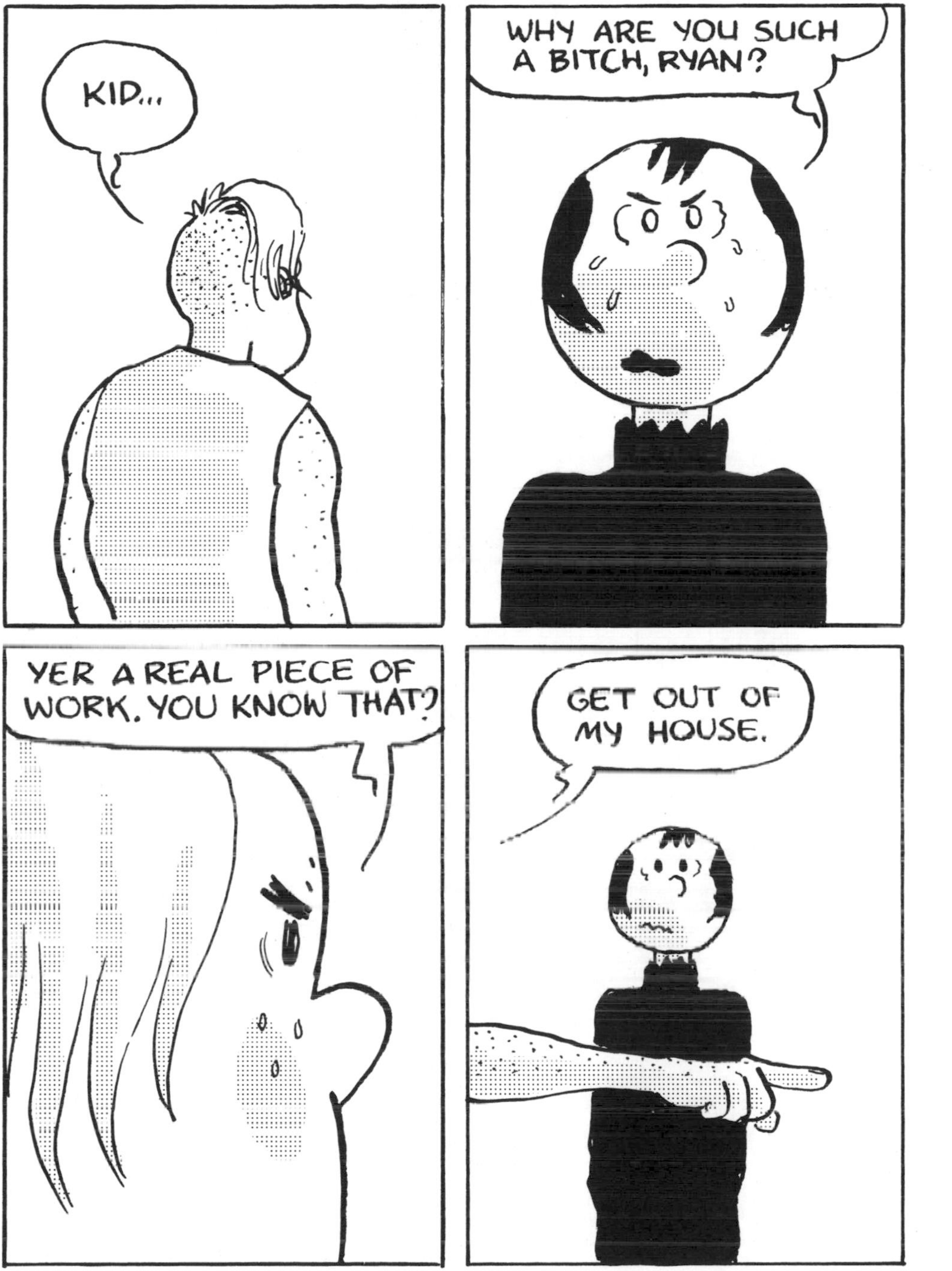
KID...
WHY ARE YOU SUCH A BITCH, RYAN?
YER A REAL PIECE OF WORK. YOU KNOW THAT?
GET OUT OF MY HOUSE.

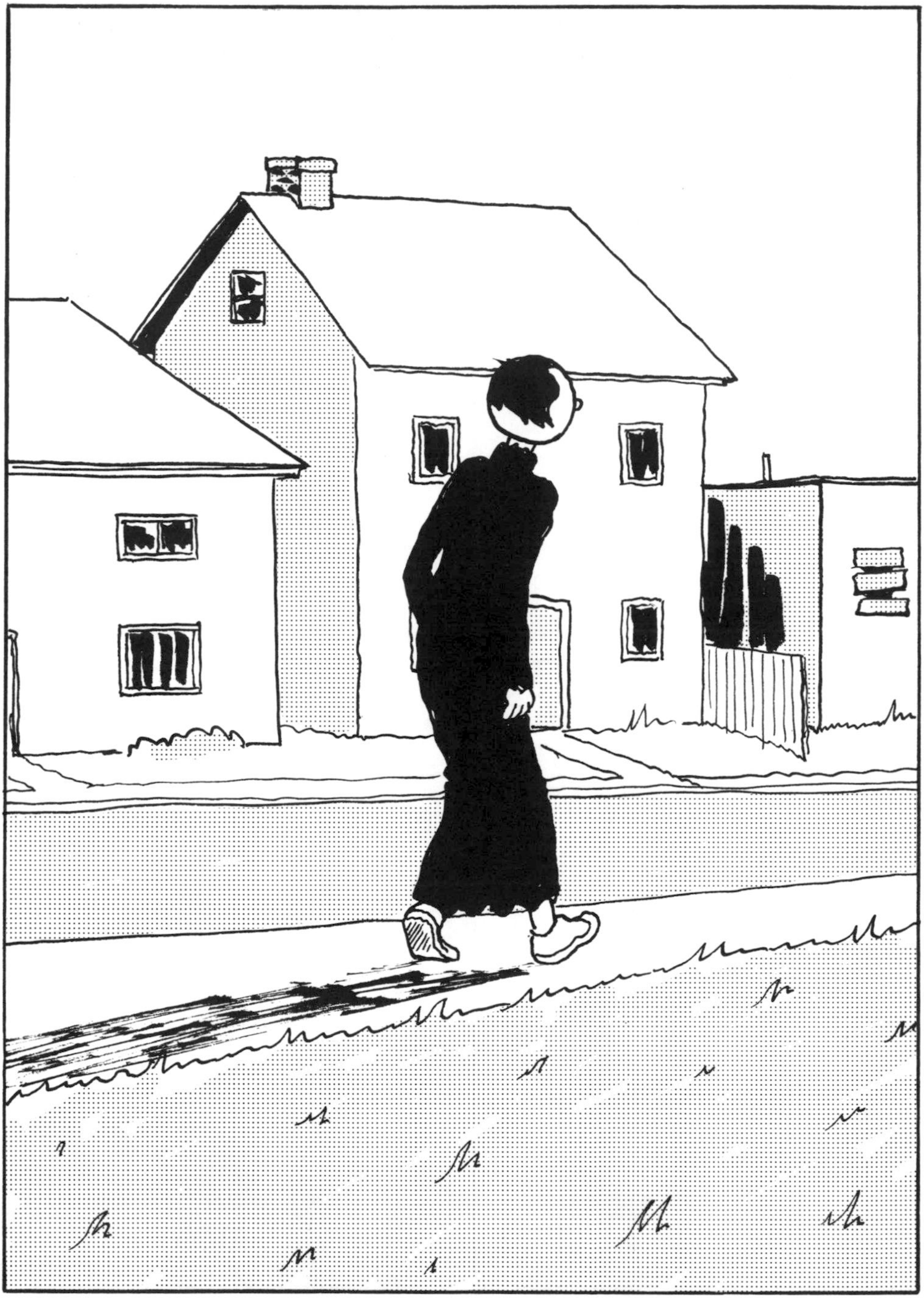

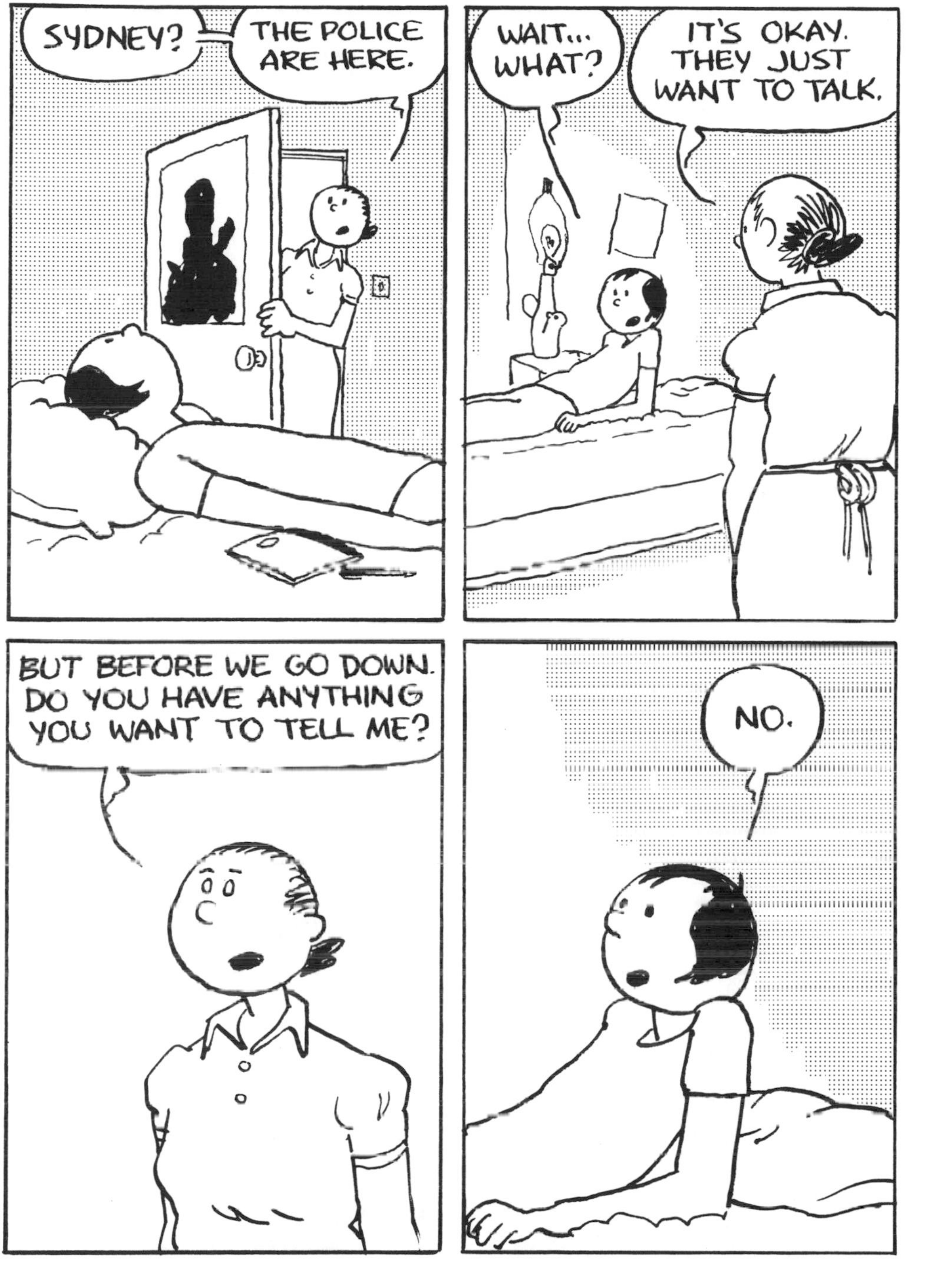
SYDNEY?
THE POLICE ARE HERE.
WAIT... WHAT?
IT'S OKAY. THEY JUST WANT TO TALK.
BUT BEFORE WE GO DOWN. DO YOU HAVE ANYTHING YOU WANT TO TELL ME?
NO.

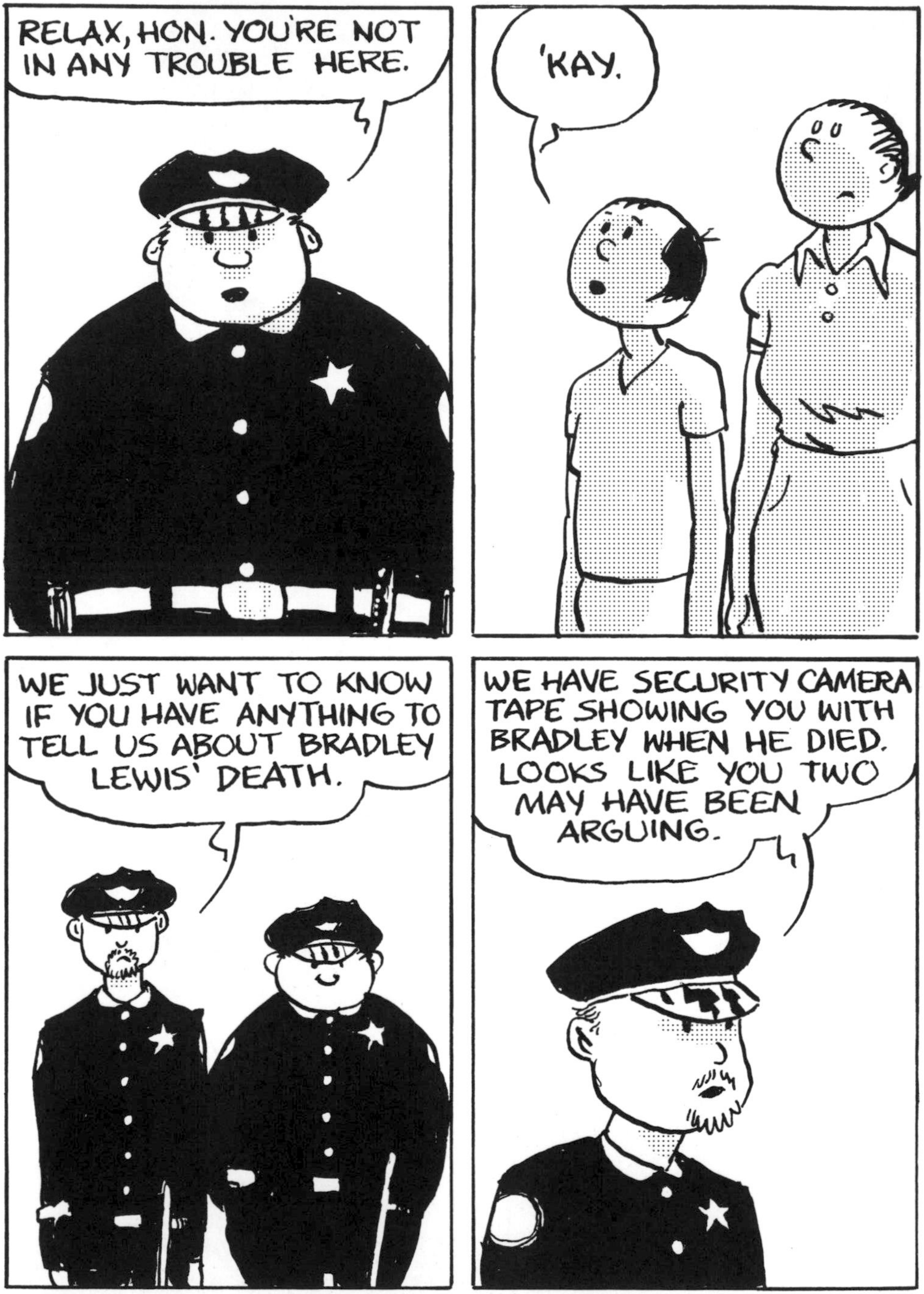
RELAX, HON. YOU'RE NOT IN ANY TROUBLE HERE.
'KAY.
WE JUST WANT TO KNOW IF YOU HAVE ANYTHING TO TELL US ABOUT BRADLEY LEWIS' DEATH.
WE HAVE SECURITY CAMERA TAPE SHOWING YOU WITH BRADLEY WHEN HE DIED. LOOKS LIKE YOU TWO MAY HAVE BEEN ARGUING.

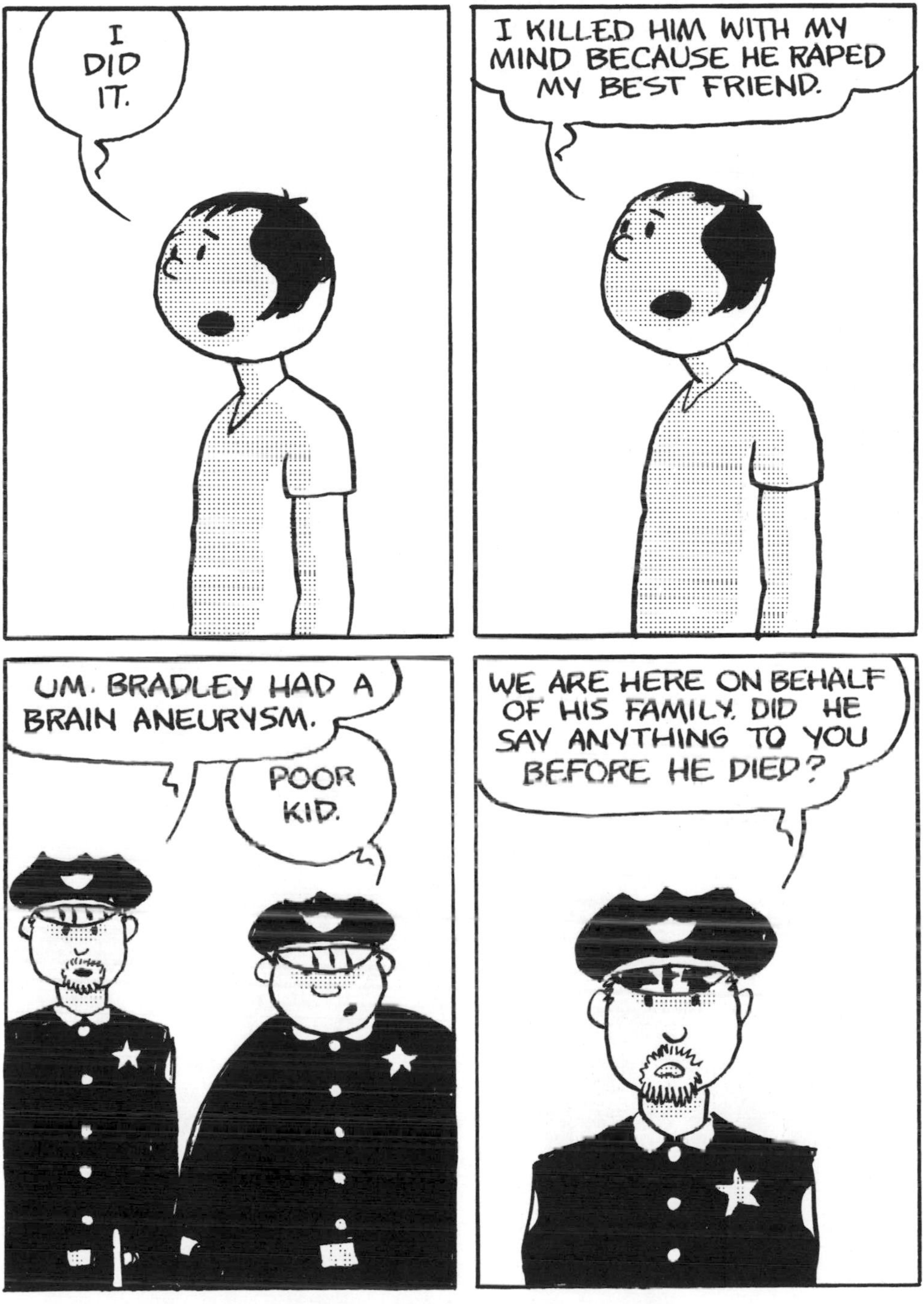
I DID IT.
I KILLED HIM WITH MY MIND BECAUSE HE RAPED MY BEST FRIEND.
UM. BRADLEY HAD A BRAIN ANEURYSM.
POOR KID.
WE ARE HERE ON BEHALF OF HIS FAMILY. DID HE SAY ANYTHING TO YOU BEFORE HE DIED?

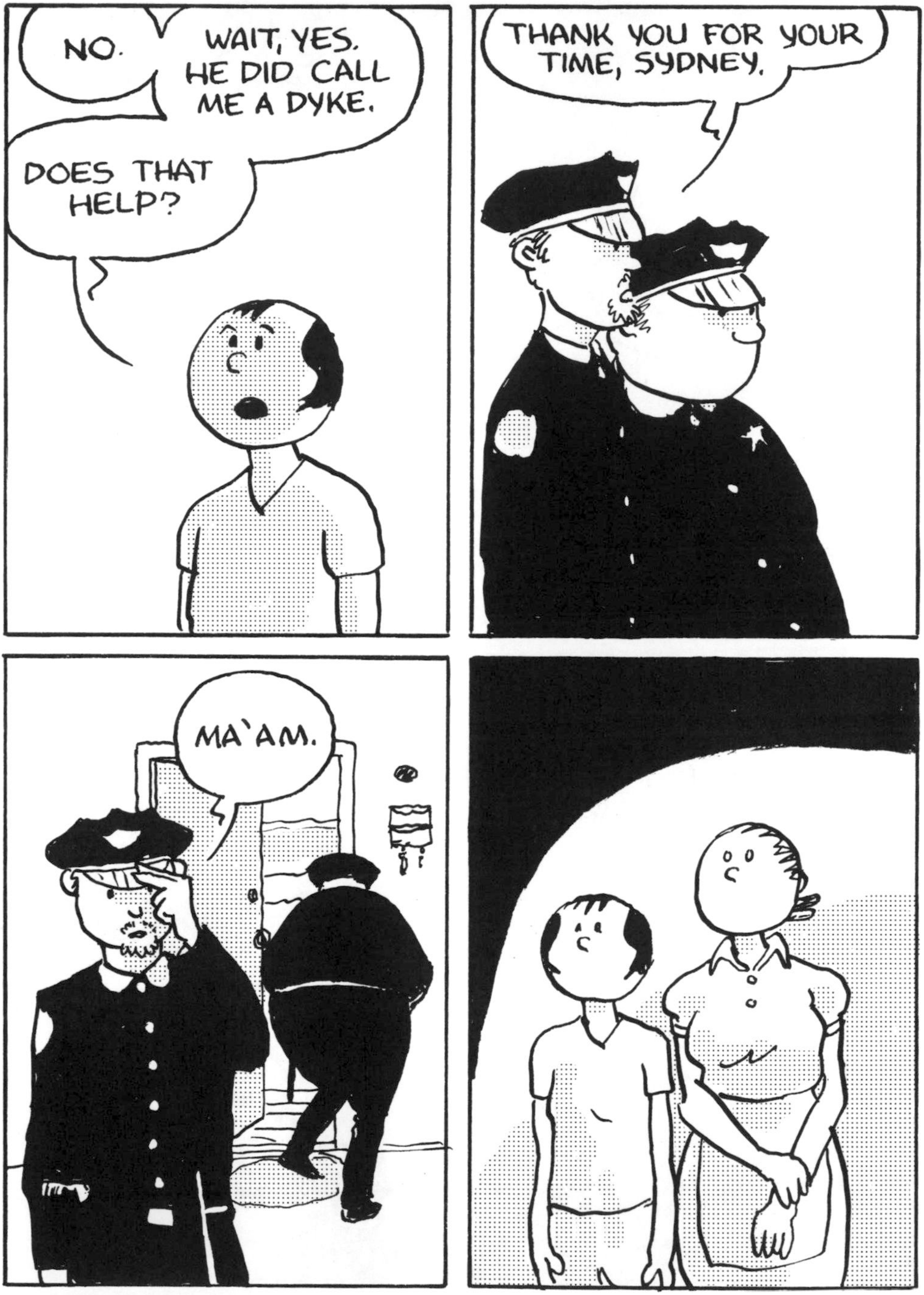
NO.
WAIT, YES. HE DID CALL ME A DYKE.
DOES THAT HELP?
THANK YOU FOR YOUR TIME, SYDNEY.
MA'AM.

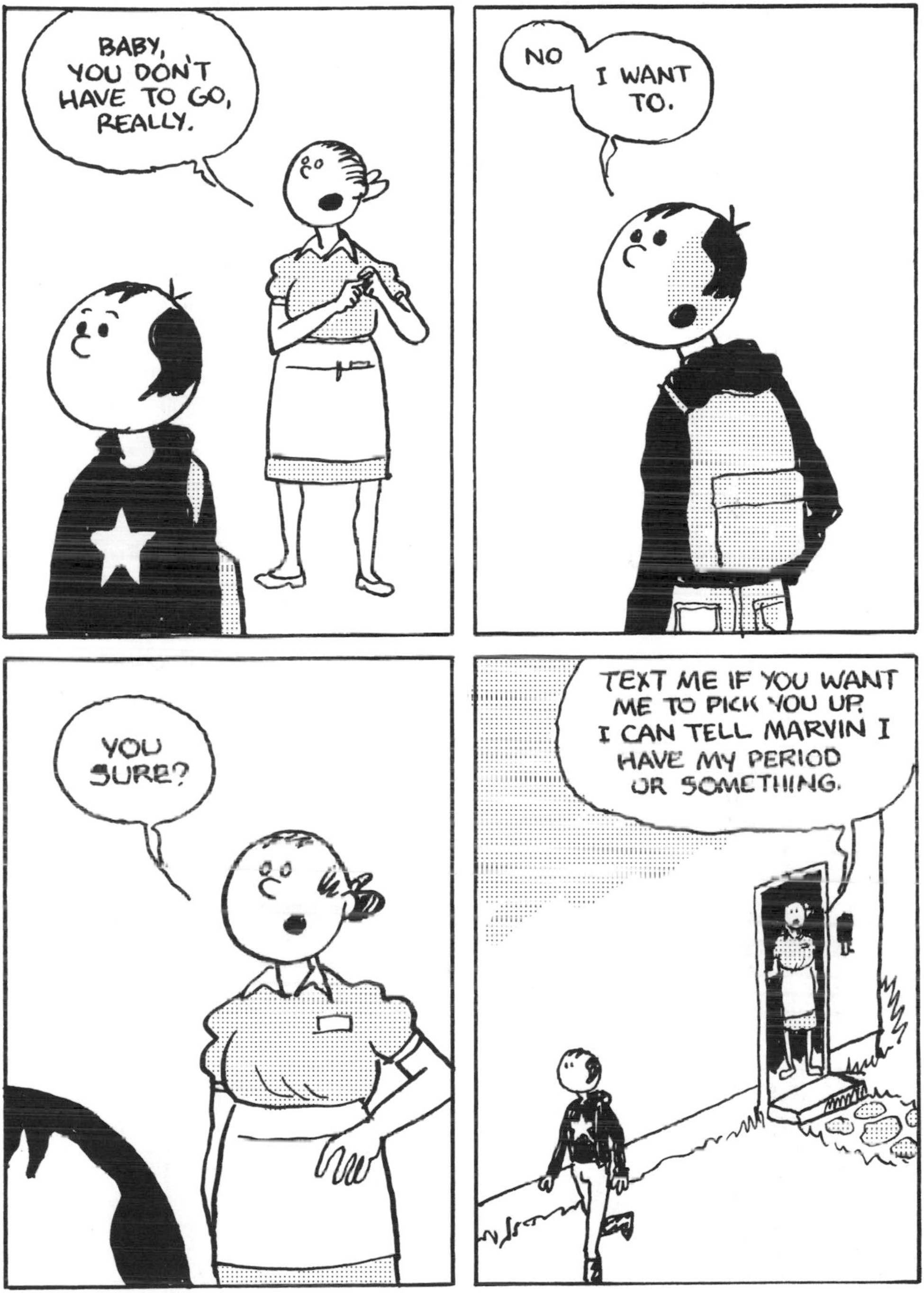
BABY, YOU DON'T HAVE TO GO, REALLY.
NO
I WANT TO.
YOU SURE?
TEXT ME IF YOU WANT ME TO PICK YOU UP. I CAN TELL MARVIN I HAVE MY PERIOD OR SOMETHING.

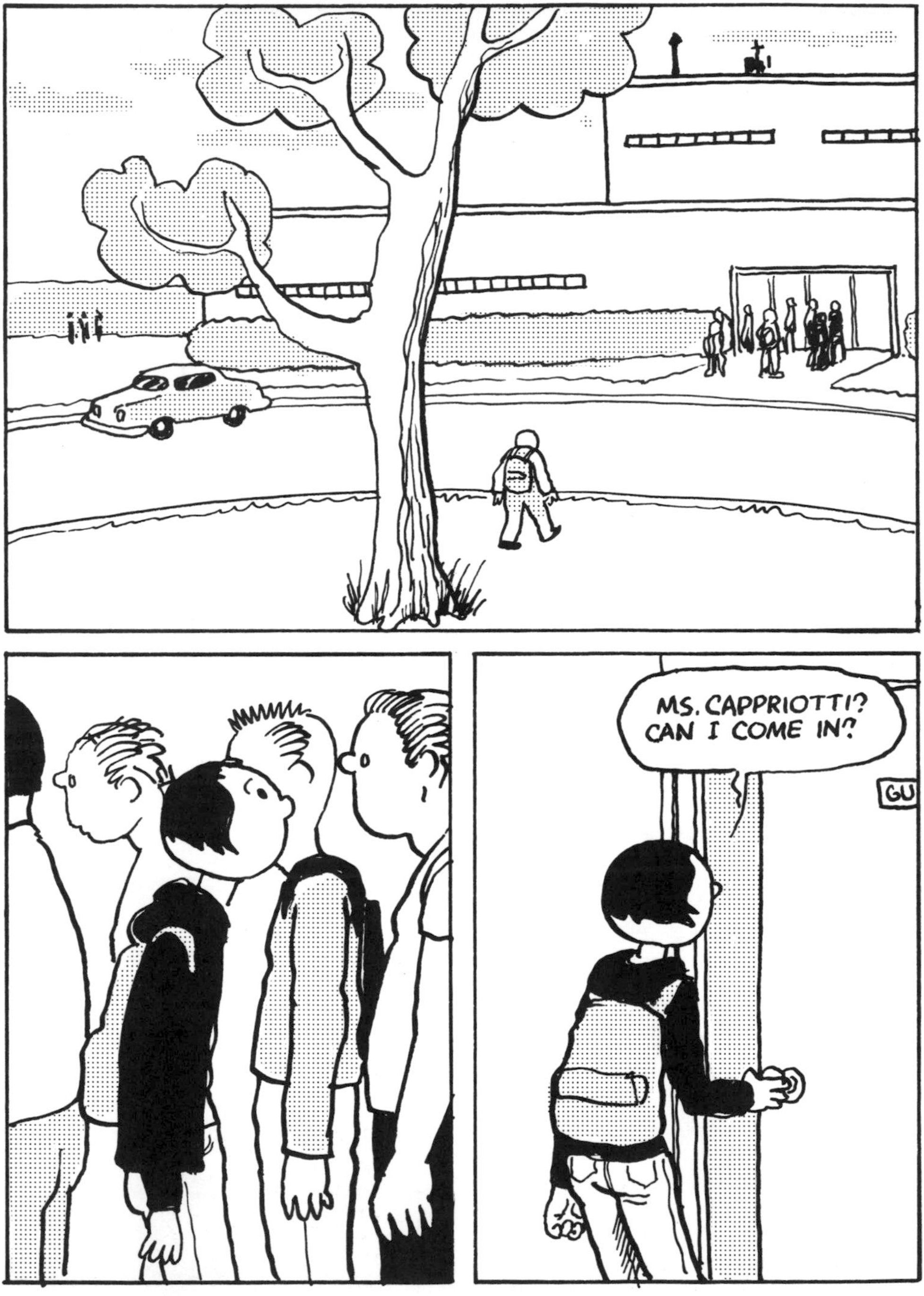
MS. CAPPRIOTTI? CAN I COME IN?
GU

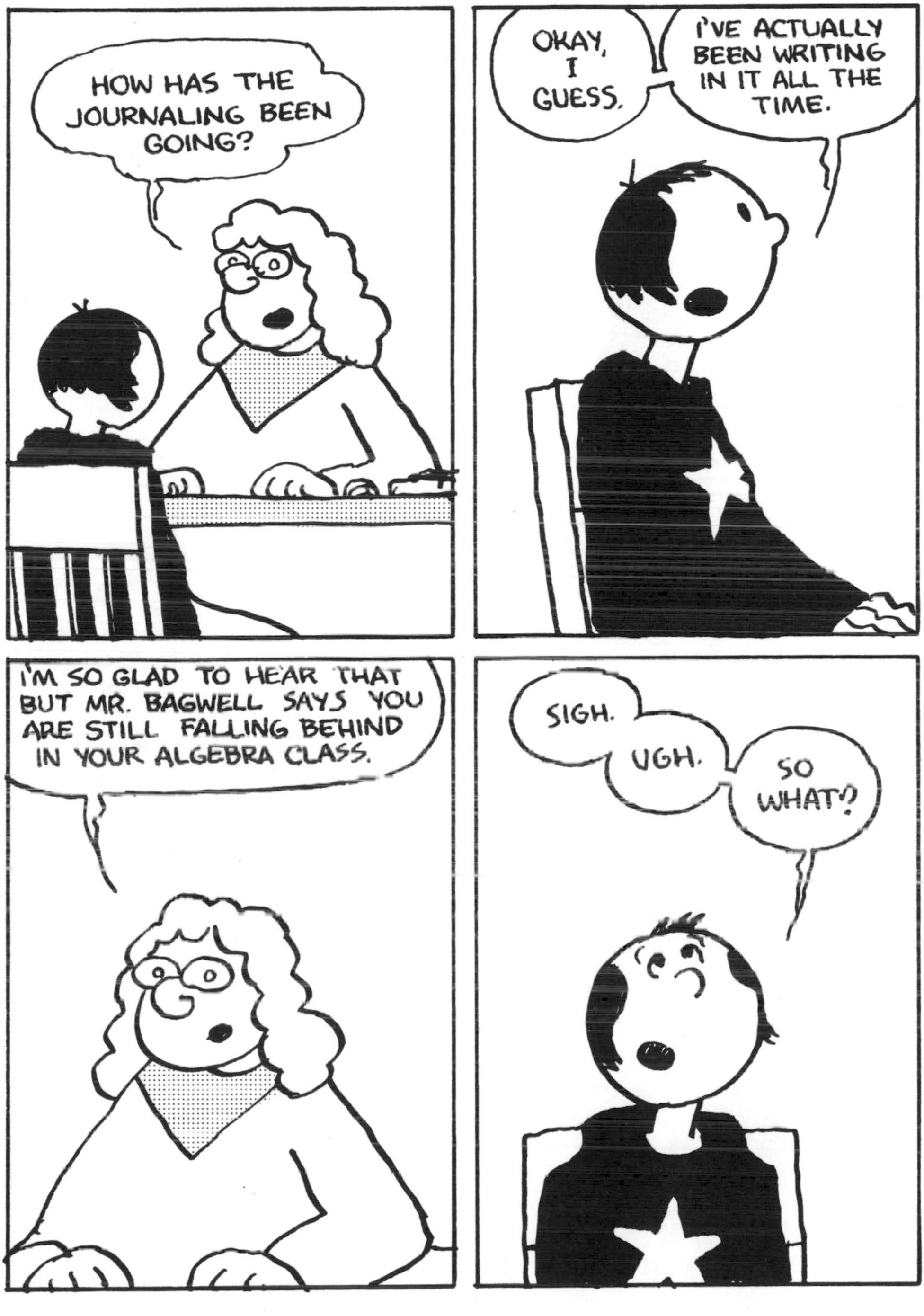
HOW HAS THE JOURNALING BEEN GOING?
OKAY, I GUESS.
I'VE ACTUALLY BEEN WRITING IN IT ALL THE TIME.
I'M SO GLAD TO HEAR THAT BUT MR. BAGWELL SAYS YOU ARE STILL FALLING BEHIND IN YOUR ALGEBRA CLASS.
SIGH.
UGH.
SO WHAT?

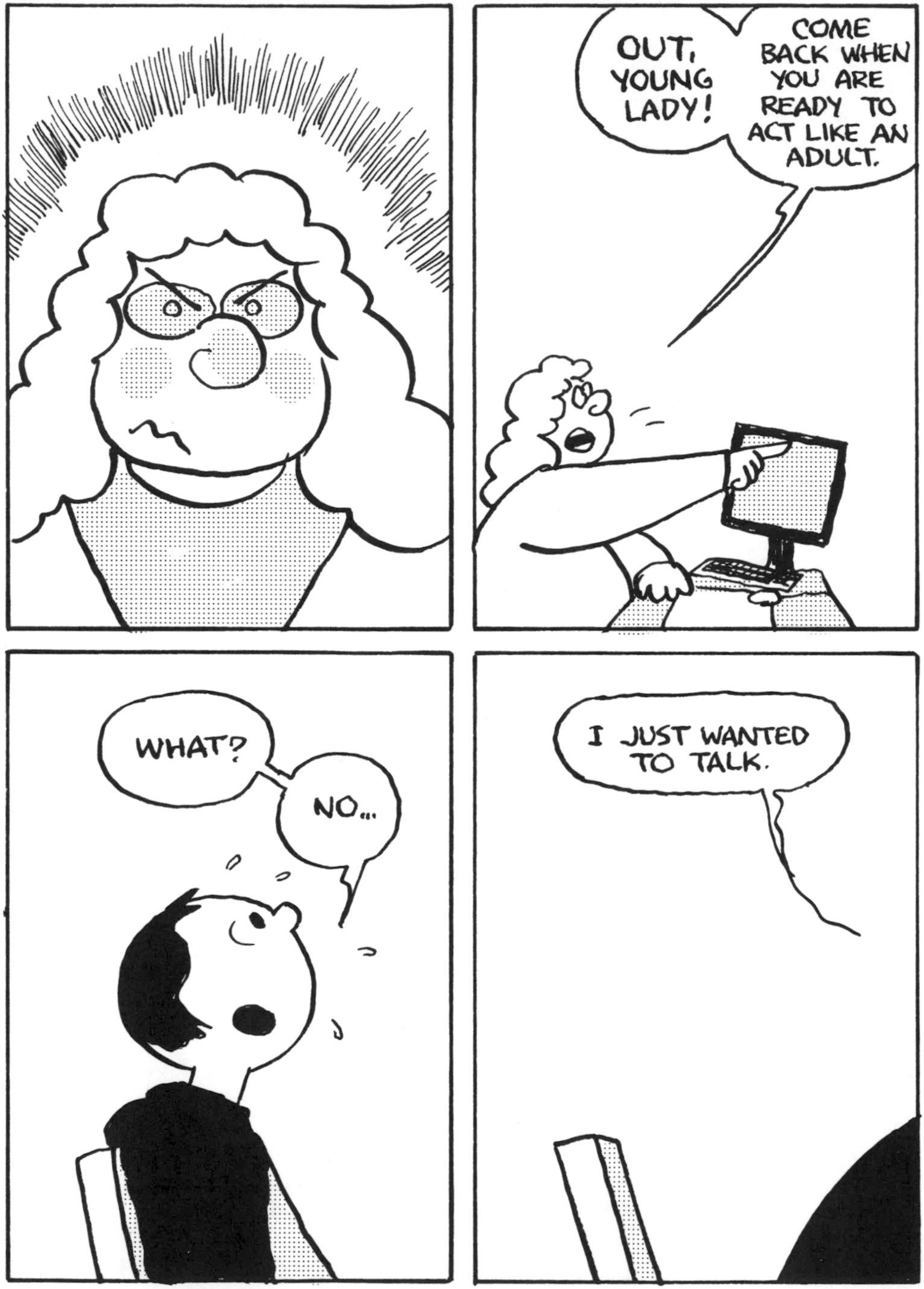
OUT, YOUNG LADY!
COME BACK WHEN YOU ARE READY TO ACT LIKE AN ADULT.
WHAT?
NO...
I JUST WANTED TO TALK.

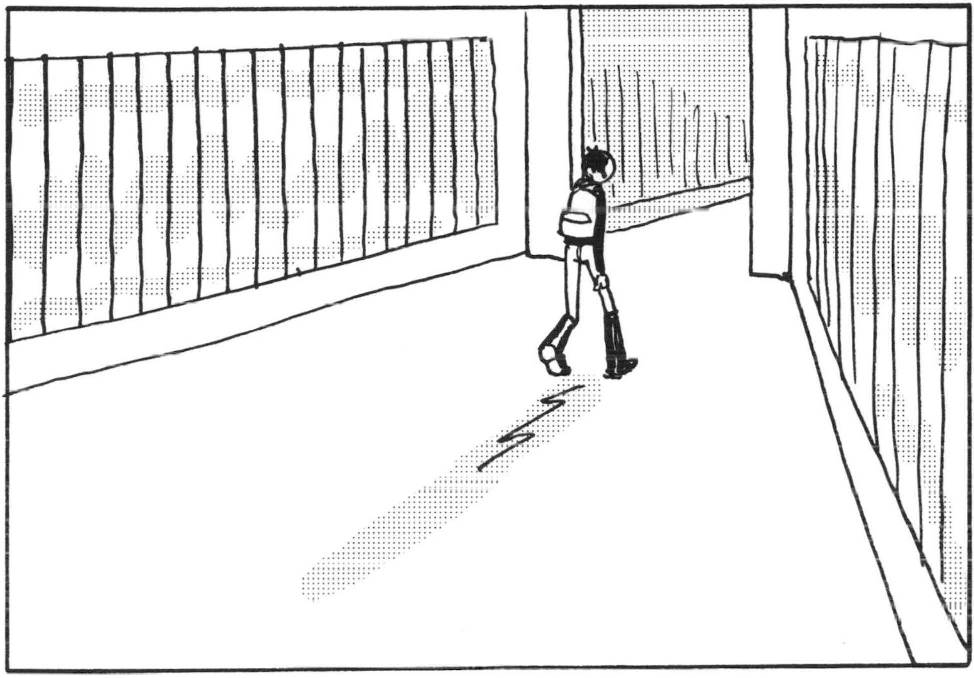

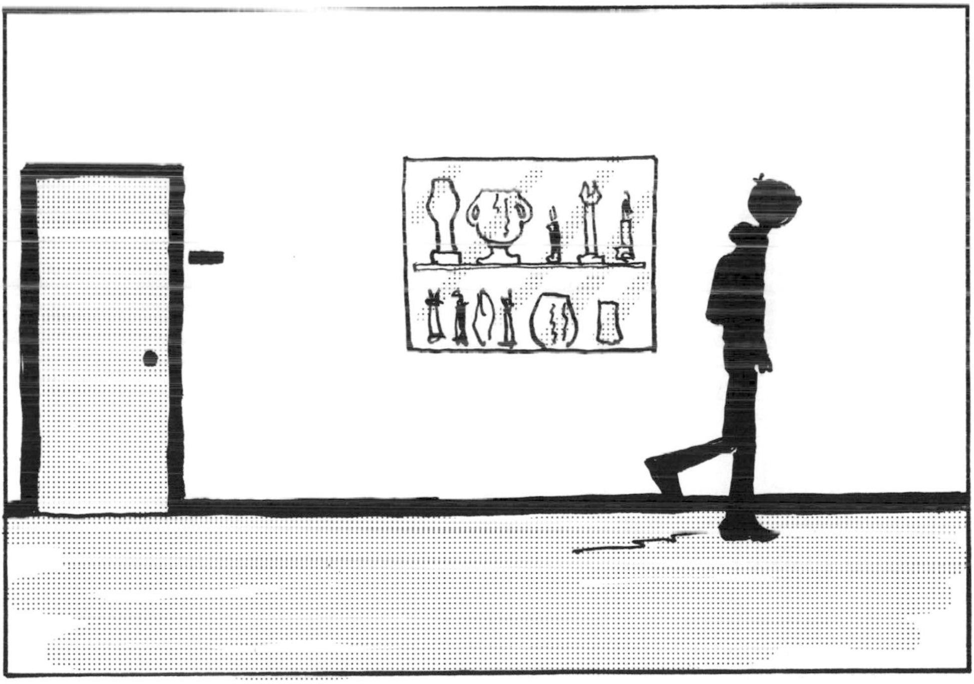

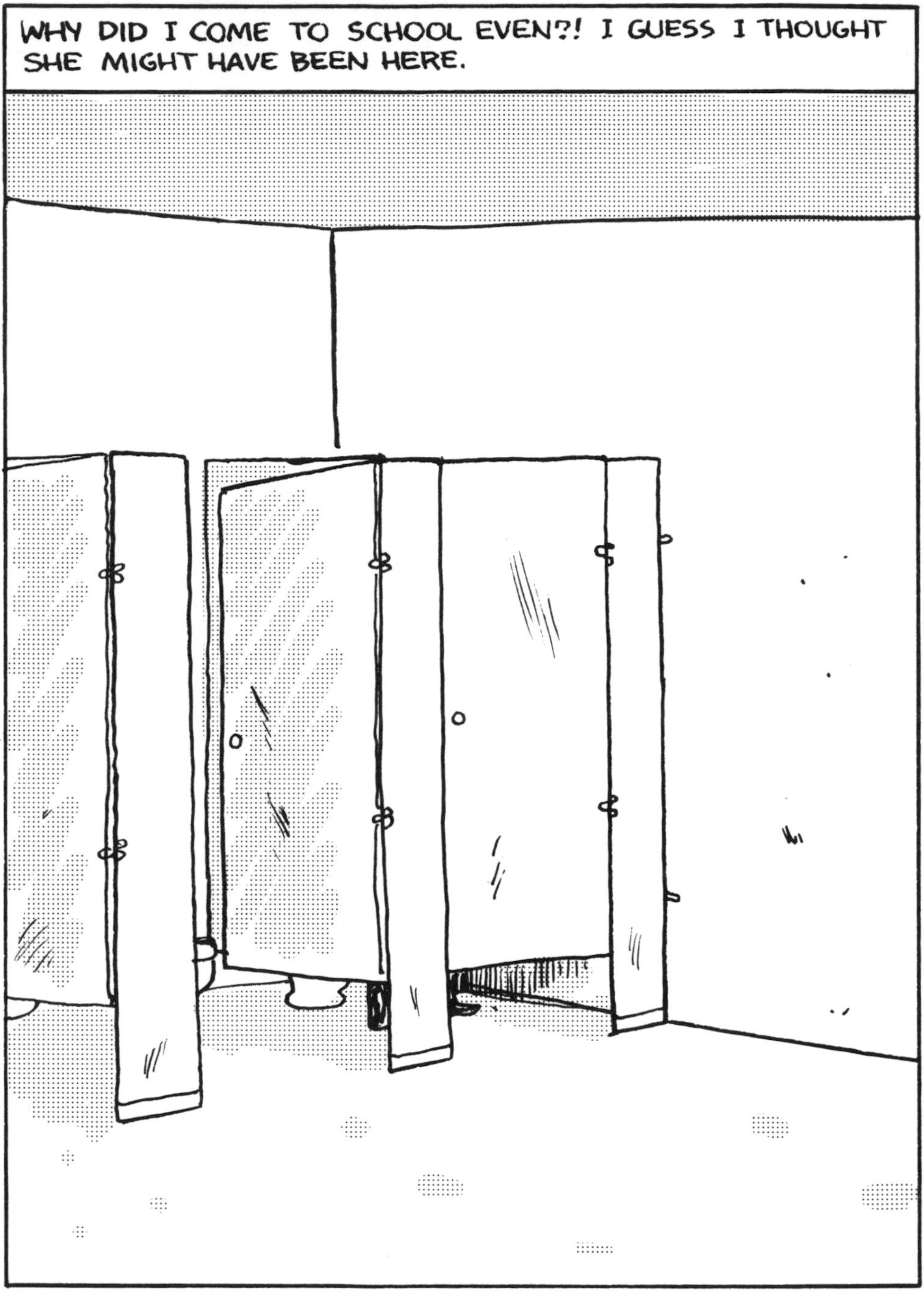
WHY DID I COME TO SCHOOL EVEN?! I GUESS I THOUGHT SHE MIGHT HAVE BEEN HERE.

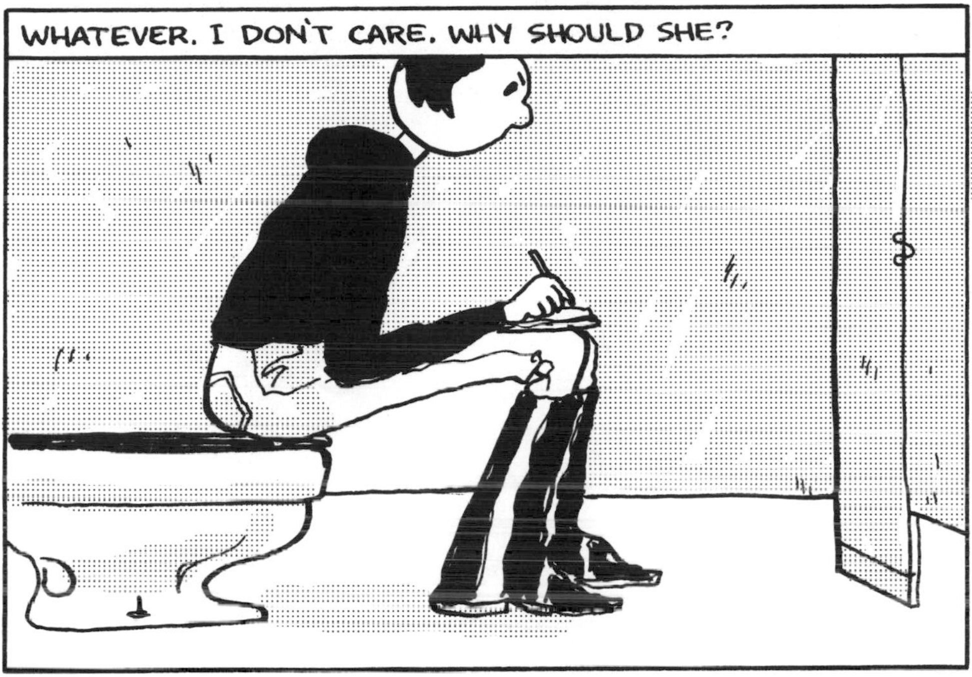
WHATEVER. I DON'T CARE. WHY SHOULD SHE?

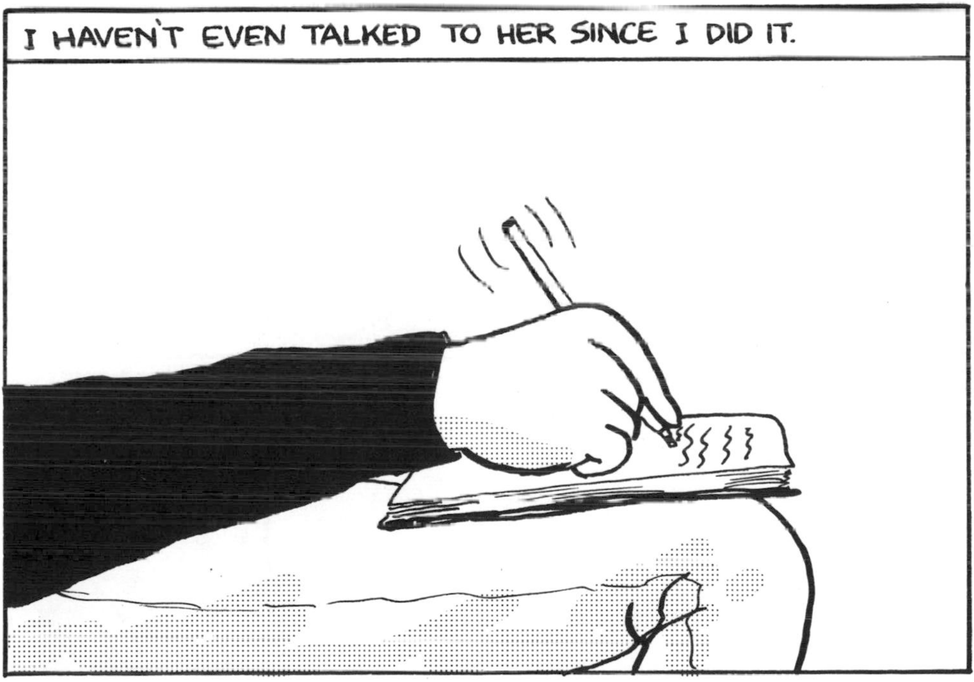
I HAVEN'T EVEN TALKED TO HER SINCE I DID IT.

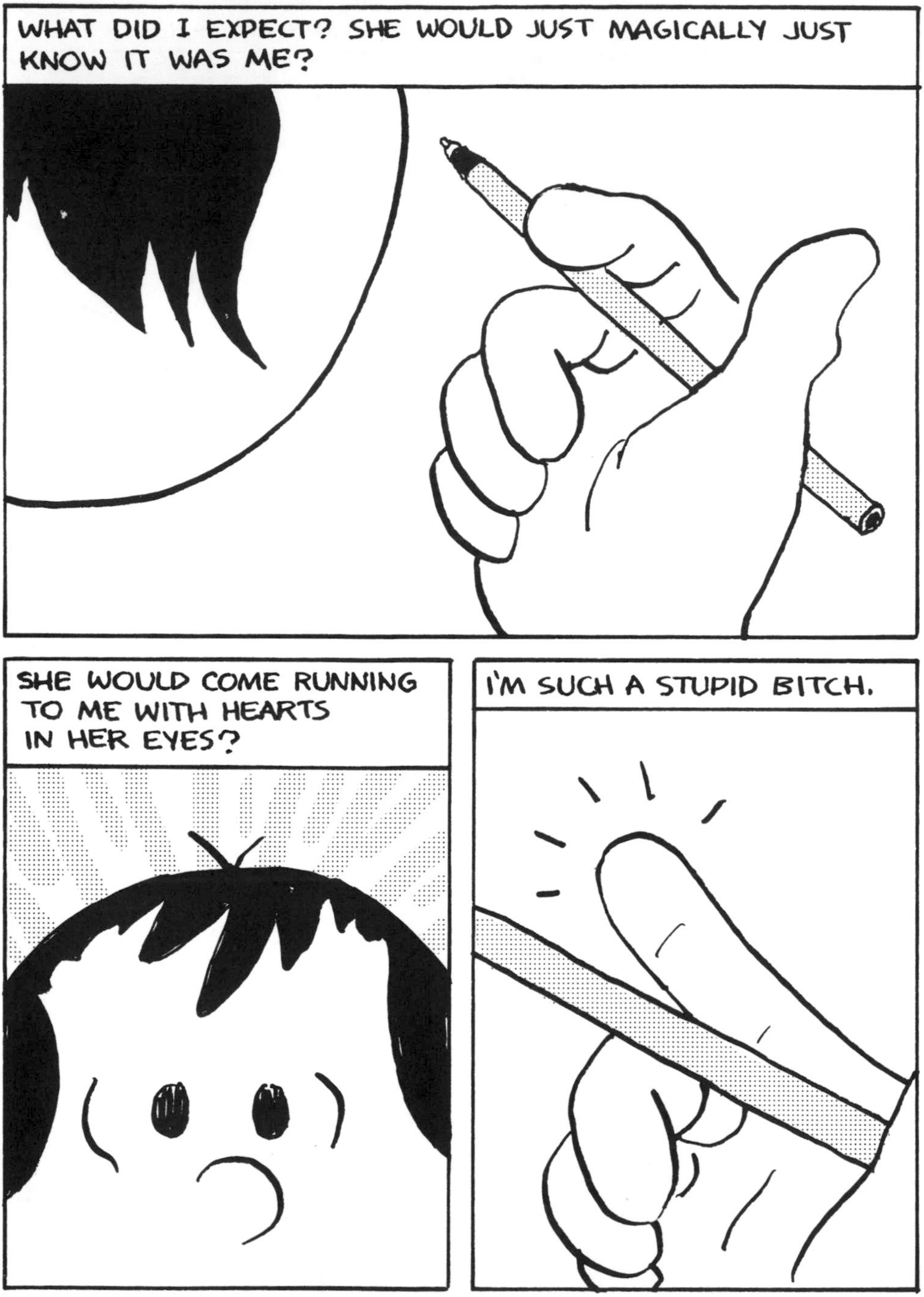
WHAT DID I EXPECT? SHE WOULD JUST MAGICALLY JUST KNOW IT WAS ME?
SHE WOULD COME RUNNING TO ME WITH HEARTS IN HER EYES?
I'M SUCH A STUPID BITCH.

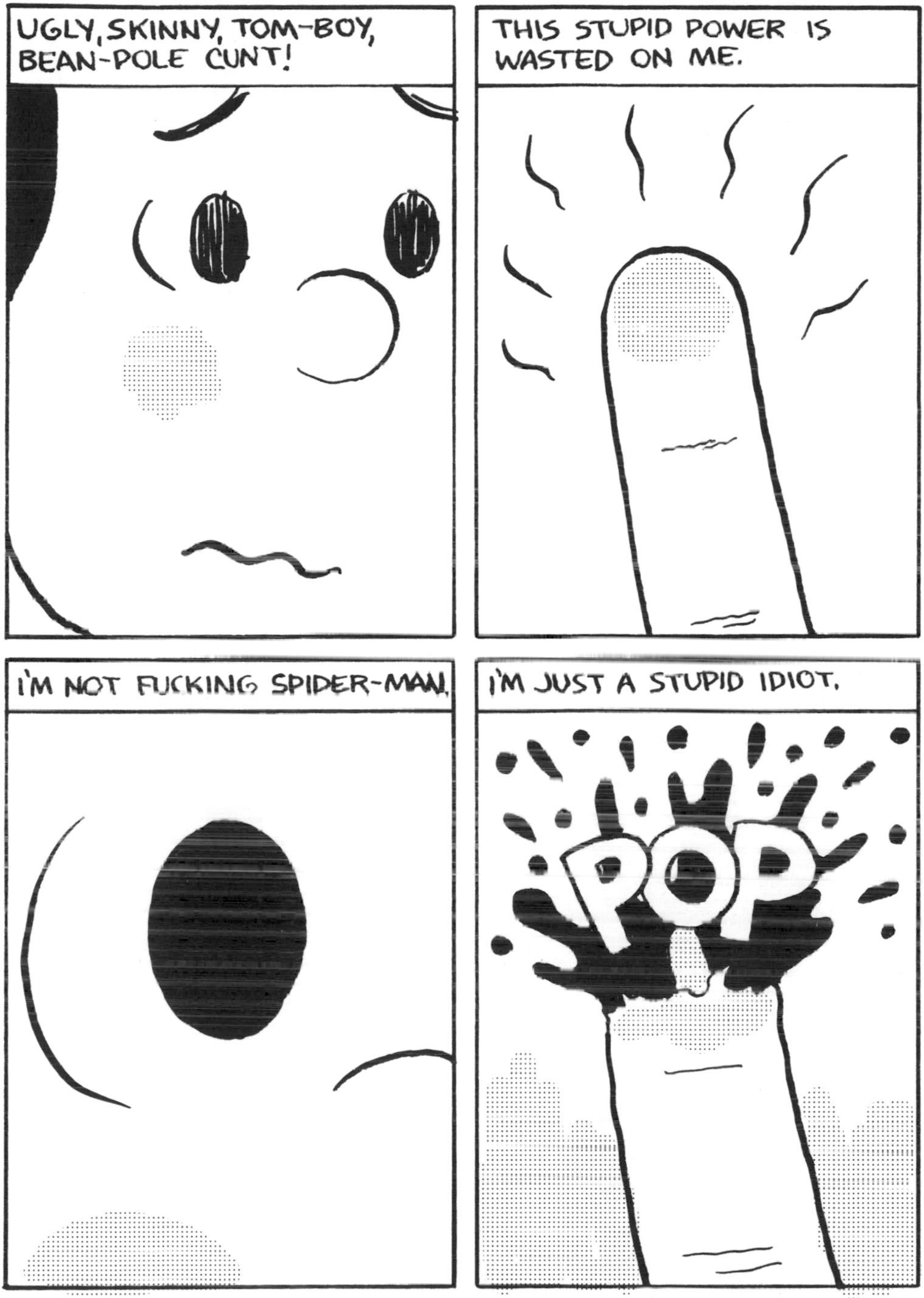
UGLY, SKINNY, TOM-BOY, BEAN-POLE CUNT!
THIS STUPID POWER IS WASTED ON ME.
I'M NOT FUCKING SPIDER-MAN.
I'M JUST A STUPID IDIOT.
POP

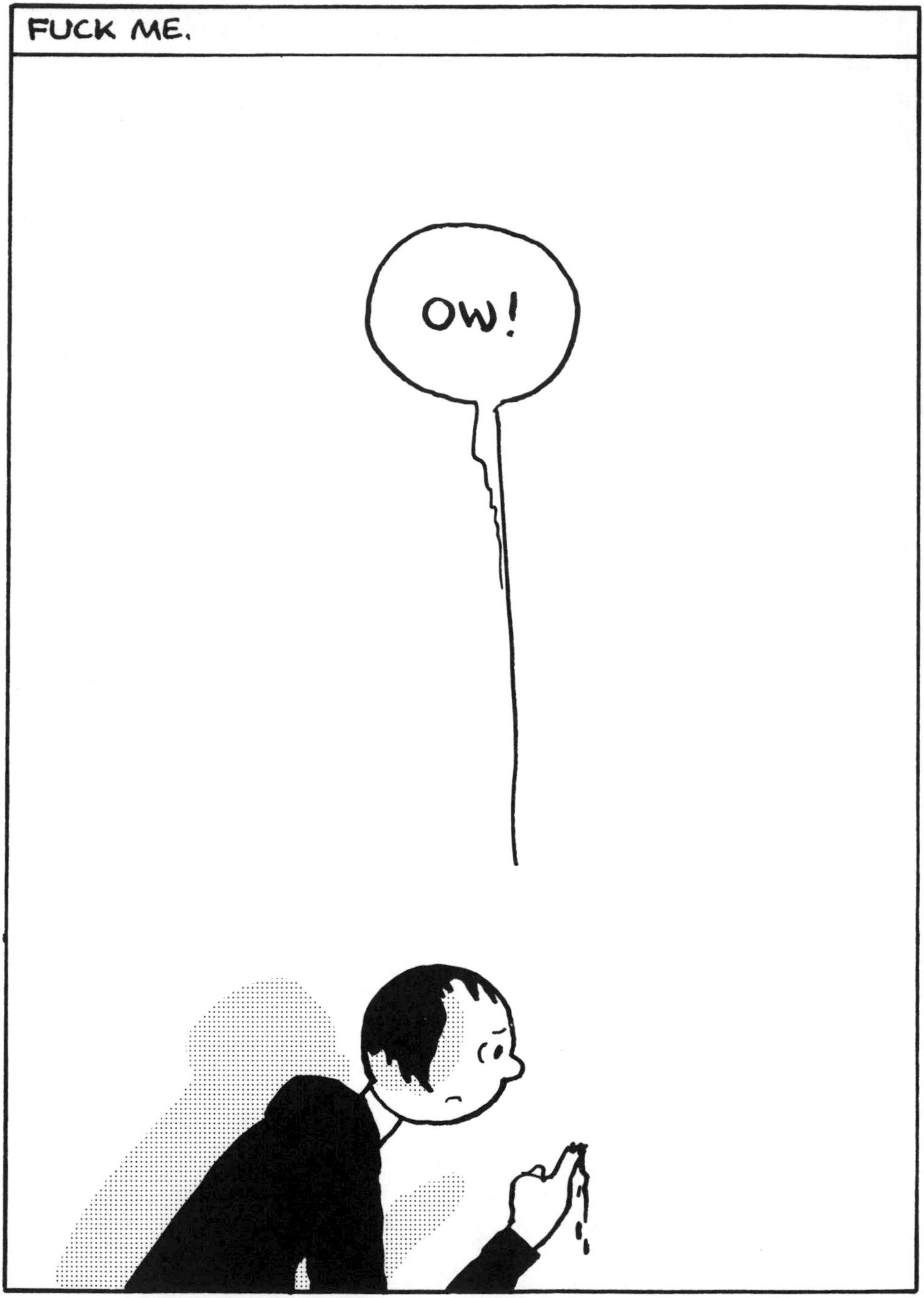
FUCK ME.
OW!

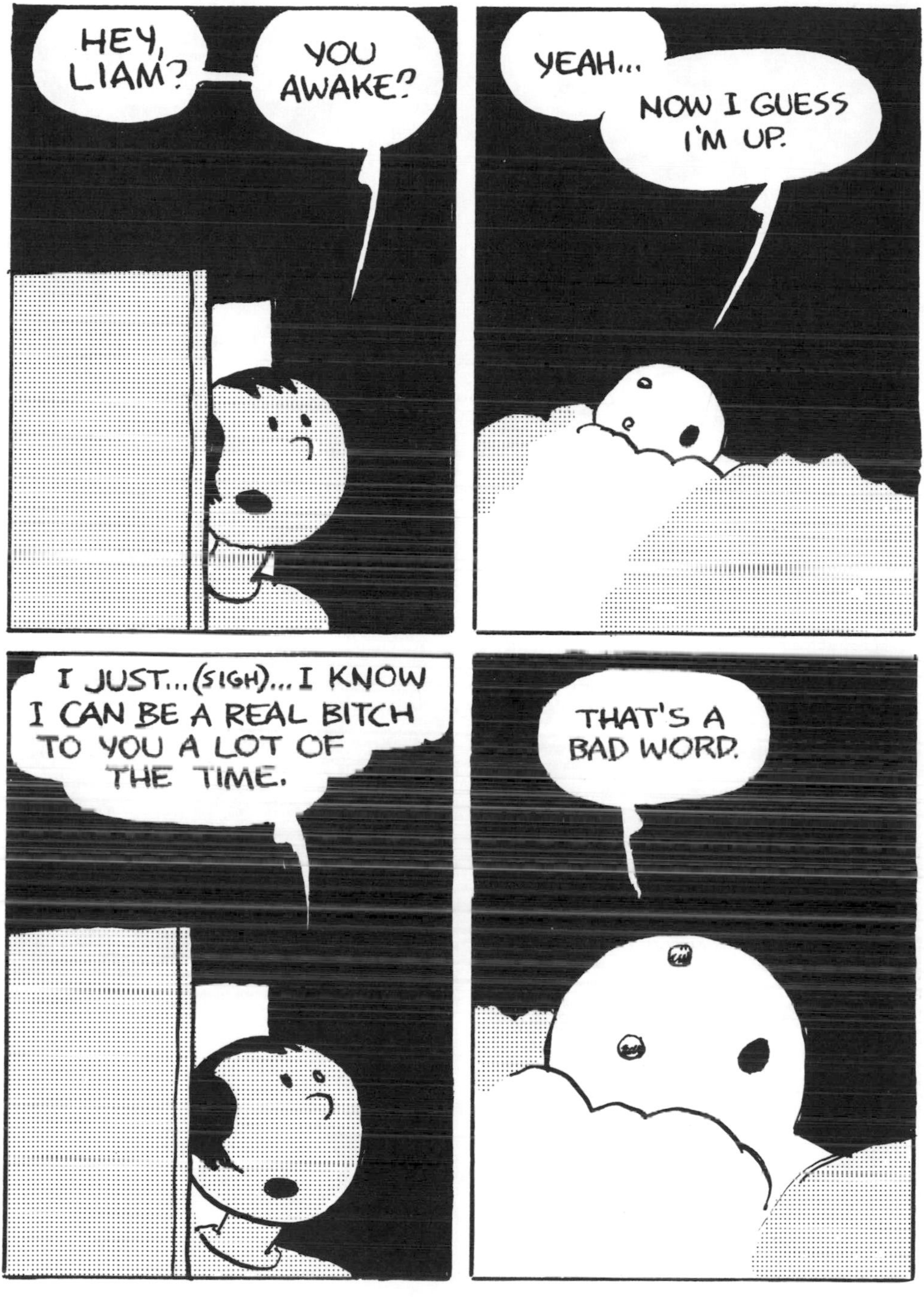
HEY, LIAM?
YOU AWAKE?
YEAH...
NOW I GUESS I'M UP.
I JUST...(SIGH)...I KNOW I CAN BE A REAL BITCH TO YOU A LOT OF THE TIME.
THAT'S A BAD WORD.

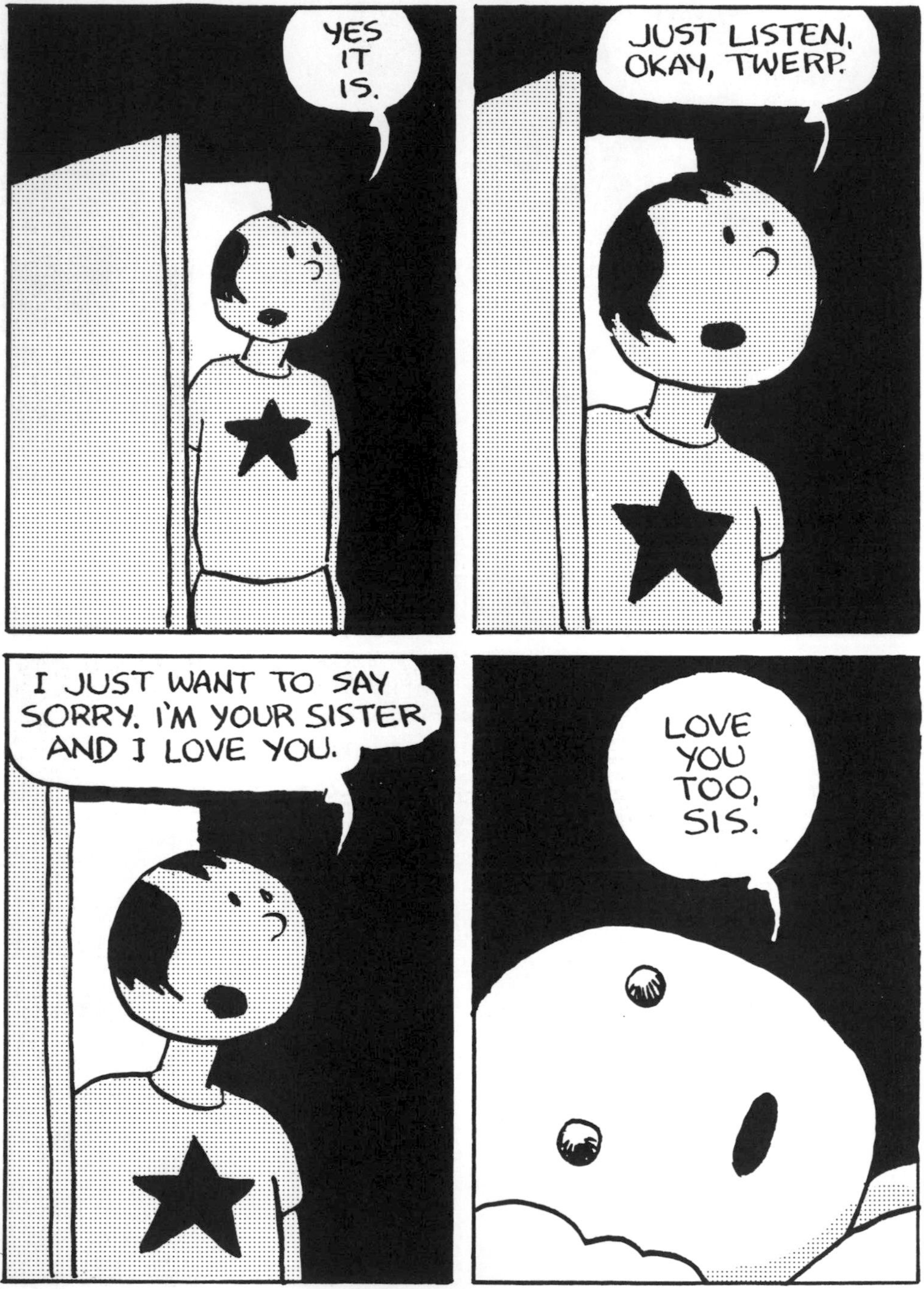
YES IT IS.
JUST LISTEN, OKAY, TWERP.
I JUST WANT TO SAY SORRY. I'M YOUR SISTER AND I LOVE YOU.
LOVE YOU TOO, SIS.

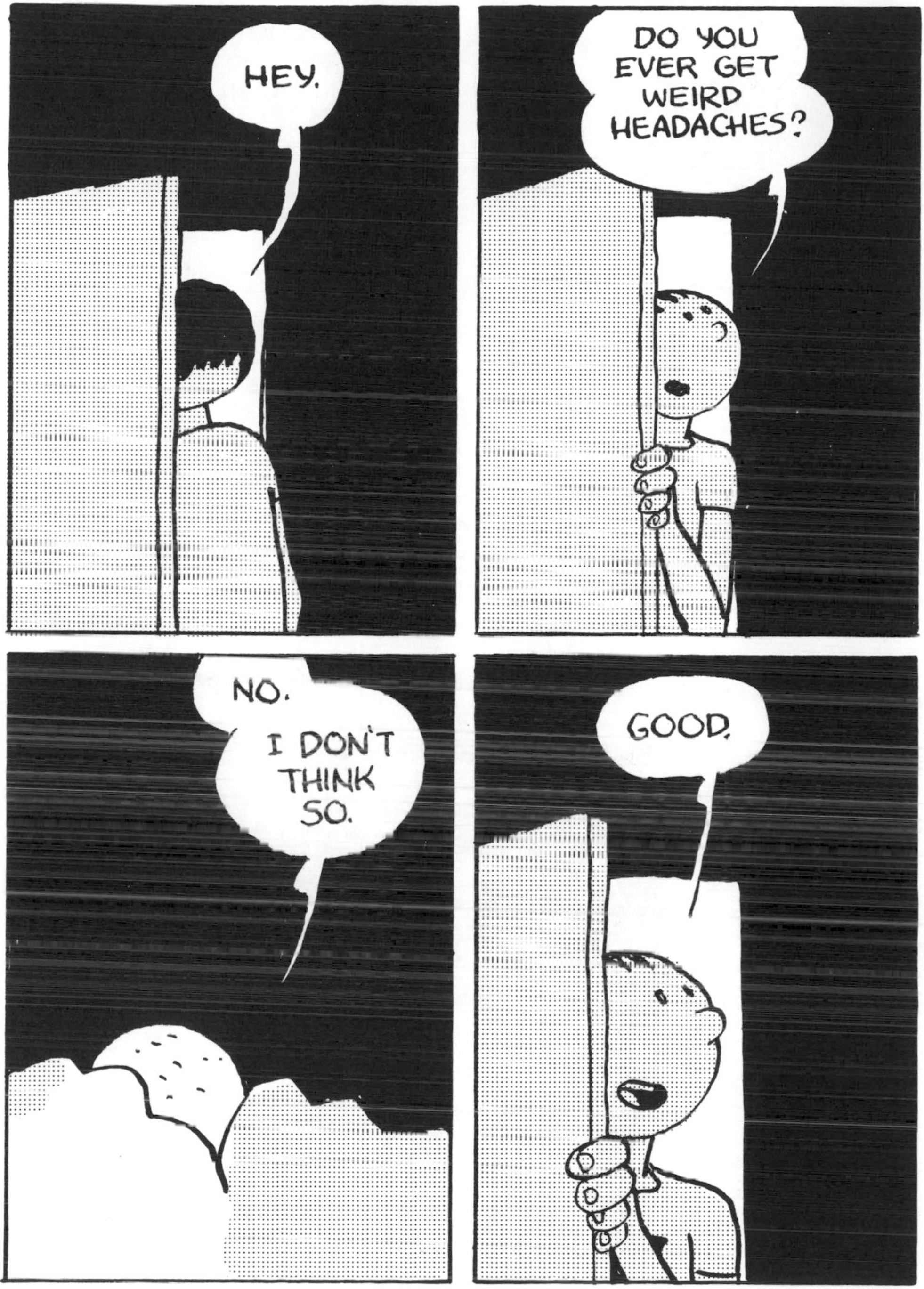
HEY.
DO YOU EVER GET WEIRD HEADACHES?
NO.
I DON'T THINK SO.
GOOD.

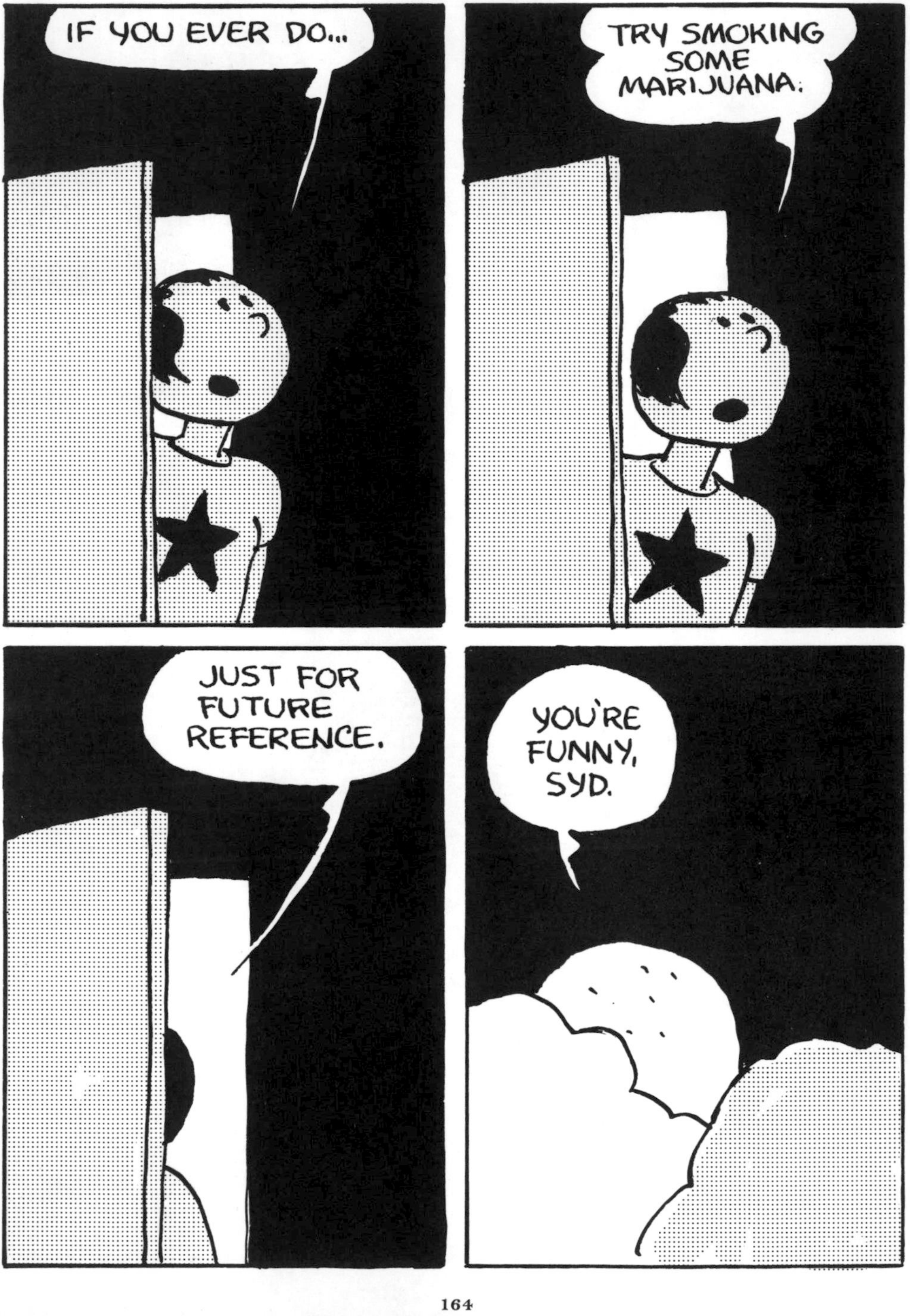
IF YOU EVER DO...
TRY SMOKING SOME MARIJUANA.
JUST FOR FUTURE REFERENCE.
YOU'RE FUNNY, SYD.

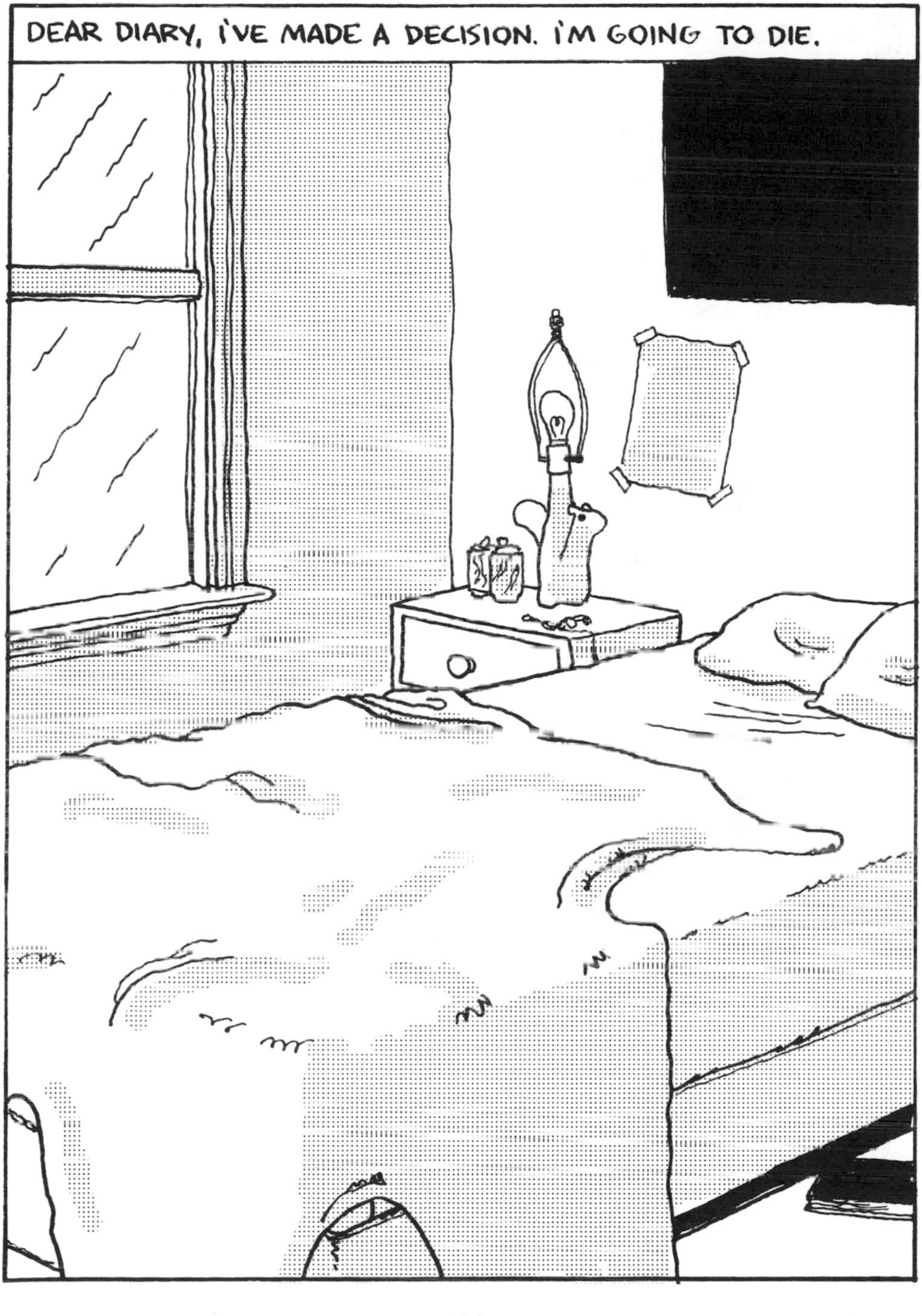
DEAR DIARY, I'VE MADE A DECISION. I'M GOING TO DIE.

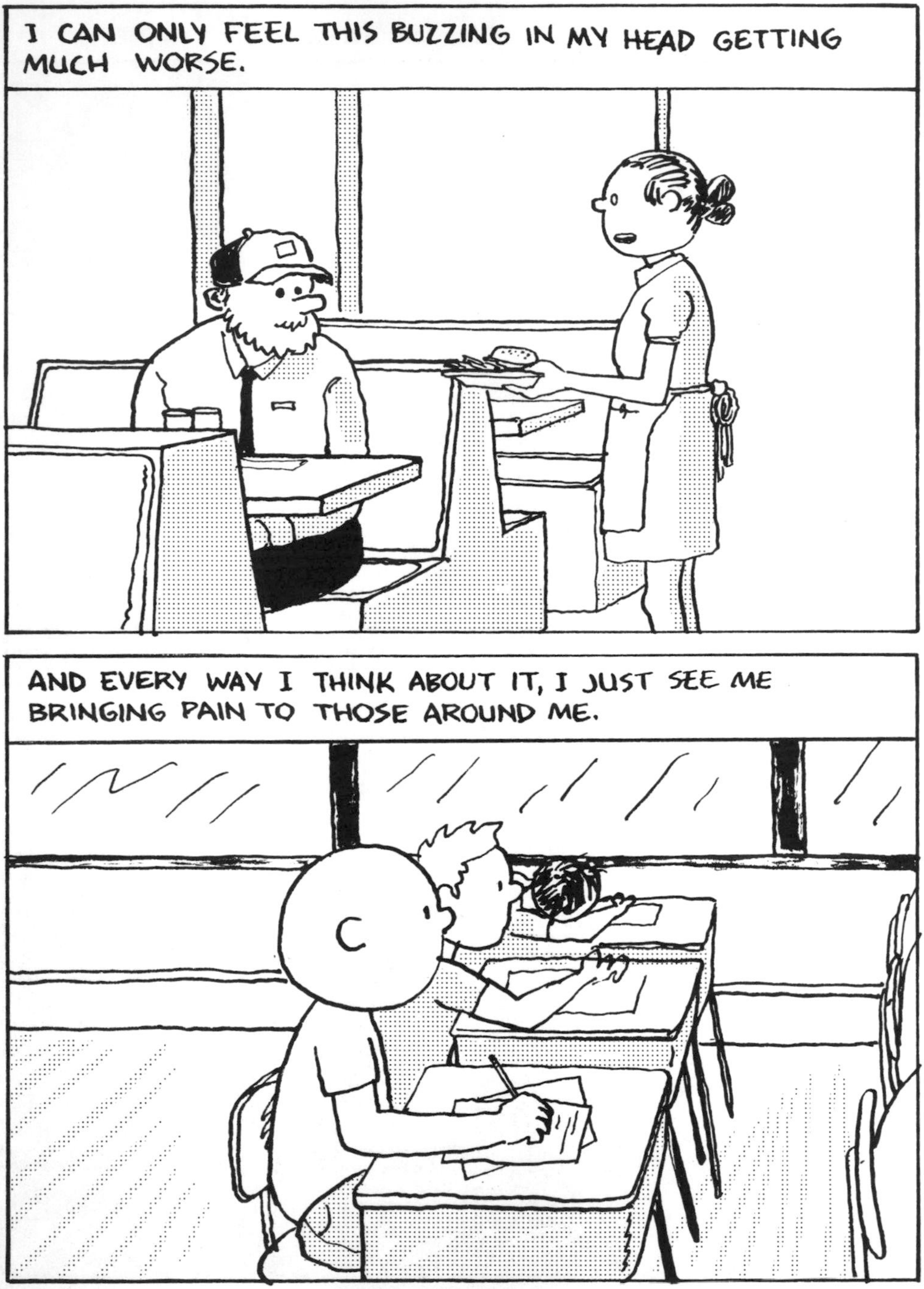
I CAN ONLY FEEL THIS BUZZING IN MY HEAD GETTING MUCH WORSE.
AND EVERY WAY I THINK ABOUT IT, I JUST SEE ME BRINGING PAIN TO THOSE AROUND ME.

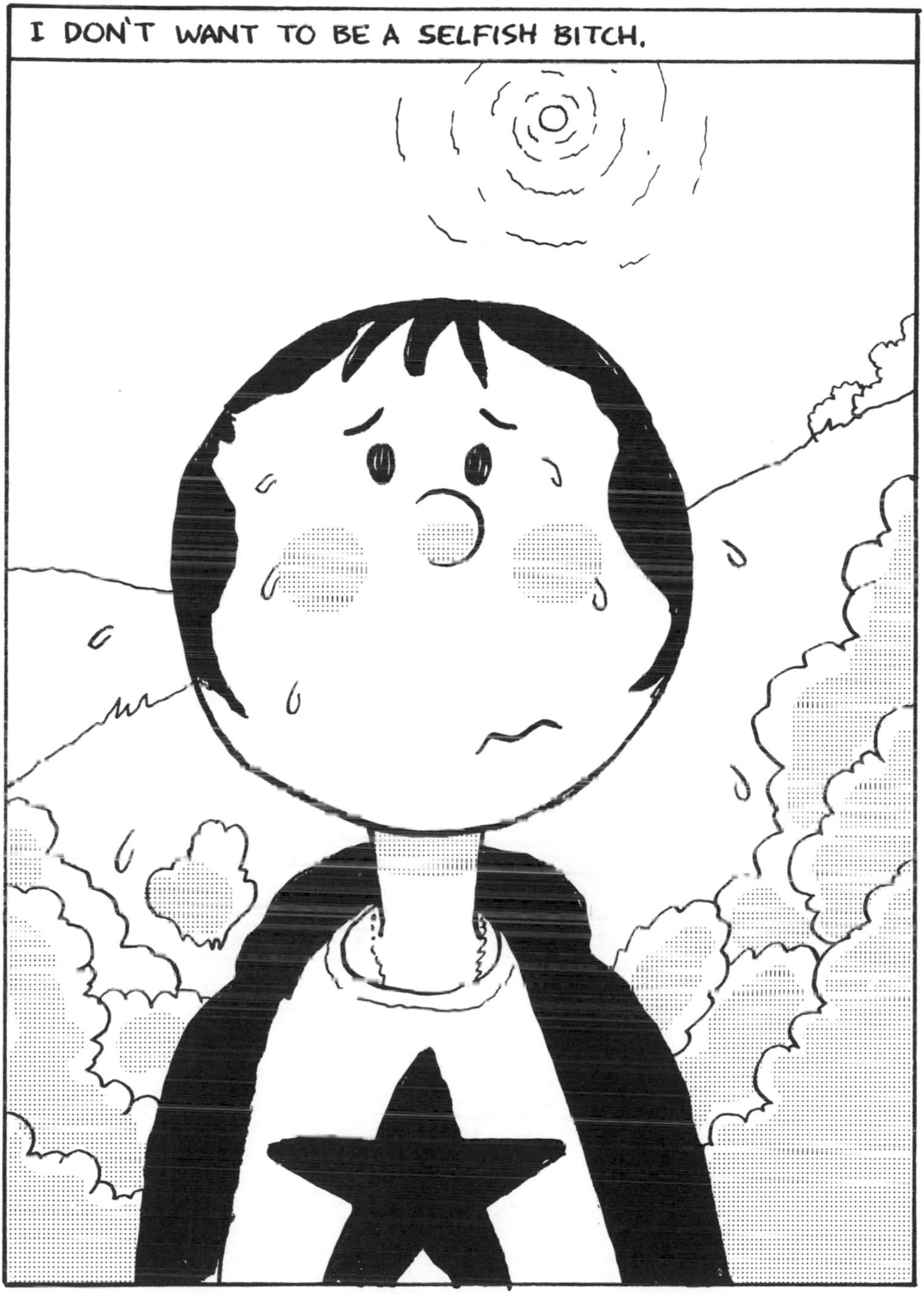
I DON'T WANT TO BE A SELFISH BITCH.

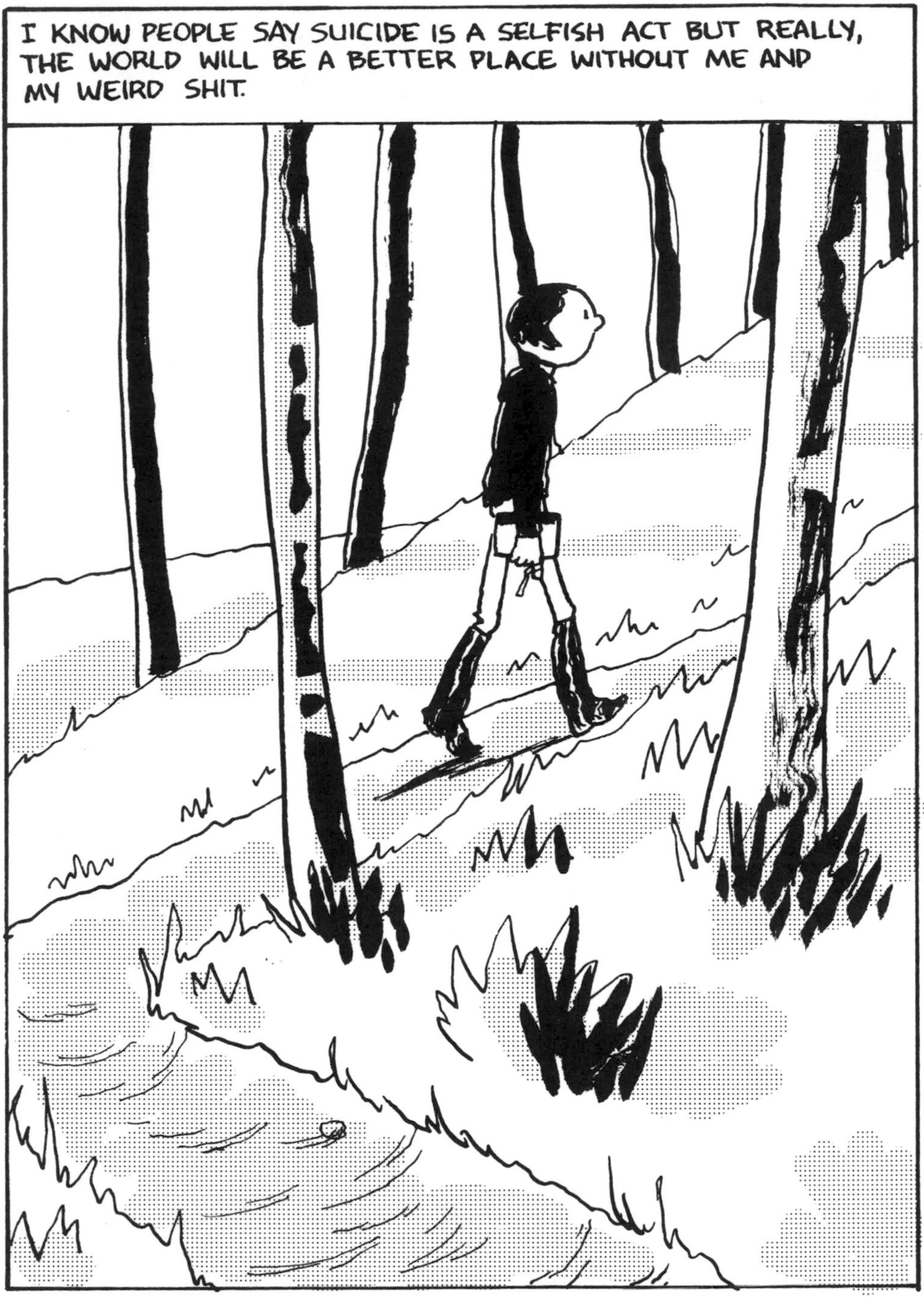
I KNOW PEOPLE SAY SUICIDE IS A SELFISH ACT BUT REALLY, THE WORLD WILL BE A BETTER PLACE WITHOUT ME AND MY WEIRD SHIT.

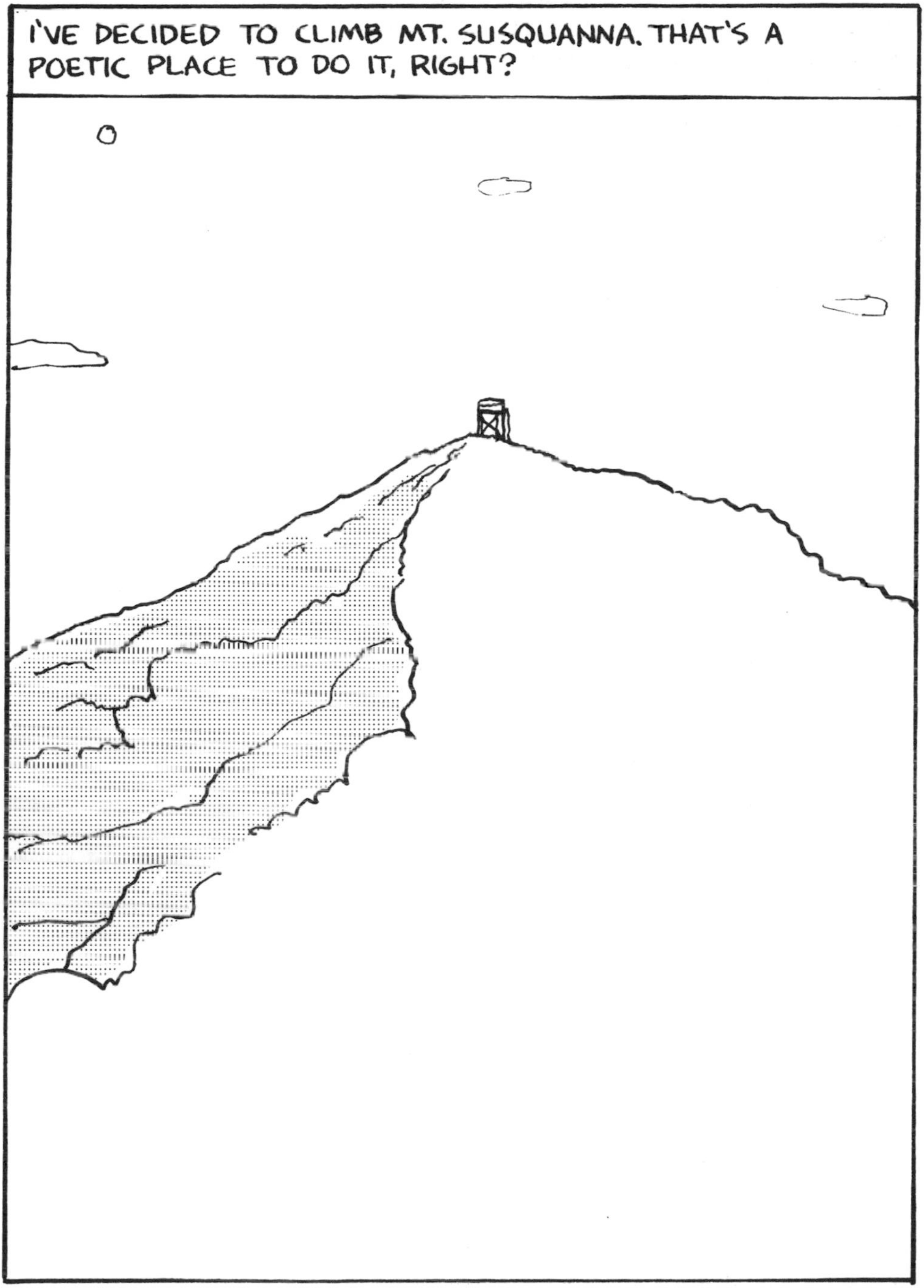
I'VE DECIDED TO CLIMB MT. SUSQUANNA. THAT'S A POETIC PLACE TO DO IT, RIGHT?

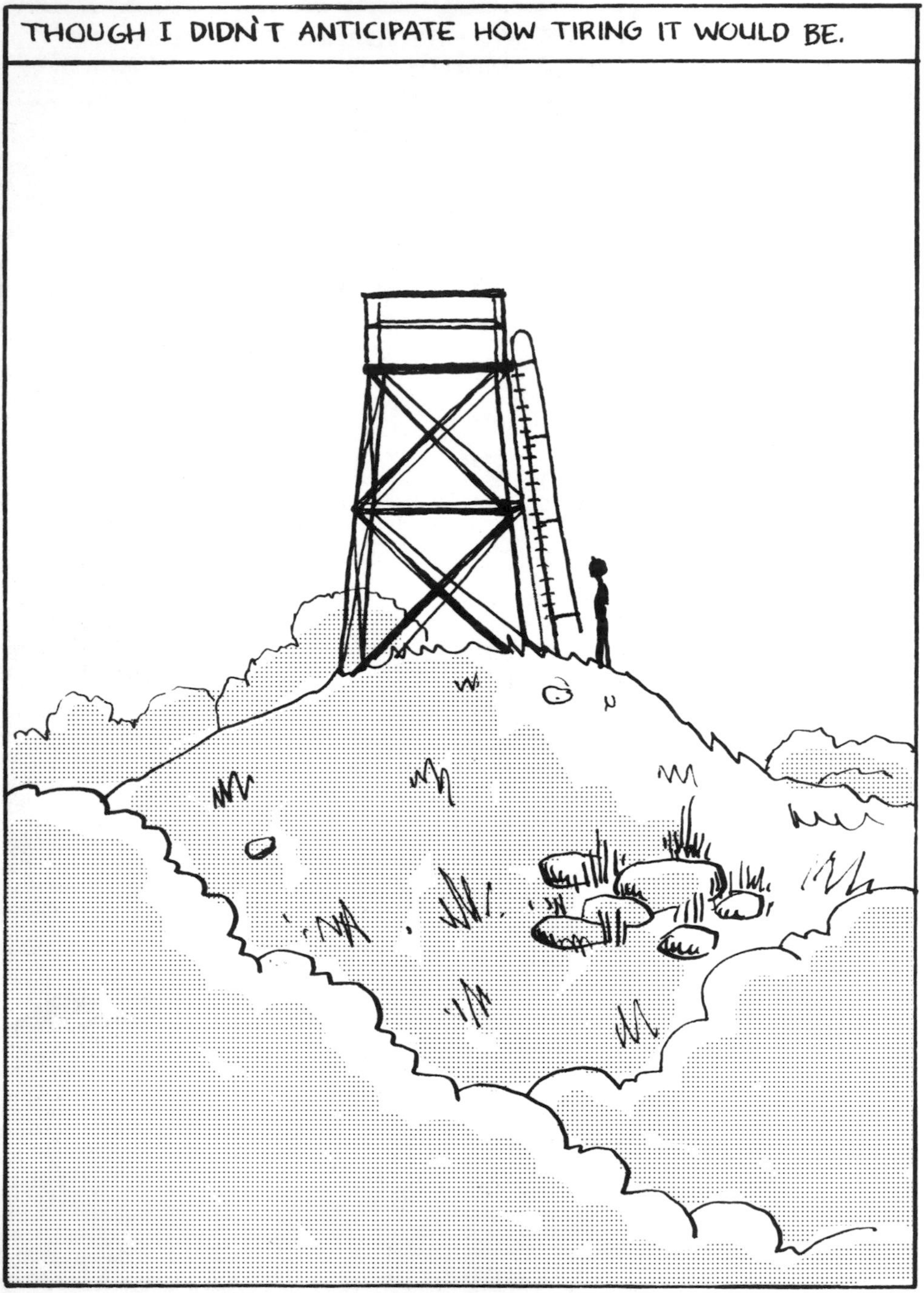
THOUGH I DIDN'T ANTICIPATE HOW TIRING IT WOULD BE.

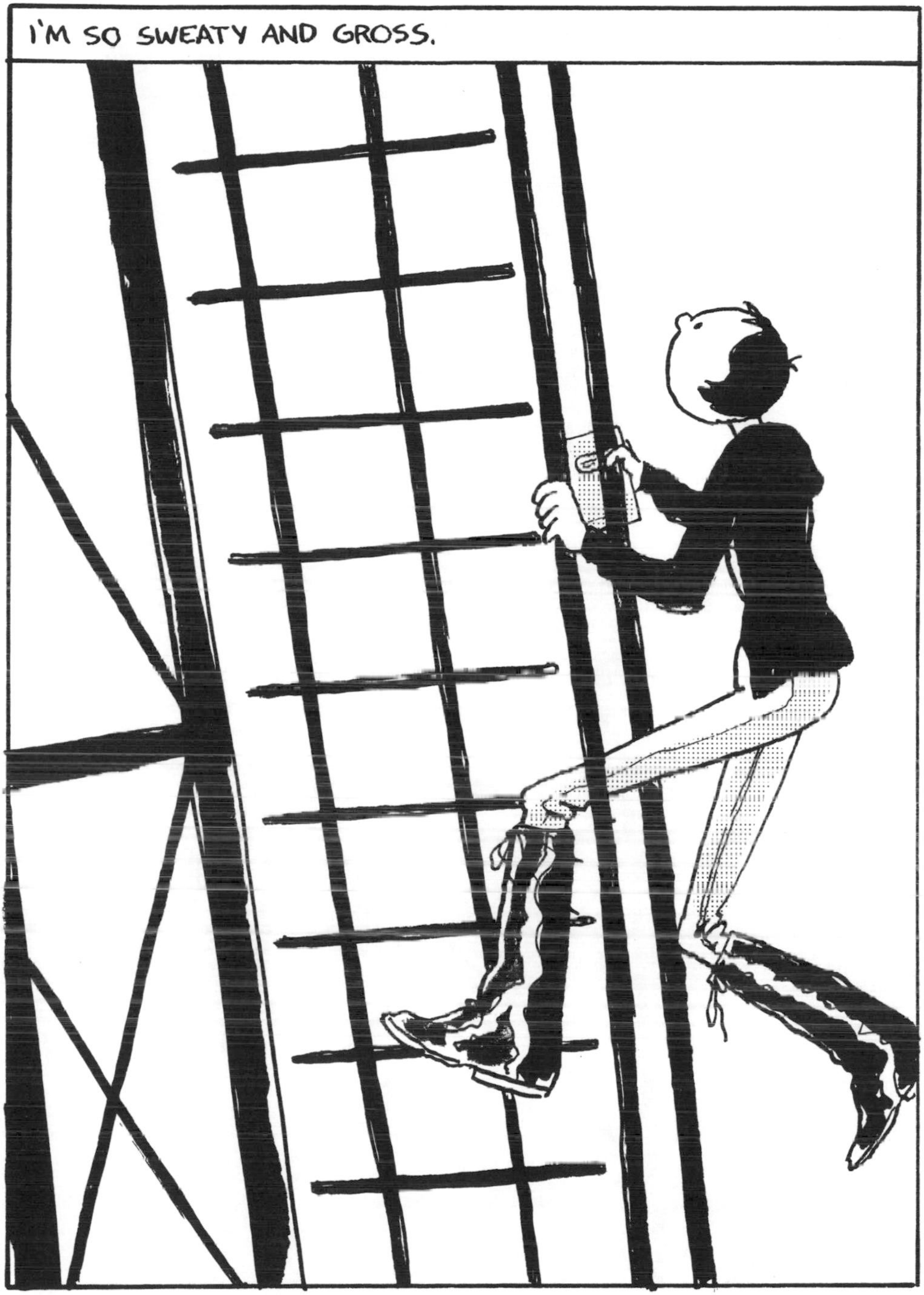
I'M SO SWEATY AND GROSS.

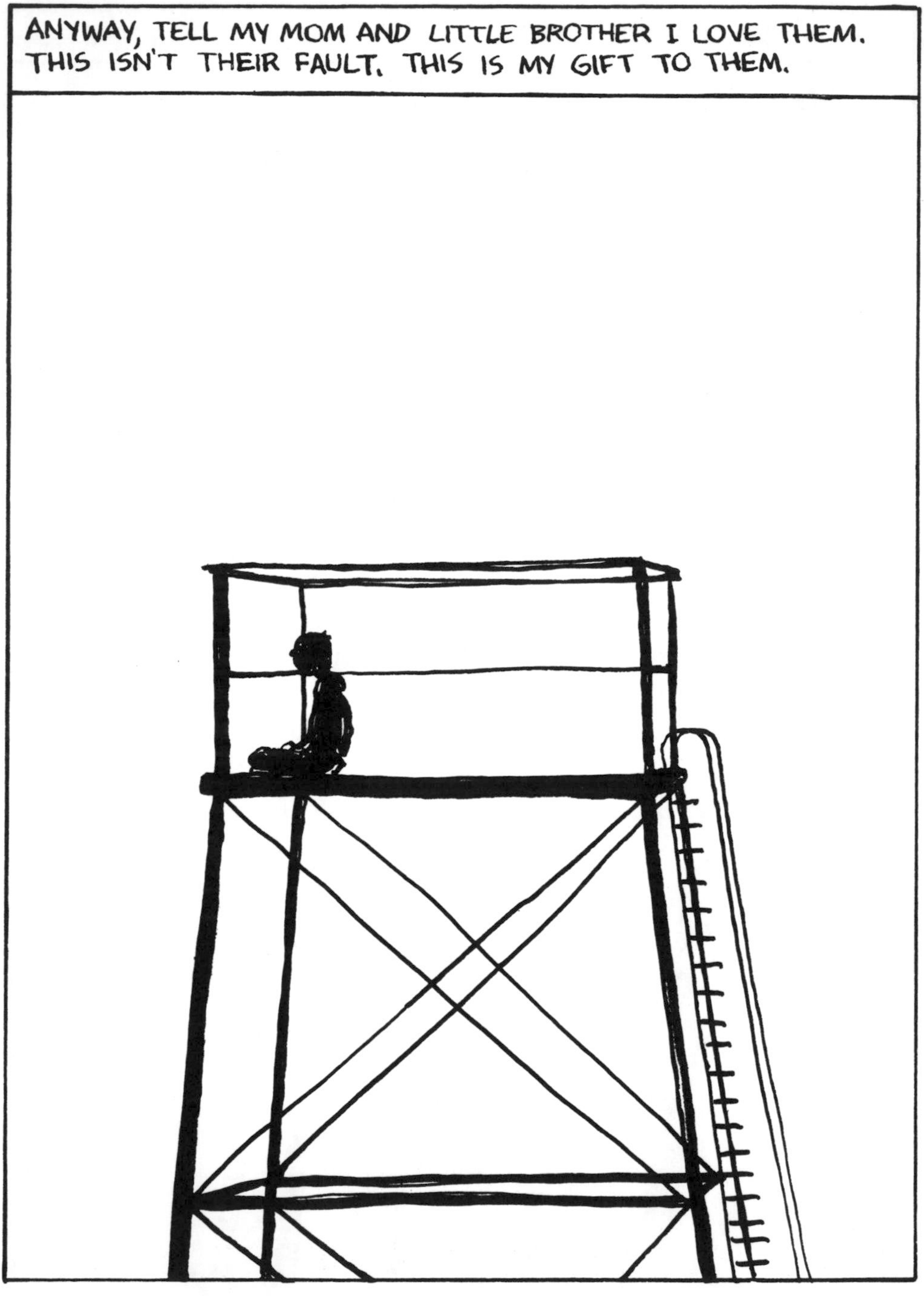
ANYWAY, TELL MY MOM AND LITTLE BROTHER I LOVE THEM. THIS ISN'T THEIR FAULT. THIS IS MY GIFT TO THEM.

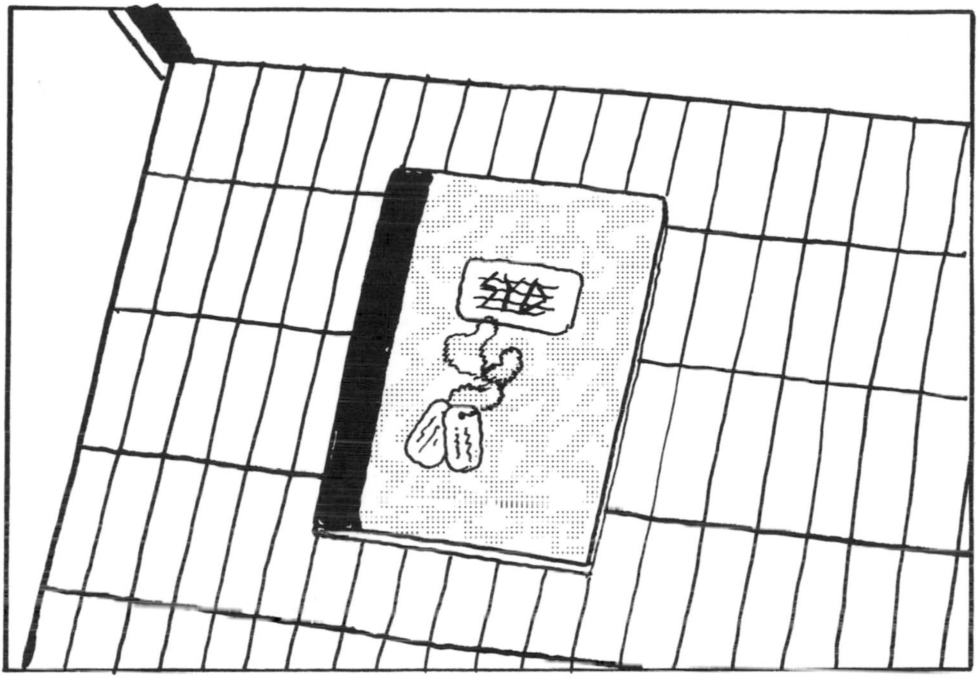

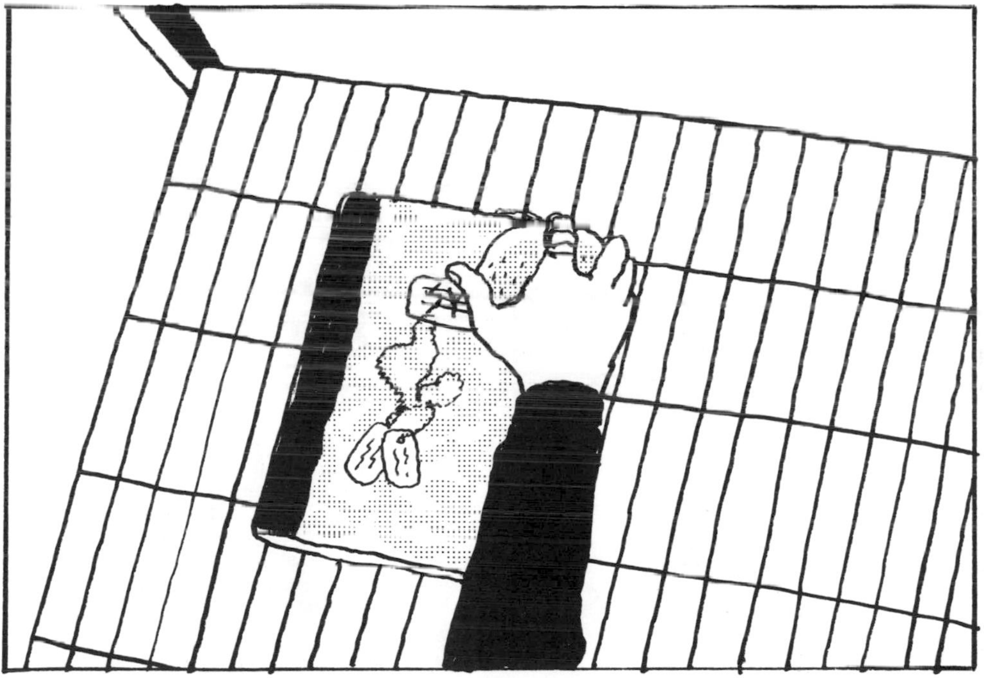

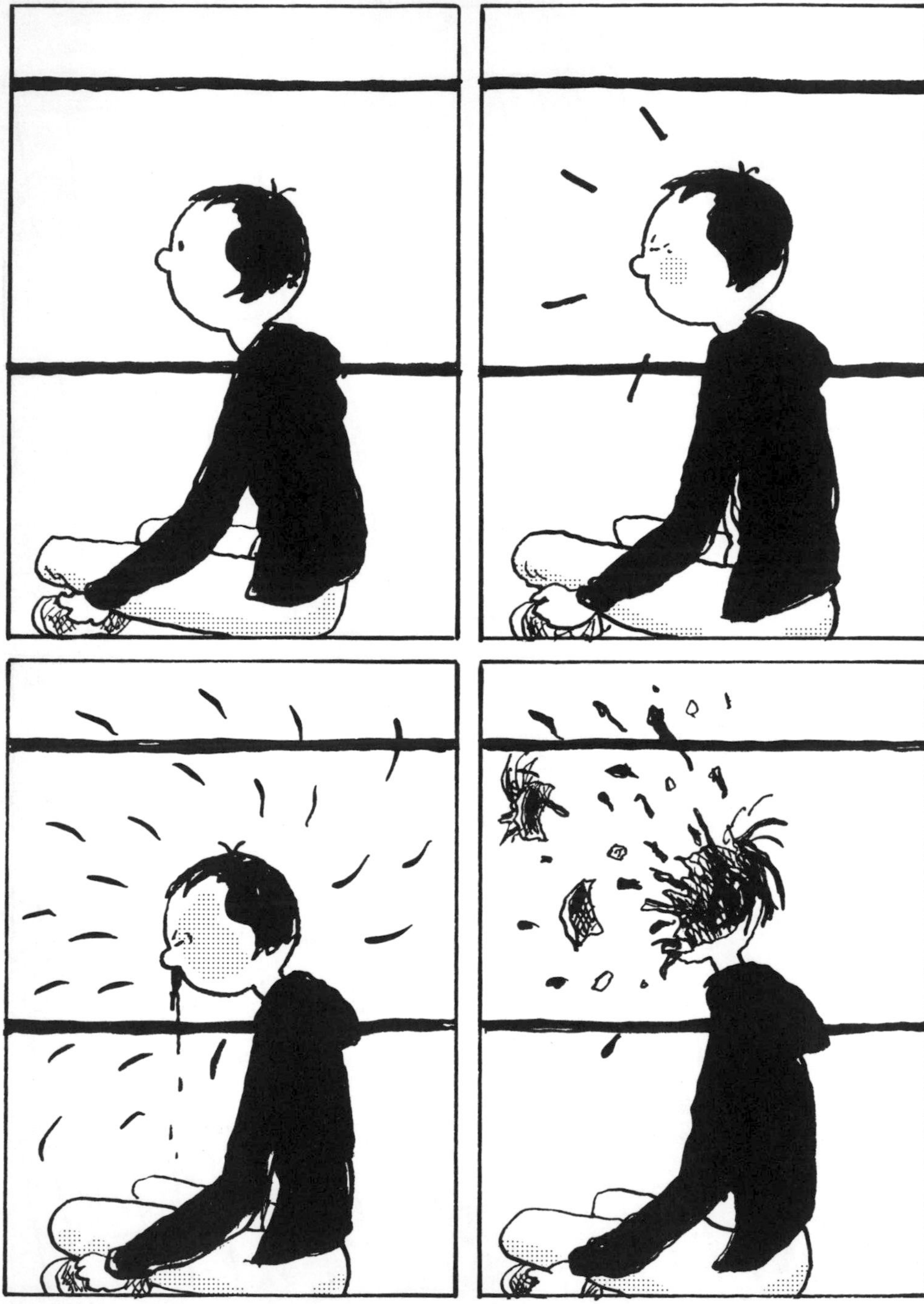

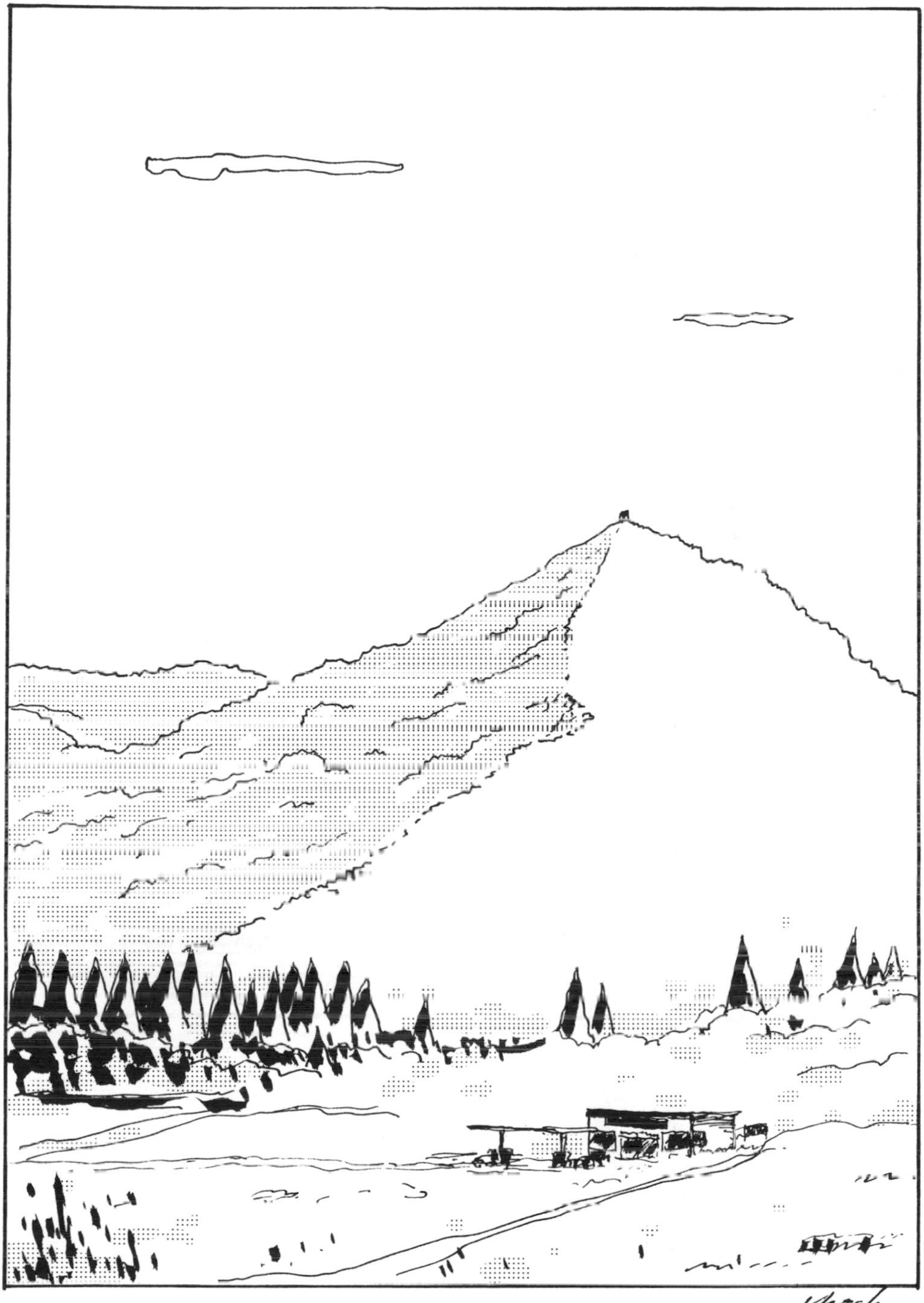

WHATEVER YOU'RE GOING THROUGH,
YOU CAN TALK TO SOMEONE.

NATIONAL SUICIDE PREVENTION LIFELINE

1-800-273-8255 (ENGLISH)

1-888-628-9454 (ESPAÑOL)

1-800-799-4889 (TTY)

SUICIDE PREVENTIONLIFELINE.ORG

PROVIDING 24/7, FREE AND CONFIDENTIAL
SUPPORT FOR PEOPLE IN DISTRESS AS WELL
AS PREVENTION AND CRISIS RESOURCES FOR
YOU OR YOUR LOVED ONES, AND BEST
PRACTICES FOR PROFESSIONALS.

EVERYONE PLAYS A ROLE IN
SUICIDE PREVENTION.